Debra

②

The Sparrow's Wing:

Maggie(2)McKinnon

Beatrice Smith Samples

Beatrice Smith Samples

PublishAmerica
Baltimore

ISBN: 1-60610-794-1
PUBLISHED BY PUBLISHAMERICA, LLLP
www.publishamerica.com
Baltimore

Printed in the United States of America

Glowing reviews of *Maggie McKinnon,* a novel of the **Reconstruction South,** the first published book of **Beatrice Smith Samples,** began to flow in as soon as the first copy of the manuscript left the computer for proofing. The clamor for a sequel immediately followed.
It makes one both humble and grateful, to have work so well received, appreciated, and enjoyed.

All Scripture in this book is from the King James Version of the Holy Bible.

All characters are fictitious, as is the North Georgia mountain town of Rhyersville. Other North Georgia towns mentioned are historical places. Songs used are in the public domain.

This book is lovingly dedicated to the memory of my mother, Della, a southern lady to the core, a woman of strength, faith, and indomitable courage—who could, at age 88, still vividly recall her first sight of an automobile, her first taste of brewed tea (other than wild sassafras, the roots of which had been dug from the red-clay banks of a North Georgia road or field), her first enjoyment of a silent motion picture, or a soap opera broadcast on a weird contraption called a 'radio.' Though she has been gone from among us for several years now, she is far from forgotten. Her smile, her brave, unselfish, unstinting, unrelenting spirit of unflappable optimism, often in the face of unbelievable odds, still live on. She has climbed the mountain—and reached the other side.

Acknowledgments:

It is indeed difficult to acknowledge all those friends and family who have given me support, aid, encouragement, and in some instances tons of help in proofreading, and making this book possible. But, here goes: My family: Son, Stephen Samples; daughter and son-in-law, Vicki and Darrell Pruitt; grandchildren, Joshua and Michelle Pruitt; sister and brother-in-law, Hazel and J. L. Peppers; brother and sister-in-law, Gene and Edna Smith; sister-in-law, Jean Smith; brother and sister-in-law, Tony and Gelaine Smith. Nieces and nephews: Laverne Ron, Connie Mullinax (and husband, Joey), Kathy Appling, Timothy Smith, Cindy Calk, Michael Smith, Rebecca Barrick, and Kevin Smith. And to very special cousins, Mary King and Charlotte Smith, thanks a million.

Friends who have offered support in numerous ways: Elaine Pruitt, Shannon Gravitt, the folks at Sherwood's, Johnson's, and Borders at Mall of Georgia. My church family at New Hope Baptist, especially Cathy Brannon, Sheila Tanner, and Rosemary Patterson.

And special thanks to all those readers who have heaped praise upon my work and who make all the hours and hours of research and writing worthwhile.

Are not two sparrows
sold for a farthing?
And one of them shall not
fall to the ground
without your Father.
But the very hairs of your head
are all numbered.
Matthew 10:29/30

Chapter 1

The Blue Ridge Mountains of North Georgia—1885

Margaret Ann McKinnon Evans sat in the kitchen of *The Sparrow*. Before her on the rough oak table set a cold cup of coffee which Maggie turned idly with one slender finger. She ran through her mind the events of the previous evening—totally unable to comprehend what had happened. Her gaze fell to the huge diamond set in a circle of rich gold—on her left hand.

What *had* happened?

Urged on by her sister, Barbara Jo, she had accepted what she thought was a harmless invitation to a dinner party—some distance from town. Then when Barbara Jo's fine carriage rolled over the crest of the low hill, and they arrived at their destination—

Maggie heaved a great sigh.

Somehow, everything had gotten all out of hand.

Not until she and her sister had actually arrived, did Maggie realize *where* this mysterious dinner party was being hosted—

—*Cottonwood!*

What memories *that* name conjured up!

Maggie rose distractedly from the bench at the oak table and carried her cold cup of coffee to the big black iron cookstove in the corner, thinking perhaps that she should pour a warm-up. Then, somehow, she found the cup of coffee no longer in her hand, and she was approaching the front door of *The Sparrow Restaurant & Rooms to Let.* She shoved up the heavy bar and swung the front door wide. Then she stood gazing out into the main thoroughfare of the small North Georgia mountain town of Rhyersville.

It was scarcely past dawn. Fog still hung over the surrounding rim of deep blue mountains and drifted down the street in thin tendrils on the light morning air. Nothing moved in the narrow, deeply-rutted red dirt street. The oak-plank buildings on either side were tightly shuttered and locked. Except that, down at the end of Main Street, Jonas Trap was just swinging wide the huge double doors of his wheelwright shop. *Jonas Trap*, she thought with the shadow of a smile, *he's as regular as a clock*. Well, at least *some* things in life were still dependable!

Behind her, Maggie heard Liza Mae Daniels shuffling about in the kitchen, humming some nameless tune. She heard the kitchen door bang shut. She knew that Benjamin Noah Daniels, Liza Mae's new husband, had also arrived. And Benjamin Noah had taken the big oaken bucket and gone out to the well for water.

Benjamin—and Liza. What would she do without them?! Her gaze fell again to the huge diamond sparkling on her left hand. If she actually *married* William Bartram Logan, what would become of Liza—and Benjamin Noah!?

Maggie's head felt as if she was drifting, floating in a bank of clouds, with no sure footing—

"Mornin', Missus. How's you doin' this fine mornin'?" Liza walked up behind Maggie, a happy lilt in her southern drawl. Maggie turned, and gazed at the attractive little Negress as if she had never seen her before. Her mind flew back to the first time she had actually seen Liza, nothing but a stack of bones with black skin drawn tight over them...

No! No! Don't go there! Don't fall into that pit of despair—that nightmare with no awakening!

As Maggie turned, Liza Mae grinned at her, a huge grin that caused the heavy coiled plaits of raven-black hair atop her head to lift half an inch. "I's 'spect this be a *fine* mornin' fer you, Mizz Maggie!" Liza wagged her head and crooned. "You'se look'd *so* bootiful las' nite! And that *Mister William Bartram Logan*!—Now tha's *one* fine gen'leman! I *knows*, Miss Maggie, dat he's will...Whut's da matter, Mizz Maggie? You don' look all that happy to Liza Mae."

"I...I have a slight...headache," Maggie lied, leaning against the open door, closing both eyes, lifting a hand to stroke her forehead, giving Liza Mae the faintest of smiles.

"Then…why don't you jus' tak' yo'self back upstairs, Mizz Maggie? And lay yo'self back down!" Liza Mae's voice rang now with deep concern. "Me and Benjamin Noah, we's cin tak' car' ob startin' da food fer da breakfast crowd. You jes' go on now—"

"If you think that you and Benjamin Noah can handle things for a while, Liza—" Maggie began wearily, feeling as if she was teetering on the rim of a high cliff. She felt peculiar. Her head spun; her vision wanted to blur. She'd scarcely caught a wink of sleep all last night—

"*Whut*, Mizz Maggie? Whut's th' matter?" Liza frowned at Maggie worriedly. "Adder las' nite, I's thought today youse would be dancin' on top da world! I thought this would be one o' da happiest days—and you, Mizz Maggie, *you deserves* som' o' dem happy days—!"

"I…don't know, Liza Mae. I feel as if I'm drowning!"

"*Drownin'?!*—Mizz Maggie?! But—"

"Never mind me, Liza," Maggie shrugged slender shoulders, forced a brave little smile, her blue eyes gazing into Liza Mae's brown ones, almost black now with concern. "I'll be…all right. It's just that…the thought of….*marrying* again… it would… entail… all *sorts* of…changes! For me…and you and Benjamin Noah…and Johnny…I wasn't expecting…." Maggie halted, no words coming to mind to express her jumbled emotions.

"Dat lil' brother o' yor's, Mizz Maggie—! Why, dat chil' *loves* Mister Bart Logan as much as any chil' could love he's own pap!"

"But he's *not* his Papa, Liza Mae—" Maggie broke off angrily in mid-sentence. Liza stood mute, staring at her, but Maggie seemed not to notice. Anger rose, flushing her cheeks.

Why *had* Papa died so young?! Leaving Mama, Barbara Jo, Maggie, and Johnny—with *nothing*—!

Papa died. Then there had followed her *terrible job, her horrible marriage. Mama's death…and Katie Ann's. Len's*—

And, then… she had heard of Mr. William Bartram Logan…and the logging operation he was bringing to the mountains north of Rhyersville.

Maggie's gaze swept the small restaurant she had worked so hard to establish. If she actually married, what would become of her business? For months she had labored as a cook at *Mr. Bartram Logan's logging camp*. She had lied, blustered her way into his camp, arguing and sparring with him—oftentimes at her wits end—in order to earn enough money to open this place—to hopefully put a roof over her brother Johnny's beautiful little head, food in his mouth—provide some sort of future—

Future—!?

"Miss Maggie…I's…don' unnerstan'…"

"Neither do I, Liza Mae." Maggie blinked wide blue eyes, wagged her head as if to clear the cobwebs from her brain. Then, as if driven by some inner impulse, she spun suddenly about, sending the full skirts of her cotton stuff dress swaying. "If you can get along without me for a while, I just might…go for a drive."

"A…..drive?" Liza muttered in astonishment. Liza Mae had never known her friend and employer to leave the premises of *The Sparrow* during open business hours—*never*.

"Yes, Liza Mae," Maggie replied, the gaze from her blue-blue eyes drifting about the room, "I think that's *exactly* what I'll do! I'm just going to run upstairs…and fetch my shawl and bonnet. It *is* late September. And there's a sharp chill in the air this mornin'."

Liza Mae Daniels stood watching—dumbfounded—as Maggie gathered up her full skirts and fled upstairs as if the devil himself was chasing her. A few minutes, and the gorgeous brunette, Margaret Ann McKinnon Evans, came drifting back down. Without another word or a backward glance, she flew out the door, and went marching down the dirt street—towards Jonas Trap's. Unable to tear her gaze away, Liza Mae watched as the slender form moved down the dirt street, her small lady's leather boots kicking up little puffs of dust. And in a very few minutes, Miss Maggie came plunging her one-horse wagon out the double doors of Trap's, and down the narrow, dusty street, driving faithful old Job as if the poor horse's tail was on fire.

"Ummmmmm! Ummmmmm! Ummmmmmmmm!" Liza Mae moaned. Wagging her head in disbelief, she turned and disappeared back inside *The Sparrow*.

Chapter 2

Wind whipping past flushed cheeks, colorful leaves flying up from beneath the whirring wheels of the wagon, Maggie flew along. The beauty of the late-summer countryside, the golden sunlight filtering through the trees, the rolling ridges of the Blue Ridge Mountains surrounding her completely eluded her. She had ridden this road so many times with Papa and Mama, and her sisters, Nellie Sue and Barbara Jo…

It all seemed so long ago. But it hadn't been all that long. What year was that, 1880?—when her eldest sister, Nellie Sue, had married the shy, handsome young schoolmaster, Thomas Beyers? Then, within months, Nellie Sue was gone. About a year later, Papa had passed. And they had lost the farm due to the terrible debts Papa had incurred after coming home, wounded and penniless, from the War Between the States— the war that had torn the country asunder.

Then, in order to find work, to put a roof over their heads and food in their mouths, Maggie had taken a job down country as companion and serving maid in a town called Cumming, near the Chattahoochee River. A few years following that awful move—and was it just this spring, May of this year of our Lord, 1885, she had lost her baby daughter, Katie Ann…?

And her husband…Len…

And though Maggie had prayed mightily about it, she still could not find it in her heart to consider Len Evans' passing anything approaching a great, mournful loss. She tried her utmost not to even *think* of *Len Evans*! God have mercy on her!—but she simply *could not* forgive him—*ever!*

Maggie bit her lower lip, then set her mouth in a firm line, feeling the anger, even now, as fresh as if it were yesterday. Forgive Len? *Never!* Not after he had ridden his prized palomino over her precious baby!

And even Len Evans, despite what he had done, his dying in such an odd and bizarre manner had left Maggie shaken, shocked to the core. How could *any* man just decide *to go and lay himself down in the graveyard*!—and *expire?!*

Maggie felt hot tears stinging her eyes, dampening her cheeks. She gave a little gasp. Almost angrily she brushed the tears away with her free hand, then re-took the reins and slapped Job smartly across the rump.

The wagon leapt forward through the cool mountain air filled with scents drifting from the tall forests lining the mountainsides, of honey locust pods and ripening persimmons that would soon turn bright orange with the first frost. Up ahead, the road was already descending through the small gap in the mountains.

And her beloved McKinnon Valley came into view.

———————————

Bart Logan tied his mount to the oak-pole hitching post in front of *The Sparrow Restaurant & Rooms to Let.* A pleased little smile on his handsome, well-tanned face, he removed his expensive felt hat and stood gazing at the little mountain country inn for a moment. Its plank front was painted with the new color, *Redwood Wonder*; its windows gleamed shiny clean and boasted white lace curtains. Evergreens and flowering shrubs hugged the front of the two-story structure, creating a lovely, narrow garden. He wondered what on earth Margaret Ann would want to do with the place after they were married. Even though it was an establishment open to the public, always the consummate gentleman, Bart rapped lightly on the front door, hesitated politely for a moment, and then pushed open the door.

"Liza Mae!" Bart smiled broadly at the little Negress whom Maggie had taken under her wing. When first Bart saw her, Liza looked rather more like a black scarecrow than a living, breathing person. But Margaret Ann McKinnon Evans' determined ministrations had changed that. And, like a mother hen attempting to save the entire world, he thought, she had also given aid and shelter to the tall, thin vagrant, Benjamin— whom Maggie had miraculously transformed into *Benjamin Noah Daniels,* hired man for the little inn. And Benjamin Noah had just recently become Liza Mae's husband.

Liza and Benjamin—two homeless freed slaves, penniless and starving, though the War Between the States had been over for twenty years. But Bart had noticed, much to his dismay, that it was not an uncommon sight, even a score of years after the War, to see straggling groups of ragged, emaciated freed slaves, prowling up and down the roads, searching for shelter—searching for a home. Even though he was a Yankee businessman from Philadelphia, it sometimes broke his heart to see what the War had done to the South. He wondered just how much longer it would be…before that War released its cruel grasp on the southern states of the Union.

But Bart determined, as he stood smiling broadly at Liza Mae, that he would *not* allow his mind to harbor such unpleasant thoughts. Not today. Not *this* day. And he hoped not for many days to come…

He was getting married—!

—To the most beautiful, most charming, most intriguing, most frustrating, most—

He was marrying Margaret Ann McKinnon Evans…

Who could charm an alligator out of a river…

And who could carve a man into *mincemeat* with her lovely blue-blue eyes, and her sharp little tongue.

"Liza Mae!" Bart began, "And just where is your lovely—"

"If Himself is meanin' *Mizz Maggie*," Liza Mae snapped tartly with narrowed eyes and a little disapproving jerk of her head, "she done to'k hurself off—in a flurry of dust an' dander—ta God-only-knows-whar'!"

"What? She's…gone?"

"Ain't dat *jest whut* I *jest* said?" Liza Mae declared, staring at Bart with narrowed, angry eyes.

"But, Liza Mae…" Bart stammered, "You seem angry at *me*."

"Well, suh! I's jest feels lak' bein' mad wif' *somebody*. And since *youse* seems ta' be da only one's here rite now, I jest feels lak' being mad wif' you!"

"Well," Bart wagged his handsome head and murmured, "I fail to see the *logic* of that. But I see, Liza Mae, that you've learned *quite a bit*…from…a certain person."

"Don't you go doin' no bad mouthin' 'bout Mizz Maggie, now! You hear me?!"

"Liza Mae," Bart Logan began very patiently, placing a tanned hand on the back of his neck as if he felt the unmistakable onset of a fierce headache,

"I would not… in *any* way… in *any* fashion…in the least…make *any* remark which could be construed as being disparaging to your employer."

"Whut do *dat* mean?"

"It means, Liza Mae," Bart explained, slowly lowering his hand, staring Liza Mae Daniels squarely in the eye, "that I *love* the woman. *I'm* the gentleman who asked Mrs. Evans to become *my wife. Last night?* Remember?"

"I's not no fool! 'Couse, I's remem'er! After all da trouble I's wents to…fixin' dat gran' meal! Youse want's a cup o' coffee?"

"What? No…thank you. Well…then…never mind. Do you have the *slightest inkling* as to where she might…Let me *rephrase* that. Do you have *any idea* where she could have disappeared to…gone?"

"How's wou'd *I's* know?!" Liza Mae put hands on thin hips, knit her brow into a brooding frown. "Nobody don' tel' me *nuthin'* 'round here! And anyhow, yo'se *too* late! Da coffee's don' col'!"

"Oh? Yes. Well. Thank you…Liza Mae…for all the…"

Bart Logan gave a little nod of his head, slammed his hat onto his head, and walked out the door.

Outside, his head in a whirl, he stood in the golden sunlight of what he knew was going to be an absolutely gorgeous day. The air was light and balmy. The surrounding mountains were more beautiful than the finest artist could possibly have captured on his best canvas. *And last night, she had said she would marry him*! Now, this morning, she was gone!

What else would he have expected—from *Mrs. Margaret Ann McKinnon Evans?!!!*

Untying his roan mount from the oak hitching post, touching the brim of his fine felt hat, Bart pulled a rueful little grin and swung lithely up into the saddle. The roan prancing beneath him, he sat his saddle for just a moment, gold-flecked hazel eyes narrowing as his gaze swept the rutted street flanked with dust-coated buildings. Then, wondering what on earth he should do next, where he might locate her, he turned his mount and loped slowly down the dirt street, the rise and fall of the roan's hoofbeats the only sound in the small mountain town fading behind him.

Maggie drove the wagon into the shade of the grove of yellow maples back of the square-log house. She sat for several minutes, gazing at the golden yellow maple leaves trembling in the light morning breeze. Then she lifted her gaze to the mountain rising behind the log house where the trees had begun to take on varying shades of reds, yellows and oranges, and the memories washed over her in a mind-numbing jumble. Finally, she stepped down into the weed-choked yard. She walked around the one-horse wagon and stood staring at old Job for a long moment. Then she put one arm on his neck and laid her head against his familiar warmth. She would never forget the day she and Papa rode over to the Stillwell's horse farm…and bought Job.

Oh, how she missed Papa! Papa always knew *exactly* the right thing to say to still the aching of her wondering heart as a child. Papa…so handsome, with his long handle-bar mustache, his twinkling eyes filled with songs and love and laughter, his dark hair parted in the middle and neatly water-combed to either side…and Great-grandpa Shawn's fiddle resting ever so lightly beneath his chin…glorious songs of Old Scotland pouring forth beneath the flying bow…

Maggie felt her throat tighten. Tears filled her eyes and one slid down a beautiful cheek. Job lifted a hoof, softly pawed the tall grass, and gave a low whicker—as if he knew and shared her pain. Then Maggie angrily knocked the tear away with the back of one small hand, turned and stared at the familiar square-log house, the logs hewn by the axe of her great-grandfather, Shawn Ian McKinnon, the spring of the year 1827, the spring following the year he emigrated from Scotland—when the Nation of Cherokee Indians still claimed this valley. Shawn and Katherine Ann had spent months living in their huge covered wagon, right here in this valley, until Shawn could get the log house roofed with stout oak shingles. Later, Grandpa Thomas Shawn McKinnon had added the second story.

Slowly it dawned on Maggie. Last evening, just after that astonishing, heart-stopping moment when he had proposed marriage, Bart Logan had informed her, his mouth warm against her ear as he danced her around the grand salon of his mansion at Cottonwood, that he would be presenting to her *McKinnon Valley. As a wedding gift…!*

Bart galloped his mount through the narrow gap in the mountains, down the slight grade, and toward the square-log house with its narrow front porch and its red-clay-chinked chimney. He dismounted, tied the beautiful roan mount to one of the front porch posts, and strode around back.

There she stood beside the small wagon, one hand on the neck of her horse, so engrossed in her thoughts she was totally unaware of his presence.

"Good morning! I thought I might find you here! How…are you…this morning? I trust…you…slept well?" He walked up and stood facing her, laying one of his own hands on the neck of her horse, as if thus making some sort of personal connection with this beautiful, mesmerizing, totally frustrating woman.

But…what he had just said…Did *that* sound like the words of a man hopelessly, head-over-heels in love…with this gorgeous brunette who now wore his diamond?!

But…it had been such a long time…since Bart had made any sort of attempt to court, or romance, a member of the fairer sex. A long time since he had felt the slightest inclination to do so. Not since—

But he pushed those thoughts out of his head. Sue Ellen was *gone*. The infant son she had borne him—gone. He had no close blood relatives still living. For more years than he cared to recall, Bart had been so achingly, painfully lonely…valiantly attempting to immerse himself in his extensive business interests…to fill the yawning void in his life. And doing fairly well at it—

—Until the day this lovely young woman came marching up the hot, dry, dusty street of the small mountain burg called Rhyersville, and made straight for his hiring table. And that, William Bartram Logan firmly assured himself, was about to change everything. He intended to marry this woman, Mrs. Margaret Ann McKinnon Evans, and if Providence allowed, rear a large family, along with her young charge, her little brother, Johnny… He certainly had the means—

"Oh, Mr. Logan." Reluctantly she tore her gaze from the log house.

When she turned and looked at him…her eyes—

As always, whenever Bart appeared her lovely face took on a startled, defensive look, her smooth brows lifted, her blue-blue eyes widened. Like a deer, Bart thought, being stalked by a determined, well-armed hunter.

He had thought…that after last night…he might have expected a different sort of greeting this morning.

Removing his fine felt hat and holding it against the breast of his gray wool jacket, Bart smiled charmingly down at her:

"Mister Logan?" he inquired with a lift of dark brows.

"What…what would you prefer…that I call you?" Maggie asked, head cocked to the side, voice low, impersonal. As if getting the work assignment for the day, Bart thought.

"Well," Bart's brows knit thoughtfully. Heart hammering, he gazed intently into that loveliest of faces, searching his mind for something… anything…to break the awkward silence.

"*'Darling'*?" Bart took a step toward her, leaned down, smiled and whispered softly. "Yes, I think *darling* would suffice very nicely."

She stared up at him, the blue-blue eyes narrowing a bit. He could tell that she was uncertain, terribly ill at ease. He could almost see her brain spinning, searching for some appropriate response. Something not too…personal.

This was not at all how he had envisioned their first meeting of this morning. He had lain wide awake most of the night, his heart pounding with the anticipation of folding her in his arms, holding her close, feeling the warmth of her. Talking with her, easily, comfortably—

—Logically.

But here she was, asking in a small, almost frightened voice:

"You're out and about so early this morning…was there something you wanted…Bartram?"

"I can't recall for the *life of me*…" Bart broke off, lifted his hand from the neck of the horse, raked it through his shock of perfectly trimmed dark hair, glanced down at the tips of his shiny black boots for just a moment in obvious frustration, swung his intense gaze back. He said slowly, his voice low, a bit sarcastic, "I don't think *anyone* has called me *that*—not since my *Mother* died."

"Well," Maggie began in a low voice, heaved a little sigh, her blue-blue eyes cast suddenly down to the tips of her own little brown lady's leather boots.

Bart stood absolutely still, determined not to say a word, not to rescue her. He stood watching her closely, letting her stumble along. Maybe, at long last, he'd get some sort of *straight answer* from this lovely creature that held his heart in her small hands—and seemed not to care one whit what became of it. In spite of the fact that he had unraveled all her lies about the *absent husband* whose grave Bart finally discovered, despite his having learned about the child she had lost beneath the thundering hooves of Len Evans' grand horse—

"That is…" She was mumbling and stammering, chewing her lower lip, "I am…" She was making a valiant effort, Bart could see, to find *something…anything…* to say to him.

"Yes," Bart finally broke the awful silence hanging between them, feeling his heart go out to her despite the way it was twisting in his chest. He loved this woman. He was willing to do…almost anything…to gain her.

"I can see that you…are…not…feeling well…perhaps…we could…talk…another time…"

"Yes," she looked up, heaved a great sigh of relief and gave him a faint smile. He could feel the tension drain out of her slight form. She looked him straight in the eye, lifted a small hand to her temple, and lied, "I have this…awful…"

"We can talk another time," Bart cut off her lie, wanting to spare her the need to lie to him, studying her face closely, attempting to read something, *anything* there that would give him a clue as to how she *actually felt* about him. If she had no feelings for him why hadn't she said so—last evening? Why had she accepted his ring? Why had she stepped into his embrace?

But that was last night. They had been at Cottonwood. With the magic of a delicious supper and the lovely glow of candlelight in one of the grandest mansions ever built south of the Mason-Dixon Line. And there had been the pleasant shock to her of her brother, little John Thomas McKinnon, Jr., fulfilling his dream, playing on his Papa's fiddle.

Had the candlelight and the music—and his own desire—addled his love-sick brain?! But, here she stood, in the full light of the morning sun, the huge diamond sparkling on her slender finger, giving testament that she must feel something for him…

The look on her beautiful face…it was the same look Bart had encountered since that first day he saw her…when she broke into his hiring line as he was attempting to round up a logging crew to send up on the mountains, that hot, dusty, dry day on the street, just in front of Trap's in Rhyersville. Had it only been this past May? It seemed that for an eternity…he had loved her…

She turned and moved away from him, stepping up onto the low back porch of the square-log house.

Determinedly, Bart followed.

This wasn't going to be as simple as Bart had supposed. Mrs. Margaret Ann McKinnon Evans was a very beautiful, very complicated lady.

"Well," Bart repeated himself, stepping up onto the low porch, speaking to her back. "I suppose, then, we'll…just talk later. Could we, do you think perhaps… darling…set a date?"

She turned.

"A…*date?*" She stared up at him, blinked her beautiful blue eyes.

"Yes, sweetheart." Bart Logan was absolutely determined to press his case—in the most gentlemanly fashion of which he was capable. "*A date*…perhaps…a day…and a time… for the wedding?"

She gazed at him for a moment, then clearing her throat, suddenly found her voice. She said in a clear, crisp, straightforward tone, each word very distinct, clipped, as if, Bart thought, she was instructing her brother Johnny to go wash up his hands for supper:

"*Mister* Logan…Bartram…darling…as you well know, I just recently lost my child…and…my… husband. I feel that to set a date now…so soon after Len's… passing…would be altogether unseemly. It would break every rule of civilized Christian conduct of which I have *ever* become acquainted…remarriage…so soon…after his death."

"I see," Bart murmured with a slight frown, "And just how long, my best beloved, will it be…until a proper amount of time has elapsed…allowing you to…emerge from this prescribed period of—?"

"Oh," she spoke up very quickly, "at least a *full year.*"

"Then, you are still in deep mourning… for Len?"

"Well…that it is to say…"

"Excuse me, darling," Bart said quickly, realizing he was being something of a selfish clod. He had a good idea that Len Evans' departure from this life had been more of a relief to Margaret Ann McKinnon Evans than a mournful tragedy. He certainly had no wish to wait…he wanted her for himself…now.

How long would that be…a year from that man's death? The month of May…he believed her sister, Barbara Jo, had told him. Len Evans had stretched himself out beside his infant daughter's grave and expired—May of this year. Shortly before Margaret Ann McKinnon Evans had shown up in his hiring line…in Rhyersville.

"I certainly have no desire to press you for a definite date…not today…but if Len Evans died in May…and I, to be quite frank, had hoped for a Thanksgiving wedding… perhaps even…or Christmas…"

"Oh, no," she said very quickly, as if stricken with consternation, vigorously wagging her head as a hand flew to her lovely throat, "Mr. Logan… Bartram…darling… I couldn't *possibly*…"

"No," Bart ducked his head, pulled a thin smile, "I suppose not. Well, this coming May, then, shall we say?"

"What?"

"We shall *both* mark our calendars, my sweet. This coming May, a year will have passed since your tragic loss—*this coming May*."

Chapter 3

A huge shopping basket swinging from her left arm, Maggie entered Moss' General Mercantile, the big oak door banging shut behind her, and approached the long counter running along the back of the cavernous building. One could purchase almost anything to be thought of—at Moss' General Mercantile. Anything from lamp oil and matches, to horse harnass and plow stocks.

"Mornin', Fred," Maggie briskly greeted her brother-in-law, Frederick J. Moss, owner and proprietor of the mercantile.

His eyes on the task of sorting the newest shipment of fine yard goods piled before him along the counter, Fred Moss, not bothering to look up to meet his young sister-in-law's gaze, only the top of his balding head visible, mumbled a reply, "Mornin', Maggie."

Well! Maggie smiled to herself. *It looks as though things haven't changed. Ever since chasing me around my own kitchen table—the chase ending when I burst a sack of fine flour over his head—Fredrick J. Moss still finds it impossible to look me in the eye!*

"Where's Barbara Jo?" Maggie smiled at Fred Moss, a cold, sweet smile that failed to reach her wide blue eyes. Maggie had never once mentioned to Barbara Jo the lustful behavior of her husband that fine spring night at the little sharecroppers' shack in the town of Cumming, down country. After all, polite society dictated that one must, Maggie thought, attempt to keep peace in the family. And what good would it have done to hurt and upset her sister? Barbara Jo had certainly not married Fred Moss because of love, but they did have a decent sort of marriage, Maggie supposed. She felt certain that Barbara Jo had probably not once remotely dreamed that her husband...

Fred Moss glanced up from the counter. For an instant, Maggie was stunned at the full sight of his face. Since the last time she had seen him…what?…just a few days ago?…Fred Moss had changed.

His light gray eyes gazed at her, bloodshot and rheumy. His long, horse-like face, Maggie thought, appeared as thin and shrunken as an old man's. *How old*, she wondered for the hundredth time, *was Fred Moss?* Deliberately setting her gigantic shopping basket directly beneath Fred's nose and atop his lovely new yard goods, Maggie stood openly staring at him.

"How…are you, Fred?" Maggie narrowed her eyes and continued to stare. How well she recalled the day she had discovered Barbara Jo and this thin, balding mercantile owner—how many…four years back?…when Barbs was a girl of eighteen, worried that she would never marry—their heads close together over the counter of his store. How she and Barbs had argued about her growing involvement with the older storekeeper! Barbs assuring her she certainly did *not* love Fred Moss, but if he asked her to marry him, she would—in order to improve her situation and escape the looming specter of impoverished spinsterhood. And they had married—

"What can I get for you, Maggie?" Fred asked in a low, muffled voice.

"Are you *sick*, Fred?" Maggie asked. She had noticed that lately, each time she saw her brother-in-law—whether behind the counter of his store or during the services at the Shiloh Baptist Church—Fred was either clearing his throat or coughing into his fine linen handkerchief. Maybe it was all the *flour* he had breathed in that night…at the little sharecroppers' house.

"I'm…all right," Fred mumbled into his thin, badly-drooping mustache.

"Good," Maggie replied, knowing he was lying, "Then, I need twenty pounds of coffee, Fred. And two dozen *fresh* eggs, if you have any that were brought in fresh from one of the farms, this mornin'?"

"Get eggs in fresh every day, Maggie. You know that." Fred coughed, a racking, painful noise that erupted from his belly, through his slight chest, and came out with a loud, sucking and gurgling that caused Maggie to cringe and put her teeth on edge. Fred struggled to catch his breath, adding sarcastically, "Twenty pounds of coffee, did you say? Folks must be powerful thirsty for coffee… these days…twenty pounds…"

This was *another* thing Maggie had always *despised* about Fred Moss—he was a curious busy-body. Watching other folks, scrutinizing their every purchase, like a hawk circling the chicken coops. Trying to mind everyone's business—*except his own!* Maybe it rankled Fred that the men of the town no longer congregated at his fine mercantile to do their pipe smoking, their tobacco chewing, their gossiping and their business transactions…perhaps putting a small dent in his trade…

"You know I need that coffee, Fred," Maggie said in a too-sweet voice, wanting to rub salt into his wounds. "You know that *The Sparrow* is now the exclusive gathering spot of *all* the farmers hereabout. *Anytime* they want to discuss upland cotton prices or Indian corn yields," Maggie gave a very sweet, sweet smile, "here they are, lounging before the big fireplace at the inn—!

"—The *Inn*…" Maggie mused, deciding right there on the spot to change the name of her business. "Don't you like the sound of that, Fred?" Maggie wrinkled her little nose and grinned at him, "It will no longer be *The Sparrow Restaurant & Rooms to Let*. Now, it will be *The Sparrow Restaurant & Inn*. Don't you think that has a *much* more sophisticated ring to it? More fitting for an establishment that hosts ladies' luncheons, birthday and wedding parties—"

Fred Moss lifted his bony, goateed chin, stared Maggie directly in the eye, and retorted, "Call th' place *whatever* you please, Maggie." From Fred's tone, Maggie could tell that the growing success of the inn did indeed rankle her brother-in-law, as he continued, "You never did bother ta listen ta anybody else, anyways."

"Why—! Fred—!" Maggie pulled a frown. *Balding old toad!* One would think he'd be happy for her—happy that she hadn't ended up a penniless widow totally dependent upon a wealthy brother-in-law…

"Anythin' else I can get for you, Maggie?" Fred's thin frame clad in a rich, soft, linen shirt boasting a black string tie and dark cotton stuff trousers that hung on him like they were two sizes too large, leaned heavily against the long oak counter. Trembling like a leaf in a high wind, as if he were in imminent danger of collapsing, he reached his right hand beneath the counter, grasped a square of linen, covered his mouth and coughed, a cough that shook his thin frame down to his toes. His eyes, Maggie thought, looked glazed and feverish. *Old.* Fred looked old. Had she ever heard? *How old was Fred Moss?*

Maggie stood, waiting and watching, as Fred held to the counter, rasping and swaying, gasping and wheezing, attempting to catch a bit of breath. Just as he had begun to collect himself, pulling his thin frame erect, Barbara Jo came prancing in the back door of the store—from her fine yellow brick house on the street just behind the huge mercantile.

"Oh, Maggie! I do declare! How nice to see you this mornin'! However *are* you?" Barbara Jo's pale, narrow face broke into a broad smile. Approaching her younger sister with light steps, giving her a little peck on the cheek, she removed her fancy ribbon-bedecked bonnet and smoothed down the skirt of her blue silk dress. Barbara Jo's light blue eyes sparkled mischievously as she swung her bonnet onto a wooden peg beside the door, twisted her neck about and asked, "And *how* is *Mister Bartram Logan* this fine mornin'? Have you two set the date yet?"

"The date?" Maggie hedged, her eyes wandering the shelves behind the long oak counter, as if intently searching for something, refusing to meet her sister's curious gaze.

"Oh, *you know*, silly! The date for your *wedding*! I do declare, Maggie! We are *all* just *so* thrilled—for you and Bart. Have you made any solid plans?"

"Plans?" Maggie echoed, glancing toward her sister, her own blue eyes wide and innocent, as if she had not the faintest notion in the world what Barbara Jo could be referring to.

"Yes, *plans*, Maggie! You sound like a *parrot* this morning!" Barbara Jo let out an exasperated sigh as she walked over to stand beside her husband. "Good grief! That's what people who are in *love* and engaged to be married do! They make *plans*!—as to where the marriage will take place, and *when*. Where they're going to *live* following the ceremony! How many *children*—"

"*Children?!*" Maggie exclaimed suddenly, eyes wide.

"For heaven sakes, Maggie!" Barbara Jo put hands on narrow hips and gazed at her sister wonderingly, "You act as if you don't have the slightest notion what I'm speaking about! You *are* wearing Bartram Logan's diamond on your left hand, are you not?!"

Quickly, without actually realizing she had done it, Maggie tucked her left hand into the voluminous folds of her dress tail.

"What's *that* all about?" Barbara Jo demanded, arms crossed over a thin chest, a frown on her face, almost pretty now, as a slight color rose into her cheeks.

"I have not the vaguest notion as to what you're referring," Maggie lied.

"Margaret Ann McKinnon!—you know *exactly* what I'm referring to! You're *supposed to be getting married*! And you act as if *you* are the last person on the face of the earth to hear the news! Oh, Maggie, what's—?"

"I have to go," Maggie said all in a rush, gathering up the big basket of eggs with one hand, and with the other reaching for the sack of coffee.

"I can bring that over," Fred Moss offered rather lamely, just before doubling over in another spasm of great, racking coughs. With great effort, he recovered and pulled himself erect.

"It appears that I may be more able than you, Fredrick Moss, to tote a twenty pound sack of coffee!" Maggie blazed out at him, hefting the heavy bag onto her free arm. "And, my dearest sister, Barbs, instead of meddling into *other* folks' affairs, why don't you tend to your own! Why don't you fix a nice garlic-and-onion poultice for your husband's chest, and go up on the mountain and gather a handful of ginseng and some willow bark—and mix in a little wild honey—and fix him some hot, healing tea!? He sounds to be at death's very door! Now!—Good day to *you both*!"

The heavy bag of coffee hanging in the crook of one arm, the huge basket loaded with eggs on the other, Maggie spun and tromped away, the heels of her little leather boots tapping angrily against the bare oak floor. She shoved her way through the front entrance, the thick plank door of the mercantile banging loudly behind her.

One step outside the door, suffering more than a twinge of remorse for her unchristian-like outburst, Maggie halted dead still. She was behaving abominably! Why on earth was she so angry with Fred Moss? It wasn't Fred's fault that he was sick. Burdened with her heavy load, she turned on her heel, pushed open the heavy door with one shoulder, stuck her head in and flashed them a dazzling smile, offering sweetly, "I'm *so* sorry you're not feelin' well. I *do* hope you'll be feelin' better soon, Fred. I'll see you later, Barbs! *Do* have a good day! Now, goodbye to y'all!"

"*Well—!*" Barbara Jo declared, lips pulled thin, picking up one of the bolts of newly-arrived cloth as the door settled again on its hinges behind the slender back of her younger sister, "That Maggie…! She will *never, never* change! One minute she's…and the next…she's…one scarcely knows *what* to expect! I wonder if Mister Bartram Logan knows *just exactly what he's letting himself in for*?!"

Maggie, the giant basket of eggs on one arm, and the heavy sack of coffee weighing down the other, hurried along the narrow street as best she could, Barbara Jo's words ringing in her ears:

That's what people who are in love and engaged to be married do…they make plans…

She had accepted the man's ring, but, somehow, she could not for the life of her imagine herself *making plans to actually marry William Bartram Logan…!*

Maggie began a recitation in her mind of her favorite Scripture verse, the words weaving themselves into and out of her consciousness, beginning:

Are not two sparrows sold for a farthing…

Ending with:

… the very hairs of your head are all numbered…

Surely, *surely*, if God cared for the sparrows, and numbered *every* hair on her head, He would help her handle this…situation…she had somehow created…with Mr. William Bartram Logan.

Chapter 4

Despite the comforting Scripture verses ringing in her ears, still in somewhat of a huff, Maggie pushed open the front door of the inn, and staggered inside. In the kitchen, she deposited the basket of eggs on the table and dropped the heavy bag of coffee atop the meal chest.

Then she soon forgot Barbara Jo's words, as her little brother, Johnny, came bounding into the kitchen, rubbing the sleep from his beautiful blue eyes, yawning and grinning at her. Maggie scooped him up into her arms, rumpled his hair with one hand, gave him a quick kiss, and hugged him tightly, so tightly that Johnny pushed her away, giving her an inquisitive look.

"Go on, sugar," Maggie smiled at him as she plunked him down onto the backless bench flanking the table, "Go on and eat your breakfast. My! That bacon and eggs looks good! Did you remember to thank God for it? And I might just pour myself another cup of coffee and join you. One biscuit or two? Liza Mae is said to bake the *very* best buttermilk biscuits in the county! Oh, by the way, I might have a bit of free time this afternoon. Between the dinner and supper crowd. What would you like to do? We haven't spent the afternoon together for quite some time now." A cup of fresh hot coffee in hand, Maggie turned to the table and sat down by Johnny on the bench.

"Bart's comin' today," Johnny gazed up at her with wide, innocent eyes, and announced between bites of his buttered biscuit.

"Don't speak with food in your mouth, young sir! Mr. Logan is coming, did you say?"

"Yeah," Johnny grinned up at her and wiggled about on the bench, swinging his little legs in a steady rhythm, munching again on his buttered biscuit and staring happily up at his sister, "He's goin' ta take me ta *th' river*! Me 'n Mr. Logan, we're *goin' fishin'*!"

"You are? Why *is it*…that *I* haven't heard one word about this?" Maggie demanded, setting her coffee cup down with a thud on the battered oak table, feeling her anger begin to rise. Did Mister William Bartram Logan think he could just waltz right in here and take Johnny… What was Bartram Logan *doing*? Trying to worm his way deeper into Johnny's affections!? Trying to get at her through Johnny? Or was he simply trying to replace his own lost son…what was his name…Joshua Bartram Logan?

What was *wrong* with her today?! Where were these thoughts *coming from*? It was clearly evident from Bartram Logan's actions towards Johnny that he loved this little boy! And Johnny probably needed more than Maggie could give him. He probably needed…

He needs Papa! Maggie thought. As if to shut out the pain, with a wrenching squeeze of her heart she put down her cup and laid her head forward into cupped hands. Papa had *been* there—for her, and Nellie Sue and Barbara Jo. Now—who would be there…for Johnny…?

"Mizz Maggie? Youse wants me ta—whut's wrong?"

"What, Liza Mae? I'm sorry," Maggie lowered her hands, gave a little lift of her chin. "I guess I… wasn't listening. What were you saying?"

"Is you all right, Mizz Maggie? Ever since… you and Mr. Bart…youse has been so…*is* you all right, Mizz Maggie?" Liza Mae's black eyes shone with concern. Her voice rang with a deepening sadness. This young woman before her had literally given her back her life. Given her back a reason to go on living in this world.

"Fine! I'm just fine!" Maggie asserted shortly, waving one slender hand about dramatically. Her voice sharper than she intended—*what was wrong with her today*?!—

"Now, don't you think, Liza Mae, since we have almost a *dozen men* congregated before the fireplace in the dining room, that we should be putting ham and sausage in the skillets…and more biscuits in the oven…and how about the coffee? Did you notice that I just brought in a new bag from the store?"

"Yes'm, Mizz Maggie. I's has meddled enough," Liza Mae sighed heavily. "I'sll git *rite* on it."

Highly ashamed of herself, Maggie rose and carried her cold cup of coffee to the dry sink, where she stood, lost in thought, staring into the sink's bottom, all battered and dented. Like me, she thought wryly.

———————

Immediately when she pushed open the kitchen door and entered the dining room—balancing a huge tray of mugs of hot coffee expertly on one arm and a platter of ham, sausage and biscuits on the other—Maggie noticed the lank form of Bartram Logan, lounging before the huge fieldstone fireplace with the other men.

As Maggie entered the room, the men all rose politely from their ladder-backed chairs before the roaring fire, and moved their seats with little scrapes and clatters, across the bare oak-plank floor to the scattering of tables.

"Good morning," Bartram Logan offered softly as he passed close enough to Maggie to touch her elbow with a warm, well-tanned hand, giving a slight bow, and a charming smile.

Feeling a surprising shock of warmth flood up her arm, Maggie pulled away from him, "Oh? And it's a fine day, then, is it?" she inquired, her Scotch-Irish temper flaring, staring at him coldly as he seated himself at one of the tables spread with snow-white cloths that had been boiled in well-water laced with lye soap in the big black-iron wash pot out back, and well rubbed with the heated smoothing iron. "And just why, now, would *that* be? A fine day for…say…*fishing?*"

"I thought I…mentioned that to you. I…seem…to have…failed…to do so?"

"No, Mister Logan…*Bartram…darling*…you did *not* mention *that* to me. Yes, you did fail to do so! I learned it from Johnny…just now…as he was eating his breakfast…in the kitchen."

"Sit with me for a moment," Bart said softly as he stood, reached out a hand and pulled out a chair, "So that we can talk."

"I, Mister Logan, *darling*, have a business to run. Biscuits will not bake themselves. They never have! And they never will! It's going to be a *very busy day!*"

"And a very *cold* one, I gather," Bart remarked dryly, dark brows shooting up as he lifted a tanned hand to the back of his neck, as if warding off a painful chill.

"What is *that* supposed to mean?"

"Nothing. *Not the first blessed thing.* It's just that…we never have any time…together."

"We're together now."

"I meant…alone…so that we can talk."

"I *might* have had some time this afternoon…but I seem to recall that you, Mr. Logan, *darling,* have made other plans."

"Why don't you come with us?" Bart asked retaking his chair, as it became obvious she had no intentions of joining him at table.

"Are you inviting *me* along? On your fishing expedition with Johnny? I haven't yet said that he could go."

"Well…" Bart stammered, "No…that is…I am most certain that a lovely lady such as yourself would not deny an innocent child like Johnny an afternoon on the riverbank holding his little fishing pole. And…Well…Yes! I think that's a splendid idea! For you to accompany the two of us! We could pack a picnic—"

"A splendid idea, did you say? But it wasn't *your* idea, now, was it? No, you two just run along. I'll find something…with which to busy myself—"

Bart leapt suddenly from his chair, sending the oak legs dragging noisily across the floor, and declared loudly:

"Margaret Ann McKinnon Evans! You *are* coming fishing with us!—*this* afternoon—or by All That's Holy!—I will *physically* toss you over my shoulder!—and *bodily* heft you—across—"

"Well! If you feel *that strongly* about it—"

"Yes!" Bart asserted loudly enough to cause every eye in the dining room to turn and stare at them, "I feel *very* strongly about it!" He bent suddenly and planted a warm kiss full on her mouth. "And now that that's settled, will you kindly fetch me another cup of that delicious hot coffee? Or would you prefer that I fetch it myself?"

At about eleven thirty o'clock, Bart Logan appeared before the door of *The Sparrow Restaurant & Inn.* He wasn't at all certain how she had managed to accomplish it, but somehow, between the time he had had breakfast and his return just now, the mistress of the small business had managed to get her business sign repainted! Bart drew the matched pair of fine steeds to a halt, alighted from the grand new carriage he had just purchased, and entered the inn.

"All ready to go?" he asked breezily, his hat before him in his hand, his heart hammering at the prospect of having *Margaret Ann McKinnon Evans* all to himself—for an entire afternoon!

"I suppose we are," Maggie was muttering. She looked lovely as usual. No, that was entirely untrue, Bart thought, his heart almost bursting. She looked even *more* lovely than usual. The dress she was wearing, the lovely bonnet that framed that beautiful face—

"Mister Logan, darling, I think we are about ready. If you would be so kind as to cease your *lollygagging* and help me with the food basket?"

"What? Oh yes, of course, sweetheart! Come along Johnny! Just wait until you see what I have just purchased!"

"What on earth have you bought now? Oh! My!" Maggie breathed as she stepped outside. She stood on the narrow porch of the inn, her mouth agape. It was *the* most lovely carriage she had ever beheld. And the glistening steeds—they looked as if they could move a *mountain*!

"When? Where? Did you get *this*....*these*?"

"The day after you accepted my proposal of marriage, I picked out the horses. And the next, I ordered the carriage. After all, we're going to be a family—"

"A family?" Maggie muttered, gazing up at Bart, cutting off his words.

"Oh, yes! Of course!" Bart moved beside her, taking her by the arm as if guiding a child, steering her firmly toward the waiting carriage and horses, "We require something decent in which to transport ourselves about!"

"*Decent*, did you say?" Maggie found her voice, cast him a rueful gaze and asked sarcastically, "How about *grand.* Or *extravagant.* Or even, perhaps, *ostentatious.*"

"Ostentatious? You really think so?" Bart mused, as he lifted Maggie into the grand carriage, then Johnny, giving the little boy a wink and a warm, tight hug.

His tall frame lithely mounting the seat, he gathered the reins into his hands and started the fine steeds off at a lively trot.

"Ostentatious..." he rolled the word around on his tongue as if tasting it. As if hearing it for the first time. "You really think so, do you?"

"*I* have most certainly never seen such a carriage!" Maggie asserted with a lift of her lovely chin. She *loved* the look that flashed across his face. Like a little boy, she thought, asking that his gift be accepted. "Not on the streets of Rhyersville," Maggie added with raised brows. "It looks to me to be more suited for the streets of…say… *Philadelphia*."

"Philadelphia, eh?" Bart mused, a little smile playing about his handsome mouth as he gazed over at her. "You know, my sweet, you're absolutely right. It would look *fine* on the streets of Philadelphia. Perhaps, then, after we're married, of course, we might just take it there. How about it, Johnny? How would you like to see my hometown, the grand city of Philadelphia, in Pennsylvania? Of course, we wouldn't carry *this* carriage. We'd, quite naturally, go by train, then rent a carriage similar to this once we'd arrived at our destination."

Suddenly, Johnny's small, beautiful face was aglow with excitement. He hung on Bart Logan's every word, constantly bouncing up and down on the seat between Bart and Maggie until Maggie felt as if she was sitting beside a jack-in-the-box. But she hadn't the heart to call him down. She had never, ever, seen Johnny so happy or excited. How could *she* possibly offer him anything like *this*? This grand carriage and fine team of horses? How could *she* possibly offer him *Philadelphia*?!

Finally, between Johnny's bouncing and Bart's laughing and talking, they were pulling into McKinnon Valley.

"I thought we'd make our way to the river…from here. Is that all right with you?"

"Me?" Maggie quipped, her little chin in the air. "Fine. Just…fine."

But *this was her place!* The river just beyond that creek and the pasture…that was where she had sat on the bank with Papa that day…so many memories here…and *none of them included Mr. Bartram Logan!*

"Are you sure this is all right?" Bart asked, his eyes dark, his voice soft with concern. He had not the slightest intention of offending her. He had thought, given the way she loved this place…. "You don't appear all that…enthusiastic…"

"What's en-thus-astic?" Johnny piped up as Bart reached to lift him down.

"And wouldn't *you* just like to know, young sir?! But there are *some* things for grownup ears only. You just remember that!" Bart teased, releasing him with a little squeeze.

He's so good with Johnny! Maggie thought, her heart aching in her chest. He knows *exactly* what to say, and how to say it. How to be firm…but gentle. He's…almost perfect. *Perhaps, too perfect!* I wonder…if he's quite…*real?* Will I awaken one morning, and find that *William Bartram Logan isn't real?*

"Margaret Ann?" she heard him saying as he reached to lift her down, "You're certainly quiet. You seem a bit upset. Are you sure everything's all right?"

"Yes," she flashed him a brilliant smile, but Bart did not miss the bright pool of tears in the blue, blue eyes. "We're going to have an absolutely fabulous time!" Then, gathering her heavy skirts in her hands, Maggie flung down the challenge:

"Race you to the river, Johnny!" And with that, she turned and bounded off. Flying like the wind, like a child, Bart thought, let outdoors after a long rainy spell. *Oh God,* he whispered, *how I love her! How I wish I understood her! Could really reach her…*

"Hey! Wait for me, you two!"

And William Bartram Logan, the Yankee businessman from Philadelphia, was racing across a North Georgia pasture knee deep in overgrown grass.

Galloping across the grass, then through the deep woods, the three made their way quickly to the bank of the river.

Maggie sank down, gasping for breath. Drawing off her bonnet, she fanned herself with the stiffly-seamed brim. "My!" She sucked in a deep draught of mountain air. Suddenly she felt like a child again. How long had it been, since she'd raced across a pasture?

Not since Papa died…

"What shall we do first?" Maggie heard Bart asking. "What do you say, Johnny? What comes first? Fishing? Or eating?"

Maggie watched Bart's face closely as he gazed down at Johnny, his heart in his eyes. Johnny needed a man in his life. Maggie realized that. He needed a man to teach him the things that men need to know to make it through life. And Mr. William Bartram Logan appeared to be making it through this life very, *very* well indeed!

Yes, Mr. Bartram Logan was wealthy. An astute businessman. But what was he like as a *man?* What sort of *husband* would he be? What sort of *father figure* for Johnny? What would he be like…*after* the marriage ceremony?

Would he undergo a complete transformation? *After* the marriage ceremony…would a different man emerge? Would he cease being kind, gentle, perfect to a fault…would everything he had told her be a complete and *utter lie*…?

Suddenly the scenes of her wedding day at age sixteen flashed through Maggie's mind. She had married the son of one of Forsyth County's wealthiest landowners. Following the ceremony, he had driven her to their new home, far out in the countryside, isolated, down a road that dead-ended at the river. Where there were no neighbors…for miles about. Except for Clem and Sarah Green…

How clearly Maggie recalled that day, her shock and dismay, when the little sharecroppers' shack came into sight. How she had stood in the tiny area that was laughingly called the kitchen and gazed at the back door— where cracks admitted enough sunlight to line the worn plank flooring…and light the little shack that had only two shuttered windows…

No! She wouldn't think of Len Evans! Not this afternoon, not with the sun glinting off the river and the trees rustling with a soft fall breeze. She was home. *Home in McKinnon Valley*. This was the bank where she had sat with Papa, as he told her about the Indians that had occupied this valley. He had taught her a lesson about loving people despite their faults, or the color of their skin.

"Should we fix a pole for you? Or are you just going to watch us men show you how to fish?" Bart was smiling down at her, little crinkles in the deeply-tanned skin at the corners of gold-brown eyes. Maggie had plunked down on the river bank in the tall grass, hands clasped about her knees, deep in thought. And Bart wondered, almost jealously, what those thoughts were…flitting through that lovely head, causing that wistful look to fall across her face, like the shadows of ghosts walking.

"Would you like to fish first, darling, or do you want to eat now?"

"What?" Maggie sat gazing up at him, standing tall above her on the river bank. She stared at this man whom she suddenly realized that she scarcely knew. What did she really know about him? What on earth could have possessed her to accept his ring!? She recalled another tall, handsome man, standing beside a lovely, rushing stream…smiling … promising always to cherish her…more than his own life…to do *anything* she wanted …anything to make her happy…

No! No! This is not Len! Do not even think about Len Evans!

"What? Oh… Whatever you two want to do, you and Johnny, Mr. Logan, darling, is fine with me." Maggie made as if to rise to her feet.

Bart reached and took her hand, pulling her up. When she was on her feet, he did not release the hand but pulled her close to him. Staring intently into her eyes, as if gazing into her soul, he commented, the words escaping him before he could stop them, "I can think of lots of thing I'd like to do. But I'm not at all certain you'd go along with a one of them. By the way, where *were* you just now?" he finished softly.

"Where? I…"

"You certainly weren't here. With me."

"I *assure* you, Mr. Logan, darling," Maggie replied in a tart, clipped voice, "I *am* here with you." Bart couldn't help but notice that each time she called him *darling*, she coupled it—in a somewhat forced manner—onto the name she had called him, *Mr. Logan*, all those days she was employed by him up at the logging camp. And the appellation *darling* as it fell from her lips sounded bright and brittle as an eggshell. As if it were about to crack. Then, a sudden change of mood. With a brilliant smile, she broke into his unhappy train of thought, waving her hands with little nervous twists, as if shooing chickens to roost.

"Just go ahead, now, you two, and see which of you can catch the biggest fish. I suddenly have a fine appetite for fried fish for supper! I think I'll just take a little stroll along the river bank."

"I wouldn't do that, if I were you," Bart said quickly, his voice sounding sterner than he had intended.

"And why on earth not?" Maggie turned to stare at him. She felt blood, hot, creeping up her neck. The handsome face of Len Evans rose before her. His voice, filled with angry, husbandly authority, rang in her ears, absolutely forbidding her to leave the little sharecroppers' shack that belonged to his wealthy father, and go walking…*I will not have you walking the roads, Maggie*…!

She had been married to Len Evans. But she was *not* married to this man!

How dared he attempt to forbid her to walk in her own pasture!? No. It was *not* her pasture. If he actually did what he had mentioned the night he proposed marriage, soon it would be *Mr. Logan's pasture*. Mr. Bartram Logan, the *timber man*, who felled trees by the hundreds, as if they were mere straws before the hungry, whining saw blades of his logging crew…

"Are you *angry* with me?" Bart cocked his handsome head aside and asked wonderingly. "Have I offended you in some way? Of which I'm totally unaware? I know I'm not very good at this."

"Good at what, Mr. Logan?"

"You *are* angry. And I haven't the foggiest notion why."

"You just *forbade* me to go for a walk, did you not?" Maggie inquired, tilting her head quizzically to one side, feeling her anger deepen, heat rising up her neck into her cheeks, which she now realized must be as red as ripe strawberries. "I am *not* a five year old child, Mr. Logan, *darling*. I have walked this pasture…" Maggie halted, her voice choked with emotion. She would not let this man make her cry! She absolutely, positively would not…!

"Forbade…is rather…a strong word. What I meant…I certainly meant no offense. I just thought…we *are* deep into the countryside. And who knows what lurks in these woods? Snakes. Bears. I just wanted you to be cautious. To be safe. I wouldn't want…*anything* to happen to you." *I don't want to lose you,* he wanted to add.

"To you, Mr. Logan, these woods may lurk with dark dangers. To me, they are as familiar as my own face, and filled with…."

"Yes?"

"Never mind."

"If you insist on talking a stroll, I would like it very much if I could walk along with you." Bart offered.

"Mr. Logan, *darling*," the biting sarcasm, the unbridled anger deepened in Maggie's voice, "I do *not* need a…*protector*."

"No. I just thought…"

"I am going for a walk. *Alone.* I will be back in twenty or thirty minutes," Maggie announced with a stern lift of her chin. "And when I return, very shortly, I shall spread our lunch. And you, sir, you have issued an invitation to a certain young man to come fishing with you. Now! Go catch yourself a fish, Mr. Logan!" With those words, she spun, and flounced off into the thick woods.

Bart could scarcely keep his mind on Johnny or on his excitement at catching a huge fish almost as soon as the worm on his pole was cast into the clear, rippling waters of the river. Bart kept watching the trees, which appeared to him as thick, dark and forbidding as a forest in some medieval fairy tale, lurking with witches and wyverns and dragons with flaming tongues of fire....

"He's a big one, isn't he, Bart?" Johnny was jumping up and down with so much excitement that his britches threatened to fall off. Bart reached down and gave them a firm yank. And Bart, despite himself, gave a hearty laugh as he showed the beautiful little boy how to remove his catch from the hook without ending up with a piece of sharp medal protruding from one of his tiny fingers.

Then to Bart's great relief, Maggie was soon back, her cheeks rosy, her eyes bright. Having gotten her way, and proven her point, whatever ghosts were chasing her she had evidently shaken off in the trees. Now she seemed eager to get into the lunch she had packed. The short stroll, Bart thought, had done wonders for her! She had undergone an amazing transformation in attitude. Joking and chatting with Johnny, now, poking him playfully in the ribs, and at one time actually falling down, rolling in the grass and wrestling with him as she caught him after a wild chase about the bank. Then she straightened her hair, tucking wisps of darkly glistening tresses behind her ears and up beneath the strand of sky-blue grosgrain ribbon encircling her locks. With swift, purposeful motions, she bent and yanked up Johnny's drooping britches; then she spread the food onto a checkered cloth, calmly handed out sandwiches and muffins and cheese and fruit.

The food all spread out, she gazed directly at Bart, and asked:

"Mr. Logan? Would you care to bless this fine repast?"

"Why...of course!"

And Bart did exactly that, mumbling some sort of Grace over the food. A thing which he had never done before. He fervently hoped that his feeble efforts came off reasonably well to those lovely ears. To say nothing of the listening ears of his Heavenly Father...

"Well...Father...we...uh...certainly...appreciate...this...uh... fine day...and this...fine food...and the...uh... lovely...company...in which...we're allowed...to partake...of it. Amen."

Until meeting Margaret Ann McKinnon Evans, Bart had given little thought to things like *prayer*. Like *faith*. Like offering *thanks* for daily benefits. But since meeting Margaret Ann McKinnon Evans, Bart had taken out his mother's Bible, dusted it off, and he had begun to develop a joy in reading its words of comfort, and hope, and love. As Maggie seated herself beside him in the lovely sunlight of a gorgeous fall day, a line from the Song of Solomon came suddenly to Bart's mind:

Behold, thou art fair, my love…

Behold…thou art fair…!

The three of them sat on the riverbank and stuffed themselves.

When she had the remains of the picnic tucked away in the basket, Maggie waved the man and boy back to their fishing. Maggie never wasted food. She could recall a time not so long ago, when she had wondered where the next meal for her and her brother, Johnny, was coming from. Then Maggie realized how very tired she was. She lay back on the riverbank. Lulled by the murmurs of the water, the sounds of Johnny's excited yips of laughter—as he leapt up now and again chasing up and down the riverbank, his britches hanging about his knees—and Bartram Logan's happy return sallies as he chased after the small boy and pulled them up, she drifted off into a peaceful, dreamy sleep.

Maggie grew quiet, and Bart glanced around to check on her. She was fast asleep. He smiled to himself, and noted that Johnny, too, seemed to be flagging. The little boy had sat still for all of the past five minutes or so, and Bart caught him yawning wide yawns, which he valiantly attempted to stifle behind small hands. He was, after all, only four—almost five—years of age. Bart suspected that Maggie ordered him to nap each afternoon. He noticed that from time to time the wide blue eyes drifted closed, full dark lashes falling onto apple-red cheeks, and the cane pole finally dropped from the little hands. Bart lifted the boy, and carried him into the shade of a tree near Maggie, where he carefully laid him down. Then he sat between the two, and Mr. Bartram Logan took turns, quietly contemplating the pair, what he hoped would soon be his new family.

When Bart turned his gaze full on Maggie, his heart almost stopped. She looked incredibly young, incredibly vulnerable, her eyes closed, dark lashes thick against rose-white skin. He found it difficult to believe this fantastically beautiful young woman, still scarcely more than a girl, had endured the heartache and suffering her sister, Barbara Jo, had described to him that night in her fine yellow brick house behind her husband's rich mercantile establishment. He also found it difficult to believe this delectably lovely young woman now wore his diamond on her left hand. A diamond, a gem that only the strongest tools on earth could break, set in gold, an element of the earth that did not fade or tarnish with age, but grew softer, brighter, more precious. Set in a circle…of undying, unending love…

So, Mrs. Margaret Ann McKinnon Evans didn't think she needed a protector!? Bart sat contemplating the future. That's *exactly* what William Bartram Logan intended to be, for the remainder of their lives.

"Oh, I'm so sorry. I must have fallen asleep. What time is it?" Almost as if she felt Bart's gaze resting on her, Maggie sat suddenly up, rubbing her eyes and self-consciously straightening her skirts. She recalled another time she had inadvertently drifted off into a drowsy, dreamy sleep—as she sat on the bench before Moss' Mercantile, waiting to be interviewed by this handsome lumberman, for the job of cook at his logging camp high in the mountains…

Bart, seated on the grass beside her, reluctantly drew his eyes from Maggie and pulled a gold watch from a silk vest pocket. He had shed his jacket and his soft linen shirt was open at the neck. His dark hair was slightly mussed, and his face shone with a slight sheen of perspiration glistening across his deep tan.

"It's a quarter until four."

"Oh, my! I need to get back! Liza Mae and Benjamin will be needing help!"

"I'm sure they can handle it," Bart offered. "And Johnny's fast asleep. I think all that fishing tired him out. And I thought that, now that we're here, you might want to go up to the house. Have a look around. Decide on what changes you might want to make to the place, once the deal is finalized."

"Deal? Finalized? You're…actually *buying* McKinnon Valley?"

43

"You sound as though this thought takes you totally by surprise, darling. Isn't that *exactly* what I told you I'd do, the night you agreed to marry me? God willing, I'm buying the valley for you. As a wedding gift."

"But...what if..."

"What?"

"I don't know. Forget it."

"I don't want to forget it. Is there some question in your mind, about our getting married? If there is, don't you think you should do me the courtesy of discussing it with me? Give me a fighting chance here, to make my case?"

"Is that what this is to you, Mr. Logan? A *case*?" The term sounded so stiff, and legal. *And binding*.

Bart immediately noticed that *this* time when she spoke, she didn't even bother to add the empty appellation *darling*, to her address of him. "It was merely a figure of speech, sweetheart. If you have something on your mind, I would very much appreciate being privy to that. I would like you to share it with me. We need to talk, if there's something bothering you."

"Talk? What good is *talk*!?" Maggie's voice dripped with sarcasm. She flounced up, refusing to meet his gaze, angrily brushing bits of weed and grass off her dark skirt. Bart, taken by surprise, still seated on the bank, his hands on his knees, listened to the angry tirade that continued, and all but tore his heart out of his chest. She blurted out: "Men's words can mean *anything. Or they can mean nothing!*" Maggie turned and stared angrily into his eyes, her own eyes dark with pain.

Slowly Bart unfolded his lank frame and stood, drawing himself to his full height, attempting to search his mind for the right words. He wasn't sure what she meant, and very evidently she wasn't about to tell him. Had he just been called a liar? Roundly insulted? He wanted to be very careful with his words, not jump to any false conclusions, not create some new issue here that didn't actually exist.

"I am as *good* as my word, darling," Bart said, his voice low and laced with hurt. "Whatever I *tell* you, as much as God allows me breath and strength, you can take as *truth*. I will *never, never* tell you anything, make any promises to you that I have no intentions of fulfilling. You have my solemn word on that. Now, would you or would you not like to go up to the house?"

"Not today," Maggie sighed, drawing her gaze away. She felt tired, drained. Weary. All the fight seemed suddenly to have flown out of her. What was wrong with her? She had no desire to fight with Bart Logan. Exactly what *were* her feelings towards this rich, handsome, almost too perfect man? There were too many emotions roiling around inside her head, inside her heart, to sort them out. Too many bad memories. "I don't think so. Later, perhaps. What did you envision that I would want to do…to the house?" she asked suddenly.

"I don't know. Whatever you please," Bart tried to stumble on. She had completely lost him. "Build on? Remodel? Purchase new furnishings. It will be *yours.* To do with as you please. I will, of course, put any sum of money you think necessary, totally at your disposal…"

He talked on. Maggie stared up into his eyes, so dark, so solemn and so earnest, and she thought of all the wealth this man had at his beck and call, right at the tips of those strong, brown fingertips…. And she wondered… *What would it feel like, to have the money to do whatever your heart desired…?* Reared on this North Georgia mountain farm that lay around them, that had been sunk in debt from the day Papa came home from the War, recalling how they had lived mostly on barter, how seldom cash money was seen or felt in the Reconstruction South, Maggie could not begin to imagine such a situation.

But if her little brother…if sweet little John Thomas McKinnon, Jr.…. was to realize his dream of becoming a physician, where could she, Maggie McKinnon Evans, possibly get the funds to make such a dream come true? He would need to be educated at a fine medical college. For Maggie, as for the majority of folks, money was still scarce in the South. The inn was turning a profit…but not *that* kind of profit…

"Not today," Maggie sighed again, picking up her basket, her brain in a whirl.

"Whatever you say, darling. I'll just get Johnny, then, and we'll be on our way."

Bart bent and easily lifted the little boy into his arms, placing him on his left shoulder. Johnny's head lolled in deep, contented sleep beneath Bart's chin. The small body melted against his chest. He could feel the boy's breath, warm and alive against his neck, the beating of the little heart, exactly as he had felt it the day he rescued the child from beneath the giant hooves of one of his logging horses. A great lump in his throat, his vision blurring, Bart tightened his grip on the boy, wishing with all his heart Johnny's sister was as accepting of his love, of his warm caresses, as her little brother. How he longed to get his arms about that lovely young woman now striding so rapidly, so purposefully up through the shaded pasture just in front of his eyes, the young woman who now wore his ring—but refused to grant him the very slight familiarity of calling him by his given name.

Chapter 5

"Maggs? It's quiet as a tomb in here! Where on earth is everyone? Where are you? I've been…oh, there you are." Barbara Jo, her face almost entirely hidden beneath the brim of a frilled bonnet, walked briskly forward, through the dining room of the inn, offering her cheek for Maggie's usual kiss of greeting.

"It's mid-afternoon, Barbs," Maggie chided her older sister good naturedly, "You know we can *always* be found out in the kitchen in mid—"

They had by now arrived in the kitchen and stood near the battered oak table. Barbara Jo drew off her bonnet. At the look on her sister's sallow face, Maggie broke off, quickly inquiring, "Is something wrong? You look peeked and pale as a ghost! Has something happened?"

"Could we sit down, Maggs, please?" Barbara Jo asked in a tone of voice Maggie had not heard for many years. Not since, in fact, they were children, and something went against Barbara Jo's expectations.

"Something *has* happened," Maggie answered her own question in a small, thin voice as she sank into a ladder-backed chair across from Barbara Jo. "What is it?"

"It's…Fred," Barbara Jo began, producing a small elaborately embroidered handkerchief from the folds of her skirt, dabbing at her eyes, and then twisting the little linen square in thin hands. "You know how he's always coughing and carrying on. Saying he's contracted another bad cold? Well, we saw a new doctor today. A specialist. Down at the hospital in Gainesville. And…he said…"

"Well, what did he say?" Maggie urged.

"Fred…..Fred has… consumption of the lungs."

"What? Oh, no…no…not that…that…*can't* be right," Maggie

47

muttered, stunned. "That's a horrid disease. A wasting away of the lungs. It robs a person of all breath. Oftentimes, of their life…I'm sorry, Barbs. I don't know what's wrong with me. I shouldn't have said that. I'm sure Fred will be fine. Maybe he just needs a few days off from the mercantile. A few days to sit in your beautiful flower garden. Or on the wide veranda of your house and just look at the mountains. And just rest and recuperate? What do you think?"

"I think that, as usual, *you*, Maggie McKinnon Evans, are being your *over*-optimistic self! Trying to assure *everyone* the sky isn't really falling, when all the time you know good and well that it is!" Barbara Jo broke off, her light blue eyes brimming with tears. "Oh, at the times I have accused that man of being a big *faker*! Putting on that he's sick, just to get my attention!"

"Has it been all that difficult, Barbs… for your husband to command your attention? That he has to….I'm sorry, I'm prying into something that is *none* of my business. Whatever…goes on between you and Fred…well…that's completely your own affair. Would you like me to heat up the coffee?"

"What? Oh, no. I don't think I'll *ever* eat or drink *another* bite of anything!" Barbara Jo blurted out, thin lips trembling, tears now filling her eyes and spilling down her cheeks, dripping onto her fine dress. She let out a long, loud wail, moaning:

"Ahhhhhhooooooooo! I do declare, Maggie! I'll just *starve* to death of this grief! Fred is *dying*! I just *know* it, Maggs! My dear, *dear* husband is dying! *Right* before my eyes! And I'm *helpless* to prevent it!"

Barbara Jo burst into great wailing, wracking sobs. It was the first time Maggie had seen her sister weep so, not since they were children and Barbara Jo selfishly didn't get her way about something. But, then, a while back, Barbs had suddenly grown up. Maybe, Maggie thought, it was all the loss they had endured—loss that, at the time, seemed to roll off Barbara Jo like ripples of water off a duck's feathers. But deep inside, she now knew, Barbs' heart had pained the same as her own at the loss of the farm, and Papa's and Mama's passing.

Her heart breaking, Maggie moved to a chair beside her sister, reached out and drew Barbara Jo into a warm embrace, as much so as she could with the two of them still seated. "Oh, Barbs! I'm so frightfully, frightfully sorry! Is there anything…anything at all I can do? No. I know I can only pray. We can only pray…that God will have mercy! And heal Fred of this…where is Fred? Is he still…working at the mercantile?"

"No. Not today. This morning… he tried to get up. He was so weak from getting hardly any sleep, from all that hacking and coughing all night… that he could scarcely stand. I insisted he get back into bed, fed him a bite of breakfast, what he could keep down. Then I left him in bed…I know…what you think…but he was so adamant that the store be opened at least for an hour or two to serve the needs of people who depend on him to be there…I thought not doing as he asked might do more harm than leaving him alone for a few hours."

"Barbs? Is there any treatment for this? What do you plan…on doing…about the store? Oh, how I wish I were free to help you! You worked so hard, helping me get the inn furnished and up and running! I feel like such a—"

"No! Now you hush that, right now!" Barbara Jo lifted her teary gaze to her younger sister's face, and began patting her eyes with her soggy, wrinkled handkerchief. "After what you went through, I think it was high time someone lent you a helping hand. And I just thank God He in His kind mercies made it possible for me to do just that. Maybe it helped make up for all that selfishness and laziness when I was a child…and you were carrying us all on your little back…"

"Oh, Barbs! No one is thinking of any of that now!"

"Well, I'm thinking about it. I think about it almost every day of my life. But we can't go back and change things, can we, Maggs? We can't go back and fix our stupid failures and mistakes. As Mama always said: *You can't put the spilt milk back in the pitcher!*"

"You were just a child, Barbs!" Maggie insisted sweetly, "And I don't really think you spilt *that* much milk..!"

"Oh, Maggs!" Barbara Jo, uncertain as to whether to laugh or cry, blubbered into Maggie's warm, fragrant hair, "What on God's earth would we all do without *you*? No one but you would forgive all those years of—"

"Now you just hush that up, you hear me, Barbara Jo McKinnon Moss! And I don't want to hear another word about it. It's all over and done. And this is another day. You have to think now about your sick husband, and what we can do to make this thing as easy on you as possible. I can come over, during off hours, and open the store for you. Now, hush your snuffling, and don't wag your head at me like that. Liza Mae and Benjamin Noah can certainly do the clean up after each meal. It will at least keep things going until…you can decide exactly what it is you need to do…about the mercantile."

"Oh, but Maggs! You don't realize all the *work* there is to be done…running a huge mercantile like that! There are inventories to be taken, orders to be placed, accounts to be kept, stock to be priced and shelved…deliveries to be made…"

"Well," Maggie replied with a firm nod of her head, "We'll just do what we can, and leave the remainder in the hands of our Heavenly Father! If He keeps account of the very *hairs on our heads*…well…Now, I'm going to fix up a couple of plates. And you can take them back with you. Get a few bites of good home cookin' into that husband of yours. Then Johnny and I will go up on the mountains, and bring down some—"

Barbara Jo wiped her eyes, nodded her head, and smiled weakly as Maggie rattled on and on. What a joy it was to have such a strong sister!

Maggie bustled about the big black iron cookstove, preparing two plates, talking on, making positive plans. Anything. *Anything*…to help Barbara Jo cope with this tragedy that had befallen her. Maggie thought with a wash of guilt of all the times she had felt envy coursing through her. Yes! Envy of her sister's fine clothes, her grand house…especially when Maggie, Johnny and Liza Mae were living in Dr. Ellis's little dirt-floored, one-room cabin down at the end of the rutted dirt lane that was the main street through Rhyersville.

Maggie turned, two plates, snow white food cloths covering their contents, extended toward her sister. "Now, you just take these and go on home. I'm going to call Johnny, and we're going on up into the mountains."

"Maggs, you don't have to do that," Barbara Jo began lamely.

"No. I know I don't. But it's something I want to do. And Johnny will love a hike up the mountain, to gather his healing herbs. You know how Johnny feels…"

"Yes. Maggs, I don't know if I've ever told you, how much I appreciate your seeing to Johnny. After Mama died, I just didn't feel…that Fred…would accept. I just didn't feel that I was capable of…"

"Hush, Barbara Jo. Take this lunch. I'll put on a pot of chicken soup for your supper. Now. I have things to do. Go on home to your husband!"

Maggie practically shoved her sister out the door. What on earth had gotten into Barbara Jo? Here she said her husband was dying! And her going on and on about her past faults and failures! It didn't make one dab of sense! But, then, Barbara Jo had never been known for being especially rational or logical. Or strong. Fred had always looked after her...he had always managed the store. How in the name of heaven was Barbara Jo going to cope with a dying husband...and what had been a thriving business...suddenly left with no one at the helm?

Clasping her brother, Johnny, by one small hand, Maggie trudged up the mountain back of the square-log house in McKinnon Valley. She turned once she had reached the little flat plateau where the graveyard lay. She scanned the log house, so serene in the valley below. It was as if, she thought wryly, the valley had lain like this for a thousand years and never in all that time been touched by tragedy. But she recalled so clearly how the cooling board holding Papa's corpse had rested across the split oak rails of the back porch—from the hour the clock on the fireplace mantel struck four that morning. How Thomas Beyers had placed the board there, then tenderly brought Papa down from his upstairs bedroom, and placed him on the board to cool. How with the coming of dawn, Mama, big with her pregnancy with little Johnny, had tenderly washed and bathed her husband, anointed him with camphorated oil, and dressed him in his fine black worsted suit that Maggie had just bought on credit from the Rhyersville Store.

Thomas!...Maggie thought with a sudden pang of...of what, she was not exactly sure. Thomas held such a special place in her heart. Not only had he once been her schoolmaster, but Thomas was the surviving widower of her dead sister, Nellie Sue. It was Thomas Beyers who had given her such help and support in her time of need, when Papa became so deathly ill. While Barbara Jo refused even to rise from her bed to as much as draw a bucket of water from the well in the back yard...as Papa lay dying...and finally...dead. But instead, Barbara Jo cowered beneath her bed covers and moaned and whined into her pillow.

She seldom thought of Thomas Beyers these days, Maggie realized with a jolt of guilt tinged with sadness. Thomas had been such a rock of strength for her, such a bulwark in the awful storm that had swept over her, over the valley, with Papa's sickness and death. The awful fact of Papa's having lost the entire amount he received for the cotton crop she and Papa had slaved to gather in from the rolling, terraced fields—five bales. All that money *lost.* And still not found until this day. Maggie still wondered sometimes, deep in the dead of night, *how could that one hundred and fifty-three dollars have simply vanished?!*

But through all that, Thomas Beyers had been there, every time she looked up. A young schoolmaster, not a farm worker, yet Thomas had taken on every job he could find about the farm. Scything wheat, bundling fodder, chopping wood.

And now, being a widower, Thomas came into the inn for a meal fairly regularly. And Barbara Jo more than once had hinted that Thomas Beyers came into *The Sparrow* for more than a good meal. But Maggie scarcely paid him any attention. She refused to hear any such nonsense. Thomas Beyers was like a brother to her, she assured Barbara Jo, and nothing more. And Maggie suddenly realized she had scarcely paid him the courtesy of carrying on a decent conversation with him, since coming back to Rhyersville and opening the inn! How very rude and thoughtless of her! She would have to make amends, make it a special point, the next time Thomas came into the inn, to sit with him for a few moments—and talk.

Then, distractedly, Maggie turned her gaze to the headstones. Shawn Ian McKinnon, her great-grandfather. And, resting by his side, her great-grandmother, Katherine Ann, the fourteen-year-old Irish lass that the young Scotsman, Shawn, had encountered on the salt-encrusted decks of *The Last Farewell,* had rescued from her despondency after the corpses of her parents had been consigned to the tossing waves of the cold Atlantic. And shortly after *The Last Farewell* dropped anchor along the quays of the port of Charleston, South Carolina, that long ago summer in 1826, just after they disembarked, Shawn had married young Katherine Ann.

Beyond them lay the grave of Mary Margaret McKinnon, Maggie's grandmother. And beside the granite headstone of Mary Margaret rose a memorial stone to Grandpa Thomas Shawn McKinnon, whose bones lay bleaching somewhere in a Virginia field or forest, where the dirty Yankees had shot him dead... Then there was Papa's grave. But Mama did not rest beside him.

At the edge of the clearing, beneath a small stand of tulip poplars lay a few scattered piles of stone. These, Maggie knew, smiling in spite of herself, were the 'graves' of her pet rabbits, and of her beautiful doll that had melted in the rain—Katie. She recalled how tenderly Papa had laid the little doll in her 'grave,' playing a dirge on his fiddle to see her to her final rest.

Maggie pulled her mind back to the present, calling, "Johnny? Oh, there you are, sugar. Let's walk on up the mountain, see if we can get something to help dear Fred."

Later that afternoon, Maggie, with Johnny firmly in hand, stepped across the wide, well-shaded veranda, and entered the fine yellow brick house behind Moss' General Mercantile. Since there were only Fred and Barbara Jo, Maggie often wondered why Fred Moss had bothered to build such a grand, spacious house. Now, Barbara Jo descended the wide, carpeted staircase, and greeted her sister with a peck on the cheek.

"Well!" Barbara Jo attempted to put on a brave mantle of cheerfulness, "I see that the two of you come bearing your ministrations before you! Chicken soup I smell, and what else is that that you have there, Johnny?"

"My med'cines!" Johnny declared with a proud lift of his little chin.

"Well..." Barbara Jo hesitated for the briefest moment, brow knitting in a little frown beneath a thin fringe of brown curls. Fred had never taken any special liking to children. They had never had any of their own, and Barbara Jo did not know why. Maybe it was the Lord's will, since God surely knew Fred didn't care for children, and she had no overwhelming desire for one of her own. But if they had been blessed with a child, Barbara Jo felt certain Fred Moss would have responded to the whole affair much more gracefully than Len Evans had handled Maggie's two pregnancies! Cold! Thoughtless! Cruel! In each instance, behaving exactly as if the expected child did not exist!

Maggie cut into her sister's reverie, drawing Barbara Jo back to the present, gazing down at Johnny, encouraging her little brother:

"I'm quite sure dear Fred cannot *wait* for you to visit him with your healing tea and your wild-onion-and-garlic poultice, Johnny. Barbara Jo, why don't we go on up with Johnny? And see how Fred's doing?"

"Oh, yes! I do declare! It is so good to…have company!" Barbara Jo smiled brightly, "Let's just do that!"

Johnny skipped up the stairs ahead of his sisters, burst into Fred Moss' bed chamber and announced:

"I'm here now, to make you *alllll* better!"

"What?" Fred Moss attempted to lift his shrunken form up onto one elbow, turned feverish, red rimmed eyes to stare at his small brother-in-law, then up at Barbara Jo and Maggie. Then he sank back down.

"Is that you, Maggie?" Fred mumbled from his plump white pillow, sunken eyes bright with fever, in an almost entirely bald head.

"Yes, Fred, it's Maggie," Barbara Jo approached her husband's bed, reached over and took one of his hot hands between her two cool, white ones. "Maggie's come to see you. And Johnny—"

"Good," Fred interrupted, his eyes gleaming hotly, "I need to *talk* to you, Maggie. There's something you and I never did finish. Some things I need to say—to you…"

"Fred! My goodness! What are you mumbling on about? What could you *possibly* need to discuss with *Maggie?*" Barbara Jo asked, perching on the side of her husband's broad bed, making small, nervous flips at his covers with pale hands. Then she again took one of his feverish hands between hers.

"Barbara Jo! Would you kindly *leave me alone!* This is between me…and Maggie!"

As if his hand burned her, Barbara Jo released it. It fell limply back to the cover of the bed. Barbara Jo rose to her feet.

"What in the world do you think he's ranting about Maggie?" Barbara Jo asked, a frown creasing her narrow brow, her light blue eyes boring into her sister's dark blue ones.

"He's sick, Barbs," Maggie mumbled, attempting to hide her confusion and dread. *Let it go, Fred!* she wanted to shout at the sick man on the bed. Instead, she said, "Who knows what goes on in the mind of a fevered person, Barbs. He probably means…uh… something about *an order* I have at the store. Now, let me see? What was it I ordered, and it still hadn't come in the last time I was in the store and asked Fred about it?"

Barbara Jo pulled her sister away from the bed, into a corner of the large room, hissing, "*This* didn't sound like anything as *ordinary* as an order of *merchandise* that Fred has on his mind, Maggie. You and Fred haven't been…squabbling…behind my back, have you? I know you *never* liked Fred. Not from *day* one. But I didn't know that the two of you harbored some secret grudge."

"Don't be silly, Barbs!" Maggie cut in nervously. "Why in heaven's name would I be on the outs with your husband?"

Suddenly Fred blurted out, "Don't you understand? I need to apologize to Maggie…I need…"

Maggie stepped quickly up beside Fred's bed, patted his hand with rapid little motions, and remarked brightly, "Now, Fred. There's no need for that. Any…any debt that is left unpaid between the two of us…I'm sure can certainly be….forgiven. Don't you go giving…it anything *like* a second thought. You just save your strength, and hurry up and get well. We're all praying for you. You know, Fred, that I …respect you like a brother," Maggie rattled nervously on, small drops of sweat now dampening her upper lip. "Now you just hush up, you hear, and drink this tea that Johnny has steeped. Doctor Johnny and I tromped *all* the way up McKinnon Mountain, just to gather these healing herbs for you. That shows…the high regard…in which we hold you. So you just hush up, now, and let our little physician minister to your ills."

"Forgiven…? Thank you, Maggie. You don't know…that's such a *great* weight off my mind… I…never intended…"

"Never intended *what*? For goodness sakes!" Barbara Jo stepped up beside Maggie, demanding in a strident voice, "*What* in the world is this all about? What's going on that I don't know about?!"

"Nothing, Barbs. Not one single thing. You know how I am. How I've *always* been. Too quick to speak my mind. Oh, my yes! Treading all over other people's toes. I must have…done something…to upset Fred….at some time. And apparently, it's still preying on his mind. But I can assure you, there's no ill will between the two of us. Not one bit! You can just *put* your mind to rest. No ill will, Barbs, as God is my witness. Whatever… it is…Fred…*can you hear me?*…all…is…forgiven."

55

Barbara Jo stared at Maggie, as Johnny, who had scooted up behind the bed, was unbuttoning Fred's striped cotton nightshirt, spreading on his wild-onion-and-garlic poultice…

Barbara Jo's hand flew to her throat. She began to inhale rapidly, catch her breath sharply, and declare:

"*Oh, my…!* That's the same stuff you put on Papa! It *stinks* to high heaven! That mess should either cure you—or finish you off, for sure!"

"Well," Maggie smiled in relief that the subject had shifted away from Fred Moss' feeble, fevered attempt at an apology to the stink of Johnny's medications. "Let us just hope for the cure!"

———————

"How is Fred today?" Maggie asked in a very quiet, very subdued voice. Maggie had attempted to keep her visits with Fred to a minimum, just enough to border on being decently interested in the welfare of her brother-in-law, telling Barbara Jo that Fred needed his rest, which is just what the specialist down in Gainesville had prescribed.

Barbara Jo seemed to accept this explanation. And she had just opened the door to admit her younger sister to her fine home. She stood holding the door, as if uncertain just exactly what to do with the thing.

"Barbs? Dear? Shall we push the front door shut…in order to keep in all that delicious heat?" Maggie inquired softly.

"Oh, yes. Of course," Barbara Jo muttered distractedly. "He didn't rest at all last night. I've had little rest, several nights, now."

"Oh, Barbs! I'm so sorry. If only there was more that I could do!"

"For goodness sakes, Maggs!" Barbara Jo fanned her face with one thin hand holding a wad of damp handkerchief, as if suddenly overcome with a flush of heat, declaring irritably, "You are seeing to the inn *and* the mercantile, *and* Johnny! How much more do you think you can handle!?"

"I don't know, dear," Maggie mumbled, uncertain as to just how to reply to Barbara Jo's outburst, "It's just that—"

"You *can't* carry the whole world, Margaret Ann McKinnon! So I just wish you would *stop making the attempt!*" Barbara Jo snapped, turning away to hide her tears.

"Barbs…I'm sorry…I certainly didn't mean to upset you," Maggie muttered.

"Oh, don't mind me, Maggs," Barbara Jo flounced back, whining, "I scarcely know what I'm doing these days. Pay me no heed. The world has gone so topsy-turvy. Everything seemed so good! So fine! Only a few weeks ago! Now Fred can scarcely *breathe* from one moment to the next! What in the name of heaven *will I do*…without him?" Barbara Jo began to weep softly.

"I suppose, Barbs," Maggie said, though not unkindly, "You'll do what all the other widows in the world do. You'll get up each morning, wash your face, comb your hair, put one foot in front of the other…and do the best you can."

"Oh, *Maggs*! If that doesn't sound *just like you!*" Barbara Jo whirled angrily on her sister. *"You have an answer for everything*, don't you!? My husband is lying in our bed upstairs…*dying!* And you offer me *stale advice and platitudes!"*

"Well, Barbs, how about this? Papa always said that bad things happen to us in life to make us strong. Papa said that—"

"Oh, Maggs! Papa said a lot of things *to you*! But, unfortunately, he said very, *very* little to me! My brain is not chocked full of Papa's sage advice! Fred is dying upstairs. And I am left with *nothing*! *Nothing* to hang on to! Papa had only *one* daughter, and you and I both know it!"

"Barbs—! I realize you're going through a rough time…" Maggie felt hurt and shocked to the core. "Perhaps, then…Barbs…" Maggie moved towards the door, "I should…leave…and come back another time. When you're in a more…"

"Oh, Maggs!" Barbara Jo wagged her head and wailed, "Don't go! *For God's sake!* Don't leave me in this house with that man that's dying in my bed! I think that if you do, I shall go absolutely, *stark, staring, raving mad!"*

"Why don't I…" Maggie removed her bonnet and shawl, draping them on an ornate stand beside the front door, "… make you a cup of hot tea…then…and I'll just go on up and see Fred…for a moment. Is someone sitting with him now?"

"Thomas. Thomas is up there," Barbara Jo muttered between wailing sobs.

"Then, you're *not* all alone are you, Barbs? You have me, and Johnny, and Thomas. Dear, sweet, Thomas…"

"Yes," Barbara Jo muttered between sobs, "Dear… sweet… sob… Thomas…who can't see the leaves on the trees because he's so lovesick over Margaret Ann McKinnon…sob…"

"Yes! Well…I'll just trot on upstairs…then…Barbs…since you don't seem all that much in the mood for either tea…or company…"

Maggie let her voice trail off, and slowly ascended the stairs, turning to stare worriedly down at her sister from the landing above the curved railing.

If Barbara Jo was carrying on like this, now, half out of her mind with grief and…whatever…what would be the state of her mind…when Fred Moss' cold, stiff form was lowered into the ground…?

"Thomas!" Maggie breathed softly as she drifted into Fred Moss' sick room that stank strongly of Johnny's concoctions. "How is the patient today? And how are you, dear Thomas?"

"Maggie! It's *herself*, so it is, in the flesh! And how is my favorite lady?" Thomas pulled a fine Irish brogue as he rose to his feet.

"I am not a'tall, a'tall in th' way of bein' sure, Mister Thomas Beyers," Maggie sighed softly, and teased in return, "that you, sir, should be addressin' me in such a manner or fashion. I am, as you well know, engaged to be married."

"Yes." Thomas Beyers' teasing mood vanished. Suddenly very serious, Thomas murmured softly, "Lucky fellow, that Mr. William Bartram Logan." Thomas pulled a faint smile, "I find it difficult to extend congratulations, because…I shall miss you. I do miss you…already."

"Why, Thomas…" Maggie sought to change the subject, "what a sweet thing to say. And how is… everything…down at the school? John Thomas will be enrolling, next fall, you know."

"Yes. I did know. I recall *exactly* the day Johnny was born. I recall…so many things."

"Yes, well, Thomas. Those were trying days, for all of us, I fear. But life does go on, does it not? And how is Fred today?"

"Could we step outside for a moment, Maggie? Just for a moment, my dear?"

"Why, certainly, Thomas."

Outside the door, Thomas guided Maggie to the far side of the landing. Then Thomas whispered, "I fear…he won't make it through the night.

And that's not the worst of it. Fred has just revealed to me…that the store is mortgaged to the hilt. And only the house remains… that is…unaffected by Fred's…unfortunate debts. I fear for Barbara Jo, when she hears this unwelcome news. And I did not feel…that it was my place to be the bearer of such black tidings. So I thought that if you…"

"Debts?" Maggie gasped. "How on earth did this happen?"

"I…" Thomas sputtered, as if unable…or unwilling…to continue.

Maggie, overcome by the news of the looming debts, did not press him for an answer.

"Oh, Thomas! How awful! But…I'm afraid…that Barbs is not in an especially receptive mood to *my* prattling today. She has just about bitten my head off. Not once, not twice, but *thrice*, since I dared enter her door. No." Maggie wagged her head determinedly, "I shall *most certainly* not be the bearer of *these* black tidings. I leave that to a more stalwart soul. Someone with…why *not* you, Thomas? After all, you *are* family."

"No." The word was scarcely more than a whisper. "I couldn't. Perhaps… then… Mr. Logan. He seems to be a man of strong temperament…"

"Well, yes, I suppose he is, Thomas…but Bart Logan could scarcely be held responsible for being the bearer of such grim news. I mean…Bartram Logan is…"

"He's the man you're about to *marry*, Maggie."

"Well…yes…but…"

"You *are* going to marry him, aren't you, Maggie, darling?"

"Thomas…I don't think this is the time…or the place…to be discussing my future plans…"

"It's a very straightforward question, Maggie. Are you, or are you not, intending to be married to Mr. Logan?"

"Well, Thomas! I have no wish to be rude…but that's really *none* of your business, now is it?! Why on earth would you care one way or the other?!"

"Because, Maggie McKinnon, I—"

"Maggs!" suddenly Barbara Jo's voice rang up the stairs, "Are you still up there? I do believe I will take a cup of that hot tea now, if you would be a dear and hurry down and brew some up for me!"

"Excuse me, Thomas," Maggie muttered, and gathering up her skirts, she slipped past him, and fled down the stairs.

Heart hammering, she dashed into the kitchen, swung the door shut as if to close out the world behind her, leaned against it and breathed:
Thomas!

Maggie stole what hours she could from the operation of *The Sparrow*, to open Moss' General Mercantile for a few hours each day. She had drawn up a huge sign, which she posted on the front door when she opened Moss' for business. And she attempted to keep those hours fairly regular. Usually Benjamin Noah joined her there, stocking the high shelves of the mercantile, hefting sacks of fertilizers and seeds and feed for stock into the storeroom in back of the store, and then into the waiting rigs of customers. All deliveries had ceased.

By nightfall, Maggie was tired to the bone. And Bart Logan watched all this extra work with a dark, angry eye.

Did she not have enough to do, he wondered in amazement, caring for the boy, running her own business? He thought of suggesting that Fred Moss put out some of the money he had no doubt been hoarding back, to hire a couple of men to operate his business.

One sunny afternoon Bart made it a point to personally visit Maggie's sister. By this time, Fred himself had broken down, and confessed his gambling addiction and his resulting financial losses to his wife—of which Bartram Logan was totally unaware. Still, Bart dreaded the encounter. He caught her just as she stepped onto the spacious veranda of her yellow brick house, to escape her husband's sickroom and catch a breath of fresh air.

Barbara Jo waved Bart into one of the four porch rockers, then tiredly settled herself and her voluminous skirts into the porch swing. Her expensively-shod feet barely reaching the porch floor, she sat dragging her toes, rocking gently back and forth. Bart sat, his tall, lean frame perched on the rim of the rocker. He twisted his hat in his hands, as he attempted to make light, meaningless conversation for a few moments, inquiring as to Fred Moss' current state of health, then Bart replied offhandedly to Barbara Jo's latest remark:

"Yes, Mrs. Moss, it has, indeed, been a...very dry fall." Bart glanced away from Barbara Jo, down at the fine felt hat in his hands. Carefully he hung the hat behind him on a post of the rocker, clasped his hands about the knees of his expensive, fawn-wool trousers. Then he leaned even farther out of the big oak rocker, and angrily broached the subject he had purposefully come to put forward.

"You realize, don't you, Mrs. Moss, that your sister—"

"Maggie?" Barbara Jo's light blue eyes lit on Bart's tanned, handsome face. She sat, waiting, for what she knew was sure to come. This man was so crazy in love with Maggie... "Yes, Mr. Logan? What about...Maggie?"

"*Mrs.* Moss! She is *absolutely, totally* working her fingers to the bone! *Could* your husband not, mayhap, employ some strong young man? Operating a *mercantile establishment* such as Moss' is, after all, the work of a *man!*"

For just a moment, Barbara Jo's thin face went absolutely blank. She slid her gaze down to her pale hands, clasped nervously in the lap of a silk morning dress. She lifted her eyes, wet now with tears, to look up at Bart.

"I don't know exactly how to tell you this, Mr. Logan. I haven't the slightest desire...no intention, whatsoever...to injure, to...reduce your faith in mankind. But, you see, my husband, Fred, he is, you understand, a *good* man at heart and he has—over the years—proven himself a very astute, very able...business person. A man of character in the community. But..."

"But...*what*...Mrs. Moss?" Bart insisted. Dark brows knit in a deep frown, brown eyes glinting with anger, he glanced away from her, into the quiet dirt street, then swung his gaze back again. "Something has gone awry in your husband's life, rendering him financially unable to employ help for the mercantile? Is that what you're attempting to tell me? In as tactful a manner as you can?"

"Yes. That's about it. You see, Mr. Logan, Fred seems to have become...oddly disturbed, distracted, about something for the past several months. It happened, in fact, about the time Maggie lost her baby...then...her husband, Len. Or maybe, it was the uprooting, the move from Cumming, up to Rhyersville. I don't know. At any rate, what I'm trying my most earnest to convey to you, Mr. Logan, is that my husband, Fred Moss, has for the past several months been encountering a... gambling...problem. And he has lost heavily. He has lost—" Barbara Jo appeared overcome with emotion, and unable to continue. Her thin face began to crumple. Her lips trembled. She lifted clasped hands in a helpless little gesture to cover her mouth. Then she straightened her face, lifted her chin, gazed straight into Bart Logan's dark eyes, and said in a flat, toneless voice, "Almost everything we had accumulated…is gone. All we have left is the house, and whatever stock we have in the store. And now this illness…it's almost as if…God is *punishing* Fred. For some sin."

"Mrs. Moss, believe me, I may be new to the faith," Bart began, leaning so far forward in the big oak rocker that he appeared in imminent danger of toppling onto the porch floor, "and I may not know much about God." His voice dropped, became gentle, dripping with sympathy, hands clasped firmly together now, elbows on knees, "but if the God of the Scriptures were *ever* to see fit…to punish us humans for all our multiple transgressions and offences, I trow that not a *one* of us would possess more than the lowliest of tinkers. I'm certain that *that* is not the case. And I'm sorry to hear that your husband…has been incurring…this problem of gambling. It can be just as devastating as the illness that is now wracking his body. If there is anything…anything at all…that I can do. If you need…anything… you are Margaret Ann's family, and I would be only too happy to—"

"Thank you, Mr. Logan, for your kindness," Barbara Jo gazed over at him, amazed at the transformation in the man, in just one instant—from harsh accuser—to proffered protector. "You are such a thoroughgoingly kind and Christian man. I declare," Barbara Jo waved a thin, pale hand in the air helplessly and heaved a great sigh, "I *can't* for the life of me understand—"

A hand to her forehead, brushing back a strand of limp brown hair—she couldn't even recall whether or not she had bothered to comb it this morning. She must look a fright. Barbara Jo broke off, before she stepped over a boundary upon which she knew she dared not tread.

"Exactly what is it, that you find so difficult to understand, Mrs. Moss?" Bart asked with raised brows.

"Nothing." Barbara Jo glanced at him guiltily. "It's nothing. I was just remarking…that I can't for the *life* of me understand why Maggie thinks she has to wait until that *Len Evans* is in his grave one entire year, before putting the man finally to rest—and getting on with her life. After all, he was such a churlish, cold and thoughtless…*cad*… you will have to pardon my language, Mr. Logan. But when I begin to think of Len Evans, words fly through my mind that no proper Southern lady could *ever possibly permit to cross her lips!"*

"He was that bad, eh?" Bart inquired, reaching up a hand to retrieve his fine hat.

"He was that bad, and worse," Barbara Jo muttered beneath her breath. Then she swallowed hard, lifted her chin and met Bart's unwavering gaze, "But, getting back to the reason for this visit from you, I wish it were otherwise. I wish we could simply close the store and forget about it…but…in all honesty, Mr. Logan…I haven't the faintest notion what it is exactly that I should do…about the store. Fred always managed everything. I'm afraid you see before you a helpless, totally useless human being. And so, I fear, I have been most of my life. Lazy and useless! Leavin' *everything* for Maggie to shoulder. And me the older by two years!" At this point, Barbara Jo leaned forward in the porch swing, brought both hands up over her face, and began a low, moaning wail that immediately erupted into tremendous, heaving sobs.

Bart leapt immediately to his feet. He stepped over, stood before the swing, twisting his fine hat in his hands. Then he reached down and drew Barbara Jo up and to him, pillowing her head on his shoulder, patting her gently on the back with his hat.

"It sounds to me as if you're berating yourself needlessly… about things…that would best be left in the past. Left to the good graces of a forgiving God. Am I not right about that, Mrs. Moss?" he asked softy.

"Yes," Barbara Jo lifted her head and gazed into his eyes. "You are entirely correct, Mr. Logan." Bart stepped respectfully back, handed her a spotlessly white handkerchief from some inner pocket, and Barbara Jo wiped her eyes and noisily blew her nose into the snowy linen square. Then she smiled up at Bart and said matter-of-factly, "I will launder this well, Mr. Logan, before returning it to you. And should you, being the fine businessman that you are, have *any* suggestions as to how I might solve the dilemma of the mercantile…any sage advice would indeed be welcomed."

"Have you considered, perhaps, *selling* the place, Mrs. Moss? If you still own the inventory, with the money received, you should be able to sustain yourself and your ill husband, quite well, for some time to come. Have you considered putting the entire stock of the mercantile up for sale?"

"No, not really. At any rate, the store building is heavily mortgaged," Barbara Jo sniffed loudly, wiped at her eyes and nose with the soiled handkerchief, "I don't know what might remain, after the bank is satisfied. And I don't think…Fred would stand for that. Selling the store. The store has always been… his life."

"Well, as I have already indicated…if I can be of any assistance…if you find yourself in need…just let me know." Bart turned, as if to go. Then he turned back.

"I'm sorry," Barbara Jo let out two or three loud, strangled sobs, capped her mouth with Bart's soiled handkerchief, wagged her head as if stunned, totally unable to accept the turn her life had taken, "So sorry, to be depending upon Maggie again. It seems that all our lives, she has taken care of things that were way, *way* too heavy for her slender shoulders to bear. I am *so* sorry, that at this stage of our lives, I am *again* proving a *burrrr…ddden…*"

"I am sure," Bart took two or three steps towards her, "your sister would consider you anything but a burden, Mrs. Moss. She loves you very dearly."

"She loves *eeeevvveeryone*," Barbara Jo moaned. "That's Maggie for you. Taking care of *eeeevvveeryone* but herself. Always thinking *of eeeeevvveeryone*, but herself. To the exclusion of…"

"Yes? You were saying?" Bart leaned forward slightly, fixing her with dark, probing eyes.

"I was probably saying too much." Barbara Jo waved the soiled handkerchief in Bart's face, as if dismissing him, shooing him on his way. "Meddling into affairs that are none of my business. It's just that…I wish, for *once* in her life, Margaret Ann McKinnon would listen to her heart, and not her head!"

When, in the kitchen of the inn, Barbara Jo informed Maggie about Bart Logan's visit, Maggie became white with rage. She simply could not wait to hustle her sister out the door, so that she could attempt to gather her senses, to decide just exactly the words she would use when the opportunity presented itself—to confront Mister Bartram Logan.

"I can't *believe* you *did* that! I can't *believe* you *said* that! You actually…*to my sister*…and with Fred sick to the point of death??!…and here you go…and try to *meddle into my affairs*…!?"

Maggie was so angry she could scarcely speak, or think, rationally.

"I was simply trying to help!" Bart Logan made a valiant attempt to defend himself.

"When…*and if*…I need your help…Mr. Logan…*darling*…I will tell you! In the meantime, would you kindly…"

"Yes, sweetheart? You were about to say…?"

"Oh, I don't know! This is *all* such a mess! Now, with Fred sick..! And raving, out of his head, talking like a lunatic! And I'm scared to death he's going to confess to Barbara Jo…"

"*Confess?*" Bart asked, gazing intently at Maggie over the leavings of his breakfast, at the table in the inn's kitchen. "You mean to the gambling? Apparently your sister is totally aware of his gambling problem. And aware that he has gambled whatever fortune he has thus far managed to acquire totally away. It appears that, except for the house and heavily mortgaged store, they are…oh, but I see by your expression…that *this* is not the *confession* you had in mind. What…then?"

"*Gambling problem?*" Maggie's mouth hung open in total shock. Her blue-blue eyes flew wide.

"Your mouth is open," Bart said softly. "What confession are you referring to?"

"Did I hear you correctly? *Fred Moss has a gambling problem?* He has lost… practically…everything…due to *gambling*? When Thomas mentioned Fred's debts, I assumed he was referring to some…perhaps…bad business practices. But…*gambling?* Why…!? I never knew Fred to risk one thin penny? How long has *this* been going on?"

"Well, from what your sister said, since about the time your husband died. About the time they moved up here, to Rhyersville. Why?"

"Oh! No! It…*couldn't* be that! *Could it*? No! *It couldn't possibly be that!*"

Bart stared at her. Maggie wagged her head in denial, her heart breaking.

All these months she had harbored ill feelings towards Fred. *Absolutely despising the man!* And now, she finally realized, it had shown so plainly to him. Each time she met him, she had slapped him in the face with the wet rags of her righteous, judgmental indignation. She had rubbed salt into his wounded spirit…

"But he has *never*," Maggie was mumbling, shaking her head in disbelief, "Never given the slightest indication that he felt remotely *remorseful, apologetic. In any way regretful of his sorry, lustful actions*!" Even now, Maggie could not keep the scowl from her face, the cold rage from creeping into her voice.

"What, *exactly*, is it you're attempting to say, sweetheart? That your brother-in-law, the head of the deacon board of the Shiloh Baptist Church, made unwelcome advances toward you?"

"I....didn't...say that! No! That's *not* what I said!"

"You didn't have to. It's very plain. On your face. In the words you *didn't* say, as well as the ones you *did* say." Bart halted, trying to collect his thoughts. Attempting to contain the anger he felt rising up in him.

"When did this *happen*? I ought to kill the fool! Was this *lately*? No, not in the past few weeks, no. Before you came home to Rhyersville? Yes. Shortly...after your husband died. Just... as your husband died."

"You certainly are jumping to conclusions!"

"I'm *not* jumping to anything! It's plain as it can be. Your husband died. Fred Moss, who had had an eye for you probably since the first day he saw you, tried his d—tried his best to take advantage of a young widow. That *pig*—*!* No wonder he drove himself to distraction. He deserves to—"

Reaching out, Maggie laid a small hand over Bart's large warm one. "Darling!" she exclaimed. And for the first time, Bart noticed that the word did not come out of her mouth sounding stilted and empty.

"What?" Bart asked, amazed. Relishing the sound of that word, relishing the warmth, the slight weight of her hand on his, "What?" he whispered.

"Remember? I don't *need* a protector."

"So," Bart stared at her, mesmerized by the softness in her eyes, the softness in her voice, in her touch. He laid his other hand atop hers. "You defended yourself against this felonious, dastardly assault, did you?"

"Yes. You might say that."

"What did you do?"

"Fred Moss had been...kind enough..." Maggie glanced down, quickly withdrew her hand from his, "to bring along for my use a fine sack of flour, amongst a few other items. Fred left my house *wearing* his fine sack of flour." She pulled a faint, pleased little smile.

William Bartram Logan threw back his handsome head and roared with laughter.

––––––––––––

Later that night, Maggie lay in bed, restless, sleep refusing to come.

Finally she crept from beneath the heavy quilts, hand-pieced, and hand-stitched by her mother, Callie McKinnon.

Earlier in the day, she had asked Benjamin Noah to lay a fire in the upstairs fireplace, the one in the corner of her bedroom. She stoked up the fire which she had already banked for the night, threw on another oak log, then drew a rocking chair close up to the fieldstone hearth. It was one of the chairs carved by the hands of Grandpa Thomas Shawn McKinnon, before he marched away, to die in that field or forest in Virginia. Gently Maggie rubbed the tip of a forefinger over the armrest, worn smooth by the touch of her grandparents' hands, her parents' hands, her own hands. The fire crackled and blazed up as the dried oak caught, sending up a welcome light that flooded the corner of the room, where Johnny lay fast asleep on his little cot.

Maggie rested her head on the back of the maple rocker, closed her eyes, and savored the heat of the fire. But even the brightly glowing fire could not drive the chill from her bones. Not even the recollection of the feel of Bartram Logan's hand, strong and warm beneath her touch. Not even the memory of his laughter, full and rich and masculine. None of these pleasant things could drive from her mind the chilling realization that she had caused the downfall of a man.

Fred Moss had taken to gambling…*because of her!* There was not a doubt of this in Maggie's mind. She recalled suddenly the guilt she had felt when her eldest sister, Nellie Sue, accepting Maggie's dare, took that awful fall off the front porch, a girl of about twelve, who would remain a cripple the remainder of her life. And who, as a young woman of only nineteen, would finally succumb to—

As a child, Maggie had attempted to pray to God, to ask His forgiveness.

Now, Maggie tried to pray, to ask God's pardon—for harboring ill-will, that had festered in her heart, and grown, and that oftentimes bordered on downright hatred. Hatred that had scarred a man's soul. *God, have mercy!*

But Papa had adamantly insisted that Maggie was not to blame for Nellie

Sue's injuries. If Papa were here now, could he reassure her she was not responsible for Fred Moss' financial and moral downfall? If Fred had gambled away all his wealth, what would become of Barbara Jo, when Fred's illness had taken its final toll?...when Fredrick J. Moss was put to his final rest, behind the Shiloh Baptist Church, whose bell tower Fred had financed...?

As Maggie heard the clock on the mantel strike one, she rose with a sigh, again banked her fire, and crawled beneath the welcoming warmth of Mama's hand-made quilts. She thought she heard the soft nickering of a horse, somewhere in the cold mountain air of the street below. She stiffened. A chill crept down her spine, even beneath the heavy quilt. Then she decided she was imagining things. She was tired. It was late. But it was not until long after the clock struck three that Maggie fell into a troubled sleep.

The lone horseman sidled his mount into the darkness of the building opposite, and watched, as a shadow crossed before the upstairs window of the inn. He saw the shadow draw back into the room, the light flickering across the curtained window, as of a low fire beyond a rock hearth. Slowly the flickering light died.

Still he sat horseback. Waiting. What was he waiting for? He did not know. Yes, he did know! He waited for something bad. For something bad to happen to her! Something terrible! So horrible as to be incomprehensible to the human soul! How much suffering, after all, could one soul endure?

He had thought that growing up on a one-horse, hardscrabble farm up a lonesome hollow in the God-forsaken Blue Ridge Mountains of North Georgia was about all the misery one poor soul could endure. More mouths about the table than Pap could possibly feed, given the poor land that had fallen his lot in life. Pap said it was always the same. No fairness a' tall in life. Them that had...got even more. How true, Pap always said, bitterness and coldness in his voice. Scripture was sure true on that one point of fact! *To them that have, it shall be given! And to them that have not, even what they do have shall be taken away.* When it should be just the other way 'round, Pap always said.

Finally, when he was about half grown, his Pap had given up trying to raise upland cotton and Indian corn, and had gotten himself a few sheep. But Pap was not, never had been, and never could be—a *sheep man*. So that venture fizzled out, like everything else Pap put his hand to.

Then came the War, and he and Pap had marched away, leaving the rocky rolling farmland behind, along with the sweetly gurgling creeks and the cool, misty blue mountain ridges that reached to the sky. There were some things here, he guessed, that could stand admiring. But he was more than glad to go. It would be an adventure, he figured. He could escape the small shack of a cabin where the cold winter winds came whistling through the cracks like nothing ever felt. Yeah, he left to escape the fields that were so steep the mule couldn't even stand up on the sides of the terraced hills to pull the plow properly. He left to escape—more than to fight for freedom and glory.

It started out as a grand adventure, all the men and boys in the vicinity gathering for the muster down at the little log school, laughing and talking and thumping one another on the back. Marching off to take the train down to that place called Norcross, Georgia…

The next thing he knew, he was being shot at, worse than any old hound dog that ever drew breath. And from there, it just got worse and worse.

Then one day he woke up to find he had no right leg. Blessed thing gone—half up to his crotch. Just a sort of half-stump left dangling from his hip. And Pap was dead and buried, they had told him, in a mass grave, in a ditch beneath a bunch of twisted, mangled, bloodied bodies.

And, no more than a snit of a boy, he ended up, with his throbbing stump of a leg, rotting in a stinking Yankee prison, where he froze in winter and roasted in summer and fought for roaches and rats. To eat.

Then, somehow, he was never certain, even to this day, more than twenty years later, never sure exactly how—but they told him one day that the War had ended, and somehow, he got back to that hardscrabble farm, up that God-forsaken hollow.

Pap was gone. Ma had died while he was away. The kids had all scattered to the four corners of the earth. All that was left… was him, with one leg, and a piece of another one—and that hardscrabble mountain farm…

But he met and thought he fell in love with a girl from a neighboring hollow. He lived with Liddy Ruth for nigh onto two years. They had a child. And, just his luck, it turned out to be a girl—when what he needed was a boy, a good stout boy that could swing an axe and follow a mule around the steeply-terraced hillsides.

Most nights, they went to bed hungry, him and Liddy Ruth. And the child. It was hard for him to work, to hunt. Truth be told, it was hard for him to even stand and toddle about, with only one leg, even with the crutch he carved himself from the fork of an oak sapling. And, the queer thing about it was that the missing leg was the one that ached all the blessed time.

So, to keep them all alive, he took to *finding* stuff, at least that's what he told Liddy Ruth. He would find a basket of roasting ears of corn, still in the shuck, in one neighbor's field, and a ripe watermelon or a sack of peas or beans in another neighbor's fields. What th' heck!? He took what he found, where he found it—and when nobody was looking. He felt that the world owed him at least that much.

But the thing that really *got* him was when he learned Liddy Ruth was *prostituting herself*—to help keep food in their mouths. When he learned that, he just about went crazy. He threw that sorry slut out of the cabin, and dared her ever to show her face in the hollow again. He almost threw the little girl out after her. But something stopped him. The child could not help being a girl. That was the Almighty's fault. Just some more of his rotten luck.

Stealing to eat, that was one thing. But a woman offering herself for sale, that... that was something else again entirely.

How many years ago had that been? He wasn't sure. He sometimes lost track of time. Sixteen...seventeen years? Nigh onto twenty?

But he was sure of one thing. Down in that valley... rich with tall grass and flowing with a wide, clear creek and a fine, rushing river filled with fish...lived that man that called himself *John Thomas McKinnon*. And John, now, he had himself a wife that worked her fingers to the bone whilst John was off fightin' the war. And kept herself spotless for him. Yeah. John got shot in the leg, too. But John didn't loose his limb. John could plow his fat horse in his fine, rich valley. John didn't have any boys, either. And for some odd reason, John McKinnon seemed right pleased with that fact.

Then one of John's girls died. And John had got sick. And John had died. And later, he had heard, John's fine-boned, honey-haired wife died, somewhere down country. Maybe there was some justice in this world, after all.

But two of John's children, no, make that *three*, three of John McKinnon's children still lived. And evidently they thrived. The girl that ran the inn that stood before him in the coolness of the misty mountain night. Full of pluck and ginger, she was. Pretty as any thing God ever made. And his one daughter? Pretty enough on the outside, but not fit for much on a mountain farm. Lazy as all get-out! And lately, she had been disappearing. For days— and nights—on end. And he wondered—if his child was traveling down the same road that took Liddy Ruth from him...

In the coolness of the damp mountain night air, his eyes narrowed, his head gave a jerk, his thin shoulders gave an involuntary shudder, and his missing leg began to throb fiercely. Finally, not being able to decide what exactly he should do about the girl in the inn, if anything, he heaved a great sigh, and turned his thin horse toward the hollow that—except for the years away at the war—he had always called home.

Chapter 6

John Thomas McKinnon, Jr. had been given strict instructions by his sister, Maggie, not to leave the confines of the back yard of the inn, where Benjamin Noah, as he straightened his strong black form from his vigorous wood splitting at the chop block, would cast a watchful eye in the little boy's direction every now and then. And every now and again, along with his wood chopping, Benjamin Noah would straighten his strong, muscular form, and take in a deep draught of sweet mountain air. And in the process of doing so, he would whisper a fervent, heart-felt prayer:

Dear Lord, I thanks ye so much, ever' day o' my lif', fer this bootiful, bootiful, valley. And fer th' bootiful lady who don' give me a second chanch in this lif'—Mizzz Maggie! Do bless that lovely soul, Lord, with the bes' that you don' has got ta bles' her wif'... which is plenty more than enough...amen.

Benjamin Noah Daniels prayed this same prayer every day, as he chopped wood. Then he would burst into some spiritual song, his grand voice rising and soaring out over the rough-planked, oak-sided buildings stretching along the rutted dirt street of the little valley town.

Now, Benjamin Noah straightened from his wood chopping, to glance about for a look-see at his small charge, Little Johnny. But as his dark gaze swept the narrow yard behind the inn, Benjamin found it empty.

"Whar' is you hidin', now, Little John Thomas? You com'on out now, d'ye hear me? It's almos' gwin' on t'ward supper time!"

No reply.

Benjamin Noah's big heart began to pound like a hammer slamming against the sides of his rib cage. He flung down his axe, and went tearing along, searching behind and between the adjoining buildings. But no sight of the boy.

Benjamin searched for several minutes, his anxiety and terror mounting. Though the day was cool, sweat gathered in great drops on his black brow and flowed freely into dark eyes. *If he had let anythin' happen ta dat chil'—!*

He peered around the corner of a building, and there, far up the next dirt alley, was little Johnny…surrounded by a pack of dirty, ill-kempt lads. It appeared that they had Johnny out-sized and out-numbered. Benjamin Noah stealthily rounded the corner, keeping to the sides of the buildings in order to determine just exactly what mischief might be afoot here. As he came on, Benjamin Noah heard the jeering taunts:

"He's jest a poor lil' orphan boy! He's not got *no Pap,* like the rest o' us. Whar's yore pap, poor lil' orphan boy?"

"I *do so* have a Papa! He's in a far better place than this dirty old alley!"

"Well, then, he's not here to see to his youngun', is he?" one of the boys, who appeared to be the biggest, taunted.

Johnny made a diving leap at the older boy. The bigger boy stepped swiftly aside, and shot out a fist, catching Johnny squarely in the nose and knocking him off his feet.

Johnny landed flat on his back with a heavy thud. He made as if to rise. But being so small, he had no knowledge of fist-fighting, therefore, no means of defending himself.

He immediately found himself face down in the dirt of the alley, a dirty, high-topped brogan across his neck.

"Whut's gwin' on here?" There came a thunderous voice from around the corner, followed by a huge black man, roaring around the side of the building like a dark thundercloud.

At that exact moment, Bart Logan was dismounting from his fine roan and tying him securely before *The Sparrow.*

Hearing the commotion just up the street, Bart sprinted over to investigate. He was just in time to hear Benjamin Noah shouting:

"Whut're ye younguns think yer're up ta?"

"Benjamin!" Bart yelled, coming at a run, to find boys scattering in every direction, at least a half dozen of them, and Benjamin Noah reaching for Johnny, as if to pick him up in his arms.

Bart stepped quickly into the alley and barked, "Leave him be, Benjamin.

A man who can take a bloody nose like that is fully capable of standing up on his own two feet, and walking out of this alley, and up the street to *The Sparrow*. Am I not right, Johnny?"

"Yes, sir!" Johnny rolled over, pushed himself up, brushed the dirt from his clothes, walked forward, past Bart and Benjamin Noah, and headed straight for the front of the inn. His little back straight, he clomped up the steps, in the front door, and through the dining room, past a startled Maggie, who greeted the dirty face, the bloodied nose, the dusty torn shirt with a gaping mouth and wide blue eyes.

Bart silenced her with a wave of one hand, and followed Johnny on in to the kitchen. "Come sit over here, Johnny, and I'll just fetch you a pan of clean water. Sometimes, when we men meet life's obstacles head on, so to speak, we need a good washing up afterwards. What do you think of that?"

Johnny crawled up on the bench beside the kitchen table. Sitting with his back to Bart, elbows propped on the rough surface of the table, with dirt-caked hands he swatted at the dark locks of hair that fell across his face and choked down his snuffles. He didn't want Bart to hear them, to feel his fear, to see the tears threatening behind his eyes.

"Yes, sir!" Johnny piped up, giving a swipe with one arm, smearing the trickle of blood from his nose all across his face, as he struggled mightily not to cry. He had been so frightened, there in that alley, surrounded by so many boys who for some reason totally unknown to Johnny seemed bent on beating him to a pulp.

He appeared so small, hunched on the bench, his feet not nearly reaching the floor, his back to Bart, listening to Bart thudding the water dipper against the oak staves of the kitchen bucket. Bart turned and looked at the boy's small back. He felt more than saw the shudder than passed over the little form.

Then Bart was stepping to the other side of the table, setting the washpan on the table before Johnny, saying firmly, "Why don't you—" By that time Maggie had come hastening into the kitchen. Again Bart raised a silencing hand. He stooped toward the boy, continued speaking to Johnny, in a low, cool voice:

"Just dip your hands in this cool water, splash it over your face. That should take care of any grime you happen to have collected—out there in the alley."

Then Bart stepped around the table, lowered his tall, muscular frame onto the oak bench beside the boy, asking in a low, slow voice, "By the way, Johnny, what, *exactly,* were you *doing* there, in that alley, all alone?"

Johnny dipped small hands into the clean water sparkling in the pewter washpan. It felt good to his cracked lips and swollen nose, as he listened to the man's voice—cool, calming, reassuring. The world was not ending. He was not dying. He was doing a very ordinary thing…washing the dust of the alley off his face.

"I didn't hear you answer me," Bart prompted, gazing at the little boy beside him at the table.

"I…was playing in the back yard. I heard voices. I thought…maybe they were playing ball…or hop-scotch…or something…I wanted to play, too. So I…"

"So you left the back yard, where Maggie had told you to stay, and ventured into unknown territory…without her permission. And for your trouble, you got yourself a bloody nose. Is that about the sum of the story?"

"Yes, sir," tears now were not only threatening, but one or two began to roll down the little cheeks. The nose still sported a few drops of bloody mucus that the little hands had not washed away in their careless dipping and splashing.

"What, if anything, have you learned from this day's doings, Johnny?" Bart asked, his voice low, his elbows propped now on the table, his brown chin resting atop clenched fists.

"To stay where Maggie says I should," sob, sob, "To…"

"That's right, Johnny," Bart lowered his clenched fists, reached out and laid a hand on Johnny's tousled, dust-coated dark hair, "You'll be *certain sure* to remember that, won't you, Johnny? The very next time you hear voices that seem to be beckoning you where you have no business going? The next time you're tempted to stray into an alley?"

"Yes!" Sob. "Sir!"

"Good. And, oh, one other thing. There are things we men need to learn, in order to defend ourselves, when, sometimes against our best judgment, we find ourselves embroiled…in an…awkward, unsolvable predicament. Or when someone wishing us ill strolls into what we feel is our safe territory. Do you know what I mean, Johnny?" Bart asked very solemnly.

"Yes, sir!"

"Good," Bart said, drawing his tall frame erect, laying a hand firmly on the boy's thin shoulder, staring him intently in the eye, "Then straighten your face, and believe me when I tell you that *the next time* you're cornered in an alley by a pack of bullies, *you* won't be the one face down in the dirt."

"Mr. Logan! *Bartram! Darling!*" Maggie, standing at his elbow, cried, aghast.

Bart again held up a silencing hand.

"There are things in life *men* need to learn," Bart wagged his handsome head, and turned his dark gaze in Maggie's direction, "that do *not* pertain to women." He continued in a no-nonsense voice. "Men," he explained, "are often faced with… situations…which they must learn not only to confront, but to overcome, *if* they are to make it through this life somewhat… unscathed. Therefore, in addition to his violin lessons, John Thomas McKinnon, Jr. will immediately begin to learn the art of fist boxing. To the Marquis of Queensbury rules, of course."

"*Mister Logan! Bartram! Darling!* Johnny won't be *five years old* until Thursday next!" Maggie shrieked, her blue-blue eyes wide with horror at the thought of little Johnny…

"Then…" Bart rose slowly from the table and confronted her, "by the time he is *six,* and beginning *first grade*, he should be able to walk about the school grounds without *being bodily assaulted and beaten to a pulp*!"

"Well—!" Maggie gasped, shooting Bartram Logan a look that could kill, before spinning on her heel and stalking out onto the small back porch.

Bart, quite naturally, and as she had hoped he would, followed her. She wanted to be able to tell him, out of Johnny's hearing, exactly what she thought of him…of this interference into her life…into Johnny's life…

Then her angry mind slowed to a mild burn. How often could she recall the boys in the schoolyard howling and slamming at one another like a pack of mad animals!? Was this something that boys and men *just did*!? This tearing into one another? Like the horrible war that had taken her grandfather's life, and left Papa with that nagging wound, an Enfield rifle bullet lodged in his left leg…!? What was wrong with the world!?

She heard Bartram Logan walk up behind her. "These things *are* going to happen, you know. And neither you nor I can prevent them. Neither of us can protect Johnny from them, no matter how much we might wish to. It's only fair to the boy, that he learn to fight, to defend himself when attacked. To fight. To fight well. But fair. Always to fight fair."

"Is that what you do, Mr. William Bartram Logan? Fight fair?" Maggie, arms crossed tightly across her chest, turned to stare up at him.

"Yes, sweetheart," he smiled innocently down at her, "It is. Always."

Chapter 7

With his tightly curled brown hair that stood on end due to its thickness, and his emerald green eyes and smooth olive skin, he could, at first sight, have been taken for a white farmer from any of the nearby valleys. But Rufus Moon knew what he was, as did the pack of freed slaves that trailed along in his wake, walking the rutted dirt roads of North Georgia, seeking the next meal, the next night's rest, the next place they could call home.

Rufus Moon knew what he was, where he had come from—but he had no idea in this world where he was *going*. For the past few weeks, he had kept searching his heart, searching the scraps and bits of Scripture that flitted about in his mind, searching in constant, beseeching prayer on bended knees, for some place for these folks trailing along in his wake—some place to find shelter, and food—and gainful employment.

None of them, not a soul of the company of freedmen in which he traveled, was looking for a handout. And a good thing they weren't, Rufus nodded his curly head ruefully, whispering, *"For they surely are not liable to find it! Not in this old world!"*

As the crowd of freedmen trudged wearily on down the dirt road, Rufus watched with tired, worried eyes as the sun sank lower over the mountains to north, east and west, the mountains that with each step the group took drew nearer and nearer, in vast, rolling misty-blue ridges.

And Rufus wondered to himself, "Why...? *What* in the name of Our Holy God and Blessed Savior is drawing me *here*?" But when Rufus Moon raised his emerald green eyes and beheld the mountains, something stirred, deep within his soul. And the scattered words of Scripture he had heard—but had not read, for Rufus could not read—came floating into his mind, like colorful leaves drifting along a rushing, clear creek. Bouncing and flopping along, atop the waters of his mind:

Beautiful for situation
The joy of the whole earth,
Is Mount Zion
On the sides of the North
The city of our great God...

What would he and his straggling group of followers find in these mountains? The dwelling of the great God? Or more homelessness...and starvation...?

Rufus wasn't at all sure that those were the correct words, or if they came in that order, in the Holy Book, but he supposed they were close enough. Close enough to keep his weary feet on this narrow, rutted North Georgia road that led him and his followers higher and higher every day.

Rufus often recalled how the pasty-skinned preacher man would stand and expound the Scriptures, in some of the white churches he had been allowed to attend, standing in the back, when he was a boy. And finally, when the War was over and the occupying Yankee troops poured into North Georgia, he recalled being allowed to take a seat in the back corner of the little wooden church house. The Yankees had even opened some schools for blacks, but Rufus, almost a grown man by then, had never found the time or inclination to attend. And, truth be told, his pride kept him out.

But what Rufus had heard in the church house, well, it had given him *hope* for this world, but much more, for the world to come. But, somehow, he had to get himself, his wife, Flora, and his two children, his two fine boys, Daniel and Abraham, through this *present* world.

Right now, he had to find them a place to leave this road, and call a makeshift camp for the night. He wondered...how much food was there left amongst his group? They would need to find some sort of work soon...mucking manure out of some farmer's barn, chopping a pile of wood, helping to gather in a crop...anything to keep them going, up and up this road...closer and closer to the mountains that loomed blue and mysterious—and beckoning him onward...north...

Rufus stopped dead still in the dusty road flanked by wild plum bushes and thorny blackberry vines growing up in surrounding fields that lay fallow and wild. A lot of land, Rufus knew, had lain fallow—since the War.

He attempted to take logical stock of their situation. The women and children could have gathered wild plums and berries, except that the season for these was already past. They might scout up a few honey locust pods in the under canopy of trees bordering the fields, or persimmons, if they had been frostbitten, making them sweet and succulent, instead of a yellow-orange fruit that, if gathered before first frost, would pull your mouth into a pucker that would last half a week! Meanwhile the men could gather firewood, and, hopefully, scare up a few rabbits or squirrels, if they got lucky. No, not lucky—if the Good Lord sent then down a bountiful blessing. They could dig up some sassafras roots, find a clear creek, and brew up some hot tea…

"What is it, Rufus?" his wife, Flora, asked, staring at her husband as he stood still as a fence post in the middle of the road, the sun setting in a bank of red and orange over the mountains that curled now from west to north to east about them.

"I…" Rufus sniffed the air, like a buck catching scent, "I believe I smell water. Yes. Do you hear that?" He smiled at Flora, showing a fine row of white teeth in an olive face that was so handsome sometimes it still took Flora's breath away. If only things had been different! Surely, surely, if there was a God in heaven, *this* man deserved better than what had thus far been thrust upon him in this life.

But Flora voiced none of these thoughts. She simply smiled at her handsome husband, her own face not that much darker than his. She knew she had a white father, as did Rufus. But neither of them had dared claim them as their own, not with their being conceived in darkness, born by attractive slave women, in the corners of the slave quarters. They had meant no more to their white fathers than mere chattel, just like their other slaves.

But wasn't that supposed to have changed, with the South losing the War, and President Lincoln declaring them all free and everything?

But…free…to do what? To go where…?

"All right, y'all!" Rufus was calling to the dark figures crowding up around him, "We'll stop here fer th' night. And tomorrow…tomorrow, we'll press on…ta wherever it be…that God in His Good Grace…is a'callin' us."

Like a flock of dark, scattered chickens, fluttering their arms and clucking to one another, they left the road, piling over the red dirt ditches filled with dried leaves, into the fields and the forest beyond, to the bank of the creek.

Campfires were lit. Low conversations flowed. Meager food was shared. A few hymns were hummed in low, melodic voices that wafted above the treetops. And, finally, night fell. Then Rufus Moon sat alone, the dying campfire before him, the dark forest behind him, a full moon shedding a silvery essence over the dark clumps of bodies strewn beneath the trees, most so exhausted they immediately fell into a deep slumber as soon as their heads hit the leaf-strewn ground.

Rufus glanced up at the beauty and wonder of the night sky, the moon, so untouchable, so unknowable. Was the God he attempted to worship, the God that he felt was leading him up this North Georgia dirt road, was *that* God knowable, touchable, or was He as lovely, as remote, as that gorgeous night sky…?

Rufus rose, his own body odor rising about him. He needed to shuck out of his clothes first thing come mornin', and have a good plunge in the creek. He heaved a great sigh, reached down and tossed a few handfuls of loose soil onto the embers of the campfire. They certainly didn't want any sparks to escape, to create any problems! Draw unwanted attention to their tattered group. Setting the woods or some nearby farmer's fields on fire!

Rufus walked the camp, making sure no fire was left forgotten. Maybe he'd just go ahead and take that bath now. No. He'd better stay close to the others. No tellin' what was lurking in these dark woods. He strolled over and stretched his tall frame out beside his sleeping family. His curly brown head resting on one bent arm, he reached out, laying the other arm across the form of his wife. Flora turned into his embrace.

Sufficient to the day, wasn't that what the Lord Jesus had said? And what else went with those words…?

Something about a man not being able to make one of his hairs either black or white? He had no power to do that with his *skin*, either. So why bother…why worry about any of the rest…?

Sufficient unto the day…the Lord said…were the troubles thereof…

Chapter 8

The days sped past. Maggie tried not to think about the passing weeks—or that month in spring they called *May*.

It was a windy, rainy Sunday. And cold. Cold for October. Despite the rain that threatened and then fell, they had attended church earlier in the day. And as they had strolled along the cold windy street of Rhyersville, Maggie could not help but wonder how Fred Moss was doing this morning. The past week, Maggie could see Fred sinking, bit by bit, day by day. Now Dr. Ellis saw Fred every day, trying to alleviate his suffering, as Fred fought for breath in the last stages of the consumption that was robbing his lungs of function. Maggie still could not shake off the feelings of guilt, that she was responsible for Fred's physical, moral and financial decline. Daily her fears and worries mounted as to what would become of Barbara Jo.

Shiloh Baptist had a new preacher, Reverend David G. Whitcomb, a young man who the congregation swore was full of vim and vigor, and apt to meet the devil on his own playground and banish the rascal from it. On the short but cold walk to church, as she and Johnny had hastened along, Johnny's little coat lapels flapping, Maggie with her heaviest wool shawl pulled tight about her shoulders, Maggie had wondered whether she should perhaps seek advice and council from the good Reverend Whitcomb, as to her guilty feelings with regards to Fred. But by the time the pair had actually reached the close warmth of the little white clapboard building with its fine bell tower—donated by Fred Moss—she had banished such thoughts from her mind. She would *do nothing, say nothing* that could *possibly* impinge the reputation of Rhyersville's most outstanding citizen—Fred Moss.

Maggie had sat quietly in the little church, and tried her utmost to keep her thoughts focused on the sermon of the day, but despite her best efforts, they kept flitting about her head like wild birds, refusing to be trapped.

Suddenly, about halfway through the service, just as the young minister was, finger wagging, declaring vehemently:

"Brothers and sisters,
let me tell you this one thing, mooooost assuredly,
God is not mocked.
Whatsoever a man sows, thaaaaatttt shall he also reap—"

It was then that Maggie had heard a rustling of skirts, a murmuring of voices. The Reverend Whitcomb ceased his sermon, and stood staring at the rear door of the small church. Maggie was aware of the iron heater in the corner. She could almost hear the oak log that some farmer had just risen, very unobtrusively, and fed into the fire, crackling and hissing. She was aware of the warmth of the small figure of Johnny, sitting quietly beside her. Of the hushed collective breath of the church congregants, as if they were afraid to take the next breath, as they all turned their heads as one, to gaze at the figure standing before the open double doors at the rear of the church.

Barbara Jo had stepped just inside the doors, leaving them wide open. Her hair loose and flowing, a cold wind whipped her locks, her thin dress and shawl. She stood, still as a statue, no heavy cloak, no bonnet. As if locked in time, her face pale as chalk, wisps of hair swirling eerily about her head, in a choked, barely audible voice, she announced to one and all:

"The Chairman of your Deacon Board, the man who has given his *all* to this church, and built for you a *fine steeple*, and hung therein a *huge iron bell* that peals out over this valley every Sabbath day of the world...!...*Has just gone to meet his Maker!*"

With that, Barbara Jo clutched her wool shawl closer about thin shoulders, gathered her full silk skirt in the other hand, whirled and stomped out the door, and down the narrow steps.

Instantly, Maggie was up, off the worn pew, dragging Johnny along behind her, his little brown leather high-tops scarcely touching the ground.

Rushing down the street, past the mercantile, around the corner, Maggie reached the yellow brick house. She let herself in, calling as she searched the house, and found Barbara Jo collapsed on a bed in an upstairs room...

Her hair lay spread about her, wild and uncombed, as it had been as she stood at the back of the Shiloh Baptist Church and made her dramatic announcement. Her face unwashed and the color of a sheet that had seen too many washdays and had turned a dingy gray in the process, she turned distraught eyes to gaze into her younger sister's concerned face. She seemed totally unable to speak. She buried her face in a pillow. Then the sobs came.

"Barbs?" Maggie sat down gently on the side of the bed. She laid a hand on Barbara Jo's heaving shoulder. For hours, it seemed, she sat there.

Lunchtime passed, unheeded, and Maggie heard the ornately carved grandfather clock in the rich entryway downstairs issue its deep chime, marking the passing of the hours. It was now four o'clock in the afternoon. Still the two of them, as if lost to time, seemed locked in the same positions.

Finally, Maggie ventured, "Barbs? Don't you think you should get up, now? I could draw up a few buckets of water. Heat you up a good warm bath? Does that work for you? Maybe, have a bite to eat? Afterwards? It's going on toward five o'clock. It will soon be supper time."

"Fred...? Fred...will need...his supper." Barbara Jo made a feeble attempt to lift her tousled head from the plush white pillow.

"We've called Dr. Ellis. *Hours* ago, Barbs. He's...seeing to Fred. Have you made any prior arrangements? Given any thought that is...to a casket...and the...type of...service...Fred would have wanted?"

"Noooooo!...Maggs! I...*can't*...I...just...*can't*! *You'll* just have to see to...*all that*...sob...sob...*yourselfffffff!*" Barbara Jo whined.

"*Barbara Jo McKinnon Moss!*" Maggie rose from the side of the bed, stood, hands on hips, and said in a low but stern voice. "You *get* yourself right *up* out of that bed. *This minute!* Do you hear me? I'm going downstairs to put on some water to heat for you a *bath*. I'm going to fix you a *hot cup of coffee* and a bowl of *sweet oats*. And you, my dear sister, are going to *get* yourself up. *Eat! Wash and dress* and walk down the street to make arrangements for your dear departed husband's funeral. Do you *hear* me, Barbara Jo McKinnon Moss?! I shall return in five minutes with the oats and the coffee, and I'd better find you up on your feet—*do I make myself clear?!*"

Fred Moss, following a simple funeral, was buried back of the Shiloh Baptist Church. His grave faced the east, as with all graves, but the little bell tower Fred Moss had purchased was within seeing distance; and when the big iron bell sounded its toll every Sunday morning, its sound swung out far over the little graveyard, Maggie told Barbara Jo, and far up into God's good heaven—where Maggie was very sure that Fred Moss, of all people, due to his generous nature and exemplary character, was certain to be in residence.

Chapter 9

The bushel basket of fall pears set on the scarred top of the kitchen table. The black iron cookstove was loaded with lighter-knots and kindling, with the wood box behind the stove stacked to the windowsill above it. Two dozen glass jars, having been scrubbed sparkling clean and then scalded to within an inch of their existence, stood lined in a baking pan atop an iron stove eye. A gallon jug of vinegar set beside the pear basket. Next to that rested a brown paper bag containing dark brown sugar. There was also a small bottle of cloves. Maggie stood staring down at the pears, kissed by the summer sun to perfect ripeness so that they glowed yellow with rosy cheeks. Then she heaved a great sigh, as she studied Mama's recipe for pear chutney.

"Look at this!" she declared irritably to Liza Mae, just heaving a heavy iron boiler to the stove top, "There is no cinnamon left on the place! Not one single, solitary stick! And you can see what it says, very clearly, right here on the recipe!"

"Yass, I's kin see it, Mizzz Maggie, but you knows good and well that Liza Mae cin't *read* it!" Liza Mae pulled an embarrassed, frustrated frown.

"I'm…sorry, Liza Mae," Maggie mumbled, putting a hand to her forehead to hide her own frustration. Why was she always forgetting? Why was there still this chasm between herself and the person she considered her best friend on earth? It rankled her that Liza Mae and Benjamin Noah still could not read even the simplest sign, or price, or instructions.

"Wu'd ye lack me ta goes ta th' sto'e, Mizzz Maggie?"

"No, Liza. I believe I'd rather that you start peeling the pears. I'll run down and get the cinnamon. Be back in a moment. By the way, where's Johnny?"

"He out back, Mizz Maggie. He done fount a puddle *swarmin'* wif

86

tadpoles. And ye'd think no boy ever in his life seed da fu'st tadpole! Dat chile!"

"I'll just scoot on out then, and get the cinnamon," Maggie said, crossing the kitchen to retrieve her sunbonnet and a light stole. It was still very early; there might be a nip to the mountain air.

The strings of her sunbonnet tied snuggly beneath her chin, her heavy cotton skirt swirling about trim ankles, Maggie stepped off the low porch of The Sparrow, and turned her eyes down the dirt street towards the mercantile. Then her ears picked up the distinct sound of nails being hammered into the solid fibers of oak. Maggie spun and began striding smartly down the slight hill that led into the shady dale where the Rhyersville schoolhouse stood. Sure enough, behind the small weather-beaten structure, stout oaken studs rose, just beneath the heavy limbs of her favorite black walnut tree. How many times had she skinned up that tree, to escape the howling pack of jackals—both male and female—hot on her trail in a rousing game of tag or hide-and-go-seek?!

But, Maggie noticed to her great consternation, that the schoolyard, a sandy expanse tromped clean of any sort of weed or vine, contained no other mode of entertainment for active children. Nor, for that matter, had it ever contained any. A few dead leaves had been blown down from the trees dotting the yard, and drifted lazily about in the breeze that always stirred down from the mountaintops, bringing with it the scents of drying leaves and mosses. Maggie recalled how, at lunchtime and recess breaks, she, her two sisters, and the other students had busied themselves with games of hand ball with a tightly-wound wad of rags, had leapt repeatedly over wild-muscadine-vine jump-ropes, and played hop-scotch in blocks drawn deep into the white sands of the yard.

But never mind that, she was here to investigate the hammering she had heard. She walked up to the new addition to the building, shaded her eyes, and peered up to see Thomas Beyers, blond hair askew, fair face flushed beet-red and dripping with perspiration that flowed into some sort of red band he had wound about his forehead.

"Thomas?" Maggie smiled and called up at him, attempting to shade her eyes from the bright morning sunlight flooding Thomas from behind, "You look exactly like a wild Indian!'

"Oh, do I?" Thomas grinned down at her. "Well, Maggie, just how many wild Indians have you ever seen?"

"Not that many, I must in truth admit, but you do appear as I would suppose one of them might have—beneath these very trees. Not that long ago."

By now, Thomas Beyers had laid down his hammer, and swung his lank form onto the hand-made ladder propped against the side of the rising oak frame.

"Well, now, let us step into the shade for a moment, Maggie," Thomas drawled, taking Maggie by the arm and leading her beneath the walnut tree. "And perhaps you would be good enough to fill me in as to what I may attribute the pleasure of your fine company on such a sweet Saturday mornin'."

"It is a fine mornin', isn't it, Thomas?" Maggie heaved a great sigh. "I have so many, many fond memories of this place. Over there…" Maggie broke off, suddenly acutely aware that her former teacher, Mr. Thomas Beyers, was staring at her so intently that his light blue eyes had taken on a distinct tint of deep sapphire. "What…Thomas?" Maggie muttered, gazing up at the tall, blond-haired man who towered over her. She had never noticed how tall Thomas Beyers actually was. Or how broad in the shoulders. Whenever she thought of Thomas, she always envisioned him exactly the way he had looked the night he strolled across the Bidwell's barn at the corn huskin' party, and asked her oldest sister, Nellie Sue, to favor him with a dance.

How long ago had that been? She had been fourteen at the time, and Nellie Sue nineteen. And Thomas Beyers? Probably not more than nineteen or twenty himself. Suddenly it dawned on Maggie how very young Thomas Beyers had been, when he first stepped foot into Rhyersville, and took on the role as schoolmaster to a bunch of rowdy mountain youngsters—some of them scarcely a year or two younger than Thomas himself.

Yet how well Thomas Beyers had filled his role. Always kind, eternally patient, soft spoken, even with the worst of the children, those from the hidden mountain nooks and coves who had scarcely seen a town—let alone a real schoolmaster. But Thomas Beyers had tamed them all, with his charm, his wisdom, his caring…

"Maggie?" she heard him saying her name, so softly she almost didn't catch it, "Was there something…?"

"Oh…no…nothing like that, Thomas. How old are you, Thomas?"

"What?"

"I asked a very simple question, Thomas Beyers. Are you suddenly tongue-tied, or can you give me a simple reply?" Maggie cocked her head aside prettily.

Thomas Beyers' breath caught so sharply he thought he might actually choke for lack of air. Maggie McKinnon had always been impetuous, smart as a whip, sharp as a honed tack—and given to speaking her mind, sometimes without first giving her words a single thought.

"I..."

"How old were you...when you first met Nellie Sue?"

"Twenty. Going on twenty-one."

"Only a year older than Nellie? And you married her within months of that first smile she gave you."

"Yes, Maggie. Who could resist that smile? Nellie...my Nellie...she was an angel sent from God. Sometimes...I wonder if she was quite real. Could any woman be that beautiful? That sweet? Was she real? Then I lost her, and it left such a great, gaping hole in my heart. But when I visit her grave..." Thomas caught himself, glanced away, running a long-fingered hand through his bright mop of blond hair, "I..."

"I've never heard you talk like that, Thomas," Maggie whispered, "I shouldn't have brought it up. Sometimes...I...say the most *awful* things. You know how I am. You must forgive me, Thomas." Maggie rattled on, "I don't know what gets in to me. I just...what difference does it make. How old you are...after all..."

"I'm exactly six years older than you, Maggie," Thomas smiled down at her.

"*Six years!* You were a *child,* teaching other children!"

"I was a man full grown, Maggie. Teaching children."

"You were *not* full grown, Thomas! Just *look* at you!"

"What? What do you mean?" Thomas frowned down at Maggie, so very aware of her nearness, of the sweet scent of...violets? Of...

"Why, you're at least two inches taller! And look how your shoulders have filled out! And..."

Thomas Byers' face had flushed as red as a ripe crabapple.

"See, Thomas? There I go again!" Maggie threw up both hands in complete exasperation with herself.

"It's only me, Maggie. You don't have to worry," Thomas chuckled in spite of himself. "You can just be yourself. That's what I've…always…loved so much about you."

"You have?"

"Yes…just as…I've…loved all the children who came into this schoolyard. But you, Maggie, you were…"

"What?"

"Special."

"Why…thank you, Mister Thomas Beyers! You are such a thoroughgoing, good man! Whatever would Rhyersville do without you!? I'll bet you prayed for us *every* night of the world!"

"That I did, Maggie!" Thomas laughed. Then his brows knit into a teasing frown beneath his red bandana, "*Especially* you! I prayed that your impetuous nature would not lead you into deep, deep trouble!"

"Did you, Thomas? How very sweet of you!" Maggie felt tears suddenly stinging her eyes. She recalled the blustery November day Len Evans drove his covered buggy through the blinding rain, to rescue her from the wet and the cold, how he lifted her in—and how that—although she had made up her mind to wait—the following Sunday morning, she had married Len Evans….

"Maggie?" Thomas gazed at her with grave concern, his eyes squinted beneath the red bandana draped with locks of shining blond hair, "Are you all right?"

"Yes, Thomas. Of course, just…something seems to have gotten into my eye." Maggie made a great pretense of batting her eyes to clear them, sending Thomas Beyers' heart into a furious flutter. "There. I was just…looking about the poor schoolyard. Such a bare place, don't you think?"

"Bare?"

"Barren."

"Barren…"

"Yes, Thomas. There's nothing here for small, energetic children to play with…or on…or whatever."

"Oh. I see."

"Well, I just thought…that perhaps…*that*…situation might be rectified…you see…before Johnny enters school."

"Johnny? How old is your little brother now, Maggie?"

"Johnny turns five…"

"Then he had another year or so?"

"Yes. But, Thomas," Maggie explained patiently, "it's not just Johnny. There are even *grown* people who could well do with an education! And what are you going to do about it?"

"*Grown*...people, Maggie?"

"Yes, Thomas Beyers! Grown people! These people may happen to be of a different race from you! Their hair may not be glitteringly blond! Their skin may not be apple-cheeked white—"

"Maggie, for pity sakes, just *tell* me what it is you're trying to say. Are you calling me a..."

"Oh, no, Thomas. No! I...just get so upset...when I see Liza Mae, and Benjamin Noah, struggling so sometimes, because they cannot read the simplest label or count money properly!"

"You would like me to tutor your employees, is that it?"

"Well...Thomas...I can see... that you are indeed a busy man. I know that school is already in session. By the way, Thomas, what is the additional room for?"

"Yes, Maggie. School *is* in session. Come Monday morning, you will see little forms bounding through those trees. The building on is for the purpose of adding another classroom, Maggie. The town's grown so that the school board had decided to hire a second teacher."

"Why...! That's marvelous. Who did you have in mind...for this...second teacher?"

"Well...no one at the moment. I'm just working on the extra room in my spare time. It probably won't even be completed for use this term, but maybe next. But if you have someone you'd like for me to interview..."

"How about...Barbara Jo? Now that...Fred's gone...she needs something to occupy herself."

"Barbara...Jo..." Thomas said, very slowly, a frown knitting his sweaty brow.

"Yes, Thomas! Barbara Jo! She would make an excellent—"

"Maggie. Does Barbara Jo know you're...? Now, look. I would do almost *anything* I could...I *know* you would like to find something to bring your sister back into the real world. But, really, Maggie, *teaching*? Do you actually feel that Barbara Jo is cut out for the world of teaching rowdy children? I've never glimpsed the *first* trait in Barbara Jo's nature that would incline me toward the opinion that she is in any way, shape, or form or fashion…fitted…for the occupation of teaching."

"It was just a thought, Thomas. I suppose I am grasping at straws where Barbs is concerned. But…about the other…?"

"Yes. All right. When would you like me to start?" Thomas asked, slowing untying the red bandana from about his head, and wiping perspiration from his face and neck.

"Oh, Thomas!" Maggie took a step forward, stood on tiptoe and kissed Thomas Beyers squarely on the cheek, tasting the salty perspiration. "You are such a dear! I haven't the *faintest* notion why some sweet, deserving lady hasn't snatched you from the yawning jaws of loneliness…and made you her own!"

"Well, Maggie." Thomas drawled with a smile, "How many of those do you see lounging around Rhyersville?"

"Not that many, I must admit. Perhaps, Thomas, you need to branch out. It's not that far over to—"

"Maggie!" Thomas held up a sweaty palm, as if to ward off an imminent blow, "Let it go! I need to step down to the creek and wash off some of this sweat. When would you like me to start?"

"Tonight? If you aren't too tired? I know it's a lot to ask. I'll feed you a free supper! When can you come to the inn?"

"I'll be there about six. Okay?"

"Oh, Thomas! You have no idea what this will mean to Liza Mae and Benjamin Noah! How happy it will make them! How very, very happy it will make me! How—"

"I know, Maggie. That's the whole idea."

"And perhaps Benjamin Noah could donate a few hours of his time…to helping you on the addition to the school. And perhaps…doing something about the barren yard."

"Oh?"

"Why, yes, Thomas. Perhaps Benjamin Noah could construct some swings—split hardwood sapling trunks, and nail in seats for swings. Maybe build a flying jenny. And a nice tree house with a ladder in that big—"

"I'll see you at six, Maggie." Thomas turned and headed toward the creek running back of the school building.

Maggie spoke to his back, "You wouldn't at least *consider* Barbara Jo, Thomas?"

Not even bothering to turn around, Thomas waved a hand in dismissal, calling over his shoulder, "I'll see you at six, Maggie."

———————

At promptly six o'clock, Thomas Beyers, freshly shaved and bathed, clad in a clean white shirt and dark cotton trousers, stepped through the front door of The Sparrow. He took his usual seat beside the huge rock fireplace, where a welcome fire blazed and crackled cheerily beyond the stone hearth. He gave his usual order to Liza Mae: a plate of steamed vegetables, a slice of hot, buttered cornbread, and a mug brimming with cold buttermilk.

Thomas smiled up at Liza Mae and asked, "What's that delicious aroma emanating from the kitchen?"

Liza Mae, hands on hips, frowned down at him and demanded, "Whut say?"

"Uh...what's that good smell, coming from the kitchen?"

"Oh. Dat. Dat be Mizz Maggie's p'ar chukey."

"Pear...? Oh, yes, chutney. Well," Thomas smiled, "I'll just have a side serving of that."

"No, suh. That's on'ly sarv'd wif' da po'k roast."

"But...Liza Mae...I don't wish any of the pork roast. Just a dish of that delicious-smelling pear chutney, to go with my vegetables and—"

"Th' p'ar stuff is only sarv'd wif' da po'k roast!" Liza Mae frowned mightily. Some folks didn't appear to understand a thing! And this man was the town's only schoolmaster!

"Well...then, Liza Mae, how about bringing me a very small portion of the pork roast, and a side dish of the pear chutney."

"Well, suh, now, I cin't do dat. You see, Mr. Schoolmaster, th' po'k roast's already been sliced, and—"

"Fine. Fine, Liza Mae, just bring me a serving of the pork roast, and...some of the pear chutney...whatever...goes with the roast."

"And your usual vegetables? Yore gwin' ta eat da roast, an' da p'ars, and da—"

"Yes, Liza Mae! Yes, I am!" Thomas smiled up at the little Negress. "And my usual mug of cold buttermilk, if you please."

"Huh!" Liza Mae lifted her dark chin, turned and stomped off, muttering beneath her breath, "Buttermilk wif' *po'rk roast?!* Some folk don't have da sense God don' give a chicken! And him da *Schoolmaster* ob da town!'"

His food arrived, as usual, very promptly, and Thomas raised the heavy mug of buttermilk to his lips and took a long, cool swig. Immediately, his eyes widened, and his heartbeat quickened. What *was* that he felt, swimming and flopping about—*in his mouth!?* Discreetly, his left hand cupped over his mouth, Thomas spat the buttermilk back into the mug.

Gazing down in disbelief, he felt that surely his eyes deceived him! A tiny tadpole swished his tail this way then that, swimming happily about in the cold, white thickness of the buttermilk. Then, Thomas' eyes widened even further, and a grin tipped up the edges of his lips. Another little fellow had swum up from somewhere in the depths of the mug, to join his friend.

The heavy mug of buttermilk in his right hand, Thomas rose to his feet and made his way towards the kitchen door. Entering the kitchen, he found Maggie just turning from the cookstove, a huge platter of ham in her hands.

"Maggie," Thomas grinned at her good-naturedly, "since when did you begin serving meat with your buttermilk?"

"What? Thomas, can't you see that I'm quite busy here! If you'd like to speak with me about something, could it at least wait—until after the supper rush is past!?"

"Well, Maggie, I'd just like to exchange this mug of buttermilk—for one that's—free of *tadpoles*, that's all." Thomas gave a charming smile and a little shrug, holding the mug of buttermilk out beneath Maggie's nose. "See?" he pointed a finger and whispered, "I believe there's at least two of them in there. Perhaps, hiding somewhere in that creamy depth, even three."

"What…on earth?! Liza Mae! Bring the buttermilk pitcher!"

Just as Liza Mae retrieved the clay jar of buttermilk from atop its resting place on the meal chest, Johnny, seated on the long bench behind the kitchen table, piped up.

"Those are *my tadpoles*, Mr. Thomas Beyers! What are *you* doin' with 'em?"

"Well, Johnny, and how are you this fine fall evening?" Thomas Beyers swung around to lean over the kitchen table and smile down at Johnny. "And as to your tadpoles, I'm not at *all* sure, young man, what I'm doing with them.

94

I almost swallowed one of the little fellows, before I discovered he was in my mug of milk. However do you suppose he got in there?"

"Yes, Johnny, however on earth *do* you suppose your tadpoles got into the *buttermilk pitcher?*" Maggie stood beside the tall form of Thomas and frowned angrily down at her little brother. "I would appreciate a full explanation, and *immediately!*"

"Liza Mae gave me a jar ta put 'em it. But I thought it was *too little*. So I found a bigger one on th' shelf behind th' stove, so I poured 'em in there! You didn't hurt 'em, did you?" Johnny frowned accusingly up at Thomas Beyers, eyes squinted, little mouth pulled into a definite pout.

Maggie stood speechless, ready to explode. Thomas held up a hand, then slid onto the bench beside Johnny.

"No, Johnny, I don't think I hurt any of them. But I don't believe they're very comfortable, living in a pitcher of buttermilk. Why don't you and I fish them out, and take them back to where they belong?"

"You mean…" Johnny's small face drew into a puckered frown, "turn 'em loose, back in th' mud puddle?"

"I think that would certainly be the *decent* thing to do, don't you? They weren't designed by God to live in a pitcher of buttermilk. I don't believe they'd manage to survive very long, in there."

"Survive? What does that mean?"

"They will die, Johnny, if you leave them in the pitcher."

Slowly, very slowly, head down, shoulders slumped, Johnny slid off the bench and started for the back door. Thomas followed, his mug in one hand, the offending pitcher of buttermilk he plucked from the kitchen table as he swung by, in the other.

He called back to Maggie, standing mute in the center of the kitchen, "Does this remind you of anything?"

"Ohhhhhhhh!" Maggie moaned, as visions of the big bunny and the birthday cake, and the raven and Mama's quilting party came flitting through her mind.

———————

Thomas Beyers, having dispensed with the tadpole-laden buttermilk, finished his supper, then joined Maggie in the kitchen, complimenting her on the delicious pear chutney. Johnny was sent to bed, muttering and mumbling angrily as his little form clomped slowly up the narrow stairway. "*I* want to learn, *too! Why* can't *I* stay up?!"

"Your time will come soon enough, sweetie!" Maggie called cheerily to his small, departing back. "How I dread that time," Maggie sighed to Thomas. "I dread the thought of Johnny growing up…"

"Maggie…" Thomas began. But Maggie held up a silencing hand, "I know I'm being stupid and silly. I'll just go on into the dining room, and leave you alone with your…students."

Liza Mae and Benjamin Noah stood close together, before the comforting warmth of the big black iron cookstove, their faces closed and dark. Neither of them could read one single letter of the alphabet. "We's be too *ol'* fer dis!" Liza Mae complained in a slow drawl, a deep frown furrowing her brow. "Da tim' fer larnin's done flew by me an' Benjamin Noah, lac' a purty bird dat couldn't be trapped!"

"Well, Liza Mae, tonight you and Benjamin Noah are going to *trap* that pretty, elusive little bird," Maggie declared with a no-nonsense ring to her voice—a voice with which Liza Mae was all too familiar. When Mizz Maggie spoke in that tone, she was just like a mule headed for the water-trough—there was no headin' her off and no turnin' her back.

"Whutever you says, Mizz Maggie," Liza Mae reluctantly acquiesced.

"Then sit down. Both of you. And Mr. Beyers, here, is ready to begin your lessons. I believe he has his Bible in hand. And how many times have I heard you two express an intense desire to—"

"I…think I can take it from here, Maggie. If you don't mind?" Thomas was smiling up at her, as he sat waiting at the kitchen table for Liza Mae and Benjamin Noah to take their seats.

"Yes…well…if you need me…"

"I don't believe these two students will become too rowdy…get too far out of hand."

"That's not at all what I meant to imply."

"See you in about an hour, Maggie. Go do…whatever it is you need to do."

Chapter 10

Bartram Logan walked around and around the little dun-colored Highland pony, checking her out from every angle. Yes, he mused to himself, she should do fine for the boy. With a compact body with a deep chest, she carried herself well. She had a thick, healthy coat, a kindly eye, and seemed of a pleasant temperament. The Highland, Bart knew, was one of the larger breeds of ponies, but this one was not full grown, thus she, Bart calculated, could grow along with the boy. He had led her about the horse farm before ever putting down a penny on her price. She followed well, docile and obedient. And Johnny's fifth birthday, so he understood, was next week. He thought the little pony would make a very nice surprise. And for Margaret Ann, a very nice surprise also, even though it was nowhere near her birthday. That, he understood wasn't until May. *May!* Bart's heart did a little flip inside his chest at the thought of that month!

"Johnny?!" Bart called as he pushed open the door of *The Sparrow* and stepped inside with his usual strong, sure stride. By the time Bart had flipped his fine felt hat onto the usual peg behind the door, Johnny immediately appeared from the kitchen.

"Ah!" Bart smiled, "There you are! And were you able to make it out of your bed this morning? Seeing that you're *one entire year older* than you were yesterday, young sir!?"

"Bart! Did you bring me somethin'?"

"Now, just listen to you! Aren't you the mercenary-hearted little squire! You're supposed to be absolutely overjoyed at merely seeing *me!*—now you require a gift from me, into the bargain?"

97

Bart had by now lifted Johnny into his arms, given him a warm hug, and set him back down.

Johnny stared up at the big man whom he had come to regard as family, more than family, as a surrogate father, and replied, "It's *my birthday*, Bart! And you're 'sposed ta give a gift—on a person's birthday!"

"Well, now...! Is that right?" Bart cocked a brow in mock surprise, lifted a hand and stroked his clean-shaven chin thoughtfully. "Now, I wonder why I haven't heard *that* before? You think I should run right out and purchase you something? What, exactly, would you like to have?"

"I can't tell. Maggie says it's not nice...ta ask for things...so I 'spose I should say I'm sorry. But if you *do* get me somethin', then that'll be all right, too, I guess."

"Well, just let me think on that, Johnny. I'll see what I can come up with. Where *is* your lovely sister, by the way?"

"Maggie's in the kitchen! We're bakin' my cake for my *birthday!* I beat the eggs and stirred the batter! You want ta come help me lick the icing pan? It's *choc'late!*"

"Absolutely! I wouldn't miss that for the entire world! Lead on, Master Johnny! And let's get this party under way!"

Johnny bounded through the kitchen door, Bart in his wake.

"Well, it sure smells good in here," Bart came up behind Maggie as she stood at the black iron stove, vigorously stirring the hot, bubbling chocolate fudge icing. She sensed his nearness as he bent to check out the icing, and it seemed to Maggie, to sniff the scent of her hair.

"We will brook no interference whilst we are in pursuit of our cooking duties, Mr. Logan, darling. So, please just take a seat wherever you can find one. Preferably well out of the way, so no one gets burned—when this fudge comes off the stove. And we must spread it very quickly, you see, so that it doesn't get all firm before we even get it on the cake. Now, everyone stand aside. And here I come!"

Maggie turned from the big black iron stove, the iron skillet of bubbling chocolate fudge firmly in hand, and placed it on a hot pad atop the oak table. "Now," she announced importantly, "we'll just throw in a pat of this nice sweet butter and a bit of vanilla, and, Johnny, you can come and begin to spread it on the bottom layer!"

"Bart's here now! So, Bart's goin' ta help me! Ain't ya, Bart?"

"*Aren't you, Mr. Logan,*" Maggie automatically corrected. "He's playing with all these children in the street. He's picking up all sorts of…" Maggie began to mumble to no one in particular.

"That's only natural. He has to see something of the world," Bart interjected philosophically. "A sprinkling of grammatical errors here and there never killed a soul, now did it, Johnny?"

Maggie put her hands on her hips, and shot Bart a scathing look, causing Bart to quickly qualify his speech with, "But, of course, we should avoid such things…in every instance… if at all…whenever…possible."

"Well," Maggie continued to stare at Bart, "I'm shocked, Mr. Logan, that you have put in an appearance on a Thursday, and so early in the day. We've scarcely finished with the breakfast crowd."

"How could I forget Johnny's birthday? And was there, by any chance, any left?"

"Any what, Mr. Logan?"

"What were we just discussing, sweetheart? Breakfast, wasn't it? Would there be a cold biscuit and a slice of ham? Maybe a cold cup of coffee?"

"Busy as you are, I wasn't at all sure that you wouldn't forget. And *cold* coffee, is it, then, Mr. Logan? At this hour of the morning? And you haven't had a bite to eat?"

"I try to eat as little, and as seldom, as possible up at the logging camp. Since you have left off cooking for us, my sweet, it's like taking your life into your hands."

"Johnny, you go ahead and spread the chocolate fudge onto the bottom layer, before it gets hardened in the skillet. If it does, we'll just add a little dab of sweet milk. I'll just fix Mr. Logan a plate. Would you like a knife, Mr. Logan?"

"A knife? You mean…to cut the ham?"

"No, Mr. Logan, I mean to help Johnny spread the chocolate fudge, before its set up like rock in this iron skillet."

"Why..!…Yes! Most certainly so! Most decidedly so!" Bart grasped the butter knife firmly. "Here, let's get on with this job, shall we, Johnny? Give it another firm push right there, and catch that blob before it pours off onto the table! Well! Well! What a fine mess I'm making of this!" Bart Logan rew back his head and roared with laughter. Johnny was giggling, dashing around from side to side of the table, and pushing the fudge around with awkward little flirts. Half of the fudge was on the bottom layer, so Bart reached and slapped the second layer on top of it. Then he dumped the remainder of the thickening fudge onto the center of the top layer. It ran down in dark brown, sweet, thickening rivulets, some finding its way off the cake plate and onto the oak tabletop. Bart, as if playing a game of handball, was valiantly attempting to scoop it back onto the sides of the layers, before it became too firm to work.

Hot and sweaty, his shirt sticking to him from the heat of the kitchen and the excitement of icing Johnny's birthday cake, Bartram Logan finally folded his lank frame into a straight backed chair, mopped his brow with a spotless handkerchief he produced from a pocket, and pronounced:

"Well! That's not a half bad job, if a couple of greenhorns like you and I did tackle it! What do you think, Johnny?"

"I think it looks *great!*" Johnny came to lean against Bart's right leg, wagging his head and admiring their creation. "When do we get to cut it?"

"Not yet, Johnny. Not until after we have lunch." Maggie gazed sternly at the two of them, raising smooth brows to emphasize her point.

"But that's a *long time.*"

"It's not that long, and I'm sure you can find some way to amuse yourself until lunch is ready. Mr. Logan, you want your ham and biscuit now? And that hot cup of coffee?"

"I *love* you, Margaret Ann!" Bart said, his voice dripping with appreciation.

"Well! It would appear, Mr. Logan, that you love me for only one thing!—my cooking!"

"That, my sweet, is not at all the case! But for now, thanks for the hot coffee, and let me at the ham and biscuit! Johnny? Why don't you hop up here in my lap, and tell me all about the week you've had, while I make away with your sister's fine cooking. I might even share a bite with you, and let you sip from my cup, when it cools a bit!"

Johnny—sitting beneath Bart's chin, wiggling and squirming, taking a big bite now and then from Bart's ham biscuit—was allowed two or three sips of cooled coffee from Bart's cup. And Bartram Logan thought, with the boy on his lap, the kitchen warm on this fine October day and smelling sweetly of chocolate and vanilla and Maggie McKinnon's rose water—he thought his heart would absolutely burst with joy.

Then Bart was wiping his mouth, setting Johnny firmly on the floor, dipping water into the pewter washpan, assisting Johnny in washing up from the chocolate icing and his share of Bart's breakfast.

"What's that...delicious scent?" Maggie turned to ask.

"Oh? This? I brought along some of the new perfume-scented soap from the mercantile. You like it?"

Maggie—recalling how each fall just after hog-killing day her mother rendered the hog fat and mixed it with wood ashes, boiling it until it harden into soap in the big black washpot in the back yard at McKinnon Valley—stared at the snow-white bar Bart Logan held in his big hand.

"It seems to me, Mr. Logan, that the unnecessary expense of store-bought perfumed soap is..." Maggie broke off in mid-sentence. Bart Logan stood staring at her. She had been on the verge of saying it was a terrible show of spend-thriftiness on Mr. Logan's part. Though Maggie was now forced to buy lard and lye, she still made her own soap. Adding dried rose petals to that for personal use, when she had them. "It smells...very nice," Maggie heaved a sigh.

"Well," Bart smiled, "if we're about finished here, I have a...small errand...to attend to, if you will excuse me...for just a few minutes."

Maggie gave him a disapproving stare, "You have an *errand*, on Johnny's birthday?"

"This...particular errand...this...is the perfect day for it." And with that cryptic announcement, Bartram Logan was on his feet, and strolling toward the front door.

Johnny tagged along behind Bart, but Maggie called to him, stopping him short of passing through the front door of the inn, calling:

"You are *not* to go out into the street, Johnny! Mr. Logan will be back...I suppose!...shortly! That man! You'd think he would make *some* effort to at least set aside *one* day—"

"Whut's tha' youse says, Mizzz Maggie?" Liza Mae inquired, making her way down the narrow stairway after having straightened the upstairs rooms.

"Nothing, Liza Mae. It's just that...that William Bartram Logan...breezes in, get Johnny all excited…and then he breezes back out again! No consideration! No consideration at all for—"

"Mizzzz Maggie! I thinks youse better com'ere!" Liza Mae, hearing a commotion out front, had walked through the dining room, and now stood in the front door of The Sparrow Inn, her eyes wide, her mouth gaping open.

"What is it, Liza Mae?" Maggie called, setting the iron skillet in the huge, white enameled dishpan, angrily splashing in hot water from the big black iron kettle.

"It's Mr. Bart! He don' bro't some new l'il hoss!"

Pushing a strand of damp hair behind one ear, wiping wet hands on the tail of her apron, Maggie flounced to the front door. Johnny trailed behind her, peering around her voluminous skirt tail, watching, as Mr. Bartram Logan came marching up the street—leading a lovely little pony.

"Oh! *No! He didn't! Please,* dear Lord!—*Tell me that man didn't…*"

Maggie reached out for Johnny, but before her fingers could clasp his small shoulder and draw him safely to her, he had bounded across the narrow front porch, down the steps, and was racing down the street towards Bartram Logan—and the beautiful little, high-prancing pony.

"Bart! Bart! Is he for…?"

Bart met Johnny half way, lifted him into his arms, giving him a huge warm hug, whispering softly in Johnny's ear as the boy lay against his chest, "It's a *she*, Johnny! Whose do you *think* she is? Whose birthday is it?"

"Mine! *Mine?*"

"Now…just a minute, here—!"

In a flash, as soon as her brain registered what was happening in the little dirt street before her eyes, Maggie was across the narrow porch, down the steps, and striding angrily up the middle of Main Street, her lovely face a thundercloud.

Bart saw her coming. And Johnny still in his arms, he stood, holding his breath, and waited.

"Just what, Mister Bartram Logan, do you think you're about to do? What is this…this…!?"

"It's…a Highland pony," Bart said softly.

"I *know* it's a *pony!*" Maggie shrieked.

"It's *Johnny's* pony," Bart said ever so softly. "His birthday gift."

102

"But…! But…! No one said *a thing* to me…! About any…*pony!*"

"It's a surprise," Bart continued calmly. "You don't say anything…about surprises."

"It's a *surprise*, all right!" Maggie ranted, blue eyes ablaze, hands on hips.

"She won't cost you a cent. She's to be stabled down at Trap's. There's a fine pasture out back, for her to romp and play in. And there's a roan mare that goes along with her."

"Goes along with her? *A roan mare…?! Goes along with her?!*" Maggie shouted, beside herself with anger, "Johnny's too small to ride a roan mare!"

"The mare's not for Johnny. The mare's for you, sweetheart."

"I…but…I…"

"So that when Johnny takes a notion to ride, you can ride alongside him. You two can take rides around town, and long rides together, out in the country. Just so long as you don't go *too* far afield. But I feel sure you're a sensible woman. You'll know where you and Johnny can safely ride."

"Well! And thank you *so* much, Mr. Logan, *darling!*—for having so much confidence in my judgment! And…"

"And why don't we just go down and fetch your mare, and my mount, and Johnny can ride along between us….we'll just circle about in the trees, outside town."

"I…didn't *say* I'd accept the mare. I…didn't *say Johnny could have…a pony!*"

"Maggie?" Johnny peered up at his sister. He appeared on the verge of tears.

"Mister…Bartram…Logan! I could…absolutely…wring your neck!"

"Maybe, after we finish our ride and have our birthday cake, sweetheart, I just might let you give it a try. Shall we mount Johnny up on his pony, then? And, come along, Margaret Ann. Walk on down to Trap's with me. Come see your lovely roan mare."

Bart set Johnny in the saddle of the little pony, adjusted the small stirrups to fit; then with a smile, he extended his arm to Maggie.

Her eyes shooting sparks of fire, her small chin in the air, Maggie stalked past him and down towards the wheelwright's shop and livery. Bart walked along behind her, leading the pony, her angry mumbles and murmurs drifting back to him on the still October air:

"…never…saw….such…a…man…absolute…and…complete…(was that *idiot*?)…no…consideration…person's…feelings…."

"Wel'," Liza Mae, standing on the porch of the inn, surmised, giving a rueful wag of her head, a broad grin on her face, "they does make a *fine* fam'ly! And they does gits alon' *so good!*"

Johnny, seated on the little pony, was in a world of his own! A pony! All his own!

"Can I go down to Trap's pasture and feed her, every day?!" he piped up to Maggie.

"Now you see what you've gone and done, Mister Bartram Logan?" Maggie shouted back over her shoulder. "Now, I'll scarcely be able to keep him indoors, a'tall!"

"A boy doesn't *need* to be indoors so much!" Bart parried, strolling happily along on her heels. "He needs fresh air and the sun on his face! Isn't that right, Johnny?"

"Yes, sir, Bart! *Every* day!"

Maggie whirled on Bartram Logan, stood stock still in the middle of the dirt street and demanded angrily, "What if it rains?"

"Then, just *wait*, Margaret Ann," Bartram Logan smiled down at her. He was enjoying this *very* much. Behind all this bluff and bluster, he wondered if perhaps she wasn't almost as pleased as Johnny.

She spun about, and resumed her march down the street, her back as stiff and straight as an iron poker, no bonnet covering her hair, that swung loose and full down her slender back. Warm and shiny and inviting, to run his hands through… "What's that, Margaret Ann? Yes, of course, the mare will be pastured at Trap's along with the pony. You won't have a thing to fret over!"

"I wonder," Maggie flung over her shoulder as she marched along, "if Job will be jealous!"

"Job?" Bart queried, "Oh! You mean the horse that—"

"Yes, Mr. Logan! The horse *that*…Papa and I picked out…"

"Did you say something, sweetheart? About your Papa?"

"No!" Maggie snapped, "Anyhow, Mr. Logan, we appear to have arrived at the livery."

"I can see that, sweetheart. Would you be so kind as to hold the reins of the pony? I think Trap already has your mare saddled…ah…here she is. I thought for a moment of purchasing an English lady's sidesaddle, then I recalled that this *is* the mountains of North Georgia, and that up at the logging camp, you always rode astride. Do you think that the skirts you have on will accommodate that? Yes, I believe they will. And just how do you find her? Do you, perhaps, find her just a wee, wee bit to your liking, Margaret Ann?"

"Yes, Mr. Logan, I *am* a country girl, and proud of it! And as to the mare!—Oh! My! She's…stunning…she's superb! I've never *seen* a more beautiful saddle mount!"

Bart walked the roan mare up close, so that Maggie could lay a hand on her. His heart swelled, as he saw in her blue eyes the deep admiration, the pure appreciation of as fine a piece of horseflesh as the South offered. "You find, then, that she meets your…"

"She's…*gorgeous!*" Maggie felt tears stinging her eyes. Never in her life had she dreamed of owning such an animal. She had seen them, of course, fine horses, prancing along the fences of rich farms. But…never…*never* did she think she could ever dream of laying hands on one that was *her own.* "I…don't know…what to say…Mr. Logan. It's not my birthday, or anything…"

"Well, Margaret Ann. Let's be logical here. Johnny can't go riding all by himself, now can he?"

"No, Mr. Logan. He certainly can't. And I do…we do…appreciate your kind generosity…" Maggie's voice grew low, and choked off.

What was happening here? *What was she doing? Should* she let Johnny accept such an expensive gift? Should *she* accept such a marvelous gift? She wasn't even sure deep in her heart what she was going to *do* about Mr. Logan. One day, she thought marriage to him was ordained of God. The next, she recalled how marriage to a handsome man had plunged her into a deep, dark well of misery and grief… All she had was Johnny…

Maggie, one hand holding the mare's reins, the other lightly stroking the handsome neck, hedged. Her smooth brow knit in a frown, she chewed her lower lip:

"On second thought…Mr. Logan…I don't know that it would be proper…we aren't married…yet. I don't know that it would be proper…for us to accept such…expensive gifts…that evidently will continue to be a great monetary drain to you…"

105

"I thought we had that all settled? I can very well afford it. And you and Johnny are family. It *is* perfectly proper. An engagement, in many countries and in many cultures, is just as binding as a marriage."

"Really?" Maggie lifted her gaze and stared defiantly up at this man whom she loved on one hand—and feared on the other. Sometimes, to her, Bartram Logan seemed a paragon of manly virtues, at other times, he appeared a total unknown—

"And in just *what* countries would that be?"

"In the Middle East…somewhere…perhaps…never mind that…Just place your foot in my hands, Margaret Ann, and for goodness sakes, mount your horse! Johnny and I are going for a ride, and I'm sure you have no wish to be left standing alone in the stables!"

Maggie did as he instructed, Bart boosting her up onto the most beautiful horse she had ever seen. Then he led the way out of the stables, after handing Johnny the reins of the lovely little pony.

Then in a no-nonsense voice, Bartram Logan began to give John Thomas McKinnon, Jr. his first riding instructions.

"That's it, Johnny! Not too tight on the reins! Lean forward a bit! Just give her her head. Don't let your legs flop against her sides like that! That's a boy! You'll grow into a fine horseman in no time. No time at all—

"—Are you back there, Margaret Ann?"

Maggie guided her mare expertly up beside Bart Logan, and then past him, riding just the way she had on Alfred Stillwell's papa's fine stock.

Maggie was seized with the insane idea of galloping off, and challenging Mister Bartram Logan to a race! Then she recalled Johnny, seated for the first time in a saddle by himself. He had ridden before, with Bart. Her heart had risen into her throat, every time Bartram Logan took Johnny up into the saddle before him, despite the fact that she knew Bart was an expert rider. Life seemed so fragile to Maggie. How very well she knew, that it could be here today—and take wings tomorrow. Of some terrible illness…or accident…

God…! Maggie prayed as the three of them jogged sedately along through the trees lining the valley just outside the town, the same prayer she sent heavenward each night as she took to her bed: *Please, please…help me to decide the right thing to do…about marrying Mr. Logan!…and please, please…don't let anything happen to Johnny!*

Then Maggie shrugged aside the cold fear that often shadowed her thoughts. It was Johnny's birthday. She would enjoy the ride, enjoy the day.

"Is Barbara Jo going to come down and join us for lunch, and birthday cake? By the way, how is your sister doing?" Bart offered by way of making conversation.

"I'm hoping she will," Maggie replied. "Though she had…a terrible…headache this morning, and refused to come down for breakfast."

"I trust no one carried any up?"

"Why on earth would you say that, Mr. Logan?" Maggie glanced over at him, unsure why she didn't confess to Bartram Logan that Barbara Jo was being waited on—practically hand and foot. "She's my sister. And by the way, just for your information, if I thought she truly needed my help…well… of course, I would see to her needs."

"Yes," Bart replied thoughtfully, "I'm sure you would. But as long as she is *not* truly ill, you should allow her to fend for herself. Give her some reason to get out of bed each morning."

"She's up…most mornings now. She even walked over to her own house and picked up a few things she needed," Maggie replied in a worried voice.

"But…she still refuses to return home, to spend the night there?" Bart asked.

"Yes," Maggie sighed, adding, "Barbs has never been strong. She's never been able to…cope with…some of…life's difficulties. They seem to absolutely… overwhelm her. But, until Fred got so sick, she seemed to be doing so well…"

"You mean, as long as her husband was hale and hearty and the mercantile was bringing in a hefty profit," Bart said sarcastically.

"Yes," Maggie replied, resenting his remark, wanting very badly to change the subject. It was Johnny's birthday. She had no desire to quarrel with Mr. Logan. Nor to dwell on Barbara Jo's difficulties, though the thought ran through her mind—what *was* Barbs going to do to make a living? She certainly couldn't run the mercantile, not on her own. Besides, the rumors floating about Rhyersville were that the bank was planning shortly to foreclose on Moss' Mercantile. And Barbara Jo never broached the subject of the future. Did she plan on doing *anything*? What *could* she do? In Rhyersville?

"Which reminds me, Mister Logan, darling, we haven't had the pleasure of seeing your smiling face amongst those of the congregants of the Shiloh Baptist Church."

"Perhaps, Margaret Ann, if you invited me sweetly enough, I just might be able to remedy that situation, Sunday next." Bart grinned over at Maggie. And Johnny, riding between the two suddenly piped up, "I'm glad you two are not fussin' and fightin' so bad today! What with it bein' my birthday, an' all!"

The stunned look that crossed Maggie's beautiful face did Bartram Logan's heart a world of good. He could not resist the jab:

"Did you *hear* what your little brother just said, Margaret Ann?"

"Yes, Mr. Logan!" Maggie replied very, very sweetly, "I have not yet gone stone deaf."

Bart reared back in the saddle and laughed, and Johnny, thinking a big joke had been made, reared back in his little saddle and did likewise.

Maggie's face flushed red as a beet. She narrowed her blue eyes, gave the mare's reins a smart slap, and took off at a fast gallop.

Chapter 11

The new young minister preached a rousing sermon on loving thy neighbor. And Maggie secretly wished he had preached on swinging one's own weight! But then, what good would that have done?! Barbara Jo McKinnon Moss was not in attendance! Nor had she been, since Fred Moss' funeral. The day of Fred's funeral, Barbara Jo had advised Maggie, her face tight, her light blue eyes squinted almost shut, that she could not abide the idea of *ever* entering the front door of the Shiloh Baptist Church—*ever again*. Not after she had stood at the front of the church and watched the lid of that fine maple coffin being nailed shut against her dear husband's face.

That morning, immediately following the funeral, Barbara Jo had marched herself home to her fine yellow brick house, marched herself up the stairs and into her rose-colored bedroom, where she flopped her thin frame atop her feather-mattressed, carved-oak bed, and shook with wracking, violent sobs that echoed throughout the entire house, until Maggie wondered if there would be anything left of her older sister—except perhaps for a wet puddle atop the plump feather bed. Finally, at Maggie's insistent urgings, Barbara Jo had dragged herself up off her bed, shuffled one expensively-shod foot behind the other, over to her cedar-lined wardrobe, and yanked out a few of her darkest dresses. "I have *nothing* in black!" she had whined to Maggie with a tearful wail. "Except for this horrid thing I wore to the funeral—!...which I intend to toss into the fire as soon as I can rip it off! I never want to see it again! Nothing else, in black! And I don't know that I could *ever* wear this *awful* color again, anyways. It does *terrible* things to my delicate complexion! Look at me! I look like an old rag that's hung too long on the clothesline! You know how I am, Maggs!" she moaned, "I could never abide..." She broke off, overcome again by great, wracking sobs.

Maggie had gone to the mirrored bureau, pulled open this drawer then that, snatching out silk stockings, lace-trimmed pantaloons, ribbon-bedecked chemises, shifts and underskirts of the softest, most expensive of linens and cottons, and flung them all into an expansive leather valise lined with red paisley silk.

The huge leather valise clutched in one hand, the bundle of expensive dresses draped over her arm, Maggie had half pulled, half dragged Barbara Jo down the stairs, across the expansive, high-columned veranda, and up the street to The Sparrow Inn.

Once inside the door of the inn, Barbara Jo had broken down completely, so that Maggie could scarcely coax her up the stairs. One step at a time. Once up the stairs, Maggie turned down the narrow hall, intending to install Barbara Jo—at least for a night or two—in one of the small guest rooms she had for rent, at the end of the short corridor.

But Barbara Jo had topped the stairs, and dragged herself lethargically to the room Maggie had claimed for herself and Johnny. The biggest room. The one with a view of the street. The one with the only fireplace in the entire upper floor.

"You don't really mind, do you, Maggs?" Barbara Jo whined with a tearful wail as she fell across the bed. "I do feel that I need a good fire. I feel chilled to the bone."

"No," Maggie smiled sweetly. Barbara Jo had just lost her husband. She would not begrudge her the bigger room, the warmth of a good fire. With a sigh, Maggie, loaded down with Barbara Jo's belongings, had traipsed in behind her sister, depositing the load in her hand and arm over the big maple rocker before the fireplace. Maggie had dutifully laid a fire in the rock fireplace, and had instructed Benjamin Noah to make certain that the wood-box in the room stayed filled to the top.

Each morning, Maggie tried mightily to coax her sister out of bed, into her clothes, and down the stairs.

But after a few days, with Barbara Jo adamantly refusing to rise from Maggie's bed, or to leave the warmth and seclusion of Maggie's room—even to take her meals or visit the outhouse—Maggie had given up.

That had been some three weeks past. And that is why Mr. Bartram Logan's comments about not taking breakfast up to her sister had rankled so with Maggie.

And this particular Sunday, Maggie had more than half looked for Mr. Bartram Logan to make good on his promise—to at last darken the door of the Shiloh Baptist Church. But Mr. Bartram Logan had not put in an appearance, either.

So Maggie had sought, for her and Johnny, a seat on a bench near the wood-burning stove in the south corner of the church. And immediately when the few people in attendance had scattered to their homes, shivering in the cold, she and Johnny had hastened home to the inn. They ate a filling lunch, which Barbara Jo did manage—in her lace-trimmed linen chemise, her face pale and drawn, her light brown hair uncombed and all askew—to drag herself downstairs to partake of. Without an offer of help in clearing away the dishes or washing up, Barbara Jo took herself back upstairs, to lay huddled beneath heavy quilts. And now Maggie lounged before the huge fireplace in the dining room, listening to the fierce howling of the winds whistling down the tall chimney, and the rain pelting against the sides and roof of the clapboard building.

She could hear Johnny muttering and mumbling, rushing madly about between rooms, literally bouncing off the walls and the narrow staircase. Then Johnny became bored with this, and with being shut indoors. He came over to her chair, and leaned his slight weight into her left thigh, until it grew numb. Maggie roused herself from her sleepy repose in the big maple rocker before the fire, and the two of them bounded up the stairs, gathered bedding off their beds and flung it down the stairs.

Then they came bounding back down, scooping up their bedding and carrying it to one of the larger tables near the fire. Here Maggie and Johnny proceeded, as they had on other wintry afternoons, to build a most respectable 'fort' beneath the dining table.

They were snugly ensconced in their quilt-and-blanket 'fort' when Maggie heard footsteps. She peered out through a tiny crack between blankets and quilts, to see two expensively wool-trousered legs above black, shiny boots.

A masculine voice inquired rather loudly: "Is anyone here? Surely so, since the front door was not even *barred or locked*, and any soul with half a notion to could have simply barged right in from off the street. By the way…" the deeply masculine voice moved nearer, demanding: "Exactly *whom* am I addressing? I see nothing, except for two small ladies' boots, below two exquisite ankles, protruding from beneath what appears to be some sort of…exactly what *is* that thing?"

"It's a *fort*, Bart!" Johnny piped out between the opening of quilt and blanket. "You want to come on in?"

"I don't know…that I should? What does your sister think, about this…gracious invitation? Is there room… in that thing…for another warm body?"

"I doubt, Mr. Logan, darling," Maggie replied smartly, "that there *is* room under here for another warm body, especially one so tall and so…"

"You were saying? So tall…and so…what?" Bartram Logan had bent and was peering in at them through the narrow crack in the fort walls, dark brows raised.

He bent and made as if to climb in beneath the table, but Maggie quickly suggested: "I think it best, Mr. Logan, if you please, that we come out there…and join you."

"You never did finish your sentence, my dearest?" Bart gazed at Maggie quizzically, taking her hand and drawing her forth, from out of the fort and close to his chest.

"You *are* in the way of being a handsome devil, Mr. Logan," Maggie teased him sweetly, smoothing down her skirts and patting down her hair, "and you well know it! So why are you here, in my inn, on a wintry November Sunday afternoon? Fishing for compliments? And after having missed church! Tsk! tsk! Vanity, Mr. Logan, darling, is a grave, grave sin!" What on earth was wrong with her, Maggie wondered suddenly. She was *flirting* with Mr. Logan!—like a lovesick schoolgirl! But she had not seen him for almost a week. And she had to admit to herself that her heartbeat had quickened at the sound of that familiar voice, and her face felt more than a bit flushed at sight of that handsome face.

To disguise her sudden feelings of…joy?…at sight of him, Maggie stepped quickly away from Bartram Logan, and began making an attempt to dismantle the 'fort.'

"Need any help with that? You shouldn't take it down. Certainly not on my account. I really can't stay long. The weather is worsening by the moment. It might even snow. Clouds are gathering over the mountains to the north. It may be an early—"

"If you can't stay, why did you even bother to make the trip in this cold, Mr. Logan, darling?" Maggie whirled about and snapped irritably. "You intend upon popping into the door from out of nowhere, and then without a by-your-leave, out you go again?!"

"Well…" Bart mumbled, not quite sure just what *this* reaction meant, "I have…these papers…that I picked up from my lawyer's office…yesterday. And I felt that they were… of some great import. So…here…I am. And…am I welcome…or not?"

"Don't talk so foolishly, Mr. Logan," Maggie continued to snap at him. Why, she had not the foggiest notion. Why should she feel affronted that he couldn't afford her and Johnny more of his time this cold Sunday afternoon? Why did the mere *sight* of this man so often set her teeth on edge, send her off on an angry tangent?!

"Pull yourself up a chair, Mr. Logan," Maggie, her beautiful face flushed, her blue-blue eyes bright, continued to speak as if on the verge of tears, "And tell us about these papers of yours—that are so important that you are out and about in all sorts of foul weather. You will, no doubt, come down with a seriously bad case of the croup—"

Bart promptly did as she asked, muttering, "Well, I suppose I shall just have to chance it." But before he seated himself, he drew a second chair near him. He gazed at Maggie and pointed now to the second chair. Johnny had disappeared back beneath what little remained of the quilt-and-blanket fort. Bart and Maggie could hear him scrambling about, humming and buzzing and muttering to himself.

"Would you please just sit yourself down beside me, here? So that we can talk."

Maggie took the chair, her heartbeat picking up its momentum. What was this? His tanned face, his dark eyes, appeared suddenly so serious. So deathly solemn.

"Has something happened?" she asked, letting her slight weight sink into the chair.

"No. Well, that's not exactly correct. Something has *indeed* happened. Nothing, thank God, that is bad. It's just…that…title to McKinnon Valley has passed into your name. And I have here something else." Bartram Logan held out toward her a large, important looking envelope.

"What…is it?"

"These papers…" Bart Logan began in a low, very calm, very serious voice, "You should put them in some *very* safe, *very* secure place. And you should advise a trusted family member or friend, as to just where they are stored."

"What on earth…are they?" Maggie inquired, staring first at Bart, then down at the huge brown envelope.

"Legal documents."

"Legal documents? Is that all I'm to be told about these mysterious papers?"

"Legal documents…setting up a trust fund for John Thomas McKinnon, Jr., and providing that, should you and Johnny…singly or together…survive me…transfer of all my financial assets…to you."

"I…transfer? What are you saying? What…if?"

"If you do not marry me, Margaret Ann McKinnon, all that I own, at my demise, will pass to you and Johnny. Regardless of circumstances."

"But…that's…madness! What if…"

"If you do not marry me…there will not be…and I repeat very emphatically…*not be*… an *if.* I love you. In my heart, Margaret Ann McKinnon, I am as committed to you *this day*…" He paused, looked down, lifted a hand and drew it through his hair, looked away, then back. His voice thick, low, dark eyes moist, he gazed straight at her and continued, "As committed to you as if we had spoken our vows, for in my heart, I have already taken my vows before a Holy God…to cherish and protect and provide for you…*always.*"

Maggie had extended her right hand, as if to receive the huge brown envelope. Now, she quickly drew it back, as if the thing would burn her skin. Nervously she eyed the envelope, then Bartram Logan. She wiped her hand on her skirt, to remove the perspiration on her small palm.

"Take it," Bartram Logan urged, his voice hoarse with emotion.

"But, what about…your family?" Maggie asked. "They might wish…to…contest any such papers…"

"*You* are my family. You and Johnny. I have no living relatives close enough who might dare to—or legally could—contest anything. Besides, these are perfectly legal, perfectly binding documents. I have a *right* to do this. I have a *right*, should I so desire, to entitle these documents to Trap, down the street."

"Trap?" Maggie stared at him.

"It was merely said, dearest one, to make a point." Despite the gravity of the situation, Bart could not suppress a little smile. He wanted very much to make a point here. Whether or not Margaret Ann McKinnon Evans was committed to him, he was to her. She had his heart for all eternity. And Bart was well aware that things could happen in this old world—a tree could fall on him, he could be thrown from a spooked horse, ravaged by an unknown disease…Now, should anything happen to him, she and her little brother had all his worldly possessions, to hold in perpetuity.

The thought of something awful happening to the strong, handsome man before her flashed through Maggie's mind. "I would…rather…that you had not done this…" Maggie felt as if she might choke. She wanted to escape. She felt locked to the chair by some unknown force. She looked away, again wiped her hand on her skirt, shook her head, refused to take the papers. Then, feeling his intense gaze like a heavy weight upon her, her eyes were drawn back to his. As if of its own volition, her hand reached out. And reluctantly she accepted the weight of the huge brown envelope.

"I want security for you, and Johnny, regardless of what the future holds." Bart Logan laid a warm, gentle hand over hers, atop the bundle. His hand firm atop hers, beneath her hand she could feel the slight bulk of a leather thong that bound the envelope shut.

Maggie withdrew her hand, laying the bundle in the lap of her Sunday-best dress. What did this mean? What had she just accepted? How did this…bind her to this man? Was this at all proper? Her eyes felt hot. Her throat felt dry as cotton. She sought for words, but none came to meet the love she saw in this man's eyes. She enjoyed his company. She enjoyed their light verbal sparring. She had found that she drew warmth, even comfort, from his nearness, his strength. She wanted security, she admitted in her heart of hearts, *she wanted security for Johnny*. But this same strength that drew her, often repelled her. She did not wish to *lose herself*, to be *swallowed up* by his strength…the very earth seemed to shift beneath her feet. She felt that she could not reach out and truly grasp hold of him…nor could she let him go…Marriage to him would demand so much. When a woman married, she gave so much. She gave her life, her body, her worldly assets, her freedom—in hopes of gaining…what?…love, a real home, family…?

Maggie pulled her gaze away from his, so full of love, so full of longing. Nervously she rose, the bundle clutched carelessly in one hand, making a pretense with her free hand of tending the fire. Then, her mind made up, she turned to face William Bartram Logan. "I'll…place them in the brown leather trunk," she said very solemnly. "I'll keep them for a while. And then…we shall see. We shall…see. Should you *ever, ever* wish them back, they are, it goes without saying, yours. To burn…or to do with as you shall choose."

"Good. I shall never wish them back." Bart couldn't help but smile with relief, as he recalled the first time he had seen *the big brown leather trunk* that had been her great-grandmother's, the day she and her 'friend' came lugging it up the logging trace, into his lumber camp…Bart wondered now about Thomas Beyers, her widowed brother-in-law, whom Bart knew the first time he saw the man was madly in love with Margaret Ann McKinnon, his dead wife's youngest sister. Did she see Thomas Beyers, now? Of course, she did. Rhyersville was a small town…they would naturally see one another…at church…at the mercantile…Thomas Beyers must come in to eat at the inn…often…she must see him…often…

"You are…sure…about this?" Maggie turned, the huge brown envelope in her left hand, her right hand resting nervously on the stairs balustrade.

"Yes."

"Very well. Then, I'll just go on up…and put this in the trunk…and, as I have just said, if tomorrow—"

"I am *sure*, Maggie," Bartram Logan said softly, "Today. Tomorrow. And *forever*." She saw Thomas Beyers, certainly, but she never, never…mentioned him…

Maggie turned and started up the stairs. She could hear Johnny, out in the kitchen. She had no idea when he had vacated the 'fort' and gone into the kitchen. Suddenly he burst into the dining room, and ran to Bart. As she reached the upstairs landing, she could hear Bartram Logan's warm laughter, echoing up the stairs.

Upstairs, Maggie entered her room. She stepped inside the door, and leaned for a moment against the doorframe. Then she crossed the room with swift, sure steps. She opened the lid of the trunk. She gazed for a long moment at the large brown envelope. Then she opened it, reached in and drew out the sheaf of documents. She scanned them for a moment, her heart pounding so hard she was sure Bartram Logan could hear it all the way down the stairs. So stiff and formal in their wording…quickly she placed them back in the envelope. Then for just a moment she simply stared at the contents of the huge, brown leather trunk. A jumble of bedding, some mementoes from the past, a few pieces of baby clothing—Johnny's, and Katie Ann's. A few little things she had sewn so tenderly for her firstborn child—unnamed. Stillborn, they had said. Maggie never knew whether it was a boy or a girl, or if Len or Dr. Holt had dressed the child, before burial, in any of the tiny garments she had made for it…. She had no idea where the little body lay…sometimes she would awaken in the night, in a cold sweat…and imagine that tiny part of her lying in an unmarked grave—in Big Carl Evans' grave plot…a world away.

Tears in her eyes, Maggie started to slam the big brown leather trunk shut. Then something caught her eye. The badly dented red tin box that had been Papa's tobacco tin. Maggie reached into the trunk, slowly withdrew the battered rectangle of tin with its hinged lid. The red tin felt warm to her touch. She recalled the day Papa had given it to Barbara Jo, his second daughter, sliding it across the kitchen table in McKinnon Valley as a peace offering to quiet Barbara Jo's mournful howls. Papa had just given the baby of the family, Maggie, a small wooden Indian he had lovingly carved. And Barbara Jo, not much more than a baby herself, had set up a loud howl at not having likewise received a gift from Papa. Hence Papa had dumped the clumps of tobacco from his tin into a pocket, and slid the tin across the table to Barbara Jo. Barbara Jo had promptly let out even louder howls—and with a smart swat of one small fist, had sent the tobacco tin skidding across the kitchen table and clattering onto the floor.

Papa had smiled, patiently retrieved it, and used it up until he became ill. Maggie thought now of flipping open the tin lid. But she didn't know whether her heart could bear the wafting out of that familiar scent—Papa's pipe tobacco.

117

She rubbed a forefinger over the red tin, then tucked the tobacco tin back in a corner, quietly closed the lid of the big brown leather trunk, and sedately made her way back downstairs, where William Bartram Logan waited.

Quickly the afternoon flew, Bart playing with Johnny at whatever came to Johnny's little hands. Maggie watched, fascinated that this man loved her brother so. If for no other reason, she thought, than for Johnny's sake, should she not marry this man?

No! Quickly she chastened herself. She would *not* marry simply to assure security for herself or for Johnny! She often wondered if that was why, in the final analysis, she had decided to marry Len Evans. For the sake of her family. What a heart-rending disaster that marriage had proven! Maggie decided then and there that if and when she married Mr. William Bartram Logan it would be because she loved him—with all her heart and soul.

She wasn't sure whether that time would ever come. She wasn't sure what, exactly, she felt for Mr. Logan, but she was sorely afraid she could not at the moment return what she saw in his eyes.

The day drew on, and seemingly Mr. Bartram Logan had no intention of departing the inn. He lingered before the fire, rising from time to time to poke at it, as if, Maggie thought, he assumed himself to be the man of the house. He even ventured out into the cold and carried in several armfuls of wood. Brushing bits of bark and chips from the spit oak logs off his expensive jacket sleeves and into the blazing fire, he would then retake his seat. Finally Maggie rose, and moved into the kitchen, to heat them up some supper.

Supper done, Mr. Logan insisted that he help do the dishes. And when he went to toss out the dishwater, he remarked off-handedly, "Look at that! Look at how that snow's coming down."

"Why, Mr. Logan!" Maggie, standing at his elbow, peered past him at the wall of white shifting down, with flakes drifting onto the narrow back porch. "I fear you have lingered overlong. You can't *possibly* ride off to the lumber camp! Not in *that*! It's already getting dark out there!" Maggie exclaimed. "You'll just be forced to stay in your old room."

"No." Bart drew Maggie back into the warmth of the kitchen and closed the door. "Not upstairs, darling. It…wouldn't appear proper."

As soon as Maggie had accepted his ring, Bartram Logan had surrendered exclusive right to his upstairs room in the inn. He would not dare, he had vowed, bring a smear of reproach on the spotless character of his beloved. If he was forced by business to overnight in Rhyersville, he counted on his old accommodations—a haystack at Trap's Wheelwright & Livery, where he had, due to the cold winds howling over the surrounding mountains and down the dirt street, stabled his mount as soon as he rode in this afternoon.

But now…with the snow setting in, he doubted that Jonas Trap was still there on the premises, to lift the heavy bars across the huge double doors and let him in.

"I could…make my way to Trap's, I suppose…" Bart began, following Maggie into the dining room where he tended the fire, building it to a bright blaze.

"You'll do no such thing!" Maggie cried, aghast. "It must be *way* below freezing out there. That huge barn will be like an icicle. There's no one here but us! You will march yourself right upstairs, and take your old room. No one will ever know."

"Oh, but, yes, darling, someone will know. *I will.* And I gave you my word. And I have made up my mind on this." He stood, one hand on the mantel, his face and tall form lit by the fire.

"Well, for heavens sakes!" Maggie burst out angrily. "If you're not the most stubborn, most pig-headed man I have ever encountered in my entire life! You *always* insist upon having your own way! Sometimes, I feel just like…"

"Well, if you're going to kill me, just do it now and get it over with. While there are no witnesses. I think Johnny's already fallen asleep," Bart laughed.

"Well. As you wish, Mr. Logan! I shall hasten upstairs, and fling some bedding down onto the floor. You can kindly retrieve it and—"

"I think that won't be necessary. I think I can just tear down the walls of the fort," Bart grinned. "On second thought, maybe I'll just rebuild it, and then crawl inside."

Maggie smiled in spite of herself. But, still, she cringed inside, to think of this man sleeping on the floor, while at least two empty beds with fine feather mattresses waited just up the stairs.

"Are you sure…Mr. Logan? We could haul down a mattress?" Maggie hesitated, glancing over at a soundly sleeping Johnny.

"We won't go to that bother. I'll be fine. I'm sure. When Liza Mae and Benjamin Noah come storming the portals of the inn before cock crow tomorrow morning, they will find me decently asleep here on the floor by the fire. Fully clothed."

"Well…"

"It's settled then. I'll just take Johnny up for you. Then I'll come down and secure the doors, bank the fire, and we'll be all set for the night."

Which is exactly what happened.

Chapter 12

The next Sunday afternoon, Bartram Logan appeared in the kitchen of the inn just as Maggie was clearing the kitchen table of lunch leavings. He breezed in, came up behind her as she stood at the dry sink, an apron about her slender middle, little strands of hair curling damply about her face, her hands immersed in hot dishwater in the huge white enameled pan in the dry sink.

"Need a hand with that?" Bart asked walking up behind her, laying his lips close to her ear.

"No!" Maggie replied pertly. "And just what, Mr. Logan, darling, brings you into fair Rhyersville, on this lovely November afternoon?"

"And just what do you suppose, my lovely one, as if you didn't already know? Couldn't Liza Mae finish up here? Then you could come and sit with me before the fire in the dining room. I have something to show you."

"It's Sunday, Mr. Logan, darling. Liza Mae gets Sundays off. You know that. And I don't have time to talk to you this afternoon. Stock needs to be put up at the store—"

"Why is it, my sweet, that everyone seems to get Sundays off—except you?"

"All right," Maggie snapped tartly. "Just let me fling out this dishwater—"

"No. I'll do that. You take off your apron, and hang it…wherever, and I'll be right back." And so saying, Bart grabbed the heavy pan of hot water, and strode out the back door.

Maggie removed her apron, hung it on a peg beside the dry sink, smoothed back her hair from a sweaty forehead, and heaved a great sigh. Why was she so tired? It seemed of late that it was all she could do simply to heft her body out of bed each morning, and troop downstairs—to begin a long, grueling, toilsome day. What with Fred Moss gone, and the store to run, and the inn—

Then Mr. Bartram Logan was banging the back door shut, and hanging the huge dishpan on its nail behind the black iron cookstove. "Into the dining room with you, darling, and no arguments about it. The store stock…or whatever…can wait. You are working much too hard. Putting in far too many hours. As if the entire world—"

"Don't even go there, Mr. Logan. I am doing—"

"I know, darling. And I don't mean to fuss at you, it's just that—"

"What *is it* you wish to show me?" Maggie interjected snidely.

From a huge leather case he had laid on one of the dining tables, Bart Logan produced a shiny-backed catalog. Pulling two chairs up before the fire, he motioned Maggie to one. When she had seated herself, her face tired and strained and appearing more than a bit impatient at this interruption of her Sunday afternoon, Bartram Logan began to flip through the colorful catalog, and to point out this and that.

"Excuse me, Mr. Logan," Maggie finally interrupted, lifting a hand to rub her brow, her voice weary and strained, "But, exactly what am I looking at here? And why?"

"Why, darling? Were you not listening just now? You're choosing your Christmas gifts!"

"Christmas gifts? These are lovely…tables and chairs…and bedsteads. Lovely, indeed. But…what am I supposed to *do* with them? The inn is totally furnished, such as it is. Not quite so lavishly as these beautiful things—that appear far better suited for a fine manor house, than for a rustic mountain inn."

"These would not be for the inn, sweetheart. They're for the log house—in McKinnon Valley."

"But, Mr. Logan…they're, as I just said, lovely. Far too lovely, too lavish, too…for McKinnon Valley."

"But…" Bart stammered, all the wind taken out of his sails, his joy deflated like a punctured balloon. "I thought…that is to say…if the place were furnished, we could use it for a weekend retreat! After, of course, we're married. I mean, sweetheart, Christmas is just around the corner. If you *want* any of these things, we must order them now."

"Weekend retreat? Retreat from what?"

"From too many hours spent on your feet down at Moss' Mercantile! From... look, sweetheart, I didn't come here this lovely November afternoon to quarrel with you. I merely wanted to present you with a nice gift, come Christmas. But it appears that you are far from being in any mood—"

"Oh! So, now, it's a *mood* I'm in, is it!?"

"Sweetheart! Darling! Just settle yourself down, would you? And at least *look* at these! They are the finest—"

"That's *just* the problem, Mr. Logan, darling. They are the finest! And McKinnon Valley, if you had taken the trouble to notice, is not the finest! It is a rustic log house fashioned by the axe of an emigrant frontier Scotsman, and finished off by his son—who never attended an institution of learning one day of his life! It does not, therefore, lend itself to the finest of furnishings. They would be ostentatious and horribly out of place!"

"Oh. I'm...sorry...sweetheart. I never thought."

"No! Quite obviously there is quite a lot you haven't thought about, Mr. Logan, darling! Like the fact that I have obligations!"

"That's just the problem, beloved," Bart said softly, having no desire to rile her more than he already had. "You have *far* too many obligations. Just look at you! You're so exhausted you are ready to drop! Snapping at me for no reason at all that I can see."

"Mr. Logan!" Maggie began, rising suddenly to her feet. Bart immediately rose, too. Maggie gazed up at him; she hesitated. The man was absolutely correct. Here he stood, his beautiful catalog in hand. Wanting to purchase for her a lovely Christmas gift. And here she ...

"I am...sorry...forgive me, Mr. Logan. I know that sometimes lately I'm irritable and..."

"You're as tightly strung as a new fiddle. But never mind, sweetheart," Bart said softly. Taking her hand, he drew her back down into her chair. "Let us forget the furniture. Let us forget the stock for the store. How about if we go for a lovely drive?"

"Drive? But it's..."

"The sun is shining. I have the carriage out front. It's almost completely enclosed. I have lap robes. Where's Johnny?"

"He's—" But Bartram Logan was off, calling Johnny's name loudly enough that the little boy could have heard it half up the mountain.

Johnny, upstairs with his huge medical book, came running. Then they were bundled into the carriage. The fine steeds set off at a fast clip. And soon Maggie was out in the country, breathing mountain air. Johnny and Bart keeping up a fast paced exchange of quips and jests. Johnny between Maggie and Bart, jumping up and down with excitement as he always did when Bart Logan was present.

Maggie settled back beneath the warm nest of lap robes. The wind off the mountains caressing her face, the smell of the fall forest wafting down off the high ridges and over the creeks and springs bringing with it the scents of damp mosses and freshly fallen leaves, all at once, the world seemed almost perfect. All at once Maggie could almost forget Fred Moss' passing. Barbara Jo's deplorable financial condition. The burden of the inn, and the store. And Barbara Jo's declining spirits. Her worry had increased, lately, about Barbara Jo. She seemed to grow more and more lethargic with the passing of each day. Instead of accepting her loss, her sister seemed to wallow deeper and deeper into her miry pit of misery and grief. Sometimes, Barbara Jo had told Maggie with a great sigh, it was all she could do to simply open her eyes and drag herself out of the bed of a morning. She had grown pale and thin.

But all that seemed to fade away, supplanted by the beauty of this fall afternoon. And Maggie realized suddenly that Bartram Logan was driving them out to McKinnon Valley. She had not even found the time to drive out to the place, since he had handed her the deed. It was still securely shut away, in the big brown leather trunk, along with the big brown envelope containing the trust fund documents—and William Bartram Logan's Last Will and Testament. All this, she had discovered in the big brown envelope...

Bartram Logan drove his fast-stepping team through the gap and down the slope. And the log house came into view. Wordlessly, Bart leapt down from the carriage, lifted Johnny down, then came around and reached for Maggie. She sat in the carriage, still as a wooden statue, eyes glued to the front of the house. The pleasant feelings of well-being fled.

Mama's flower boxes were horribly infested with weeds. The entire front yard was overgrown with weeds. She knew that up on the hill back of the house, the entire little graveyard was almost certainly overgrown, also. Probably wild muscadine and sweet honeysuckle vines had twined their creeping green tentacles around all the McKinnon tombstones… the scene before her overwhelmed Maggie with a deep sadness, made her sick to her stomach. She held the deed to the place, but she had neither the time nor the energy to enjoy it. So much work was needed here. The place needed several pairs of busy hands, to make it appear…not so…dilapidated…and forsaken. Void of all human touch or habitation…

Just as Bart reached for Maggie, she clasped her hands over her face, and burst into wracking sobs.

"Darling!" Bart cried in great alarm, reaching up and lifting her down and enfolding her firmly against his chest, tucking her head beneath his chin, soothing her as if she were a small child:

"What, now… What's all this, now? I thought it would cheer you up! To drive out and see the place! It's *yours* now!"

Maggie could only mumble and sob. Why could this man not understand?

Finally, she pushed away, and stood gazing up at him. Her face, she knew was a mess beneath the brim of her winter bonnet. She dabbed angrily at her eyes. She was acting as badly as Barbara Jo!

"It was very…thoughtful…of you, Mr. Logan," she muttered, sniffling and swiping at her eyes with both hands. "And I'm an…unworthy ingrate! But…just… *look at the place*! Mama would turn over in her grave…should she be looking down to see this! And Papa! Always…they kept things so neat…"

"Margaret Ann…! My dearest…!" Bart began. He tipped his hat back on his forehead, then reached into an inner pocket and handed her a handkerchief. He felt he must say something, but knew not quite where to begin. Then in total exasperation he blurted out, "Look at you! You're wearing yourself thin to the bone attempting to take care of the living! Now, are you also going to take onto your slender shoulders the responsibility of pleasing the *dead*!?"

"That's…!" Maggie gasped. She stared up at him, absolutely speechless. Her mouth hung open in horror at what he had just said. "That's…*cold! Cruel!* What a *heartless* thing to say!" She felt like slapping his handsome face.

"Darling! I'm…sorry," Bart mumbled. Why was it that his mouth was always coming up with the wrong thing to say to this woman? She was right.

He was behaving like a cad. It was all too evident that the state of the place was breaking her heart. And she felt totally powerless to change it. She already had more on her than most humans could bear. And here he had gone and said such a callous…

"It was thoughtless of me, to make such a statement," Bart offered, reaching for her hand. Maggie moved away. She fairly leapt up into the carriage.

"I want to go home!"

"Home? I thought…that this was…"

"Tell me, Mr. Logan, *darling*, does this look like *home* to you?"

"Oh. You mean…the inn."

"Yes, Mr. Logan! What *other* home do I have!?"

"Of course," Bart replied, calling, softly, "Johnny! Come on, son! I think we're… leaving now."

"*Son?!*" Maggie glared at Bart as he climbed into the carriage after having lifted Johnny in.

"Just…a figure of speech, dearest," Bart Logan cocked his hat back toward his brow, picked up the reins, and heaved a great sigh, "Just a…figure of speech. Getty-upppp there…!"

"Goats, Boss?" Stephen Giles, head foreman of the Logan Lumber Company, stood in the tiny company office, and gazed at Bart, then turned his eyes away from all the pain he saw there. "Half a dozen…*goats*? That is…if I heard you correctly."

"You heard me correctly, Giles. At least *six* goats. Very *hungry* goats. That can consume voracious amounts of weeds and grasses. And if they have not accomplished the job in short order, then we shall purchase another half dozen, and so forth, until McKinnon Valley is completely clean and free of grass and weeds."

"Yes, sir!"

"I look to you, then, to see to their immediate purchase. And to seeing that they're carried out there to the place…and securely chained, so that they're not roving off, eating some neighboring farmer's gardens and fields. Do I make myself clear?"

"Yes, sir, Boss! Perfectly clear!"

"Then I want plants purchased, and put along…in the front of the house…or whatever."

"Plants…Boss?"

"Yes. Plants! Giles! You know, those things that grow out of the ground…and have blossoms and berries and the like on them. *Plants!*— Giles!"

"Any…particular…type…or whatever? Of…plants?"

"I…don't know. Whatever type it is that Mrs. Evans has growing about The Sparrow, I should think…yes…that should just fill the bill…"

"Well, sir, I'll git right on it. Gittin' th' goats…and having a look at th'…plants growing about th' inn…"

"Yes, Giles! See to it that you do. When next I carry her riding out that way, I want an entirely different picture to come into view! Do you understand what I'm getting at here?"

"Yes, sir. I believe I do."

"Good. Then how are the…"

They went on to discuss the business of the lumber mill. But Bart's mind and heart, Stephen Giles could clearly see, were not on current inventory or profits.

"You going to be around, most of the day, Boss?" Stephen Giles finally asked his boss.

"No. No, I don't think I will."

"Oh? You got something else goin'? Besides th' flowers… and th' goats?"

"Yes, Giles. I believe I'm going to try my hand at a bit of *woodworking*. And, oh, by the way. You do know, don't you, to chain the goats out of reach of the flowers and shrubs, when they're put in? We don't want all that work to be eaten to a thin stubble before she even gets to see it!"

"Yes, sir, Boss. I believe I can see to that. Woodworking, did you say?"

"Yes, Giles. I'm sure I've never mentioned it, and you may not be aware of the fact, but I do pride myself on being something of a fine furniture maker. Was rather good at it once, when I was but a lad of a boy. Spent two or three summers at Grandfather Logan's furniture factories. The one in Philadelphia…no…two summers at the one in Philadelphia…and one summer in Boston, I believe it was. He thought it would do me a world of good, he said, to learn to use my hands—as well as my head. So, I'll be wanting you to personally choose out some nice pieces of oak…and maple…from the mill. Some sweet-smelling cedar pieces, too. Pieces….that are already well seasoned, if we have them. Ready immediately to be turned, routed, sanded, and so forth. You know what I need."

"Should I do this…before…or after…I git th' goats? And th' plants?"

"Do it *first*, Giles. I want the stuff loaded onto a wagon. I'll be carrying it out to Cottonwood. *This* afternoon."

"To…Cottonwood…Boss?"

"Yes, Giles. I have a fine woodworking shop already set up out there. I go there, sometimes, on rainy afternoons. Dabble about in it, from time to time. Grandfather Logan was right. It…gets…my mind…off things." Bart thought, but did not say, *It helps me to meditate. To center my mind on the Almighty. It helps me to pray.* He wondered why he found it so difficult to discuss his faith, to perhaps *share* his faith, with other people. He had not the faintest notion whether the man standing before him, tall, handsome and dark blond with a ruddy complexion that never tanned to any great degree…he had no earthly idea, that if a tree accidentally felled his head foreman, that the man's soul would be secure…He recalled how naturally the discussion of things spiritual came to Margaret Ann McKinnon Evans. Like a second breath. Maybe, for him, someday, if he persisted in the way…meantime, *God keep Stephen Giles, and all his logging crew, safely in the hollow of His hands…*

"These *things*…you go out there, to get off your mind…are *they* why you're makin' th' furniture? And buyin' th' goats, and flowers?"

"Stop talking like an idiot, Giles! You know *exactly* why I'm building the furniture—and buying the goats—and planting the flowers! Because I *love* her Giles, and I want to see her happy! Is that all right with you!?"

"Fine, Boss! I admire…yes, I do, so greatly admire a man that sets his eye on a thing, and then goes *right* after it. If I could find me a fine woman…like Mrs. Evans…I might even…"

"Yes, Giles. Your point is taken. Now, how about getting your mind off your lack of a love-life, and onto that lumber. And throw in a bunch of two-bys and four-bys. For spindles and posts. Well dried, you understand?

Ready to work? I don't have much time, here."

"Sure, Boss. I'll get right on it. And…Boss…"

Bart had turned to stroll off, to hitch up a wagon. Now he swung rather impatiently back to his head foreman, turning out the palms of his hands, his dark brows raised quizzically. What more needed to be said here!?

"Nothing, Boss…" Stephen Giles mumbled, glancing down at the tips of his logging boots, then up at Bart, "Just…good luck."

Bart pulled a grim smile, "Thanks, Giles. You do *know her well*, don't you?"

––––––––––

Bart drove the wagon loaded with the finest maple and oak boards and posts of differing dimensions into the drive at his mansion at Cottonwood. He leapt down from the high wagon seat, flung open the double doors leading into the huge carriage house, and drove the wagon in.

Scarcely had Bart begun to unload his materials, than one of his stout loggers, Tad Horton, appeared at his elbow.

"Horton?!" Bart cried in great surprise. "What on earth are you doing here?"

"Just wanted to let you know. Just closed th' deal, Boss, on a half dozen goats. Simmons is chaining 'em in th' yard—over there in th' valley. They sure appeared to me to be skinny and hungry as all get-out."

"Fine!" Bart observed curtly, "Fine. But that still doesn't explain your sudden appearance at Cottonwood. Everything going all right, up at the mill?"

"Right as rain, Boss. But Mr. Giles…he thought you might need…some help."

"Help?" Bart inquired with a slight lift of dark brows.

"Yes, sir!" Tad Horton beamed at his boss. "You see standin' before you one o' th' finest furniture makers in th' entire county!"

"Well! Bless my soul!" Bart Logan pulled a huge smile, raised his hands heavenward, and strode purposefully through the huge carriage house doors, "Then let's you and me get right on it, shall we?"

Tad Horton followed his boss into the cavernous carriage house. But Horton immediately noted that the place was filled to the brim, what with a huge, dust-coated carriage that must take a four-in-hand to pull it, and a small, lighter rig that could easily be handled by two fine steeds. Beyond them, beside them, behind them, an array of tools and implements that would boggle the mind.

"You plan on doing a lot of work…in here, Boss?" Horton asked wonderingly.

"Yes. What's wrong with the place?"

"If ye'll pardon me sayin' so, Boss. It's a bit short on space. Fer workin'…that is. Didn't I see a big barn out back? Set back there, ag'inst them mount'ins? What's wrong with us cartin' this lumber, here, some o' these tools—just th' ones we'll be apt ta be usin', out to that big…I mean..with th' two of us workin'…we'll be walkin' on one t'other toes, so to speak."

"I suppose you're right," Bart sighed. "Which means we'll have to *reload* all this material I just had the poor judgment to throw off here in the carriage house."

"Won't take but a minute, Boss. I think Mr. Giles plans on joinin' us, later in the afternoon. And then, we'll fer shore need more space ta work!"

"What's this?" Bart turned and stared at Tad Horton. "Giles…plans on coming out? Who else, by the way, plans to get in on this…particular operation? Anyone else I know?"

"Well…sir…" Tad Horton cast his gaze down at his dirt-covered logging boots, then up at his boss, who stood gazing at him with amazed eyes. "There's Simmons….and Boots Jones…and…"

"Who's going to be left to run the logging camp?!" Bart cried.

"Well, they…all the men…that is…they all had a meetin'…this mornin'…and well, sir, the fact of the matter is…they all prayed *real* long and *real* hard…for a fast, pelting rain. I mean buckets full, Boss, a jim-dandy downpour. Maybe even a storm…"

"I get the idea! My Lord!" Bart threw up his hands in amazement. "Do they all …I mean…"

Bart floundered about, seemed totally out of words.

"Yes, sir!" Tad Horton swore, "They…that is…we… all think th' world of Miss Maggie! And we all want her…and you…"

"Thank you, Horton. I…don't know…what to say. I've never had…"

Seeing that his boss was totally overwhelmed with emotion, to spare him any need to respond, Tad Horton kindly averted his gaze, bent to the work, and began vigorously tossing boards and posts back into the wagon Bart had so laboriously just unloaded.

"If'n ye'll pick and choose th' tools ye' think we'll be a'needin', Boss..."

"Yes. Horton. Thank you...for that...suggestion," Bart mumbled, making his way, almost blinded by tears, to the crowded workbenches lined along the back of the carriage house.

All this time, he *had* a family...a very large family...and he just *now* had begun to realize it...

Chapter 13

From the huge barn back of the fine mansion at Cottonwood, the sounds of saws, hand-held routers, and adzes rang out over the quiet overgrown fields of the plantation whose vast fields lay fallow, as they had since soon after the commencement of the War Between the States, when Cottonwood's mistress passed away, and the master, overcome with grief and remorse, freed the slaves and fled Cottonwood, to take up residence in Charleston, South Carolina, where he lent a mighty hand to the war effort—by purchasing two fast sloops to sail up and down the coast, and run the Yankee blockade.

But the master, William Bartram Hurston, had passed, and the plantation, mansion and fallow fields now rested in the hands of his only grandchild, William Bartram Logan, son of Robert Japheth Logan, a Pennsylvania Yankee—who had eloped with William Bartram Hurston's only daughter, Eleanor.

Oftentimes when Bart would take a slight break from his woodworking—which he felt free to do quite often, given the amount of help he was receiving—he would walk outside the entrance to the cavernous barn, gaze about the endless fields stretching away in every direction, and heave a sigh. Cottonwood had been a large, working plantation, a village of sorts, containing everything necessary to sustain life for scores of people. In addition to the big house, the barn, the carriage house, there were the three dozen or more cabins, the wash house for laundry, the well house, the smoke house for curing meat, the corn cribs for storing grain, the smithy, for repairing carriages and wagons and shoeing horses, a buttery, a cobbler's shop, and several other structures that Bart had absolutely no idea what function they fulfilled. So much land, so many buildings going to waste, he thought, and with so many mouths going hungry. Now and then, as he made trips to take care of business, he observed freed slaves walking the roads, even remote country roads. And the thought would cross his mind that someone, somewhere, should do something. And Bart Logan considered himself as altruistic, as generous hearted as the next person, but, he could not, Bart told himself, become like Margaret Ann. He could not feel a crushing responsibility for the welfare of the entire world! He was one man. What could he do?

Bart knew absolutely nothing about running a huge plantation. He would stare at the empty dwellings, at the overgrown, fallow fields choked with cockleburs and a plant southerners called 'broomsedge' that seemed to sprout up everywhere there was an empty inch of ground, along with a forest, here and there, of small pines that threatened to engulf the entire place, even in the field roads. Then there was this little vine that crept along the ground of all the fallow fields, amongst the wild plum and blackberry and dewberry vines. Something Tad Horton termed "maypop" vines, and a host of other wild plants, including, Bart had noticed lately, persimmon trees and sassafras bushes. If Maggie were in residence here, she would have a pure out fit, Bart thought with a grin.

Well, maybe, when the weeds and grasses were thinned out at McKinnon Valley, he might just turn that herd of goats loose on the fields about Cottonwood. But, here, Bart thought wryly, he would need at least four or five dozen of the ravenous little animals. That was about all he felt that he could manage for now, what with the lumber mill to run, the factories to manage at some distance from Philadelphia and Boston, the Charleston properties he had inherited from his father—and with the property he had just learned he was on the verge of inheriting in the *South of England*… from some great-uncle or other of his mother's. An elderly man whom Bart might have heard his mother mention once or twice when he was a child. But who had entirely slipped his mind—until he received that letter from a firm of London barristers just recently…

He hadn't *dared* tell Margaret Ann about any of these properties. For fear that she would feel overwhelmed by it all, given the way she cringed at the thought of store-bought soap, hoarded potato peelings and tomato skins, pieces of brown wrapping paper, strands of stout cotton twine—which she carefully unwound from all her purchases that were secured with them and then rewound into one stout, round little ball…in the likely event, she had patiently explained to him, that she ever needed a piece of twine, she wouldn't have to go out and purchase a skein…!

Bart heaved a sigh, and went back to his woodworking. He wanted to make sure everything…everything…was ready by Christmas. "Horton!" Bart called as he re-entered the barn, "Do you by any chance think you could scrounge us up some fine cedar planking? Was there any in the load we just took off the wagon?"

"Cedar, Boss?"

"Yes, Horton! *Cedar!* With which to line some fine wardrobes!"

It was more than two weeks before Bart found time, between his duties at the lumber mill, his Sunday visits at the inn with Margaret Ann and little Johnny, and his woodworking duties, to ride over to McKinnon Valley and take a look at the results of the goats and Stephen Giles' efforts with the plants.

As Bart rode through the gap and down the slight incline, his mouth dropped open in stunned amazement.

The place had been transformed! It was beautiful! The square-log house sat in a nest of holly, with a row of low cedars flanking the sides of the front yard. The flower boxes were free of weeds, and sported some sort of spiky plants without blooms, but that Bart felt sure with the first warm days of summer would blossom their heads off. A few rose bushes, now barren nubs of thorns, waited for the first blush of spring. Evidently, the entire logging crew—not involved in the woodworking project—had been busy working overtime in McKinnon Valley. Evidently they had gleaned plantings from throughout the community! Other plants Bart could not even begin to name, adorned the property.

Even the pasture about the barn lay clipped to a dull greenish-brown stubble, free of tall grass and weeds. The hinges on the barn door had been properly mended. The cow trough had been rebuilt, new stanchions installed, and a small, low stool hung sedately on a peg beside the barn door, as if waiting for the mistress of the farm to come out with her pail and tend to her morning milking.

Behind the house, and to and beyond the outhouse, the yards were weed free. But gazing up the mountain, where Bart Logan knew the little graveyard lay, weeds were still in high command. He'd have to speak to Giles…about the graveyard…

———————

"What is it, exactly, Boss, that you want done…up here?"

"I want the goats chained here on this little plateau. At enough distance, you understand, that they do not trample atop the graves themselves. That area can be cleaned by hand."

Stephen Giles wandered about for a few moments, pushing the grass and weeds aside with huge logger's boots and hands. Finally, he rubbed his clean-shaven chin with one hand, and commented off-handedly, "That's odd. Miss Maggie's Papa seems ta be lyin' here, but where th' heck is Mama McKinnon?"

"That's…a long story, Giles," Bart heaved a great sigh. "I'm not exactly sure where Mrs. McKinnon is buried. Near some little church down on the Chattahoochee River, in Forsyth County, I believe Margaret Ann's sister told me. In the grave plot of a man that…"

Bart halted, his heart pounding as the memories came rushing back…the things Barbara Jo McKinnon Moss had told him that night in her fine yellow brick house…

"Why…Boss…don't we move Mrs. McKinnon? Up here with her husband and her kinfolk?"

"I…I hadn't really thought of that. But you're right, Giles. It could be done. Maybe…we'd have to get…a court order. Take several days…there and back. But that certainly can be done! Have to give up your weekend?"

"Right, Boss! Got nobody awaitin' on me. When do we get on it?"

"You think the furniture is far enough along…?"

"Everythin's almost done, far as I can see. Ceptin' maybe finishin' th' pie safe and meal chest for th' kitchen. All th' upstairs and stuff is done and varnished. And the settee and side tables for th' downstairs parlor—"

"Yes, well," Bart mumbled, "We don't want to plan on designing *too* many pieces for the front fire room. She does have that *gigantic* brown leather trunk…that she might wish to move back in some time!"

"Sure, Boss, and don't I recall *that* thing!'

"Shall we leave for Forsyth County, then, say first thing in the morning?" Bart gazed at his head foreman with raised brows.

"Tomorrow's Saturday. Suits me just fine."

———————————

The two riders made their way rapidly down country, stopping only to feed and water their mounts, and to catch a bit of sleep beside some creek or spring. Eating bread and cheese and fruit and drinking spring and creek water.

"Amazing, that there're no inns or taverns along this stretch of country," Bart mused. "Nothing but woods and streams."

"Used to be taverns along this route. This is th' old *Federal Road* that the soldiers used to canter along, to enter Indian Country. But with th' Indians all moved out, th' soldiers quit marchin' through. So th' federals' need for th' road declined, and the taverns and inns just naturally disappeared along with th' soldiers and th' Injuns."

So it was they made their way into Forsyth County. Asking directions, Bart and Stephen Giles had no difficulty whatsoever in locating the residence of *Big Carl Evans.*

At Bart's firm knock on the door, a lady appeared. Thin, even gaunt, her hair entirely gray and pulled back into a tight wad at the back of her head, she squinted up at Bart in the early morning light, pulled a faint smile and asked politely, "Yes? May I help you?"

"Mrs. Evans?" Bart muttered, not able to believe he actually stood here, on the porch of the Evans' home that had once, he could see, been a mighty fine place. But here he stood, talking to the mother of that foul human being she had actually been married to…who had called himself *Len Evans.*

"Yes?" the thin, gray-faced lady peered curiously up at Bartram Logan through the barest crack of the door. "Oh," she then muttered. And with a flutter of thin hands to her throat, she pulled the huge oak door open a bit wider. Bart could not help but notice how poor and faded the cotton dress that hung on her thin frame. Her skin appeared as thin and fragile as paper. "You will have to excuse me, sir. But…you see…the fact of the matter is…I wasn't *expectin'* any…company. And I seem to have *entirely* forgotten *all* my manners! Won't you be so good as to step inside?"

"No, ma'am, I don't…believe I will trouble you with my presence…that long. I wish…that is to say…I need to see your husband…on a matter of some…important business."

"Oh?" the faded green eyes flew wide, "Has something happened? Has someone been hurt? Do I know you? Are you a friend of Mr. Evans? My husband?"

She's lonely, Bart thought, and bent on extending this conversation.

"No, ma'am. I wouldn't say that. Not a friend. No. But…that is to say…we do… we have a…mutual…acquaintance."

"Oh!? And who might that be?"

"Margaret Ann McKinnon…" Bart paused, refusing to add the *Evans*.

"*Maggie!* Why..! Well…! Why didn't you *say* so, good sir!" Instantly at the mention of that name, the great door flew wide. "And just how is Maggie!?"

"She's fine, ma'am, except that she works too hard," Bart muttered in reply, feeling every inch the fool. He should not be standing here on *Big Carl Evans' front porch*, discussing Margaret Ann's state of health. It was demeaning to her, and far, far beneath him…

"Please…" the faded gray-green eyes were pleading, "Please, *do* step inside and visit for a spell." The thin, pale hands fluttered about, like two broken wings of a little bird. "I do so want to hear all about dear, dear Maggie. I have *worried* so…about her…and the little boy…Jonson…I believe…I heard…was the child's name…"

At that, Bart Logan's heart almost broke. Her son had been married to Johnny's sister, and she didn't even know little Johnny's name…

"John Thomas, Mrs. Evans," Bart gently corrected her, his heart going out to this woman, so evidently lonely. "But, no ma'am. Again, I must most respectfully decline your very kind invitation to come inside. I fear, ma'am, Mrs. Evans, that when your husband learns the…nature and intent of this call…I might not be welcome in his home."

"Well…For goodness gracious sakes…I can't imagine *that!* And just what… Mr.?"

"Logan. William Bartram Logan. And I'm here to see to the moving of Margaret Ann's mother…from your husband's grave plot, to their family site. On their home place, you understand. I have a signed request, from her oldest living daughter, Mrs. Fredrick J. Moss."

"Well…of course…" She appeared entirely and completely flustered. And Bart soon knew why. Bart heard heavy footsteps approaching from behind Mrs. Evans' thin form. Then the front door was suddenly snatched from her thin hand, and flung back hard against the front wall. So hard that the entire front of the huge house seemed to shudder on its foundation.

"What th'—" Such foul curses erupted from Big Carl Evans—who had evidently heard every word that had just passed—that his poor wife, standing in his shadow just beyond the door, gave a little gasp and blanched white as cotton.

But William Bartram Logan merely stood hard-faced, hands clenching the brim of his expensive hat, and listened.

"If you have quite finished, Mr. Evans," Bart finally found an opportunity to inject, "The moving of Mrs. McKinnon *can* and *will* be accomplished. With or without your…kind cooperation."

"*Not on your life, Mister*! You set *one* foot onto my grave plot, you *or* that tall, lanky rogue you got skulking out there along with you, out there, trespassin' on *my private property*, and I'll have the sheriff onto you two, before you can say *scat!* Then you two will find yourselves cooling your fine heels in the Forsyth County—"

"Let me assure you, Mr. Evans, it will be totally unnecessary that you contact the local sheriff. I intend, the moment I leave this porch, to do just that very thing myself. There is such a thing, Mr. Evans, as I'm sure you are very well aware, such a thing as a *Court Order*, to see to just such needs as this."

"Remove yourself from my porch—and from off my property—this minute, else I'll take my shotgun to you, and to that friend of yours lurking out there in my yard! And then we'll see who gits any *dratted court order*!"

"Good day, to you, Mrs. Evans," Bartram did a low bow in the direction of Ida Evans, hovering in her husband's shadow, "I shall inform Margaret Ann that you were kind enough to inquire after her health and welfare."

"Good day, to you, Mr. Logan!" Mrs. Evans found the courage to call out very softly, "And *Godspeed!*"

By nightfall, Court Order in hand, the pair were on their way, the precious cargo in a sweet-smelling cedar casket, loaded onto a wagon which Bartram

Logan drove, Stephen Giles riding mounted guard, Bart's mount secured to the rear of the wagon.

"We'll have to see to the ordering of a tombstone. Properly engraved, Giles. We'll talk to Mrs. Moss about what's to be engraved on that, as soon as the opportunity presents itself!"

"Sure thing, Boss! Boy, *that Big Carl Evans*—! That man's sure a *mean* piece of work!"

"You don't know the half of it, Giles! Not the *half* of it! Gettty upppp, there!"

Chapter 14

"Well! If it isn't *Mister Logan*! And didn't *you* make *yourself* scarce this past Sunday afternoon!" Maggie lifted the heavy bar and flung open the door to the inn, only after Bart had knocked insistently—three times.

"Darling?" Bart bent and planted a kiss, light and soft as the fluttering of butterfly wings, on Maggie's left cheek.

"So!" she whirled away from him in a huff, striding across the rough oak flooring. "Just where *were* you, this Sunday afternoon past? Johnny waited all the live-long afternoon for you," she flung over her shoulder. "Moping and almost crying! Until finally, shortly after dark, he gave it up, and agreed to go, very unhappily I might add, up to his bed. Where he—"

"Missed me? Did you, then? I am *so* sorry," Bart muttered, carefully choosing his words, very carefully closing the front door, hanging his hat on a peg, crossing over and taking a chair before the fireplace in the dining room, but not until after Maggie had dropped into the adjoining seat. "I suppose…I should have at least sent word…"

"Sent word?" Maggie stared at him, leaned her head against the tall back of the oak rocker, and snapped angrily. "And just where *were* you, Mr. Logan, darling, that you would have found it so necessary to, as you choose to put it, have *sent word*?"

"I had some…very…pressing…business to attend to…that took me…out of town."

"And was this *business* of yours, Mr. Logan, so pressing as to be worth the breaking of a little boy's heart? What on earth *was* it?"

"Oh, just digging up…one thing or another…I am sure…that young Johnny will…quickly recover. Children always do. And by the way, yes, the…errand was…that important."

"Errand?" Maggie tilted her head and cocked an eyebrow at him. It had been almost *two weeks* since they had seen hide or hair of him! She was so put out with him. So angry, she simply could not let it go.

"Oh, did I say errand? What I meant was…"

"Yes, Mr. Logan, *darling*….you did indeed say *errand*. Would you like a few minutes then, to compose your thoughts…so that you might come up with what is a somewhat more…believable excuse for your unexplained absence?"

"No, my sweet, I would not. I was unable to be here this Sunday afternoon past, for which, as I have already said, I am most deeply, most frightfully, regretful. Shall we, then, just let it go at that? And where is Johnny, by the way? I believe today is the day for our lessons, both fist boxing and violin."

"Well, if that is all the explanation you have to offer for yourself, then I suppose we shall let the matter drop, and I will go and summon Johnny. Would you, Mr. Logan, like a cup of hot coffee, while you wait?"

"Yes, sweetheart. A hot cup of coffee might just be the thing—to relieve the awful *chill* in the air—in here."

"What is this holiday we're supposed to be celebrating?" Barbara Jo asked Maggie in a small, stilted voice.

"It's called *Thanksgiving*, Barbs," Maggie explained patiently.

"Well," Barbara Jo said tiredly from her bed, where she lay propped up on several pillows, staring into the fire, "I don't ever recall us, as children, celebrating anything called *Thanksgiving*."

"No. But we learned in school about how the earliest English settlers gave thanks, remember? But it was a sporadic celebration, at best, after that initial one. Until…Look, Barbs," Maggie began very patiently. "Here's an article that Mr. Logan gave me. It says that President Abraham Lincoln, in the very year of your birth, 1863, proclaimed the last Thursday of every November a National Holiday…a day for giving thanks. You want to hear the Proclamation?"

Not giving Barbara Jo an opportunity to decline, Maggie hastened to read:

The year that is drawing towards its close, has been filled with the blessings of fruitful fields and healthful skies. To these bounties, which are so constantly enjoyed that we are prone to forget the source from which they come, others have been added, which are of so extraordinary a nature, that they cannot fail to penetrate and soften the heart which is habitually insensible to the ever watchful providence of Almighty God. In the midst of a civil war of unequalled magnitude and severity, which has sometimes seemed to foreign States to invite and to provoke their aggression, peace has been preserved with all nations, order has been maintained, the laws have been respected and obeyed, and harmony has prevailed everywhere except in the theatre of military conflict; while that theatre has been greatly contracted by the advancing armies and navies of the Union—

"You do *realize* ..." Barbara Jo drew her weary gaze from the fire, and to Maggie's face, angrily interrupting Maggie's reading, "You do realize *that the man* who spoke those words, was the *same* man who ordered *Yankee soldiers* into battle against us? And those men shot Papa, and killed Grandpa Thomas, and thousands more southern boys and men, and laid waste to the South?! And the South will *never* be the same. I don't recall *Papa* ever celebrating this holiday."

"I suppose with Papa just back from the War and all, Barbs, and times being so hard, like you just said, the South being in such a mess and muddle," Maggie attempted to explain very patiently. "Truth be told, with people just striving to stay alive, and Rhyersville being so cut off from the rest of the world..." Maggie hesitated, heaved a sigh, then muddled on. "Anyhow, a day was set aside ... it has been set aside...for the whole country. And, Barbs, the War is over, and we're a part of the country. So, I suppose we might as well just go ahead and act like it! It surely won't do us any harm to observe a day of giving thanks to God for all his marvelous blessings!"

The anger had drained away. Barbara Jo stared at Maggie, eyes dull and glazed, her voice hollow and lifeless. "Like what? Driving men to gambling— so that they lose their entire fortunes? Leaving women penniless widows in their *early twenties?* With no means of support, or any hopes of finding any? Are *these*, Maggs, the *blessings* for which *I* am to be so thankful on this day of which you speak? The mercantile—with all its contents—heavily mortgaged," her voice caught. "*Soon lost! Everything...*"

"Surely, Barbs," Maggie sought for the proper words here, spoke softly. "Surely you can't blame *God*...for Fred's gambling problems."

"Then...*whom* should I blame, Maggs?" Barbara Jo flared in reply. "Fred...he was always so thrifty. Always so careful with every penny. Every nickel. You know how he was the joke of Forsyth County, for being such a tightwad. What drives *a man like that*...to gamble away a sizeable fortune? Tell me that, Maggs. *What?*"

"Surely, Barbs, you don't blame *me* for that?" Maggie gazed at her sister, her eyes guarded.

"*You?* That's an odd...no...that's a downright *peculiar* thing for you to say, Margaret Ann McKinnon! Do you think I have completely lost all the little sense God gave me? Why on earth would I blame *you?!*"

"No reason. No reason at all, Barbs. I was...just making conversation."

"And *weird* conversation at that! Let's stick to reality, as closely as we can here. I mean...*Good Lord!* I may have said some things...out of line...to you...during all my grieving. But..."

"Well, Barbs, you seem of late to blame me for so much..."

"Let's just drop it, shall we?" Barbara Jo gave a weary toss of her chin, snapped angrily, "I'm sick of this line of talk. Let's talk instead about this holiday of yours."

"It's not just mine, Barbs. It's set aside for the whole country. I thought I might send Benjamin Noah turkey hunting, up in the mountains. A fine bird, I understand, is usually the main course for this meal."

"Where is this celebration to be held, here at the inn?"

"I'm not really sure yet. Bartram Logan mentioned something about having everyone out to Cottonwood. He seems to feel an obligation to include his logging crew in this celebration."

"Oh, I see. I might have known it was that *Yankee's* idea. I'm not sure whether or not I'll even attend this great event. I can think of very little, at this moment, to be thankful for. Would you, Maggs, be kind enough to close the door on your way out?"

"Are you not getting dressed...and coming down to the kitchen for a late breakfast? I'm sure Liza Mae can heat you up—"

"No. Not today," Barbara Jo moaned into her pillow, "I'm just not up to it yet. Could Liza Mae, perhaps, on her next trip upstairs, bring me a cold biscuit and a cold cup of coffee?"

"So," Maggie stared straight at Bartram Logan, "you do, then, plan on holding the Thanksgiving celebration at Cottonwood?"

"I thought, in view of the number of people that might be in attendance, it would be better there. Yes. If that's all right with you?"

"I am very open to any suggestion that might make the holiday more enjoyable for all of us," Maggie sighed, "But…"

"But what? Is there a problem…of which I'm unaware?"

"It's…Barbara Jo. She has…intimated…that if the meal is held at Cottonwood…"

"That she will not be in attendance? And why is that? I will be here, hale and hearty and full of good will, to transport any and all souls—"

"I don't know that it's a matter of…transportation."

"I thought…I had formed the slightest inkling of an idea that your sister found me a bit to her liking. Has something changed?"

"With Barbs, I fear, Mr. Logan, darling, that a great deal, as you so aptly put it, has changed. She refuses to honor a Proclamation issued by the Yankee president who… and…she has sunk into a pit of black despair, and I am at my wits end as to how exactly to extricate her from it."

"And just what form or manifestation is this dark despair taking?"

"You are fully aware of how she absolutely *refuses* to return to her own home. She cannot abide, she says, the thought of being in the house alone. Without Fred. She refuses to rise from the bed. My bed, actually. She—"

"Your bed? You mean, your sister has taken over your room?"

"Well, she seldom comes downstairs, even in the middle of the day. And the other rooms are fine for sleeping, when one is swaddled beneath a bundle of quilts. But on cold wintry days, the rooms are not especially comfortable…when one is forced to rise to take care of…necessary things."

"Where does she take her meals?" Bart asked.

"In my room. For the most part."

"And just *who* is doing all this waiting on Mrs. Moss? Hand and foot, it would appear! Building and tending her fire? And just *who* is toting her chamber pot, if I may be so indelicate as to ask?"

"Liza Mae. And when Liza Mae is otherwise occupied, me."

"Margaret Ann! My dearest! Your sister is taking great advantage of you here! Can't you see that? You must insist—"

"Insist what? That my only living sister is not welcome here in what passes for my home? That I am so cruel and heartless…and she is still in deep mourning…"

"She is taking advantage of your kindness, of your tender heart, of this thing inside you that apparently keeps telling you that *you* are responsible for the ills of the entire world!"

"You are the second person to tell me that, Mr. Logan! And let me tell you most assuredly, that I do not appreciate it. Especially coming from you!"

"And, Margaret Ann, may I make so bold as to ask why that is? Why do you seem to resent this coming from *me*—more than from this other person who seems to remain nameless? This wouldn't by any chance be Mr. Thomas Beyers, now, would it?"

"No! Mr. Logan! It would not! What an odd thing to say! If you must be such a curious busy-body, it came from my sister! The one who is lying, soaked in deep grief, on a bed of intense suffering…and whom you seem to feel that I should callously…"

"I'm sorry," Bart murmured. "That was rude and thoughtless of me. Let's not quarrel, shall we? We see so little of one another. By the way, where is our young Johnny?"

"Our young Johnny, as you so flippantly refer to my brother, is—"

"Margaret Ann. Margaret Ann," Bart began softly, his eyes filled with concern, "Would you, perhaps, prefer that I simply leave? And come back some other time?"

"No! I mean…no. It's just that…the store is…"

"The store is being sold. Along with all the stock within it. So I understand." Bart gazed for a moment down at the tips of his boots. Then he rose to poke distractedly at the fire.

"Oh? That's odd. Barbara Jo hasn't said one word. But…good," Maggie murmured from her rocking chair behind him. "That's at least one load off my shoulders. I wonder if Barbs got a fair price for it? There was an awful lot of very nice, very expensive merchandise…in that mercantile. Fred Moss only carried the best."

"I'm sure that…whoever…bought the place gave a fair price," Bart mumbled, failing to meet her gaze as he turned from the fireplace.

"Who was it? Do you know? Someone of my acquaintance?"

"Yes…I suppose…you might know the fellow. Ah…Johnny," Bart cried in great relief. "Ready for your lessons?"

"Well," Barbara Jo surmised from her bed of deep suffering, "at least I am no longer sunken deep into debt, along with being totally penniless. At least a bit of something was paid above the debts on the store. Enough remains, perhaps, to settle up Fred's extensive medical bills."

"That much?" Maggie looked at her sister stunned. It had been Maggie's understanding that the place was mortgaged to its rooftop and beyond. What idiot, what financially ignorant fool would pay more for a place than anywhere near its indebtedness!?

"Who…on earth …bought…the mercantile?" Maggie asked, stunned.

"I never did know. Thomas Beyers saw to the entire deal."

"Thomas?" Maggie queried her heart beginning to race. "Since when is Thomas Beyers involved in—is that the check you have in your hands, Barbs? Could I see it, for just a moment?"

Maggie reached for the check. Barbara Jo willingly handed it over.

"It's drawn on a bank…in *Philadelphia*!" Maggie gasped.

"I couldn't care less, Maggs, where or what bank the thing is drawn on, just as long as it will at least pay off our remaining debts."

"Yes, well, I'm…very pleased for you, Barbs." Maggie rose as if to leave the room. Barbara Jo gave her a look of such abject desolation that Maggie's heart almost broke.

"Yes. The debts will be paid. But I just don't know, Maggs. Whether or not…I just don't think I can ever, *ever* spend another night in that yellow brick house. I'm thinking of putting it on the market."

"Well! What a *surprise* that is. Where…on earth…" Maggie began haltingly, even more stunned than about the announcement of the unexpected largess from the mercantile. What was Barbara Jo trying to tell her? That she had no intentions of living alone, of attempting to pick up the pieces and making a life for herself?

Where in heavens name did her sister intend spending her remaining years?

"Well, Margaret Ann, are you more rested and of a more amenable frame of mind, now that the burden of the mercantile has been lifted from your shoulders?"

It was warm for late fall. Maggie and Bart Logan were seated on an oaken bench on the small back porch of the inn. Johnny was racing about the miniscule back yard, in vain attempts to corner a toad.

"Why, yes, Mr. Logan, I suppose I am. Strange, though, Barbara Jo showed me the check. It seems she received *way* over and above the amount of debt on the store, and *way* above what the stock itself could logically be valued at. It seems she will even be able now to take care of Fred's medical expenses."

"Well! And how very fortunate... for your dear sister!"

"Yes, fortunate indeed," Maggie quipped, turning her blue-blue gaze directly on Bartram Logan. "And, would you believe, Mr. Logan, that of all the places on the face of this earth where banks are located, the one upon which Barbara Jo's generous check was drawn—was in *Philadelphia!?*"

"Well, well!"

"Why didn't you tell me, Mr. Logan," Maggie's voice sounded hurt, "that you were buying the place, and getting my sister out from beneath a mountain of debt—into the bargain! And what on *earth*, Mr. Logan, with the lumber mill to run, and Cottonwood, what on *earth* Mr. Logan, are you going to do with a mercantile filled with racks and storerooms and reams and bolts and sacks of expensive merchandise?!"

"I don't know...I hadn't really thought that far."

"This...then...this purchase...was not from the *head* of a fine Philadelphia businessman?"

"No, my dear, I fear I must confess. No. It was not!"

"And just how long, Mr. Logan, do you think your grand fortune?...just how vast is your fortune, Mr. Logan?...no....don't tell me. I have no wish to know. But just how long do you think, Mr. Logan, it will last? If you foolishly invest it in…businesses for which you have no acumen or expertise?"

"I…believe…I can…handle the mercantile, Margaret Ann. I do have *some* experience in merchandising."

"And from just *where* do you have all this *experience* in merchandising, Mr. Logan, from counting and selling board feet of lumber?! This *mercantile*, Mr. Logan, is an entirely…an entirely different situation."

"No. Margaret Ann. I don't know exactly how to tell you this, except to just go ahead and say it outright. I have this merchandising experience from a half dozen or more factories—I believe that there were eight or nine at last count—I have strewn up and down the Eastern Seaboard of the United States. And as to my financial stability, I have just recently received notice— I might just as well go ahead and out with this, also— I have just recently received notice, Margaret Ann, that I have inherited a vast estate—located in the South of England. The place comes to me from a great-uncle I have never seen, on my mother's side of the family. I believe it's called *Windsfield.*"

Her eyes wide, her mouth agape, unable to utter a single sound, Maggie flounced up out of her chair, and made a bee-line for the back door, which she slammed with such a vengeance that Mr. Bartram Logan's eyeballs fairly rattled.

———————

"Well, what do you think about her, Johnny? Have you chosen a name for her yet?" Bart asked with a smile over at the little boy. The three of them were jogging along on their mounts, along the tree-lined dirt road immediately outside town, as Bartram Logan had appeared at the door of the inn shortly after lunch, insisting that the animals needed exercising. Though Barbara Jo's situation weighed very heavily on Maggie's heart, she had joined Bart and Johnny. Someone had mentioned to her in passing that ponies could oftentimes be deceitful and stubborn. She had seen neither of these traits exhibited in Bart's birthday gift, still she was not willing that Johnny ride off on the pony without her. Whatever was she to do…about her sister? How to get her up, out of bed, and gainfully employed!?

Maggie glanced over at Bart Logan. Mr. Logan might well give Barbs a job in the mercantile. But, Maggie seriously doubted that her sister's inordinate pride would allow her to accept such a step down in Rhyersville society—from mistress of the mercantile to a lowly clerk receiving a wage for standing behind the long oak counter and doling out eggs and flour, coffee, bacon and beans.

The store on her mind, Maggie said: "The mercantile seems to be operating rather seamlessly, Mr. Logan. You made a good choice in the store manager. Mr. McAlister seems to know his way about the merchandise. Where on earth did you find him?"

"I'm glad you're pleased with the service rendered by the mercantile, my sweet!" Bart smiled over at Maggie. "Mr. Andrew McAlister is, in fact, a relative of one of the men at the logging camp. He had the unfortunate luck to suffer an accident from a...misplaced chop with his axe...and is no longer able to follow a plow. But he *is* able to take inventory and to man the counter of the mercantile. His wife, as you may have noted, works alongside him. Then he has two growing boys that are more than willing and able to lend their father a hand."

"They seem a fine Christian family. At least *they* have not missed *one Sunday* of being in church, since arriving in town."

"Well! You don't say!" Bart replied with a little smile.

149

Chapter 15

The day that had been declared in the Year of Our Lord 1863 a National Day of Thanksgiving by the nation's Yankee president, dawned bright and clear. Maggie and Johnny were up early, to dress in their best for the Thanksgiving feast. Then Bartram Logan was at the door of the inn, lifting Maggie and Johnny into the front of his fine carriage. Liza and Benjamin he had transported to Cottonwood the day before. Liza insisted she needed to be in the kitchen at Cottonwood at the crack of dawn, and a day early, to make proper preparations for the feast. Liza Mae, Maggie had not failed to note, spoke often and most glowingly of the kitchen at Cottonwood.

"I see," Bart remarked wryly, "that your dear sister, Mrs. Moss, could not tear herself from her bed of deep suffering, to join us."

"No, she couldn't," Maggie replied above the whir of the carriage wheels, "and you don't, Mr. Logan, have to be so sarcastic about it."

Bart had noticed that since he had let the cat out of the bag about his vast holdings, Maggie McKinnon no longer tacked on *darling* to his term of address. Now, as he had been when she was in his employ, he was simply *Mr. Logan*.

It's very late November. The months are ticking off—towards May. And sometimes, I wonder, just which direction we're heading in, here. Forwards? Or...backwards? Bart wondered rather dismally.

But it was a beautiful day. And a beautiful lady rode at his side. And a sweet, handsome little boy grinned up at him and wiggled and squirmed until Bart wondered if there'd be any hide remaining on his right thigh—by the time he had escorted Johnny McKinnon all the way out to Cottonwood.

Bart tried to make small talk. Johnny jumped and jabbered and whizzed, as was Johnny's customary and expected behavior. Bart often wondered if somewhere there wasn't a spring that had been wound too tightly, in little Johnny's chest.

Finally the big white mansion appeared over the crest of the hill. And Bart was almost relieved. He enjoyed nothing more than keeping company with Maggie McKinnon, but today…there seemed to be a broader gap than usual between them. And Bart wondered just how he was ever going to lessen that gap, and finally, to breech it.

Cottonwood was abuzz with a bevy of men in light rigs and on horseback. The loggers. Some had brought their wives and children. Several others had escorted a lady friend. Bart was the perfect host. And Maggie found herself, much to her chagrin, seated in the hostess' chair. From which, Bart smiled pleasantly to himself and immediately decided, she reigned perfect and serene.

But Maggie did manage to set Bart Logan's heart into a sudden flutter, when she leaned over at table and whispered in his ear:

"Whatever has come over your crew, Mr. Logan? They are all looking at me as if they are the cat that just captured the little bird. Is something going on that you haven't *told* me about? As is usual with you, Mr. Logan? Any more *grand surprises* up those very, very expensive sleeves of yours?"

"Why, my dearest, Margaret Ann! I do believe you are something of a snob!" Bart accused in a shocked whisper.

"A snob?! I?"

"Yes, Margaret Ann. You! Do you always look down your pretty little nose at people whom you perceive to have more than you? Thus putting these poor people in a *lower class* than yourself? I mean, *who do these people think they are*!? *They* haven't struggled and starved and done without! *They* haven't spent hours in the cotton fields and the corn rows! *Their* hearts don't break and *their* families don't die and leave them!"

Maggie did not look up. She kept her blue-blue eyes glued to the abundance of food on her sparkling china plate. "All right, Mr. Logan. That's enough. That will do. You have made your point."

"Good. Then let's just enjoy the bounty the Good Lord has so graciously provided—to each and every one of us? Shall we, darling?"

"Yes, Mr. Logan, I think we indeed shall."

"Then…let us say Grace:

"We thank thee, most abundant God and our Great Savior, for thy bountiful blessings throughout this year. May, in the coming years, thy

blessings, health and healing, rain on all those gathered about this table, family and friends, and may these blessings wing across the surrounding community, the state, and the nation. Amen.

Maggie realized with a guilty little start, that Bartram Logan had just prayed for a great personal, and national, healing.

The Thanksgiving feast concluded, there followed an afternoon of merriment. Games of horseshoe-pitching, tug-o'-war, foot races, and hurdle jumping.

And music swelled over the Blue Ridge Mountains from an assortment of instruments. Bart Logan brought out his violin, and Johnny played on Papa's fiddle. Two of the loggers brought banjos. One had a guitar; another produced from his coat pocket a juice harp. Tad Horton even brought along an Indian water-drum, a section of hollow log filled with water and topped with a hunk of taunt deerskin, upon which the tall, lank logger thumped and bumped and kept perfect rhythm with all the other players, shaking his drum vigorously now and then, to keep its top thoroughly wet. Maggie wondered whether dark-haired, dark-skinned Tad Horton had inherited his water-drum from some Indian ancestor.

When Tad Horton began thumping out one particular tune, the other players all joined in, and Maggie, knowing the tune well, could not keep from clapping her hands and voicing the familiar words. But Mr. Bartram Logan, she noticed, did not place his violin beneath his handsome chin and join in; he just narrowed his dark eyes slightly, tipping up the rims of his lips in a slight grin, as she sang:

> *Oh, yes, I am a Southern girl,*
> *And glory in the name,*
> *And boast it with far greater pride*
> *Than glittering wealth and fame,*
> *We envy not the Northern girl,*
> *Her robes of beauty rare,*
> *Though diamonds grace her snowy neck*
> *And pearls bedeck her hair…*

Hurrah! Hurrah!
For the sunny South so dear;
Three cheers for the homespun dress
The Southern ladies wear...!

———————————

Maggie mounted the narrow stairs and entered the room she had taken down the narrow hall from her own. Slowly, she prepared for bed. It had been an amazing day. As she blew out the lamp and settled beneath the cold quilts, Maggie realized that she had spoken the words, had committed herself to marriage to this man with whom she had just spent the entire day. The words, they had felt so right, had slipped so easily past her lips that night, sitting at the sumptuous table, in the grand mansion, beside what she now knew to be an extremely, *extremely* wealthy man.

But, at night, when she lay, like this, alone in The Sparrow Inn, she wondered to herself: *Why* on earth did a man like Bartram Logan want *her?* With his looks, his charm, his wealth, he could easily have any woman he set his mind on. He was, as Maggie often reminded herself, almost too perfect to be true. Had she, this time around, really found a man who would love her, *truly love her, with all his heart?* This man who had the world at his fingertips? He spoke of a huge estate in England! A land she had only dreamed of, or read of in story books! What did this estate entail? Acres and acres? *Villages and vassals?* No, the era of vassals was long past. *But tenants, no doubt. Who was this man whose ring she wore on her left hand!? Sir William Bartram Logan?! A man who could pray so feelingly, so glibly, for the healing of an entire nation.*

Feeling as if she were a character in a fairy tale, Maggie stirred and tossed on her bed.

And Barbara Jo! What on earth was she going to do about her? She could not—she simply *could not*—toss her sister out on her ear!

Maggie rose now, lit a taper and walked across the icy floor, down the chilled hall to the room where a fire was banked and Barbara Jo slept soundly, Johnny on his cot in the corner. But Johnny had insisted, since Barbara Jo had taken up residence in the room, that for his male privacy, he should have a curtain. So Maggie had rigged a wire with a blanket strung over it across his corner. Maggie gave a peek behind the blanket. The soft yellow glow of the taper revealed the slight form of little Johnny, stretched beneath the heavy covering of quilts on the narrow cot. On the snow-white pillowcase, short dark hair spread about his head, his face the picture of contentment. Maggie's breath caught in her throat at sight of him. He appeared so…tall…lying there. Johnny was growing up! On her own, how could she ever hope to place him in a fine medical college? And …*boxing lessons!*

Maggie turned and padded down the cold hall, to crawl back into her strange bed. She curled herself into a tight ball, and tried to pray. But the questions pounding in her head and in her heart spun her round and round— and back around again.

There simply seemed no *real* solutions…

———————————

The horseman sat slumped astride his mount, well hidden in the shadows of the buildings. But not so well hidden that he couldn't keep watch on her window. So, she was up late again! Good! Let her know what sleepless nights felt like! Let her toss and turn, this lovely, righteous offspring of John Thomas McKinnon—with his fine children, his fine two legs and his fine blond-haired wife and his fine valley farm! One of the children was a *boy!* Yeah! Now, he suddenly recalled. That lucky son-of-a…! *John McKinnon had sired a son!* Birthed after John lay molding in his grave, true, true. But still, even in death, some men had all the luck…!

It was late. He was cold. He was hungry. His thin frame shook with tremors of rage, and of fear. The growing season was over. Nuthin' much to scrounge from the neighbors' fields, nowadays. Even the gleanings were slim. What was this new thing everybody was talkin' about, celebrating a day of *Thanksgiving!?* Bah! For him, when the cold months came, he called it 'the starvin' season.' And on top of everythin' else, the girl was gone again. God only knew where she went this time. When…that…is… *if…* she ever came back home, he'd take a leather strap to her back!

He took one last glance up at the darkened window, drew his worn coat about hunched shoulders, turned his thin horse, and rode towards the hollow.

Chapter 16

The weeks leading up to Christmas were filled with work and wonder for Maggie. Work, to keep the inn going, and wonder at what on earth was to become of Barbara Jo McKinnon Moss!

Barbara Jo still refused to join Maggie and Johnny downstairs for her meals. She still lay abed most of each day, and required waiting on with the chamber pot, and firewood and water for her pitcher and bowl. The washtub out back had to be lugged up the stairs for her baths, and Benjamin Noah was hard put carrying all that hot and cold water up and then back down the stairs.

Maggie was about at her wits end, that Sunday, the Sunday before Christmas, when Bartram Logan made his weekly visit, and was sitting down with them to lunch. Maggie sat at the table, her gaze on the narrow stairs, the food growing cold on her plate.

"What's the matter? What are you waiting for?" Bart suddenly asked, even though he knew the answer.

"I…was just wondering…I don't believe Barbara Jo's coming down, though I have called her twice." Maggie made as if to rise.

"What on earth are you doing?" Bart demanded.

"Well…I suppose…I should carry up a plate…for my sister…"

"No," Bart said simply.

"What?" Maggie asked.

"Why don't you solve your problem…by simply refusing to wait on her hand and foot!" Bart surmised with a wise lift of brows. "*Believe me* when I say that your sister is *not* going to starve herself to death, by refusing to come down for meals. Neither is she going to wallow, for a very long period of time, that is, in her own filth, with no bath and no cleaned chamber pot! Leave off all this cow-towing to her, and she will find her way back amongst the living!"

"Oh, Mr. Logan, I don't know…about that…I mean…" Maggie stuttered and stammered on, "She only just lost her husband—"

"Would you be so kind as to tell me something, Margaret Ann?" Bart Logan slowly put down his fork, and stared at her. "When your mother lost *her* husband, did she take to her bed in total despair? And did you wait on her like a hired servant?"

"Well, no! Of course not! Mama would *never* put another soul out, with a bunch of fetching and toting—"

"My point, *exactly*!" Bart gave another wise nod. "And when *your*…husband… died, and you also lost your child…did you, my dearest one, take to your bed and moan and whine into your pillow all the live long day!?"

"No!" Maggie shouted. "How on earth could I!? I had *things* to see to! I had Johnny, and the house, and someone had to—"

"Again, my point exactly! *Someone had to—! And if there is no one else there to pick up for us, to tote and fetch for us, then we are, quite naturally, forced to do it for ourselves! Now, will you please, Margaret Ann, retake your seat, eat your lunch, and…would you please excuse me…for just one moment?!*"

And having uttered those words, Bartram Logan unfolded his lank, tall frame from off his chair before the warm fire in the dining room, and went bounding—two at a time—up the narrow stairway of The Sparrow Inn.

As Maggie picked up her fork and began to eat, she heard a loud, rattling bang, as a door was apparently thrown violently back against a wall, and then came a rush of loud voices clearly heard all the way down the narrow stairs.

"Well, Mrs. Moss! And a good day to you!" Bart entered the room that should have been Maggie's, slamming the door back against the wall with a roar.

"What—? *Mister Logan!* What—?!" Barbara Jo, clad only in a thin chemise, sat immediately straight up at Bart's explosive entrance, and for decency's sake snatched her mother's quilt far up beneath her chin, and blinked at Bart in the dim light.

Completely undeterred, set upon his mission, Bartram Logan marched on into the room, over to the window, where he flung the curtains wide, and jerked the lower window sash up, to let in a cold, blustery, winter breeze.

"A little air, so they tell me, does a body's constitution a world of good!" Bartram Logan announced with a dry smile. Then he reached and clasped a strong brown hand firmly about the handle of the pewter water pitcher; another hand swept beneath the foot of the bed, drawing out the white enameled chamber pot. Then Bartram Logan bowed low to Barbara Jo Moss, and announced with a very gentlemanly flourish:

"I understand, Mrs. Moss, that your lunch is awaiting you. You can join the rest of us downstairs, and eat it now, warm. Or you can come down at your leisure, and you will find it waiting. Cold. On the back of the stove. It appears that all the members of this household are totally occupied with other matters, this fine day. And *no one*, as I understand it, will be *up* to wait upon your wishes and desires, or to serve you, today. Or on any of the days following. Unless you choose to carry wood, your fire will grow cold. The water pitcher and the chamber pot will still, quite naturally, be at your daily disposal, just as long as the procuring of the water and the emptying and cleaning of the chamber pot are accomplished by you, yourself. We shall, then, I trust, Mrs. Moss, see you downstairs shortly?"

And with that, William Bartram Logan, rich Philadelphia businessman, water pitcher in one hand, chamber pot in the other, whirled and stalked from the room and down the stairs.

Maggie stood open-mouthed at the foot of the narrow stairs, holding onto the balustrade with one hand, as if she was about to fall in a dead faint.

Wordlessly Bartram Logan strode past her, and out onto the narrow back porch, where he proceeded to empty the pewter water pitcher into a nearby flowerbed with a determined splash. Then on he marched to the outhouse, where he proceeded to push wide the door, and then to empty the stinking contents of the white enameled chamber pot down one of the round holes sawed very roughly into the oak boards. Then he marched back toward the inn. The empty chamber pot he dashed, then, with a bit of water from the back porch water shelf. Then he flipped it up to dry in the sun, on the edge of the porch, far away from the water shelf.

Then Bartram Logan marched back inside, washed his hands thoroughly with store-bought soap, and advised Liza Mae, who had just stopped by for lunch, and stood dumbfounded in the kitchen doorway:

"Mrs. Moss will, I believe, should I have discerned correctly, be down shortly for her mid-day meal. No one, and I mean *no one* is to assist Mrs. Moss in the preparation or serving of her food. *From this time forth.* And, *from this time forth*, she is to take *all* her meals at table, like every other self-respecting member of this household. The firewood, the chamber pot and the water pitcher, Mrs. Moss is, also, to fetch and carry, if these particular items are to be carried at all. Do I make myself clear, Liza Mae?!"

"Yas suh! Mister Logan! Suh! You shorely, shorely does. And may I add, Mister Logan, Suh, that it is about time sommmmmbbudy in this place *don' seed da light ob da day!* Hit's time sommmmebuddy don'…"

"I completely agree, Liza Mae. Now, after we finish our meal, I will be taking your mistress for a ride in the carriage. And I trust that *whatever* is to be done about the inn, you and your dear husband can accomplish, this one afternoon, without your mistress's help."

"Yas, Suh! And I *does* believes I sees a *sartin'* person, making her way down th' stairs! Wal' *halelujah,* and *praise* da Good Lord!"

To which Bartram, with a broad smile and a warm hand on Liza Mae's thin shoulder, added, *"Amen!"*

———————

Following lunch, Bart quickly bundled Maggie and Johnny into coats, scarves and gloves, and hustled them out to the carriage.

"Does this mean…that should you and I…that my sister would not be welcome…in our home?" Maggie asked.

"No, Margaret Ann, that is *not at all* what this means. What this means, my sweet, is that Barbara Jo McKinnon Moss is family. And any time she is in *need* of anything in this world, you and I, my sweet, together, shall see that she is provided it. Whether this means things monetary, or things emotional, or if it be even remotely within our power, things spiritual. Should she be in need of clothing, food, or a sound roof to shelter her head, she is *more* than welcome—to any of these—at any time. For, as I have just said, she is *family.* But she will *not* be allowed, from *this* day forth, to be a burden beyond all caring. She *will,* as much as the Good Lord gives her power to do so, move under her own power and beneath her own steam. Else, Barbara Jo will sink into a deep pit of depression and despair—from which neither you nor I nor the angels of God above can ever redeem or extricate her. Do we have an understanding here?"

"Yes, darling."

"Well. Then, good." Bartram Logan replied, a broad grin on his face. "Oh, by the way, Johnny, we are on our way to the road leading up to the logging camp. You haven't been this way for quite some time. Now, have you?"

"No, sir, Bart! Not since…wal' you know when."

"Yeah, *I* know when!" Bart smiled, putting on a southern drawl, recalling very vividly the day Maggie and Johnny vacated his logging camp. *That* was the day Margaret Ann McKinnon Evans totally demolished his camp kitchen! Slinging, piling everything she could lay her pretty little hands on—onto the two long puncheon tables running the length of the cookshack. It had taken a month or more to get everything all sorted out!

"Is there, Mr. Logan," Maggie ventured, "some particular point to this afternoon's jaunt…some *reason*, that, today, we are driving toward the logging camp?"

"Yes, my sweet, there most certainly is. I saw the most *gorgeous* cedar tree, growing along beside the trail—just as the logging trace starts up the mountain. And, I thought to myself, the day I first spied that fine cedar, now, wouldn't *that* just make a *fine* Christmas tree for *The Sparrow Inn!*"

"A Christmas tree? We're going to cut down a *Christmas tree*? How tall is it?"

Johnny jumped up and down in his excitement, until Bart thought for sure he would have to pull the team off to one side of the road before the little boy quieted enough to sit in his seat—and not plunge himself headforemost into the traces of the galloping steeds.

"Where is it? Will you tell me, Bart? When we get close?!"

"That I will, Johnny! That I will! And I brought along a small handsaw. Just the thing for helping to fell a fine cedar for Christmas! And I'm sure Maggie will be more than happy to help you make all sorts of lovely decorations—to hang on the thing."

"Maggie?…Did you say, darling? How about *Bartram Logan* lending a hand, too. This was, after all, *your* idea! Or, perchance, *you* are far above such mundane tasks?"

"No, sweetheart! Not at all! But, it's been such a long time! I think I've forgotten everything I ever knew about celebrating the Birth of our Lord and Savior."

"Bart! Darling!" Maggie cried, "You...haven't had...*Christmas?*"

"No, sweetheart. Not for a long time now. Not since my parents died. I was away, remember? At school. All the other boys, at least most of them, went home for Christmas. But, mostly, I just stayed in my room, watching the snow fall, or whatever. Then later, for a few years, with...but no...not since then. It's been a long, dry spell, in my life, for any sort of Christmas cheer."

"Well! Mister William Bartram Logan! We shall endeavor with *all* our hearts to make this the *best* Christmas for you *ever*! Won't we Johnny?"

"We sure will, Bart! What would *you* like for Christmas?"

"I don't know, Johnny. I really hadn't given it much thought. But...I think I just received it."

Chapter 17

The Sparrow Inn fairly buzzed with excitement and activity. Even Barbara Jo was pulled up from her couch of suffering, and managed to make herself available for the icing of Christmas cookies and the gluing, with home-made flour-and-water paste, of paper chains for the tree. She sat with Johnny at the kitchen table for hours, cutting and pasting and then they trooped into the dining room to hang their handiwork high up on the lovely cedar that stood in the corner farthest from the fireplace and reached to the ceiling of The Sparrow's lower floor. Bartram Logan even managed to put in a morning or two's labor—hand-dipping sycamore balls into a big bowl of snow-white flour, then tying them here and there on the cedar's fragrant green limbs. He hoisted Johnny up on his shoulders the day the lovely star was finished by Johnny with his best yellow stick crayon. After Johnny successfully hung it on the treetop, Bart laughed jubilantly, swung the little boy down into his arms, and hugged him tightly, surmising softly, "I love you, Dr. John Thomas McKinnon, and it is indeed, going to be the very best Christmas of my entire life."

"I loves you, too," Johnny breathed in the scent of the man, of pine and cedar and leather, squeezed Bart's neck and grinned in reply.

Reluctantly Bart set the little boy down and turned to gaze at the place.

A fire glowed in the huge corner fireplace of the inn's dining room. The tree stood tall and bushy and decked in all it hand-made glory. From the kitchen of the inn wafted the scrumptious scents of roast fowl, baked ham, candied yams, green beans and a salad made of canned fruits and winter berries. And black walnut jamcake. Then Maggie and Liza Mae took turns ferrying the dishes in from the kitchen. Maggie motioned that they should all be seated.

"Mister Logan, would you please do the honors, of saying Grace?" Maggie asked sweetly. Adding, "And now, on this most auspicious occasion, let us all join hands."

Bart tucked Maggie's small hand in his right one and Johnny's tiny warm one in his left.

"*Heavenly Father*," Bart began, his throat so full he could scarcely speak. He glanced around the table, closed his eyes, cleared his throat, "*We thank you for this day, for these, our loved ones, our family, gathered about this table. We thank you for the lovely spread of food, and for the hands that prepared it. Most of all, Dear Father, we thank You—for Your gracious gift of Your Son and our Savior, sent to rescue a sinful and dying world. Teach us thy will. Keep us all ever in the center of Your kind and loving mercies. Amen.*"

"Well," Maggie gave Bart's hand a warm squeeze as she smiled across the table at him, her eyes bright with tears, "that was…a lovely Christmas prayer, Mr. Logan, darling. And now would you care to carve…?"

The fire crackled. The food and the conversation flowed across and around the table.

Finally Bart reared back in his chair, rubbing his lean middle with his right hand, wagging his head, "I don't think I shall *ever* feel the need to partake of any food… whatsoever …ever…ever…again."

"We'll just see about that," Maggie teased. "Come the next morning you appear at the inn, we'll just see who wants a ham biscuit and a cup of hot coffee."

"Is there…perhaps…any more coffee?" Bart chuckled.

"Yes, Mr. Logan, darling, there is plenty more in the kitchen. And we shan't even add that to your bill! Now, and just what do you have to say to that?"

"You are a most kind and gracious hostess. And I'd rather be here…on this fine Christmas day…that any other place in the world I could even dream of!"

"Then drag your chair over close to the fire, won't you, Mr. Logan, darling? And we shall have a go at all that pile of gifts beneath the tree. Johnny? Ready to open presents? Just let those dishes wait, Liza Mae. Call Benjamin Noah in from wherever he has disappeared to. And come join us."

"I think he's gwin out fo' a'nuther load o' firewood, Mizzz Maggie." Liza Mae strode through the kitchen, threw open the back door, and screeched:

"BENJAMIN!?? We's is ab'ut ta open da gif's! You wants anythin'— you's better gits your lazy self in hy'ar!" Liza Mae gave a pleased little wag of her head as she returned to the dining room to inform those staring at her, "I'm sure he'll be in—in a minute."

"Yes," Maggie smiled, "after that!—I'm sure he will! Ah! Here he comes!"

"You don' call't me?" Benjamin Noah came hustling into the dining room. Carefully depositing his armload of wood in the wood box beside the fireplace, he hurried over and lowered his muscular bulk into a chair at the end of the table. With a broad grin showing a fine row of white teeth in a coal-black face, he reached and enfolded Liza Mae's thin left hand into his large calloused right one. Benjamin Noah found it difficult to believe—given the dreary way he had spent Christmas last year, shivering and starving in some farmer's barn—that he was actually here, in this warm, cozy inn, with his new wife...and his friends.

"Johnny?" Maggie smiled fondly at her small brother, "Would you care to pass out the gifts?"

The next several minutes were filled with soft oooossssss and ahhhhhsssss at the hand-knit scarves, sweaters, and gloves for all—from Maggie. Then new dresses all around for the ladies—specially ordered by Bart with the aid of the ailing Barbara Jo, along with a heavy wool coat and fine britches for Johnny. Not much was heard from Johnny, however, when he was presented with his new coat, a new scarf and mittens lovingly knit by his sister's busy hands, and a new shirt from Barbara Jo. Barbara Jo had tucked back enough funds to purchase wool cloaks for Maggie and Liza Mae, and for Bart and Benjamin Noah, leather work gloves. Liza Mae had hoarded back scraps and strings of fabric and oat and flour sacks, soaked and boiled free of lettering and dyed in stunning colors, and had woven each of them small, colorful rag rugs, "Ta keep a body's feets warm, when deys hits da flo'r of a mornin'," she declared.

Finally the last package was announced as belonging to Benjamin Noah. With calloused black hands, Benjamin Noah slowly unwrapped a huge brown bundle from which he lifted a thick wool coat, a cotton shirt and a fine pair of heavy cotton britches—all from Bart. His black eyes welled with tears. "T'anks, youse all," he muttered, swiping at his black face with balled fists.

Blue eyes shiny with tears of disappointment, Johnny, nursing his scarf and mittens, his new coat, shirt, britches, and his rag rug, looked none too happy.

Bart rose from his chair, stretched his back muscles, strolled leisurely over and poked up the fire; then he sauntered over behind the huge green bulk of the fragrant cedar, and rolled out a big red wagon. A loud yelp from Johnny almost curled everyone's hair, and put the finishing touches on the gift giving.

Then, as twine and brown bits of wrapping papers were being picked up by Maggie, and the table cleared of Christmas dinner by Liza Mae, Bartram Logan suddenly suggested completely out of the blue:

"Why don't we all pile ourselves into the carriage, and onto the saddle mounts, and ride on out to take a look at McKinnon Valley? What do you think of that, my sweet?"

"Well…I don't know, Mr. Logan, darling," Maggie hedged. She had not ridden out to the farm in several weeks, the longest time she had gone without visiting it since returning to Rhyersville. But the last time she and Bart and Johnny had ridden out, the poor state of the place had overcome her, sent her into a spasm of racking sobs.

"This is Christmas…" Maggie said lamely.

"Yes," Bart replied, "And we have all been shut indoors *far* too long. Get your wraps then, everyone, and I'll just walk on down to Trap's and get the carriage and, I suppose, we can borrow Job and your wagon…does that work for you, Margaret Ann? I thought it might. Benjamin Noah, wrap that new scarf tightly about your neck, get your new wool coat, and you and Johnny can just come along, and help me with the transportation."

"Yasss, Suh!…Mr. Bart!"

Johnny was loath to go off and leave his new red wagon, but he gazed up at Bart for a moment, then rolled his new treasure safely back behind the tall cedar, and shrugged himself, with Bart's help, into his new coat. Then Bart was pulling the front door closed behind them.

"Are you coming with us, Barbara Jo? You of all people need to get out into the air. I don't see for the life of me…how you endure the continual confinement—!" Maggie began.

Barbara Jo lifted her small chin, flashed a broad smile and interrupted her younger sister: "You couldn't keep me from *this* outing *if you tied me to a tree!*"

"Well…!" Maggie's eyes went wide with surprise, "Who on earth has put a burr beneath your saddle?"

"Wouldn't you like to know!?"

And with that, Barbara Jo flounced up the stairs, and soon returned swaddled in a bundle of warm clothing. Her new red scarf that Maggie had knit tightly wrapped about her throat, she flounced over and lifted the front door latch.

"Well?" she asked Maggie tartly as she stood holding open the front door, two heavy lap robes folded over her arms, "You comin' or not, Maggs?"

Liza Mae, swaddled in her new sweater with her new wool cloak over it and a big black bonnet atop her plaits, plodded along bringing up the rear.

"This is shore some fin' C'ristmus. Uhmmm, uhm.....thank ya' Lord!"

With that announcement, Liza Mae pulled the front door of The Sparrow Inn shut with a firm bang, and marched behind the others, to be loaded into the coach and Maggie's wagon.

Well fortified against the cold by plenty of hot food and warm company, the group made their way towards McKinnon Valley, Benjamin Noah bursting out with a fine rendition of several Christmas Carols, with which the others all joined in, and which echoed back over the carriage and the wagon, and up over the surrounding mountains, driving all thoughts of cold from the travelers' hearts and minds.

And before she knew it, the little gap leading into McKinnon Valley rose before them. Maggie set her mouth and steeled her heart—for the ravaging pain she knew would grip her as soon as the poor farm appeared. But Bartram Logan seemed as festive as if he were going to—

They rolled through the gap, and started down the slope. Maggie's eyes flew wide. There was no gaggle of tall weeds and grasses choking the sides of the road. The pasture alongside the road was cropped to a fine greenish-brown carpet. She noticed a herd—*of goats!*—munching merrily on what grass remained.

Then the yard and the house came into sight. Maggie audibly gasped. The front yard! How lovely! Cedars flanked the yard. Holly bushes loaded with red berries grew along the base of the front porch. And what she instantly recognized as rose bushes and hydrangea—barren now, out of season—stood proudly awaiting spring in the empty flower beds.

"Oh! Mr. Logan…! I…" Maggie was speechless, as Bartram Logan drew the carriage to a final halt, leapt down, and snatched Johnny out. Then he raced around the carriage to lift Maggie down. He stood for a long moment, his hands still about her slender waist. Then he came to himself, swung away to the back, to aid Barbara Jo in alighting.

Then Bartram Logan was leading Maggie inside.

A fire glowed in the fireplace. The front room sported a fine settee—made of curved log arms and with cushions of some sort of dark, rich fabric that appeared plush as feather pillows. A table stood beside the settee, a table carved of oak with some of the bark still on it, then rubbed and varnished and polished. Perfect for the log house. Then on into the kitchen…where stood a hand-carved, hand-rubbed oak table that looked as if it had hosted meals in this very self-same kitchen for as long as the square-log house had stood.

A pie safe with double tin doors stood in one corner. In another corner, a huge meal chest of maple, rubbed and hand-finished to appear that many a bread tray had been knocked about its top. A bread tray!—A maple bread tray—! Just like the one hand-carved by Grandpa Thomas Shawn McKinnon—!

Had Bartram Logan not kept a firm hold on Maggie's elbow, she was certain she would have collapsed in a dead swoon.

Then he was leading her up the stairs. Mama's and Papa's room—a fine big bed of carved oak, with vines twining across its headboard. A plump feather mattress into which a person could sink and never be found—topped with a snow-white counterpane and two of the fattest pillows Maggie's eyes had ever beheld. Beyond it, a gigantic wardrobe that reached to the ceiling, carved to match the bed. Maggie stepped over and swung open its doors. The sweet, sweet scent of cedar greeted her nostrils, and inside…the cedar grain was rubbed and polished.

The bureau to match stood in another corner, a vast, gleaming mirror above a polished top, and below huge drawers carrying the scroll of vines.

A big hand-carved rocker sat beside the bed, a plump snow-white cushion adorning its bottom, inviting the room's occupants to sit and rest themselves as they drew off their shoes and stockings, for reading or for a fine night's repose on the softness of the huge bed.

Then Bartram Logan was drawing Maggie, speechless and overcome, down the narrow hallway, to view the other rooms. In what had been the small spare room, a child's cradle occupied one corner, and a small narrow bed, another, evidently for the child as it grew. A little dresser, a chest for clothes or toys. Even a cushioned window seat.

The other bedroom, beautiful with log furniture exactly to the scale of the room. Fine for two or more children, Maggie could see.

She turned, tears in her eyes, and gazed up at Bartram Logan.

"I don't...understand..." she whispered "...when...*why?*"

Bart drew her into his arms and whispered into her ear, "Merry, merry Christmas, sweetheart!" Afraid that she might actually pass out on him, he held her close, as a rousing cheer rose from the lower floor of the square-log house and roared up the narrow stairway.

"What on earth...?" Alarmed, Maggie pushed away from Bart, dabbing at her eyes with her fingertips.

"Come on," Bart whispered, leading her back down the stairs.

Packed into the front room and spilling out into the kitchen—the entire logging crew of the Logan Lumber Company.

"OH!" Maggie cried.

"Merry Christmas, Miss Maggie!" the loggers all roared.

"Yes! And now, there will be punch, cake and coffee in the kitchen! Or on the porches! Or in the front room! Or wherever you wish to have it! Everyone!—just help yourself! My sweet?" Bart drew Maggie close against him, peering down into her swimmingly-blue eyes, "Would you care for a cup of refreshment, to settle your nerves?"

"I could just strangle you, Bartram Logan! You know that, don't you, sir?"

"Yes, ma'am, and frankly, my sweet, I can scarcely wait for the very day that you try that! Now, two cups of punch, coming right up!"

Bart was back with the punch. Maggie had sunk onto the fine log-armed settee. Reveling in the softness of the cushions, she laid her head back and enjoyed the warmth of the fire beyond the familiar hearth. How many wintry afternoons and evenings had the McKinnons gathered about this worn hearth? Four generations...of McKinnons.

And Bartram Logan and his logging crew had refurbished and refurnished the place—it was more than a dream come true. More than she could possibly have imagined in a hundred years! This man—

"I thought, that...after you rested for a moment...and had your punch...we might walk up the mountain, my sweet? What do you think?"

"Oh, Bart!" Maggie sipped the delicious drink and wagged her head. "This is all so much, and to visit the graveyard...that is what you mean?...and it is Christmas..."

"We'll linger but a moment. I wanted you to see it, since the men have it all cleaned off. So nicely, you understand?"

"Oh, all right. I suppose we could walk up there and at least take a look. All that they have done...all that you have done...I don't even know where to begin...how do I ever..."

"You don't. You don't even try. Come on, now, sweetheart, and it's a climb up the mountain for you. Get your heart to pumping. Your blood to stirring."

"Should my heart pump or my blood stir any more than it already is, Mr. Logan, I think I should keel over absolutely, finally dead!"

"On your feet, now. And we'll have no such talk as that."

And so saying, Bartram Logan led Maggie through the lovely kitchen, out the back door, across the back yard that sported a fine flower garden about its border, and up the mountain back of the log house.

"Everything...looks...oh, it's just so perfect. It makes me want to just sit myself down in front of that fireplace, and never move—except to drag myself up the stairs to that great, soft bed. Oh, Mr. Logan, darling, everything...everything...is so perfect...except that..."

"What, my sweet?"

"I only wish...that Mama could be here...could see it."

Bart's grip tightened on her hand, as he led her along at a fairly good clip, almost, Maggie thought wonderingly, dragging her up the mountain. What on earth was Mr. Logan's rush?!

"Well, here we are!" Bartram Logan was then announcing, as he stood

168

holding her hand. The cold mountain air swirled about them, carrying the scents of yellow pine and cedar and spruce, of leaf mold from centuries of fall leaves that lay carpeting the forest on the mountains above them. The golden winter sun was just right, Bart thought, rendering the world, at this moment in time, absolutely perfect.

Then Maggie slipped her hand from his, and began to stroll absently about. All at once, a hand flew to her mouth. She let out an audible gasp. There, in the empty space beside Papa's grave...a lovely marble headstone...!

Callie McKinnon
Faithful Wife
Loving Mother
Born April, 1846
Joined her Savior
December, 1884

"Oh, my!" was all Maggie could gasp out. "How in the name of all that's holy...! When...?"

"Do you recall the weekend I failed to make my usual Sunday call? And how you chided me, for upsetting young Johnny so? Well, that week, Giles and I...we made a visit to the little town of Cumming. We looked up a certain Mr. Carl Evans. He was, to put it nicely, a bit uncooperative. It required a Court Order to receive permission to exhume her...but all that...the details...they don't really matter. All that matters, my sweet, is that your dear Mama's come home."

"Oh, Bartram! Darling!" Maggie's heart squeezed with guilt; a hand flew to her throat. "You are...and I am...such a heartless, cold, thankless clod of a person! And to think how I *behaved* that Sunday...! Why on earth do you put up with me? Why on earth do you put up with my sharp tongue and my boundless temper?!" Maggie burst into sobs.

"Come here, my sweet," Bart pulled her close. Producing a handkerchief from some inner pocket he dabbed at her eyes and said softly, "Blow your nose now, and just hush. I wouldn't, not for all the tea in China, not for all my fortune, change one blessed thing about you, Maggie McKinnon! You are perfect, just the way you are! See how well you fit into my arms! And, sweetheart…"

All the rest, whatever he said, Maggie failed to hear. She was overcome with…every emotion that she could ever have named. She was a black sinner…saved by grace…yes, but she was sure she was only *scarcely* saved, at that! Holding grudges, unable to forgive. She was far too quick to sit in judgment, far too quick to open her mouth and spit out hateful things at those she loved. Far too…she was not half good enough for the man who was holding her so tightly against his chest.

And Maggie wondered when on earth William Bartram Logan was going to wake up—and figure that out!

Chapter 18

"How far can we ride today?" Johnny was jostling along on the pony that he had named Apples, because of the way the little animal greedily devoured this fruit every time Johnny offered it to her. She would whinny and stamp a small hoof in gratitude and appreciation, black eyes wide, head and mane tossing.

"How far would you like to go, young sir?" Bart Logan teased, glancing over at Johnny, such love and pride in his eyes.

"Let's go on down and see the big wheel, spilling the water on down the creek! Can we, Maggie?"

"But…Johnny…sweetie! That's all the way down at Johnson's Corners. No, I don't think so. We did make a late start. And it will soon be supper time…at least by the time we make it back to Rhyersville, stable our mounts, and reach the inn. No, sweetie, not today…I don't think so."

"As a matter of fact," Bart put in, "we may have gone about far enough for this afternoon. What do you say, Maggie?" Bart looked over at Maggie, so beautiful in her new emerald green riding dress with its high-buttoned bodice and long-tailed over-jacket with leg-o'-mutton sleeves, with bonnet to match, part of his Christmas gifts to her.

"I think, for once in your life, Mr. Logan, darling," Maggie teased with a faint smile, "I may just be able to agree with you. My, what's all that racket from just up ahead?"

"I don't know," beneath the shadow of his hat brim Bart's smooth brow wrinkled in a worried frown. A bit farther up the deeply rutted dirt road lay a patch of dense woods that Bart knew had a creek running through it. Oftentimes, because of the easy availability of fresh, clean water, the place had become a camping ground for vagrants and other travelers—mostly freed slaves with no place in particular to go and nothing in particular to do.

"You two just wait here," Bart ordered curtly, then he urged his great roan forward at a fast trot.

Bart Logan disappeared over the brow of the slight hill. Then to Maggie's distressed amazement, Johnny was urging his little pony forward at a gallop.

Maggie took after him.

By the time she caught Johnny, she found that they had entered the deep woods, and were surrounded on every side by a rag-tag array of makeshift tents and shelters. Maggie quickly noticed that they were mostly old blankets and quilts strewn about on tree limbs, apparently to ward off night damps. And these same coverlets, Maggie was certain, were removed from the limbs by night, and used for meager guards against the biting chill of the wintry mountain air. Low fires fueled with rotten limbs glowed. Meager fires they were, that could in no wise chase the cold from this ragged camp. Women and children stood about, dark, paper-thin skin stretched over faces drawn and slack with hunger, their eyes rheumy and void of hope. Equally bony, dark-skinned men lounged here and there about the thin fires, staring up suspiciously at Maggie and Johnny with wide black eyes.

Suddenly a chill ran up Maggie's spine. They shouldn't be here, she realized. These were clearly freed slaves down on their luck. Years of freedom had not been kind to them. They appeared to be down to their last crust of bread—or lower. They were clad in rags and tatters, some with pieces of shoes clinging tenaciously to dark feet. Most with no shoes at all. And oftentimes, Maggie was well aware, desperate men were wont to take desperate measures to fill their yawning needs. But…where was Bart? Surely, he had ridden in here ahead of them? Then she caught sight of him, talking to some fellow standing beside a campfire that sputtered and flickered and threatened any moment to extinguish itself for lack of fuel.

Maggie urged her mount forward, saying softly to Johnny, "Come along, sweetie, and let's just see what Mr. Logan is up to."

Maggie and Johnny rode the fifty feet or so to where Bart had dismounted and stood talking. Maggie turned her gaze to the face of the man Bart was engaging in such serious discussion.

Maggie gave a startled gasp, and almost fell off the beautiful roan.

Len Evans!

Len Evans???!!!

But...it couldn't be! Len Evans was dead...!

"Oh, there you are, sweetheart," Maggie then heard Bart exclaiming, swinging his disapproving gaze toward her and Johnny.

Maggie urged her mount, Johnny firmly in tow, close to Bart's, and murmured, "I had no choice. When you disappeared over the knoll, Johnny just took off..."

"It's all right. This man was just explaining to me the terrible situation he finds himself and his family...and friends...in."

"Oh?" A chill creeping up her spine, Maggie turned her gaze full on the man Bart was speaking about. And upon closer examination, Maggie could see that...no...this was not Len Evans, or Len Evans' ghost. But the resemblance to Len was absolutely uncanny. He had the same dark, chestnut-brown curly hair that stood almost straight up from his head with its abundance and swirl. His eyes...they were Len's eyes...

"And what...is your...name? If I may ask?" Maggie looked the fellow straight in the eye. His skin...dark...but not black. No. He was almost white! He could easily have passed for a North Georgia farmer deeply tanned by the sun.

"It be *Moon*, Ma'am. Rufus Moon."

"And...just...where...Rufus Moon, do you happen to hail from?" Maggie asked.

"Margaret Ann..." Bart's voice, low but stern, reached out at her, and his gaze locked on her in a peculiar stare. But Maggie paid him absolutely no heed.

"*Where*, Rufus Moon?" Maggie sat her saddle in her fine emerald green riding dress and insisted.

"Well, Mistress, of late jus' ab'ut anywhars ye could care ta name. But I's 'as borned on down near the Chattahoochee, in Forsyth County."

"Do you by any chance, Rufus Moon, know a woman by the name of *Liza*?"

"Ma!? You, Mistress, you kno' *Ma!?* "

"Rufus Moon, I am very well acquainted with a woman from that part of the country. Whether or not she is your mother, I have...no way of knowing. But she is a dear friend, who is employed at my place of business, The

Sparrow Inn, just a piece on up this road…up in Rhyersville."

"Glory—! *Glory be ta th' Good Lord!*" Rufus Moon's green eyes welled with tears. "I don' searched fer tha' woman… all these many years…"

"You do understand me, Rufus Moon, when I say that this may be another Liza… altogether. But Liza did happen to mention to me, purely in passing, that she had a son who had taken the surname for himself…of Moon."

"Where?" Rufus Moon was stuttering, "Could I come up ta sees her? Wuld tha' be awright, wi' you, ma'am, that is?"

"You can come to the inn anytime you please, Rufus Moon. It won't be hard for you to find. Just follow this road on up to a little mountain town called Rhyersville. We're located right there on Main Street. Plain for all the world to see. But I won't say a word to Liza Mae. It might be, Rufus Moon, that this good, kind, sweet friend of mine is no kin to you at all. No kin, at all, you do understand, Rufus Moon? So I wouldn't want to get either her or your hopes up too high."

"No'm, and I shorely won't do that. If she be my Ma, then praise be to' th' Good Lord. And if'n she not be, then I's jest keeps on alookin'"

"That sounds fair enough. We'll be looking for you then, one day soon, at the door of The Sparrow Inn." Maggie gave a slight nod, and without even a glimpse towards Bartram Logan, she turned her mount and rode out of the camp, back towards the road, calling sternly over her shoulder, "Come along, then, Johnny, and leave these good people to the fixin' of their suppers."

Bart gave a curt nod to Rufus Moon, mounted his roan and struck off after her, his anger almost blinding him. She had just come riding into the very midst of this camp of Negroes—that appeared to be so poor, so bedraggled they probably had not eaten in more than a week! And she in a fine new dress, riding an expensive mare, and the boy, Johnny, seated on a pony that if roasted over one of these fires would feed this camp of fifty or sixty people…

By the time Bartram Logan had caught up to Maggie and Johnny, which took no more than a minute or two the way he was pushing his mount, his anger at the boiling point. She had risked so much…exposing herself…and the boy…

"Margaret Ann!" Bart was shouting at her, before his mount ever drew abreast of hers.

"Yes, Mr. Logan?" she turned cool blue eyes on him.

"And just *what*, may I be so bold as to ask, possessed you to come…and what was that…making conversation with a freed slave that is on the verge of imminent starvation….as if he were some…"

"I do think, Mr. Logan, that *Rufus Moon* may just be…my brother-in-law."

"Your…what?!"

"I don't suppose you know this…no, there's no way you could know….but Liza Mae was a slave on Big Carl Evans' plantation there in Forsyth County. She…shared with me…how she bore a child…when no more than a child herself. The first, I believe, she told me….when she was no more than eleven years old—to Big Carl Evans. I do believe, Mr. Logan, that Rufus Moon is the son of none other than Big Carl Evans, Liza's master. I do believe that would make Rufus Moon my dead husband's half-brother…and thus…"

"Surely…surely…this is some sort of sick…"

Maggie drew her mount to a halt. The roan shifted nervously beneath her rider, as if sensing the solemn, the dreadful mood settling over Maggie McKinnon's heart.

"No, Mr. Logan, this is not a jest…not even a very lewd, cruel one. It is a mere fact of life. I am not at all proud to say that things like that went on… on some southern plantations ….where beautiful black children…girls and young women…were helpless captives of cruel masters who had their way with them whenever and wherever they chose, then yanked up their fine trousers and walked away. Putting their own sons and daughters to the fields and the plow and the slave traders' blocks. It is not at all an uncommon thing, Mr. Logan. Not at all."

Maggie yanked the reins of the roan, and cantered off.

Very slowly, very thoughtfully, Bartram urged his mount alongside hers. Riding abreast of her, he said, "I'm so sorry. I had no idea. That poor soul. Those poor people. We shall have to pray for them. Yes, they are so wretched and homeless and ragged, we must pray for them." Bart's dark brows knit in a frown.

"Yes, Mr. Logan," Maggie glanced over at him and snapped, a knowing look in her blue-blue eyes. "We shall indeed have to pray very hard—that the Good Father of Mercies will open up his heavens and rain down upon them wagon loads of corn meal and bacon and beans. A few milk cows would be nice, too. Yes, let's all pray for that! And some fine fields that now lay fallow that could easily be broken and cultivated and could produce food for the owner and sustenance for the sowers. And while we're at it, Mr. Logan, let's pray for shelters, cabins…no matter how mean or small…that at least have roofs on them to shut out the rain, and tiny hearths where they might kindle small fires to warm their bones and bake them a pone of bread…"

"Yes," Bartram muttered, his voice low and choked with emotion, as the vision of cabins setting empty, their doors banging in the winds, the fields about them growing rank with grass and broomsedge and maypop vines flooded into his mind. "I think, darling…I might ride out to Cottonwood tomorrow, that is…right after I send McAlister's two sons down to that camp with a couple of wagon loads of supplies. I just might ride on out to Cottonwood…and take a look around. There are at least three dozen or more stout cabins, there. Might need a bit of repairs. But there are tools in the…"

"Tools in the barn? And plows and turning forks? I do believe, Mr. Logan, that the Good Lord had just heard our prayers! And them not even out of our mouths."

"Yes, sweetheart," Bart grinned over at her, "He may just have. But, mind you, I really *do not* have it in my heart…to become some sort of… *landlord*…"

"Maybe, should we pray hard enough, Mr. Logan, God might just see fit to put *that* in there."

"Would you, perchance, sweetheart, like to ride out to Cottonwood with me? Should I drop by… say at…eight?"

"I shall be waiting by the door, Mr. Logan, darling, my bonnet and my shawl in my hands."

———————————

"It's…pretty bad…isn't it? Terribly run down. I'd never actually thought of human beings inhabiting these two-room cabins again. Therefore, my dear, I've expended absolutely no money or effort towards their upkeep.

Look at all the cobwebs! And some of them actually have holes in the roofs. Rain has been coming in at least four or five of them. Swallows have stopped some of the chimneys with their huge nests. It would be a task of gargantuan proportions—to make them even remotely livable—!"

"Mr. Logan," Maggie fixed her gaze full on Bart, standing at her elbow in one of the open doorways, the door shutter hanging by one rusty hinge. She began patiently, as if explaining to a small child, "Did you, perchance, take a good…I mean a very, very *good* look about that horrid place those poor souls choose to call a camp? They are *totally* without *any* sort of shelter…leaking or not leaking. They have nothing that even resembles a chimney, be it stopped or unstopped. There are no doors to hang off any hinges, for Mr. Logan, darling, there are no walls to support doors or roofs, or—"

"Your point, my sweet, is well taken." Bart heaved a great sigh, tipped his hat back on his forehead, as if finally accepting the inevitable. "So, when do we go down and make the offer of Cottonwood to them? With all its terrible flaws and—"

"I would say, what is wrong with this afternoon? I am sure they will find this place a veritable Paradise on earth, after that filthy, cold, cramped, raw, windswept—!"

"Yes," Bart smiled down at her, taking her arm, as she rattled on, and leading her to their waiting mounts, muttering small replies in all the right places.

"Yes, my sweet!

"Yes, you are most assuredly, absolutely correct in all your assumptions.

"And yes, I will attempt to recall to mind…to do that very thing.

"You think *that* is necessary, also, do you? Right. Right—!"

———————

Down in the freedman's pitiful camp, great excitement reigned, as two wagons heavily laden with sacks of flour, corn meal, dried beans, ground oats, sugar, coffee, salt, and hickory-cured sides of bacon and salt cured hams rattled into the midst of the camp. Two stalwart young white boys, named Sam and Seth McAlister, asked in clipped but cordial tones, "Just where would y'all like this stuff offloaded?"

Women and children, their black eyes wide, clucking and cackling like a gaggle of hungry geese, clustered about the wagons, snatching off the smaller bundles of coffee, sugar and salt, while the men hefted the heavier sacks of corn meal, flour and oats. A few cold crocks of butter were handed down, along with several brimming canisters filled with fresh sweet milk. Two barrels of winter apples, some cabbage and potatoes and turnips dug up from storage cellars.

Out of crates and baskets, miraculously appeared sturdy metal plates, forks and spoons. Small bowls and cups replaced the empty tin cans from which the freedmen had been drinking their creek water. Soon there wafted out over the camp the scent of boiling coffee, steaming in huge pots that appeared from out of nowhere along with some of the largest iron skillets these people had laid eyes on for quite some time.

Frying bacon and warming ham sizzled and popped, while roasting hoe cakes rose, adding to the heavenly aroma. Not an hour after the wagons departed, the women and children ladled out food for the waiting men. But before a bite was consumed, Rufus Moon gave a loud holler, "All right thar, now all ye gather yoreselves 'round, and we'll just say a bit of thanks ta th' Good Lord above for this blessing and bounty!"

"Did we send thanks ta th' good man who paid for all this stuff?" a man at his elbow inquired of Rufus.

"Since we had *sarta 'n* visitors jest yestidy adfernoon, I'm shore we all know who that good man is," Rufus replied with a wide grin. "And should we git th' good fortune to meet that man and his lady ag'in, we wants to all be shore we thank 'em *real* good. Now, fall to. And don't nobody overstuff yoreselves…or ye'll all be sick as a foundered houn' dog!"

Two days later, the woods about the creek lay empty and quiet. No tattered and torn quilts whipped their faded and filthy cotton in the cold winds. No children cried about dwindling campfires for a sip of milk or a bite of bread.

The woods lay empty and still, the cold winter winds from the mountains moving down and removing every vestige of the stink of a camp that had been inhabited by sixty or more souls whose tired, unwashed bodies stank of weeks on the road, and were racked by starvation and scurvy.

At Cottonwood, the nearby woods rang with the sounds of newly-sharpened axe heads biting into stout oak and hickory trees. Beneath the wintry skies, children romped and played before the row of cabins, strutting cocks, fryer chickens and laying hens clucking and pecking for the grains of dried corn strewn about their feet. Atop the roofs, dark-skinned men knelt, hammering on well-dried oak shingles. Women with long poles poked and prodded at the chimneys of the cabins, and straw and mud, grass and twigs, came tumbling down from dirt-dauber and swallow nests, to be swept into baskets and hastened outside.

Out in the cavernous depths of the barn, men and boys scrambled and searched amongst a jumble of piled and dusty farm tools and implements, which had overflowed from the tool shed. Shovels and rakes, a few rusty two-man cross-cut saws, along with age-grayed plow stocks were dragged out into the thin rays of a slanting winter sun and the webs and mud knocked off them. A long rack of hoes stood like waiting soldiers, idling against a wall.

And in the newly cleared pasture, a herd of milk cows grazed, and past them, some mules and plow horses lifted their noses to sniff the cold winter's air, knowing by the scents greeting flared nostrils that surely, surely spring was just around the corner. So enjoy this fine leisure while you may, for as certain as the sun rises, spring plowing and planting is just around the corner!

It was a cold January day. Liza Mae grumbled and muttered and bustled her way out the back door of The Sparrow to dash out the lukewarm dishwater. No hogs here, so no need for saving slops. Her tepid dishwater disposed of, she stomped her feet, drew her shawl about thin shoulders, and made as if to hasten back inside.

"That you, Ma?" Liza Mae heard a voice that sounded as if it peeled off the back of the well shelter, flew through the winter air, and hit her square in the forehead, almost taking her breath away.

"Who dat?!" Liza Mae whirled about, black eyes flying wide. "Youse come on outta dar', and sho' yoself...or I'se wil'—"

"It *is* you, ain't it, Ma?! It's *me!* Yore son, Rufus!"

179

"Rufus? *Rufus! Oh, de Good Lord done be praised! It's my boy!*"

Then Liza Mae was squealing and bawling like a new-born calf, and being squeezed in a great bear hug that took all the breath from a thin frame that never seemed to put on an ounce of fat no matter how ravenously she ate. Then, long black face filled with wonder, she pushed Rufus back; with tear-filled coal-black eyes she gazed up into his face. "Jest *look* at you, now! You's don' *all* growed up, ain't ya, boy?!"

"I 'spect so, Ma," Rufus grinned down at her, showing a fine row of white teeth.

"I's...never thot' ta see ya alive ag'in', boy...not in this here ol' world!" Liza Mae swiped at her eyes and almost choked on the words, and on the happiness bubbling up in her soul. Eyes as black and shiny as chinquapins, tears spilled down thin cheeks. Memories came flooding back—of that hot summer day Big Carl Evans come for her boy, aged nine. He sent him off with the overseer. The next day, the overseer came back—alone. The boy had grown to resemble too closely the Master's youngest son, Len. He had become an embarrassment; he had to be sold off. After the War, word reached her through the freed slaves' grapevine, he was somewhere in South Carolina.

"Whar' on earth did ya' come from, Son? How'd ya ever fin' me?"

"I guess it wuz th' hand of th' Lord, Ma. He don' led me up inta these here mountains. I met a fine lady, out whar' we wuz campin', a few days back. And she and her gentl'man friend, they don' brought us ta th' promised land."

"Whut ye talkin' 'bout, Rufus?! You don' lost yore mind?! Whut promis' lan'?"

"No, Ma. It's real! It's a place they call *Cottonwood!*"

"*Cottonwood!? O, da Lord don' be praised!*" Liza Mae clapped her hands, flung back her head, and danced a little jig. *"I shoulda knowed it! Ye don' met Mizz Maggie!—and Mister Bart!"*

Chapter 19

Johnny picked up the buttered biscuit from amongst the scraps of grits and eggs left on his plate. With the biscuit tucked securely in one hand, he picked up his every-day jacket from the end of the oak bench and stuck the biscuit in his mouth while he wiggled both arms into his coat.

Then Johnny's short legs carried him around the table. Next he ventured out the back door, and sat down on the lower step of the porch, to finish off his delicious biscuit filled with melted butter and a big dollop of dark brown sugar.

The late January sun, just rising over the mountain ridges back of town, felt good on his face. Johnny grinned, as his eyes picked up a furry ball slipping around the well curb, then leaping atop it, to perch atop the closed lid and stare at him with open curiosity.

A kitty! A tiny kitty as bright yellow as the sunlight breaking over the mountaintops. "Here, kitty! Here, come here! Do you hear me? Want a bite of my biscuit?"

Johnny pinched off a few crumbs of the delicious biscuit, and flung them down between the porch step and the well curb.

Just as he had hoped, the kitten leapt off the well lid, and bounded toward the buttered crumbs.

Cautiously, so as not to frighten the tiny animal, Johnny stepped gingerly off the porch step, and into the yard. The kitten arched its back, and moved a few steps backward. "Want some more?" Johnny coaxed in his little-boy voice, "Just one more bite? Or two? What's your name?"

Johnny tossed another piece of sugar-and-butter coated biscuit toward the tiny animal. It seemed to relax, and approached, very cautiously, toward the tempting morsel.

"You got a name? Why don't I call you *Sunshine*?" Johnny knelt before the kitten, whispering, "Sure! Come here to me, Sunshine! I don't have me a cat! You want to be my cat? Maggie might let me give you a little more to eat. This here biscuit's about all gone. You still hungry?"

The kitten, having gobbled down what little was offered, suddenly sat up on its haunches, cocked it small head, eyed Johnny very suspiciously, then spun about and shot behind the well curb.

"Come here, kitty! Kitty!?"

Johnny crept around the corner of the well curb.

The kitten gave a mad dash across the narrow yard—and vanished into the trees that led across the valley, and then up the mountainside.

Immediately, without a backward glance, Johnny took off in hot pursuit. "Kitty? *Kitty!*"

Exactly how long he'd been in the woods, or how far he had run, Johnny was not at all sure. He was only sure of one or two things. He was very tired. And he was getting very cold. When he looked up into the sky through the barren winter tree limbs, each tree looked just like the tree beside it. He was lost in a thick stand of hardwoods completely barren of leaves, and sprinkled amongst the oaks and maples and poplars, an occasional pine reared fragrant limbs heavy with dark green needles. And underneath his feet, layers and layers of dry leaves rustled and rattled in Johnny's little brain as loud as claps of thunder with each step he took.

Attempting not to panic, Johnny stood perfectly still and gazed about him. Which way had he come? He wasn't at all sure. And the little kitten had long ago disappeared from sight. Maggie would be furious with him. And Mister Bart, he had warned him about leaving the yard—

"Kitty?!" Johnny screamed, screwing up his face in a frightened scowl, "This is *all your fault!*"

Had Johnny given in to his first impulse, he would have fallen to the forest floor and burst out in wracking sobs. But Maggie had taught him well. If you made a mistake, if you did something wrong—or stupid—you stopped, carefully considered what you had done, and rectified your error—tried your best to do what you could to make it all better. "No use," Maggie had drilled into his little head, "cryin' over spilt milk! That's what Mama always told me. You must remember that, Johnny. Just pick yourself up, brush yourself off, and set your face toward the best thing to do for *everybody* concerned— and that, young sir, includes, most of all, *you!*"

Johnny screwed his little face into a scowling frown. What would be the best thing to do?

He could try calling Maggie or Liza Mae or Benjamin, to see if they could hear him. He could walk around, and see if he recognized any of the trees he had passed, or any stump or rotten log.

When his throat was raw from calling and he felt that he couldn't move his legs another step, Johnny couldn't believe his eyes, the little yellow kitten was peering out at him from behind a rotting log!

"Come here, kitty!" Johnny called.

And she came, slowly, deliberately placing one soft paw before another, her little head cocked sidewise, peering curiously at him.

Then Johnny scooped the tiny form into his arms, and placed his cheek against the soft warmth of the yellow fur. The kitten began to purr. Johnny could feel the pulsating rhythm of its little heart. He wondered if the kitten was cold. He tucked it into the front of his jacket so that only its head could be seen beneath his chin.

Then Johnny sat down.

Johnny knew that when the sun was almost exactly over his head, it was about lunch time at The Sparrow. He knew they would all be looking for him. They had probably been looking for him for hours. He was thirsty. He wondered if there was a creek or spring nearby...did he recall leaping over a stream...not once, but twice? He'd backtrack, and look for that.

Johnny stumbled wearily from the dense woods into a thick cane patch, and he knew the creek was near. Just a bit farther on he could get a drink, and think what he should do.

Holding onto the kitten with his left hand, with his right he fought his way through cane that reached far above his head. Suddenly, his foot struck something soft. Johnny peered down, to see that he had stumbled onto a huge black bear—that had prepared a bed for hibernation deep in the thick cane.

Shiny black as burnt charcoal and huge as a small mountain, the bear reared up in a drunken, half-stupor, threw back its head and gave a maddened roar.

Towering black! Sharp white teeth and a wide red mouth…!

Clutching the kitten frantically to his chest, Johnny gave a frightened yelp, whirled and fled as best he could, back through the dense cane brake. Behind him, he could hear the bear, angry at having been roused from its deep slumber, crashing through the cane right behind him.

"Jesus! God! If'n you're up there today…" Johnny was too scared to finish his prayer.

Miraculously, he broke free of the cane brake, and found himself running through the forest, dried leaves crackling and rustling beneath his feet like rifle shots.

Johnny stumbled and fell. He felt the sting of pain as the kitten's claws sank into his chest, as it frantically attempted to dig its way out of his jacket. In the same instant, he heard rustling as the bear broke free of the cane, and rumbled across the leaf-strewn forest floor—!

"—Magggggggie!"

––––––––––––––

Maggie hurried along the street, calling as she ran. "Johnny! John Thomas McKinnon!—*You answer me*—!"

"What is it, Maggie? What's happened?"

Having opened the door in answer to Maggie's furious banging, Thomas Beyers stood in the door of the schoolhouse in his shirtsleeves, a worried frown on his face.

"It's *Johnny*, Thomas! He's vanished! We haven't seen hair or hide of him! For two hours or more! I thought sure I could cry the town and find the little rascal. But I've called until I'm hoarse…and…there's…no answer."

"No one has seen him?"

"No, Thomas! No one has seen hair or hide of him! I've asked at every business. Benjamin Noah has searched every alley. We've even searched the woods immediately back of the inn. He's been gone since right after breakfast. I…I'm worried sick. I don't know where else to look. What else to do!"

"Just let me get my coat, Maggie. And don't worry," Thomas called, disappearing inside the little schoolhouse for a moment. Then he was back, stepping out the door, drawing on his hat and coat, and pulling the oak door closed behind him.

They had gone over the town again, street by street, alley by alley. They scoured the woods behind the inn. The sun now stood toward the west.

"Maybe we should return to town," Thomas suggested. "Organize a search party, before…"

"We've got to find him, Thomas! We've got to find him before it gets dark!" Maggie shrieked, her nerves as taunt as fiddle strings. "I can't stand much more of this! Not knowing…where he is! If he's…all right!"

"Of course, he's all right, Maggie," Thomas said confidently. "We'll find him. It's just a matter of time."

"But, Thomas…time's what we may not have! You know how cold it gets here in the mountains at night. It'll be way, way below freezing…once the sun sets…"

"But you said, Maggie, that he had on his jacket?" Thomas asked.

"His jacket, yes, Thomas! But what good will that do against freezing temperatures, and bears and mountain lions! And—it might rain, it could freeze!"

"I don't believe it's going to rain, Maggie, darling. We need some way to track him," Thomas gazed anxiously at the sinking sun, painting the sky red and orange over the western band of purple mountains. "Jonas Trap's got several hunting dogs. Maybe his hounds—"

Jonas Trap hooked bony thumbs in the leather belt holding up his baggy britches and gazed at Thomas Beyers with squinted gray eyes sunken far back into a narrow head capped with a fur hat. He squinted dark eyes, turned his head, and spat a long stream of tobacco juice to one side, barely missing Thomas' shiny black boots. Then Jonas surmised, "Soon's you come by here this mornin' alookin' fer lil' John, Maggie, I sent a man up to th' loggin' camp. Mr. Logan should be ridin' in, any minute now."

"Oh," Maggie said, wondering why she hadn't thought of sending for Bart, immediately when she had found Johnny was missing. But she hadn't thought of Bart. She hadn't thought of anything…but finding Johnny. Then she had gone to Thomas…

185

"Oh." Maggie mumbled, gazing over at Thomas.

"Good," Thomas muttered. "We'll need all the help we can get."

"And speak of th' devil…" Jonas Trap spat another stream of tobacco juice into the dirt street, just as Bartram Logan came thundering up in a cloud of dust.

"What's going on? Johnny's missing? Since when?" Bart Logan sat horseback, his sweaty mount prancing beneath him as he glared down at them.

"Just after breakfast," Maggie replied.

"Just after breakfast!?" Bart shouted, staring down at her with dark eyes filled with questions. He swung his tall frame out of the saddle and approached her. "Why didn't you send for me?"

"I don't know! I wasn't thinking!" Maggie moaned, tears filling her eyes. "I thought he was just playing hide-and-seek! I thought any minute he'd pop out from behind some building, or tree!"

"Trap," Bart turned to Jonas, "I see you have your hounds ready to go?"

"Yeah, it was Beyers' idee ta take th' hounds along. Maggie fetched along one o' lil' John's shirts. Maybe, after catchin' a whiff, they cin sniff out his scent."

"If we just follow the dogs—" Thomas began.

"The boy's been gone since early this morning. Close on to five or six hours. No telling how far he may have wandered in that amount of time. You have a mount?" Bart turned on Thomas, a scowl on his face.

"No."

"Thomas can…" Maggie began, her gaze moving from Bart's dark, closed face to that of Thomas Beyers.

"Jonas," Bart ordered, "Saddle Mrs. Evans' mare. Beyers can ride her." Bart stepped into the saddle. "Maggie, I suppose you'll want to come along?" His eyes were dark and unreadable. His tanned face closed.

"Well, Mister Logan, you suppose *exactly right*!" Maggie stared up at him and snapped angrily, "I can ride—"

"Put your foot in the stirrup and give me your hand," Bart ordered.

Maggie did, and Bart lifted her up before him in the saddle.

Jonas Trap appeared with Maggie's mare and a mount of his own, calling to his hounds as Thomas Beyers swung into the saddle, and the foursome roared out of the wheelwright's yard.

His arms encircling the slight form of Maggie McKinnon Evans, the crown of her winter bonnet touching his chin, Bart tried to push down the anger that had almost choked him, when he had ridden up to find that in her hour of crisis, it was *Thomas Beyers* she had summoned to her aid.

Maggie sat stiff and silent, her mind churning. If anything happened to Johnny, she would never forgive herself! But he had slipped out the back door, when she was upstairs—

"If only I hadn't…gone upstairs…and left Johnny alone in the kitchen to finish his breakfast," Maggie muttered, sobs not far beneath the surface.

Bart tightened his hold on her, drawing her back against his chest, "It's not your fault. Don't go casting blame where none is due. It's no one's fault. You can't watch Johnny every single moment of the day. The boy has to learn—" He felt her stiffen in his arms, and knew he was treading on dangerous ground. He drew in a sharp breath, and continued softly:

"It's not your fault. Johnny's too young to know the dangers of wandering off. He'll learn. He'll be all right. Wait and see."

"But the dogs…they just keep running about in circles!" Maggie sighed.

"Maybe that's because Johnny did the same thing—ran about in circles. But he's just a little boy, afoot. He couldn't have gone so far that we can't locate him…soon."

"You really believe that?" Maggie asked, her voice quivering with fear. "What if—"

"Now, don't start that, or you'll go wandering down too many dark trails with no turning. Trust me, love, we will find him. And soon. Trap, what do you think they've found?"

"Oh, they's picked up young John's scent, alrighty. Just a matter o' time now, 'til we run up on th' lad, I figure."

"How many ridges have we ridden across!? Could he have come this far?" Maggie worried.

"Yes, my sweet, I fear he not only could have, but he indeed did. Our little John Thomas has been on the move today. The question is, what on earth drew him into the mountains? I'd say that without a doubt, we'll soon discover one tired little boy."

"Maybe he came searching for herbs for his healing potions," Maggie muttered in a puzzled voice.

"Don't you two usually do that together?" Bart asked.

"Yes, we do. Always. Johnny knows *very well* the woods are forbidden. He knows very well…"

"Yes, well," Bart surmised, "sometimes we humans know things very well, but then, we get drawn off course so easily."

"Oh?" Maggie bristled, "Are we still speaking now of Johnny, or of humanity in general, or of—"

"No one in particular," Bart said crisply. "Just making conversation."

"Well, it sounds to me as if you're…angry."

"I'm not…angry. Let's…just drop it, shall we."

Maggie felt a chill start at the top of her head, and travel down her spine, to the tips of her toes.

"I'm so frightened!" she fought back a sob. She had to admit that she felt better about the situation, now that William Bartram Logan was on the scene. He seemed so strong, so confident. But, *"Please, God! Let Johnny be all right!"* She whispered the little prayer almost without realizing it.

"Trap! Anything promising yet?" Bart shouted to Jonas Trap, who had now taken his hounds and ridden a bit ahead, strands of thin gray hair whipping about from beneath the fur of his cap.

"Creek and a cane brake just down the bottom of this rise. Looks like somebody or somethin's been thrashin' 'round in thar. Could be th' boy. Could be a bear."

"A…*bear*!?" Maggie shrieked.

"You yoreself know, Miss Maggie," Jonas Trap laid his head to the side as if reasoning with a child, "Them b'ars, they like ta snuggle down in a mess of thick cane tops fer their winter bed, wif a good stream nearby, so's they cin stagger up and git theirsefs a good swig of cold, clear water onct in awhile."

"A bear?" Maggie shrieked, louder.

"We…don't…know for sure, Maggie," Bart said in a calm, level voice, "that there's been a bear—"

"I'd say that thar's not th' exact fact o' th' matter, Mr. Logan," Jonas Trap drawled slowly. He stared at them for several moments with dark, narrowed eyes, then he leaned aside to spit a long stream of dark-brown tobacco juice into the dried leaves beside his mount's front hoof, "I see his—or her—probably her—bed a bit farther on. But th' b'ar, she's done ups and gone."

"*Bart!*" Maggie felt as if she would faint, her hands clasped tightly about those of Bartram Logan, as if holding on for dear life.

"It's all right, darling," Bart drew her closer, trying to stop her quivering, enfolding her so tightly she wondered that she could breathe. But somehow, she felt his strength, his closeness highly comforting. "We're going to find Johnny," Bart whispered in her ear. "And he's going to be all right."

But he was glad he had stuck his rifle into the scabbard of his saddle. "Where to now?" Bart turned to gaze at Jonas Trap, his dark eyes begging the man to find Johnny—and to find him soon.

"Th' hounds seem ta be onto somethin'," Jonas surmised, turning his head aside to arc a long stream of tobacco juice into the tall cane. "Okay, fellows! *Sic 'em!*"

Johnny stirred, and wondered just how long he'd been hanging on to the huge pine limb. Just how much longer could he stay awake, and hold on? If he fell asleep, if he fell from the tree…him and his kitten, Sunshine…

The kitten purred, then wiggled and squirmed in a valiant attempt to escape the trap of Johnny's coat, but Johnny held it tightly against his scratched chest. With wide blue eyes he gazed down to where the black bear waited below. It appeared at times to be in a deep slumber, its dark, furry form all stretched out, its head resting on its front paws, which the bear would chew and lick at from time to time, as if starving…honing its appetite for a good meal…

"You go away! You hear me?!" The sun was almost down! Maggie would have his hide! His stomach rumbled loudly. He had missed lunch! And supper!

The black bear lazily raised its head, wagging it dazedly from side to side, before lowering it back to those big, wet paws.

"*Johnny!?*"

"*Maggie!?*"

189

He saw the dogs first, running madly about in circles, around the big black bear. Slowly the bear lumbered to its feet. Mister Bart produced a rifle from his saddle, and aimed it above the bear's head. The shot rang out through the forest like a clap of thunder, sending birds aloft by hundreds and causing the horses to stamp and shy about.

The bear eyed the dogs, then the man with the gun, then she turned and lumbered off, turning back once to growl her disgust at the lot of them, before disappearing into the barren trees and over the next ridge.

Bart guided his mount beneath the pine, in between the branches. Then he spoke softly to the coal-black stallion, "Whoa, there." He stood in the stirrups, and lifted Johnny down into Maggie's arms. "All right, everybody, let's go home."

––––––––––––––

Maggie stood peering out the kitchen door. She reached for her shawl, hanging on a wooden peg behind the door, and stepped out into the cold mountain night. She could see the moon, a full moon, hanging high over the mountain ridges. She could make out the line of the trees flanking the mountains. A sound drifted up from a far ridge, and sent a shiver down Maggie's spine. It looked so peaceful, so absolutely, perfectly beautiful. But she knew that danger lurked in the mountains, once night had fallen. The cry had probably been that of a bobcat.

Maggie was aware of Bartram Logan moving up behind her. "Is he sleeping?"

"Yes," she laughed, a light, tinkling, relieved sound that set Bart Logan's heart to hammering.

"I'm glad."

"You…I want to thank you…for today."

"Thank me? You sound as if…"

"What?"

"Nothing. Never mind."

"No. I do mind. Tell me. How do I sound to you? You're angry."

"No, I'm not. Don't be ridiculous."

"Am I? Being ridiculous?"

"Why should I be angry?"

"Perhaps because…Thomas Beyers…"

"I'm sure Mr. Beyers is a fine man. He was simply attempting to help a neighbor in distress. I admit that I was a bit…put out…when I rode up…and saw you with him. And learned how long Johnny had been missing, without your giving a thought to sending for me. If it hadn't been for Trap sending me word…"

"It was a mistake, not sending for you. But…I was so upset…"

"I'm not angry. Not at all. I'm just happy. Relieved. That Johnny is all right. I'm not at all jealous of…Thomas Beyers, if that's what you're thinking. There…for just a moment…I must admit… but I trust you. I love you. And I trust that you love me." Bart reached and took her hand.

"Yes," Maggie sighed.

"Yes," Bart smiled. "Now, what do we do about Johnny? Does he get to keep the kitten?"

"After what he *went through* to get the poor little thing, don't you feel that he's *earned* it?"

"That's *exactly* the reply I was expecting. And I *thoroughly* agree." Bart squeezed her hand, "Have you ever seen a lovelier moon?"

"You know, I recall Papa saying almost those exact words to Mama— on the back porch of the log house," Maggie leaned against Bart's shoulder for a moment, then she turned and gazed up at him, and to her utter delight, he murmured:

"Why don't we just forget about supper, and go for a little walk in the moonlight?"

Chapter 20

"Mizzz Maggie, I thin' ye better don' come to the doh *yoself!* " Liza Mae called to Maggie that cold February morning.

Maggie reached the back door and stood peering out into the cold, drizzling rain.

There on the narrow back porch stood a young girl. Frowsy, red-blond hair hung wetly about a face that was pale, dirty, and sprinkled with freckles. The hair didn't appear to have seen such a thing as a brush or comb for a very, very long time. Lips blue with cold, no cloak or coat, clothes a tattered, soiled mess that clung to thin shoulders and draped over a huge, mounded belly, the girl stared at Maggie. Suddenly, a violent shiver shook her from head to foot.

"What on earth—!" Maggie gasped. "Why are you out in this? What has *happened* to you, my dear?" The girl looked to be expecting a child!—any moment! And she was scarcely more than a child herself! "I'm sorry! Keeping you standing in the cold. Do come in."

The girl stood in the open doorway, eyes lowered, wagging her head tiredly, teeth chattering so she could scarcely push the words out. "No. I cin't rightly…see ma wa' clear…ta doin' nuthin' so for'ard as that, ma'am. If I culd jest trouble ye…fer a bit o' food. Just a cold…hunk o' bread—"

"Nonsense!" Maggie reached out, grasped the girl by the arm, and practically dragged her into the warmth of the inn's kitchen.

"What on earth are you doing out in this weather? Where's your family? Your…father? Your…mother?" Maggie's angry gaze fell to the girl's bulging middle. She banged the back door shut, and demanded: "Your…*husband,* for pity sakes?!"

"I ain't got no mama. Nor I ain't got me no husban'. And as ye cin see plain as day, ma'am…tha's my whole troubles. And Pap…when I got in th'

192

fam'ly way… wal, ma'am, Pap said I wuz a devil and a sinner. He don' throwed me out th' cabin."

"*What?!*" Maggie breathed in disbelief. The girl glanced toward the door. "Won't you come on in, and find yourself a seat. By the way, what's your name?"

"Bethany Lee, ma'am. That's e'nuf name…fer now." The girl hung her head.

"Do you…" Maggie began, reaching out, taking one of the girl's cold-stiffened hands, drawing her on into the warmth of the kitchen, seating her on the oak bench beside the kitchen table, "Do you live around here?"

"N'm. Not so close's you would have any chanch ta know 'bout me. We, that is…Pap…he's got a farm, on up th' mountains. Up a cove off th' road toward Hiawassee way." The girl ducked her head, refusing to meet Maggie's intense gaze.

"Hiawassee?" Maggie's eyes grew very wide. "Why, that's way over…"

"No'm, not all th' way ta Hiawassee, but, yes'm, it's a pert long ways off."

"How long…when…did your …Papa…put you out?"

"I don't rightly know, ma'am. Week or so back, maybe near ten days, I 'spect."

"A week or ten days? For a week or more you've been out in the elements? In those rags? Without food or shelter?! Look at me!"

The girl gazed up shamefacedly. "Yes'm. Do'ya think I c'uld have a…"

"Oh, do excuse me. I was so taken with what you had said. I'll get you a plate. And a cup of hot milk. A cup of coffee? Do you drink coffee?"

She stared at Maggie tiredly, "Rite now I'd drank most anythin' ya gives me."

"Oh, yes. Right." Maggie turned her back, bustling about the stove, pulling out sausage patties from the warming oven, a biscuit still dripping with butter. A jar of wild blackberry jam. A cup of milk. Hot coffee.

Maggie sat down opposite the girl as she wolfed down the warm food like a starving thing and took long appreciative gulps of coffee then the milk.

"How long…that is…if I'm not prying into…too personal an affair…when…is your child…due?"

"I don't kno'. Could be 'most any minute naw, I 'spect. That's why Pap put me out. Said he was a God-fearin Baptis'… not abut ta have no bastard borned 'neath his roof."

"Most any minute, now?" Maggie breathed. "What are your plans? You have someone…surely…some relative or other…?"

"N'm, I don' s'pect I do. Have nobody, that is."

"Well, in that event. We need to get you out of those wet things. Why…don't you just spend the night here, dear girl, and then tomorrow will be another day. And you can make plans…for whatever you think best…for the future of yourself…and your baby."

"Plans, ma'am?"

"Well," Maggie stared into the girl's gray-blue eyes, "Yes. Well, we can discuss all that later. Why don't we bring in the tub, and get you a nice warm bath? A good night's sleep upstairs on a feather mattress, and tomorrow when the sun rises and the skies clear, I'm sure the world will look to be a much brighter place. And let us just pray, my dear, that your father comes to his senses! A Baptist, indeed! What God-fearing Baptist father puts his daughter out in the winter's icy cold?!—and her no more than a child, and on the verge of giving birth to his *grandchild*! Just answer me that?"

"I…wouldn't be aknowin', ma'am." The girl's thin shoulders slumped; she stared at Maggie with weary gray eyes. "Makes no sense ta me. No sense a'tall."

By the time winter's darkness had settled for the day over the Blue Ridges, the girl was washed, dressed in one of Maggie's nightshifts, and fast asleep in one of the upstairs beds.

And not a moment too soon, for about midnight Maggie was awakened from a deep sleep by moans of pain.

Before Maggie could even think of summoning help, the child who could not have been more than fourteen or fifteen, brought into the world a beautiful little girl, with a rose-bud mouth, perfect hands and feet, with ten fingers and ten toes. Perfect little body, and a head full of dark hair that glistened in the soft yellow glow from the kerosene lamp.

"Oh! She's perfect! Isn't she beautiful, Bethany Lee?" Maggie crooned and cooed over the baby. The girl just turned a pale, freckled face to the wall and wept as if her heart would break. When Maggie tired to comfort her, she turned to stare at her:

"Whut in th' name of Job am I ta do with that little thin'?" she wailed, her eyes filled with fear. "I got nobody, and no place ta go! And not a *soul in the' whole world*! Not a soul in th' whole world keres if'n I live er die!" She buried her face in the quilts.

"Now you listen to me," Maggie rolled the girl onto her back and peered at her sternly. "You have a beautiful little child, here, who is going to be looking to her Mama—and that's *you*. She'll be looking to her Mama to feed and clothe her and provide her a home. Now, just who, I want you to tell me, is the *papa* of this fine, precious child? You did not...I never knew of a girl yet...who somehow managed to get herself in the family way without some man involved! And now, Bethany Lee, you are going to tell me exactly who this...man....is ...This man who..."

"No, ma'am!" The girl's light gray eyes widened in alarm. She shook her head, "I cin't do that! I...don't ritely kno', who th' ... who...her Pap be!"

"How on earth could you not know? You are *shielding* some man, my dear girl! I can see it in your eyes. And whoever he is, he is not worth it. Do you hear me? Now, this man is responsible for this child. And he is responsible for the rip and tear of your life. If he refuses to marry you, he should be...horsewhipped. He must assume *responsibility* for your care and the care of his child! Now, Bethany Lee, tell me—"

"No'm. I cin't tell ya!" The thin face crumpled.

"Oh—!" Maggie muttered in great frustration, her heart twisting for this girl who had sunk herself into such a mess. "Well, we won't press the point. Not today. But sometime in the very near future, when you are out of that bed and on your feet again, you must come to terms with the consequences of his...and *your*...actions...that have brought this child into the world! Just remember, Bethany Lee, *whatsoever a man sows, that shall he also reap! And, my dear girl, that most certainly includes women!*"

The girl stared blankly at Maggie.

"Oh, you poor thing! Don't tell me, child, that you are so totally ignorant of any learning of the Holy Scriptures?!"

"Yes'm. I s'pose I am." The girl stared guardedly at Maggie.

"Fine God-fearing Baptist, your father is, *is he*? And his daughter not even knowin', then, the *least* little thing about the Scriptures?! God save me from these religious folk who never crack the door of a church nor as much as lift the lid to knock a bit of dust off their Bibles! Nor bother to lift their voices in one moment of prayer!"

With that, Maggie was out the door of the little bedroom, and flouncing down the stairs into the warm kitchen of the inn. She walked over to the black iron stove, and poured herself a cup of coffee, setting the coffee pot down with a bang that echoed about the kitchen, so upset, her brain in such a muddle that she didn't even know whether the black brew was cold or hot.

This! This, Lord! Maggie grumbled beneath her breath, *This is all I need. More nonpaying, disabled guests at the inn. Two of them! Occupying another room that is not free to let! Further reducing my meager income…!*

Immediately the words were out of her mouth, Maggie was contrite, stricken with guilt. How on earth could she grumble about *income*, when that poor, homeless girl lay upstairs, flat on her back, a fatherless babe at her breast?!

Of course, she would have to give a room over to the girl and her baby, until she could get her on her feet, find her some other lodgings. And there was still Barbara Jo. Not willing to carry wood for a fire, she had surrendered Maggie's room, but she was still in residence at the inn…and making no plans to return home.

With a heavy heart, Maggie rose, walked out the back door, and dumped her coffee into the yard.

As Maggie stood in the yard, she felt a drop of moisture hit her cheek. Then another. She gazed up into the barren tree branches, to see whirling crystals of white drifting down in thickening sheets. "It's snowing!" she shouted.

Bart Logan appeared in the door, a huge grin wreathing his handsome face that managed to retain a deep tan even in winter, so many hours did the lumberman spend outdoors.

"Should it keep this up," he laughed, "you and Johnny will be able to build yourselves a fine snowman come morning!"

"Johnny and me? How about you, Mr. Philadelphia, you ever build a snowman?"

"Don't be silly, darling. Of course. I've rolled hundreds to their frozen feet!"

"Feet?! That doesn't sound like you know a great deal about snowmen!" Maggie teased, enjoying the feel of the snow drifting down against her face in cold, icy drops. "You built snowmen with feet?"

"You know very well *exactly* what I meant! You're just trying to ruffle my Northern feathers, so to speak. Well, I'll have you know, young lady," Bart was beside her now, drawing her close against him in the cold air sparkling now with so many flakes the world had gone absolutely white, "I have stood many a snowman on his—bottom—that has lasted for weeks and weeks in the frozen Pennsylvania winters. So there! Can you match that!?"

"No, Mr. Logan. I cannot match that! For down here in the mountains of Georgia, the snow comes, we enjoy it for a few days, then the sun pops out and melts it all away. So, you see, Mr. Logan, that again our horses and buggies and wagons can travel, so that we can go to the mercantile, the mill, and attend church! Melted snowmen or no!"

"Oh, yes, I see. And I simply love it—down south. All the beauty…and warmth…speaking of warmth, shall we step inside, my love? And mayhap come back out on the morrow, when the snow is thick enough to really enjoy. I just can't wait!"

"For what?" Maggie smiled up at him.

"I can't wait to help Johnny and you. We'll make history, on the morrow—we'll build our first snowman. And we'll have out first snowball fight!"

"And maybe we'll invite the entire town!" Maggie laughed, "And throw a party! Everyone could bring a covered dish! We could—"

Bart smiled down at her, "You look absolutely lovely! Absolutely radiant! How on earth could I not love you!? You always want to include the entire world—in whatever good is happening in your life, don't you, darling?"

"Right at this moment? No."

"Come inside, and we'll talk about it."

"By the fire?"

"By the fire."

"I'll brew us up a fresh pot of hot coffee."

"You brew up whatever it is that you wish."

The inn was crowded to overflowing. Good food and good conversation flowed, as it does when neighbors come together in a Georgia mountain town. The older children chased one another about the tables laden with food. The older men and women clustered close to the comforting warmth of the huge fireplace piled high with burning oak logs. The younger children napped in their mothers' laps, or on quilts folded and placed safely out of harm's way along the walls, and beneath the tables.

Then, the food cleared away, Bart brought out his violin—and he sent Johnny to fetch his Papa's fiddle. Together, the two of them, man and boy, set the air afire with their glorious tunes of old Scotland. Soon other instruments miraculously appeared. Memories floated about the inn, from room to room, and up the narrow staircase, and Maggie thought of Papa, and Mama, and Nellie Sue, of Grandpa Thomas and Grandma Margaret Ann. Of Great-grandpa Shawn Ian McKinnon, the man who had the vision to leave his beloved Scotland, and journey far across the sea, to a land called *America*, and to a state that would come to be called *Georgia*, and to a little North Georgia mountain town that would come to be called Rhyersville...

The music seemed to enter Maggie's heart, and lift it, and let it float about the room, amongst the warm-hearted, solid, hard-working country folk that filled this town.

But, then there had come an outsider. Wealthy. A Northerner. Cutting down the trees that had stood along the mountainsides since time immemorial.

Now, that man, who had taught Johnny to play Papa's fiddle, had taught Maggie's heart to believe that she might at last find the strength, the courage, the faith, to trust again. Maybe, to even love...

"All right, everyone not asleep or over eighty, grab your coats and come outside! We're going to build the biggest snowman ever seen in this part of the mountains!" Bartram Logan was calling.

A riot erupted, of arms and legs being shoved into coats and heads being covered with hats and scarves. Gloves were snatched on, by those who had them. A mad rush ensued—for the back door. Young and old piled out, into the wintry afternoon. There followed a raucous pummeling with snowballs. All were fair game. Maggie hit Bart squarely in the small of his back, causing him to whirl on her, and chase her madly about the yard, the two of them dashing here and there amongst the other combatants, until no one knew who exactly had been their assailant, amongst those flying orbs of ice.

Then the snowman was built, so big and thick and solid they all stood about in stunned amazement. And Bob Starling, the local post master, finally swore, a hand to his heavily-bearded chin, that the thing would still be standing when the first crop of cotton was picked come next August!

Sleds were produced, and hauled up the side of the slope back of the inn, and the cries of happy children rang over the mountains. Not until dusk settled over the hills and dales and lamps began to be lit, did the people bid one another a fond farewell, and head home.

———————

The following Sunday afternoon, after a lunch at which they were still lingering at table—Bartram Logan, Maggie and Johnny, Barbara Jo, Bethany Lee, and the baby cradled in her young mother's arms—Bart Logan drew Maggie aside and whispered into her ear:

"And just how many *lost souls* do you suppose this small inn will shelter, and leave you enough space to keep The Sparrow Inn open for business?"

"And just what, exactly, was I supposed to *do* Mr. Logan, darling? Scold the homeless girl—big as a barrel and on the imminent verge of bringing a child into the world—in the middle of a wet, icy winter? Scold her, yes, and say, 'Begone with you...you vile creature! There's no room in *this* inn for the likes of you and your fatherless babe! Is *that* what I was supposed to say to the girl, Mr. Logan!? Isn't that exactly what happened to the Christ Child?"

"My sweet, I won't even *begin* to go there! But...did she...perhaps...divulge her little secret, to you?"

"Her little secret, Mr. Logan?"

"Yes, my dear, like...for instance...who the *father* of this darling little babe might be?"

"No. She did not find the will in her heart to let me in on that little tidbit of information, though I did prod and probe with all my considerable might. She adamantly refuses to divulge the name of the sorry fool."

"Sorry fool? Those are rather strong words, aren't they, my sweet?"

"Strong?...Mr. Logan, darling? Strong, did you say? To leave a poor, penniless, wretch of a girl to wander the wintry hills and cold streets? Homeless and...?"

"Yes, I know, sweetheart. But could it be that she hasn't even told this person…whoever he is…that he is a father? Has that thought ever occurred to you?"

"Why on earth wouldn't the girl tell the terrible sod?" Maggie grated from between clenched teeth.

"Well, maybe he's not free…to marry her?"

"Free?"

"Yes, my sweet, maybe the poor fool…is married."

"Married…I never thought of that. That would mean…that he will *never* step forward. Because he *can't*. He'd be absolutely ruined."

"My point *exactly*. And, come to think of it, this *is* a small town. I'm sure this…person…knows exactly where the girl is. I'm further sure that he is well aware that he is the father of a lovely little baby girl. And, if I were to hazard a guess, I'd say that he is absolutely terrified that the girl will spill the beans, so to speak, on him. He could either be a young boy, old enough to father a child, but far from old enough to support a wife and baby. Or there is the very real possibility he could be that other sort of person. A man already bound to a wife. Therefore, my sweet, I wouldn't stand and scan the porches too closely, looking for the missing father of the child to miraculously appear, and assume his heavy responsibilities. It's perfectly clear that if this…person…"

"Oh, Mr. Logan!" Maggie wailed softly, "It never occurred to me, that some man already bound could be so *unthinking*, so *awful*, so *uncaring*, so *vulgar* as to…"

"Yes, all of those are, of course, very apt descriptions of such a cad. But calling him names will not bring the missing father forth out of the woodwork, so to speak."

"*Cad?!*" Maggie fairly shouted, "That's a mild sort of name for such a…Oh! What am I to *do* about her? And the child?"

"Feed them? Cloth them? House them?"

"And for how long?"

"I would not begin to know, my dear. I suppose until God in his good mercies finds them another home. Should you find yourself in need of funds, I would be more than happy to lend some support to—whomever you see the need, sweetheart, to take beneath your roof. Fear not. I shall not allow a one of you to starve! By the by, did I mention how well things are going out at Cottonwood? Rufus already has the men into the spring plowing," Bart went on, moving the conversation along to other subjects.

"I know. Liza Mae, bless her jubilant heart!...has been giving me glowing reports of the progress being made. You have taken an entire village of people beneath your broad wings, Mr. Logan! And here I am complaining about one sister and one homeless girl with a newborn at her breast."

"Well, my sweet, I did not do it without some prodding and urging, remember? And you have cause to complain. Whereas there are what... three...four bedrooms in this inn. Cottonwood had those rows of empty cabins that just cried out for occupants. And these men and women are not only willing, but now that they are eating regularly, they are more than able to swing their own weight. I expect the place to be turning a profit for them, before the year is out. Some of them have been in the woodworking shop, building crude pieces of furniture from all the scrap left over from the furnishings for the log house at McKinnon Valley. And I'm starting immediate construction of a sort of commissary...or store building...or what have you...Rufus Moon is to be in charge of it, solely on the barter system, as Rufus cannot count money, and besides that, not a person of the freedmen possesses any. At least, they will have a small store, where they can trade their produce, handiwork, and so forth, for things like lamp oil or candles or matches. And the other necessities of life, close at hand for them."

"A store? You're building a *mercantile* for the freed slaves, Bartram? Oh, how very, very *wonderful!*" Maggie was overflowing with emotion, which, with Maggie was not all that difficult to achieve, as Bartram Logan had learned.

So Bart hastened to add, "Don't get yourself too excited. Not a mercantile, really, sweetheart. Just a sort...of small...miniscule...really... country store."

"But...still...a *store*, Bartram! Soon you'll have your own little *town*, out there at Cottonwood! What shall we call it, Mr. Logan?... How about *Logan Town?*"

And from that day forth, Maggie began to laughingly refer to the freed slave settlement rapidly growing about the grounds of the big mansion, Cottonwood, *Logan Town*. And the little store became known as the *Logan Town Store*.

Chapter 21

Maggie rose at the crack of dawn. From somewhere within the environs of the little mountain town of Rhyersville, she heard the shrill, insistent crowing of a rooster raising the daily alarm from his domain in a small yard or garden behind some house on down the street.

Maggie slipped out of her warm nightshift and into a work dress she had thrown over the rocker before the fireplace the night before. Slipping on her heavy cotton stockings and little leather boots, Maggie did not bother to light a fire in the upstairs fireplace. She knew she would not have the leisure of spending time upstairs in her cozy bedroom. Not today. The Inn would be open for business, serving three meals, then accepting whatever lodgers offered themselves for the night.

There were potatoes and yams to peel, cabbage heads to be chopped, chicken to be slaughtered, gutted, plucked, singed over the open coals, cut and fried. But…before that…came the fat slabs of hickory smoked ham, the thick patties of home-made sausage, the fresh eggs…biscuits to be baked. Pots of jam, jellies and preserves to be placed upon the tables strewn about the dining room. And she hoped that Liza Mae and Benjamin Noah had already made their way along the cold street of Rhyersville, into the back door of the inn. And that Benjamin Noah had already kindled a fine fire in the big black iron cookstove in the corner of the downstairs kitchen, and one in the huge fireplace in the dining room.

As Maggie began her rapid descent of the stairs, she felt the welcoming warmth of the dining room fireplace, and saw the yellow-orange glow of the fire sweeping over the scattered tables. Benjamin had also lit each oil lamp on each and every table. Soon, Maggie knew, loggers and farmers would be breaking down the door to get into The Sparrow Restaurant & Inn. Several of Bartram Logan's loggers up at the camp on the mountain had recently gotten together and designated one man as courier for the camp. His job: to arise in the predawn of the night, rush down the mountain with his sturdy cart, drawn by a stout mule that could navigate the logging trail in what was oftentimes pitch blackness, to be standing on the narrow front porch of The Sparrow Restaurant & Inn, his huge crate in his hands, in which to cart back up the mountain a few dozen biscuits filled with butter and jelly, ham, or sausage, along with a big black bucket of grits seasoned with honey and butter. He also carried a huge milk tin, which he trusted that Maggie would fill with hot coffee, and which he hoped to somehow manage to transport back up the mountain—without spilling its delicious, steaming black contents. When he reached the logging camp, everything would be re-heated. And ravenously consumed.

Occasionally, the noon meal was handled in somewhat similar fashion.

Maggie sighed now, as she heard the loud banging on the front door. She walked through the dining room, hefted up the heavy bar, and swung the oak door wide.

"Is that you, Tad Horton? How on earth did it fall your lot to make the trip again today? Didn't we just see you down here on Tuesday, for chicken and potatoes and apple pie…was it…for lunch? Or was it supper?"

Dark hair swinging almost to his shoulders, sweat-stained hat held before him in one hand, Tad Horton grinned, "Makes no never mind when it is, they just gobble it up whenever they cin git it, Miss Maggie! Should I just drive the cart 'round back?"

"You just go ahead and do that, Tad," Maggie smiled. "Liza Mae's been baking biscuits and frying ham and sausage since about five o'clock this mornin' I do believe. And coffee's boiling in a pot big as a washtub."

"That sound's great, Miss Maggie. Well, I'll see you around back, I s'pose. And Miss Maggie, Mr. Logan said to tell ya 'Good Mornin'… and some other stuff…"

"Yes, thank you, Tad," Maggie smiled despite herself, "I believe I get the gist of the message. Just drive your cart on around."

As Maggie pushed the front door firmly shut, she heard a small, insistent cry from upstairs.

203

The baby was awake, demanding to be fed. What on earth was wrong with Bethany Lee? The small, insistent cry of ravaging hunger came again, tugging at Maggie's soft heart. Maggie cast an eye to the kitchen, where so much needed to be done, the cart for the loggers loaded…

Maggie turned and tromped quickly up the stairs. Reaching the first room to the left, she shoved open the door and bellowed, "Bethany Lee!!? Can't you hear your little daughter begging her Mama to be fed?!"

"What, Mizzzz Evans? I don't feel none too well this mornin'. I don't know that I can feed this chil'. She stinks, too. Needs changin', and a bath, I 'spect." The girl's hair was tousled, her light eyes swollen with sleep.

"Yes, Bethany Lee," Maggie said, impatiently flinging back the covers. The tiny little girl, perfect but for the howling scowl on her red face, peered up at Maggie with beautiful blue eyes brimming with tears of angry indignation, hunger, and discomfort. Her tiny hands were balled into fists that trembled and shook with outrage.

Maggie scooped the baby into her arms, cooed to her for a moment until she grew quiet, then turned to the young mother who had turned her back on Maggie and the baby, evidently planning to sink back into the warm folds of peaceful slumber, minus the problem of the tiny infant howling ear-splitting cries.

"Bethany Lee…" Maggie began, "I know your milk should be down by now. I'll take her downstairs, heat up some water and clean her up and change her. Then, when I bring her back to you, I expect you to roust yourself up and let this child nurse! Do you hear me, Bethany Lee?"

"Yes'm…" came the muffled, resentful reply.

"And another thing," Maggie called to the girl from the door. "*Today* you are going to choose a name for this beautiful little girl. She is three days old today. And in all good Christian conscience, we cannot allow her any longer to be called simply *Baby*. Are you awake? Do you hear me, Bethany Lee!?"

"Yes'm. But…I's don't kno' whut ta call her…."

"Well, see if you can stay awake for fifteen or twenty minutes, at least? And give this very important matter a bit of consideration!" Maggie flung back over her shoulder very sarcastically, as she swung angrily down the stairs, the little babe in the crook of her left arm. Reaching the warmth of the kitchen, her right hand free, she snatched up the pewter washbasin and slowly poured in some warm water from the big black iron kettle on the back of the stove.

She searched on a shelf in one corner of the kitchen for a clean cotton cloth with which to bath the tiny infant, who felt in the crook of Maggie's arm, as light as a feather. If Bethany Lee didn't revive herself up, if she didn't begin to consume enough food to form milk for this child, how would the tiny thing survive? She certainly knew of no wet nurse that might be available. Then suddenly Maggie recalled the little herd of goats roaming and cropping the pastures out in McKinnon Valley. Maybe, this afternoon, when things quieted down, she'd either ride out there herself, or send Benjamin Noah, to see if he could find a nanny goat that was in, that could be brought back and maybe chained in the back of the inn, in the grass line along the trees that grew up the slope of the mountains. Probably not enough wild forage growing there, though, to feed even one hungry goat…

Suddenly the day yawned before her. She doubted very much that with all that was going on at the inn there would be enough hours in the day to accomplish what needed to be done…what with Barbara Jo still abed about half the time…and Johnny needing some bathing up and breakfast…and with all the meals for customers to prepare… And Maggie felt a huge, yawning guilt, at the lack of time she spend lately with Johnny. There seemed, since Fred Moss had gone to his eternal reward, sending Barbara Jo into an emotional tailspin, and Bethany Lee had shown up on the back porch of the inn, no time to do anything with her small brother any more.

Perhaps she'd involve Johnny in the washing and dressing of the infant. He was so interested in everything living. And what was more alive than this lovely, perfectly formed little girl that howled and wiggled and protested so vigorously in Maggie's arms at this very moment?

Maggie turned to Johnny. His little head resting on one hand, as if he was not yet wide enough awake for his body to support it, he sat at the table half asleep, a bowl of sweet oats before him. His spoon halted mid-air between bites, Johnny looked up and grinned at Maggie.

"That Baby…she *sure* is…noisy…" Johnny mumbled, oats dribbling down his chin.

"Don't wipe your mouth on your sleeve, Johnny," Maggie smiled at him. Then she looked at him and asked, "You about finished there? Okay. Why don't you drink your sweet milk, and then come on into the dining room. I have so much to do lately, with this new babe here with us and all, I sure could use your help with her." Maggie gave him the full force of a worried frown, as if, without his help, care of the infant would surely fall through the cracks of the floor.

Even as Maggie was speaking, Johnny grabbed up the cup of milk, drained it in three gulps, then leapt down off the bench, and was by her side, gazing up with wide, excited eyes.

"Can I hold her, Maggie? Can I help you, by totin' her into th' dining room so she will be warm beside the fireplace for her bath? Is that what you want me ta do?"

Maggie gazed down at the beautiful little face, so earnest, so filled with concern, little hands hanging by his side. She wondered absently just how many folks those little hands would heal—should Johnny actually grow up to be a doctor. "That's exactly what I want you to do. Put out your arms, Doctor John Thomas McKinnon, Jr. You are about to have your first lesson in the care and feeding of infants. What do you think about that?"

"Wow! Gee! That's…great!…put her right here…right here on my arms. See how strong I am, Maggie? Boy! She don't weight nothin' hardly!"

"She weights hardly anything, Johnny," Maggie corrected.

"Yeah! Ain't that what I just said?!"

"Yes, sweetie. You are so strong!" Maggie smiled as she laid the tiny infant of a few pounds across Johnny's small, outstretched arms.

The little girl seemed to know something was different. She hushed her howling, opened perfect blue eyes wide and wider, and peered up into the face of John Thomas McKinnon, Jr. And Maggie could have sworn that despite her tender age, the baby had just smiled at Johnny.

"She likes me! Maggie? See? She likes me!" Johnny was beside himself with excitement, as he held this fragile piece of new life.

"Okay," Maggie bent toward Johnny, a hand resting lightly on his small shoulder. "Now just turn, and take small steps, very small, very careful, not letting your arms droop one tiny bit, until we reach the chair beside the warmth of the hearth in the corner of the dining room. You know the one."

"Where she had her bath yesterday? And you dressed her in that new dress you made."

"Yes," Maggie whispered, her heart twisting painfully in her chest. One of the small garments she had sewn during those awful months of waiting for

206

the birth of her first child…in the little sharecroppers' house…

With small, sure steps, Johnny, the tiny babe cradled securely in his arms, marched straight-backed around the kitchen table, through the door and into the dining room, up to the chair Maggie had placed near the hearth. Maggie followed close behind, carrying the pewter washbasin filled with tepid water.

"Hold her for just a moment, more, sweetie," Maggie said, as she made her way to the side of the huge fireplace, tossed on a new log, and gave the fire a poke or two.

Then Maggie spread a folded quilt on the corner of the table near the fire, bent and picked up the small stack of clean clothing she had place on a chair in readiness for the bathing session, laid it onto the corner of the dining table, and said, "Now, Doctor Johnny, if you will kindly give the baby to me…"

Maggie laid the tiny little girl gently on a clean sheet spread over the layers of quilts, and turned to Johnny. "Now, let's begin, shall we? And would you, Doctor McKinnon, like to wash Baby's face for her?"

"Sure, Maggie," Johnny pulled his beautiful little face into an important looking frown and asked, "Where do I start?"

"First you take this very, very soft cloth…"

The tiny baby, somehow sensing that she was the center of attention, cooed, wiggled and kicked her legs, and waved her arms frantically in the air.

"Dip it into the warm water, and twist it, like this, getting all the excess water out so you don't drown the poor little thing and wet this quilt padding. Then…you just gently drape it over your hand. That's right, Dr. McKinnon, then you take your fingers and spread them out beneath the cloth, and you touch it to the baby's face, and you begin to rub and rub…in all directions, even the hair and all behind the ears. Now the neck. And I think we need to rinse the cloth out and make a new beginning. But, my, Dr. McKinnon, you are doing an excellent job!"

"Don't we use no soap? Even the kind ya put flower petals inta?"

"No, sweetie. Not on a baby this young. Her skin is very fragile. Very tender. For now, after we wash her all over, we'll just rub her with a bit of sweet oil. To keep her skin soft. But in a few more days, yes she will require a bit of soap."

"Seems like ta me," Johnny announced with squinted eyes and wiggling nose, "she could use a swipe or two of it now. She sure does stink!"

"Oh, Johnny! She's a baby! She uses the bathroom in her cloth diaper! And she will, young sir, for quite a while yet. Just the way you used to do!"

"*No*, I didn't!"

"Oh, yes, you did! We all did! And then her Mama will have to take the cotton squares and boil them in the big iron washpot out back. At least, I hope her Mama will do that! Then rinse them very, very clean of soap, and hang them in the sunshine to dry. Then she'll be all fresh and clean with each new change.

"And now that the face, hair and neck are clean, we'll move on to the little hands and arms."

"I can do that, too," Johnny announced with a stern wag of his head.

"Yes, dear, I'm sure you can. Just be very, very careful to rub gently between each tiny finger, and in all the little folds of her skin. That's right, so she doesn't get a rash, or anything. You must keep a baby very, very clean, to keep her healthy."

"Well!" Johnny announced smartly, "We sure want her good and healthy! So she can grow up and help me scout the mountains, for ginseng and ..."

Oh, no! Maggie murmured to herself, *I do hope she won't be here that long! I hope I can get her mother to divulge who the father is...*

"Well! Well! It's bath time, is it?"

"Why, Mr. Logan! I never expected to see you at this hour! Scarcely after dawn, and before breakfast is even on the table! From what Tad Horton said, the greeting you sent, I thought...you were up on the mountain for the day."

"Well, I just decided to come on down into town and check on the mercantile and a few things."

"Is something amiss at the mercantile? With Mr. McAlister?"

"Not with McAlister himself, but I understand he's having a bit of a problem with one of the lads. It seems he and his father had a falling out, and he has gone missing."

"Oh, I'm sorry to hear that. Now, moving right along. Johnny, maybe I'd better take it from here. I have to remove her undershirt and diaper, and I'm not at all sure that you gentlemen want to be in on that...rather soiled affair."

"We're tough, aren't we Johnny? Go right ahead, sweetheart, we can take it. Or, if you'd rather, I'm sure Johnny and I can handle the remainder of this little job ourselves."

"Oh, you can? Well, then, Mr. Logan, I find that I am suddenly needed very urgently in the kitchen! Here, beside the washbasin, awaits Baby's little bottle of sweet oil, her clean diapers, her change of undershirt, tummy band, and nightie. Call me, will you, when she's ready to be carried back upstairs...to her mother."

Bartram Logan watched Maggie's slender back quickly disappear through the kitchen doorway. And the next instant the swinging shutter closed with a firm bang.

"Well, sometimes I find we men don't have the good sense to keep our fool mouths shut! What do you think, Dr. McKinnon? Are the two of us up to this tremendous task?"

"Sure, Bart!" Johnny piped up. "But...I'll wash her chest and back, and she sure does stink. So I'll leave you the other parts."

"Oh? Yes, well. I might have figured as much. Just let me remove my coat jacket here, and roll up these white shirtsleeves, while you're finishing your part of the job. Did you get into the little folds of skin beneath the back of her neck, Johnny? Seems to me I detect a speck of cotton fuzz in there."

"Got it, Bart!" Then, wiping his nose on his arm, Johnny asked very softly, "Bart?"

Bart glanced down at Johnny.

The small boy was staring up at him, very earnestly, "Where did Baby come from? One day she wasn't here. And the next day...she was?"

"Well...Johnny," Bart's tanned brow knit in a deep frown as he stammered about, searching for the proper reply. "She came from God, like all the rest of us."

"But...Bart...how did God git her here?"

"You have a Bible, Johnny?" Bart asked, a smile tilting up the corners of his full lips.

"Sure. I keep it in the kitchen, where I can find it real easy, come Sunday mornin'"

"Then, Johnny, why don't you just go and fetch it?"

Johnny bounced into the kitchen, snatched his Bible from its place on a shelf.

"What are you doing?" Maggie asked, her back to Johnny, as she stood at the big black iron cookstove.

"Bart's going ta show me where Baby com'ed from."

"He...*what!?*" Maggie whirled about, wiping sweaty palms on her snow-white apron, and followed Johnny as he bounced through the door to the dining room.

"Well," Bart's gaze met Maggie's look of concern, "Let's just open the Book to the 1st Chapter of Genesis, Johnny." Bart took the small Bible and flipped open its leather lid. "Ah, yes, and here we go. See, Johnny, right here, it says, and I quote:

"And God said, Let the earth bring forth grass,
the herb yielding seed, and the fruit-tree yielding fruit
after his kind whose seed is in itself, upon the earth:
and so it was."

"But, that's trees...and stuff..." Johnny's beautiful little face drew into a puzzled scowl.

"Well, sure, but, Johnny, you see, God made men, also, and though the Bible doesn't say it here, specifically, He put seeds in them, too."

Maggie stood gazing at Bart. She recalled very vividly what Mama had said to her, when, as a little girl of seven or eight, she had asked that crucial question. *God gives every man a little sack of seed. And when the season's right, Maggie, he...plants them,* Mama said...

Gazing now into Bartram Logan's eyes, Maggie realized that every man, no doubt Bartram Logan included, had this God-given urge—to grow a man like himself. Bartram Logan wanted a son.

"Oh," Johnny shrugged a small shoulder, "now what do we do next, with Baby?'

Giving a wag of her head, Maggie turned to head back into the kitchen.

"Well! Now, I just suppose we sort...of flip her over...here..."

"You have to hold onto her head all the time. Maggie told me that."

"Yes, well. I knew that."

"How, Bart? How did you know that?"

"I...had a little boy of my own...Johnny. He's gone now. Had he lived, he would have...been about your age."

"Where is he now, Bart?"

"Up in Heaven, Johnny, with his mother."

"That's him, ain't it Bart? In one of the little graves behind the church?"

"Yes, Johnny, it is. But it's been a long time now. And new babies are born, and the clocks on our mantels tick on."

"I know, Bart," little Johnny heaved a big sigh. "Like my Mama and Papa. I remember my Mama, a little bit. I try to remember her. But, Papa...I never have seen my Papa"

"Yes, Johnny, you have, son. Every time you look into the mirror. Our blood continues to flow; our lives go on, Johnny, in our children. Your Papa's blood, and his seed, they're in you."

"Wouldn't you like to have some more babies, Bart, some live ones, like Baby here? But she is noisy. And she does stink."

"Maybe the Good Lord will, one of these fine days, see fit to bless me...to have some live ones, Johnny. And this one here, she won't stink. Not for long. Now, if you're finished with the upper parts, we'll just remove these pins here. Let me see if I recall just how to do this. Then we remove the belly band—"

"What's that for?" Johnny peered close and looked on as Bartram Logan gently removed the narrow band of cotton cloth that had been snugly wound about the perfect little body.

"I suppose, since you're an up-and-coming physician, Dr. McKinnon, you should be privy to these things. That is wound about her to prevent any bulging out, or any rupture or injury to her little belly, Johnny. You see this black, dried-up looking thing? That will drop off in another day or so. In fact, it looks as if it's about ready to come off—this very day." Bart bent closely and stared at the dried end of the cord. Gingerly he closed two fingers about it, and gave a tiny lift. "Ah! And there we go! It's off, and she is flat as a flitter, and clean as a whistle! Now, just a gentle swipe with our clean cloth, and then you can rub on a few drops of oil, just a drop or two, Johnny, on your fingertip. And that should do it. Then we go to other things. Hand me that clean diaper, there. We must have everything in complete preparedness, for this part of the operation. We certainly don't want to tarry at it overlong!"

Bart opened one diaper pin and removed it, then the second, and laid back the boiled cotton cloth.

"Phhewwwwweeeee!" Johnny snorted, suddenly grasping his nose.

211

Her blue eyes gazing straight up at him, her minuscule hands pounding the air viciously, as if she were afraid she was about to be dropped, Bart was taking the little form with his big warm fingers by its tiny feet, and raising the little bottom out of the stinking mess that lay pooled about her. With deft motions of the clean ends of the swaddle of the diaper, Bart removed as much of the soiling as he could. Then he lowered Baby's feet back to her quilt pad and proceed to wash the remainder away, oil the areas well, and swaddle her in a clean diaper.

"Now, Dr. McKinnon, if you would please just work that clean gown or frock or whatever it is, over her little head, I think we're about done here! And I do believe we're not one minute too soon. I believe she's about fed up with this entire operation, and wanting to be returned up the stairs to the warmth of her mother's bosom and bed!"

"Yeah!" Johnny moaned in disgust, "Look at 'er! She's tryin' ta eat her hands!"

Bart gave a hearty laugh, cradled the infant up beneath his chin, and laid a big hand on her head and back for firm support. How long, since he had done this? Held a newborn infant against his chest? Five years....five...long...years...

Suddenly the kitchen door swung open. Maggie walked slowly into the dining room. There stood Mr. William Bartram Logan, a pleased grin on his handsome face, a clean-smelling, perfectly washed and oiled infant swaddled against his chest.

"Well! I suppose you're right proud and pleased with yourself!" Maggie cocked her lovely head aside and teased.

"That I am, my sweet. But I fear I can't take all the credit for this beautiful little production. I did have some help from my very able assistant, here. I believe you are somewhat acquainted with the well known physician, Doctor John Thomas McKinnon, Jr., from over Rhyersville way?"

"Yes," Maggie smiled, enjoying the game they were playing immensely, thinking how natural Mr. William Bartram Logan looked, a newborn infant clasped to his muscular chest, a glow of love in those gold-flecked eyes. It seemed there was nothing this man before her could not accomplish—when he set his mind to it. He was just too, too perfect to be quite real... "I'll take Baby up to her mother. Before she gnaws her little fingers to the bones. And you, *Papa* Logan, why don't you make your way into the kitchen for your hot breakfast and waiting coffee?"

The words were out of her mouth before she could stop them. Why on earth had she called him *that?*

Wagging her head, Maggie made her way up the stairs and along the narrow hallway.

"Well, here she is. Your lovely little daughter! All cleaned and ready for breakfast. Bethany Lee!" The girl lay unmoving as a log. Holding the baby in the crook of her left arm, Maggie reached and flung back the covers with her right hand. "Bethany Lee! Turn yourself over here, and feed your daughter! And while she's eating, try to collect yourself enough to settle on a name for this beautiful little child!"

Maggie tenderly deposited the perfect little form onto the feather bed covered with freshly laundered sheets. Maggie thought it such a beautiful picture, if only Bethany Lee would comb her frowsy red hair, and remove that ugly scowl from her pretty face, and at least put on a pretense that she loved and cherished this warm, tiny bundle.

With a long sigh, Maggie turned and made her way back downstairs, to find Bartram Logan seated at the kitchen table, enjoying a fine breakfast, Johnny at his elbow. And the two of them were keeping up a running conversation on boxing moves, the coming violin lesson, and the pony, Apples. Oftentimes Maggie felt the slightest twinge of resentment, that Bartram Logan had wormed his way so thoroughly, so warmly into little Johnny's affections. It was becoming clearer by the day to Maggie, that her small brother all but worshiped the tall, handsome, strikingly rich Bartram Logan. And it bothered her greatly. Should she marry Mr. Logan, what would be the effect on Johnny of all that attention heaped on his small head by this Philadelphia businessman, this owner of a vast estate in England, what effect would it have on the simple life she and Johnny were accustomed to leading?

Maggie realized with a start, as she gazed now into Mr. Bartram Logan's gold-flecked brown eyes, that she, Maggie McKinnon Evans, had never been farther south than the tiny country village of Cumming, Georgia, down on the Chattahoochee. Nor farther north than the small mountain village of Hiawassee. Nor farther east that the Logan Estate of Cottonwood—now the growing little farming community called Logan Town. Nor had Maggie gone farther west than the Stillwell horse farm! Hers had been a limited world, indeed, when compared to that of Mr. Bartram Logan…and the other disparities in lifestyle that loomed between them. To Maggie, one hundred dollars was an entire fortune. To Mr. Bartram Logan, Maggie now knew, it was a mere flash in the pan, chicken feed, something he would plunk down onto a store counter or spend on a fine suit or a fine meal, and never give it a second thought. Could Maggie ever live like that? Did she wish too? Did she wish that sort of life for Johnny? But…then…there was Johnny's dream of attending medical college…

"Well, that's certainly a somber look on that lovely face of yours this morning, sweetheart!" Bartram Logan mused, rising from his chair as she stood gazing down at him. Gallantly Mr. Logan pulled out a chair, and with one strong brown hand motioned her towards it. "Aren't you joining us for breakfast? Or, was I horribly impolite to begin the meal, without asking you beforehand? Johnny was starving, and Liza Mae tempted me with this plate…is something amiss, my sweet?"

"No," Maggie slipped into the chair upon whose back Mr. Logan's firm grip still rested. Suddenly she felt very tired, overwhelmed, when she thought of this man, standing here gazing down at her with those warm brown eyes, and of the small boy, greedily gulping down his sweet oats. And of her older sister, recently widowed, and it appeared, firmly of a mind to languish away the remainder of her life, her lassitude broken only by short trips between the kitchen, the outhouse, and her bed. Then there was the girl, scarcely more than a child herself, a newborn infant beside her in one of Maggie's beds… A child the girl seemed to regard as more of a pest and a nuisance, than the beloved fruit of her body.

"Want a bite of my biscuit?" Bartram Logan teased, not at all pleased with the look on that lovely face. "I'm always happy to share. Especially with such a beautiful breakfast companion. Margaret Ann?"

"What? Oh, no, thank you. I might just get another cup of coffee…and a biscuit of my own…"

Bart was up out of his chair, and in a moment back, holding in his right hand a plate laden with scrambled eggs, a huge sausage patty, a biscuit as big as his fist dripping with butter and jam.

"And just how, my sweet," Bart grinned at her as he retook his chair, "does that strike your fancy?"

"Really, Mr. Logan, darling," Maggie snapped tiredly, "you don't have to wait on me! I am perfectly capable…"

"You are tired to the bone," Bart said softly. "You are worn out from carrying the world on your lovely shoulders. Even you, Margaret Ann McKinnon, are not up to fending for the entire creation."

"No. You are entirely correct, Mr. Logan. I am not. And I fully intend…"

"What, exactly, is it that you *do* intend, my dearest?"

Maggie chewed and swallowed thoughtfully, attempting to frame a reply, before raising her blue-blue gaze to meet Mr. Bartram Logan's gold-flecked stare.. "I don't really know…yet. But…I intend making some sort of *decisions*…and soon."

"Yes…well…" Bartram Logan mused thoughtfully, "in the meantime, have you given consideration to taking a holiday…from all your…many and varied responsibilities?"

"A *holiday?*" Maggie gazed at him as if he had just suggested flying to the moon.

"Yes, my sweet. I…find…that…I must shortly take ship for England. It seems that I must make a journey there in person, to the barristers' offices, you see, to take care of this business about the inheritance from my mother's great uncle."

"England? You're…taking ship…for England? But…when?"

"Sullivan & Sullivan, the firm of barristers handling the entire affair have their offices, I understand, in the heart of London. It is to London, then, that I must go, and to their offices located just off Trafalgar Square, on Fleet Street. I need to book passage immediately." Bartram Logan was staring intently into Maggie's blue-blue eyes.

Maggie reached very thoughtfully for her cup, took a long sip of the delicious hot coffee, raised her gaze again to Bart's eyes, and asked simply, "And just where, Mr. Logan, darling, is this conversation leading?"

"Well…sweetheart…here's what I came to say to you…today…"

"Yes, Mr. Logan? Please…do go on."

"I want you, and of course, Johnny, to come with me."

Maggie's heavy pottery cup hit its matching saucer with a loud clatter. She felt an odd fluttering in her stomach.

"Surely…you…don't…you can't mean…?"

"With a *chaperone*, of course, sweetheart. Anyone of your choosing."

"And just whom, do you suppose, from this small village in the mountains of Northern Georgia, I could choose to accompany me *to London, England, as chaperone*?!"

"How about…your sister…Mrs. Moss?"

"Barbara Jo? She scarcely draws on her day clothes, or leaves the familiar confines of her room! Do you, then, Mr. Logan, darling, suppose that such a reclusive creature as Barbara Jo has become, is going to be chomping at the bit, so to speak, to make a journey across the wide Atlantic Ocean, to the gigantic, cosmopolitan megalopolis of *London, England*?! You must be out of your mind! You do not *know* Barbara Jo! If she thought for one instant I actually *wanted* her to go…"

"Then, don't let on that you actually *want* her to go. You could pretend that you find the whole idea absurd, and that it is only a passing fancy. That I put forth the notion to you, and you immediately brushed the entire thing off—a trip of a lifetime, that you are certain she would find totally obnoxious to all her sensibilities?"

"I don't know why we're even…having this ridiculous conversation," Maggie rose from the table and flounced over to the dry sink. Her back to him, she gripped the edge of the dry sink stand, to keep herself from swooning away. *A trip to England!*…he had just said? Was that what the man had just said?! How often, even as a child, had she dreamt of just such a thing? And here the man stood, his heart in his eyes, offering to take her and Johnny to *London*! An ocean voyage! Across the vast Atlantic! *London!*

Then Maggie straightened her shoulders and lifted her head. Her gaze rose from the dry sink, stacked high with dirty dishes, and swept the kitchen of The Sparrow Inn. And upstairs lay Barbara Jo…the girl…and her fatherless babe…

"I…couldn't possibly…it sounds…wonderful…but I couldn't possibly. I have the inn, and Bethany Lee, and the baby…"

"Bethany Lee and the baby are not your responsibility, Margaret Ann," Bartram Logan interjected sternly. "Besides, the girl will be well on her feet, and well able to feed and see to the infant by the time our ship sails. And as to the inn, Liza Mae knows all the ins and outs of running the place. And

Benjamin Noah. And if need be, I'll hire one or two persons to come in and assist. You are without excuse, my dear. Would you like me to broach the subject to your sister, or would you prefer to do that yourself?"

"Will you, Mr. Logan, be staying for a while, and say, joining us for lunch? Barbara Jo should be up and about…by that hour, I would expect."

"Yes. If you think that best, I shall indeed busy myself about the place for the space of the next few hours. And Johnny and I shall find ourselves a quiet corner, where I propose to show him a book I have on the place, so that he will be somewhat familiar with what his young eyes are about to behold."

"Pretty certain of yourself, aren't you, Mr. Logan? Pretty certain of having your own way. Getting exactly what you want?"

"I do…work at it, yes, my sweet. I do that very thing. And I have no intentions of denying it. Now, will you be gracing us with your sweet presence, as we peruse the lovely books I have brought?'

"Books?…is it, then?" Maggie cocked a smooth brow at him, and Bart grinned.

"London, such a large city. Palaces, and towers and cathedrals…and the surrounding countryside, so diverse in landscape and in the products from its factories and fields."

"Any particular fields, you had in mind?"

"Yes, sweetheart, as a matter of fact, I had in mind the countryside south of London. The lovely rolling fields and hills of West Surrey. From there, when the weather is fine, so I understand, one can take coach into London for a fine day of shopping and dining. And, of course, for you and Johnny and me, fine, fine days of sightseeing. London is chock-full of magnificent historic sights that dazzle the mind and blind the eye. Or, so I'm told."

"Yes," Maggie muttered up at him, "I have read about it in books. But I never dreamed once in my life…I'll just go on up then, and see if Bethany Lee is yet of a mind to give that lovely little babe a name."

Maggie flew away up the stairs, her brain in a whirl. It was a stunning dream, a surreal vision, the idea of seeing London, England. But, she assured herself with a brisk shake of her head that it was no more than that. She couldn't possibly…actually leave the inn for…weeks…it would take weeks to make such a trip…and how long did Mr. Bartram Logan plan to linger, looking after this business of his?…assuming ownership of this new estate?…sightseeing through the beautiful streets of historic London…? And *the cost…*

Maggie pushed open the door to the room Bethany Lee was occupying, to find the girl snoring softly, blissfully oblivious to the baby grumbling and rutting against her, as if half starved.

"Oh," Maggie rushed forward, lifting the baby and cradling her in her arms, cooing, "You poor little tyke. Bethany Lee! Rouse yourself up here, girl! Did you, or did you not, make a sturdy effort to get this child to nurse?!"

"She sucks and sucks on me, but she never seems to be satisfied. It's beginning to wear on my nerves, it t'is."

"Wear on your nerves? Your child is starving, and that is all the comment you have to make about this awful situation. Wear on your nerves?"

"Well, what's it ye 'spect me ta say?"

"Well!" Maggie snapped, "Certainly something with a little more concern, a bit more heart in it. Are you going to come downstairs for breakfast? If you moved around a bit more, ate more, drank a bit more sweet milk—"

"Don't got no appetite…fer no food much. And I never did cotton to drinking much milk. We never seed non', in th' cove."

"Well, Bethany Lee, sometimes, when someone has a need greater than our own, we just have to force ourselves to lift our chins up, square our jaw, and to do things that might not exactly suit our fancy. Have you given that fact any thought at all?"

"No'm, cin't say's I 'ave."

"Well, then, there you go! And have you given any thought to a name for this lovely little babe of yours?"

"Yes'm," Bethany Lee's faded eyes lit up for an instant, "Yes'm, I've sure gone and done that. I'm agonna call 'er *Sam!*"

Maggie stared at the girl, her mouth half open, "*Sam*?—Bethany Lee? But…*Sam*…that's a boy's name. A *man's* name. Just because someone gave you a man's name…"

"You mean 'Lee? Well, my Pap done wanted a boy, not no girl, so he said at least I could have one boy's name. So he tacked on the name of the Gener'l."

"Robert E…."

"Yes'm."

"But, Bethany Lee, *Sam*? Surely you must mean Samantha?"

"No'm." Bethany Lee's eyes had resumed their blank, hollow stare, as if whatever spark the name *Sam* had kindled had just as quickly died away, and with it all hope. "But if'n tha's whut ya want ta make of it, you can call her *Samanthie*, but *I'll* be a callin'er *Sam*."

Bethany Lee glared at Maggie, a deep frown wrinkling her pretty brow, light eyes squinted almost shut in angry defiance. "She is, adder all, *my* chil'!"

"Well, yes. Of course…she is…but…" Maggie began haltingly, scenes flitting through her mind of a lovely little dark-haired girl skipping about the schoolyard, being teased and tormented unmercifully, the other children chanting at her heels: *Saaammmm! Saaammmm! Oughta be a man…*

Maggie pasted on a weak smile. The baby cradled against her, she turned, saying, "Ummmm…well…I'll just carry little….*Samantha*…on downstairs, and see if there's any milk of any sort we can drop into her mouth. To try to fatten her up a bit." Maggie felt all sorts of conflicting emotions as she descended the stairs, the tiny bundle warm against the crook of her arm. She felt the need to protect this child from her own mother! And at the same time, the need to get this mother and her child out from beneath her roof, and beneath the roof of the man who had planted a seed and grown this child, and then forsaken all his responsibilities. The need to speak to Barbara Jo… And would there also soon be the need to begin packing?…and this was Sunday morning. And it was clear to Maggie that there was no way under heaven she was going to make the church service. Not with the baby and…

Maggie reached the kitchen, a frown on her face, the baby in her arms. She asked Liza Mae to draw up the sweet milk from the cool depths of the well. How on earth would they get it into the child?

As Maggie stood pondering and murmuring about this dilemma, Bartram Logan offered, "There is some sort of…bottle…things…down at the mercantile. I hear that now some mothers, when the need, of course, arises, use them to replace…"

"Oh?" Maggie turned and stared at him, her ire rising. "You, Mr. Bartram Logan, never cease to amaze me. You have an answer for *everything*! Don't you? You are just a *bottomless repository* of little bits and pieces of various kinds and sorts of knowledge. And just what other information are you privy to, that might help me in this disastrous situation!?"

219

"Johnny and I could stroll down to the store, and pick up a few of those bottle…things…then after lunch, maybe we could ride out to McKinnon Valley, and look over that little herd of goats. Goat's milk, so I've been told, sets well on the stomach of some infants. Better, perhaps, than that of the cow?"

"Yes! Well! I've thought of goat's milk, but the opportunity to check on it has somehow failed to present itself, with everything else that's going on hereabouts!" Maggie snapped, "Well, go on, then, the two of you! What are you waiting for? Can't you see this child is starving? Liza Mae, do you have that milk up out of the well yet?! Put a bit into a pan, then, so we can warm it on the stove. Hopefully those two won't dawdle too long, and will be back here with the…bottle…things…Lord only knows whether little Samantha with take to such an odd…contraption!"

Little Samantha, who was starving, had taken immediately to bottle feeding, but Bartram Logan sat at the end of the kitchen table of the Sparrow Inn, picking at his food. Maggie noted that for a man of such usually ravenous and appreciative appetite, Mr. Bart Logan appeared more than a bit off his feed.

Maggie felt about the same way. Not half a dozen words had passed around the table, since Maggie herself had offered up a short word of thanks to the Lord for the food. Johnny sat gazing with wide blue eyes from one face to the other of the grownups, wondering which of them would first broach the subject of the coming trip to London. He and Bart had brought back the needed bottles with rubber caps, and then had settled themselves into one big rocker before the fireplace. Johnny, boring deep into Bart's muscular left thigh with his elbow, had leaned eagerly against Bart to get a better look at the picture books about London. He was hungry and making ravenously at his food. Let the grownups do as they pleased; he intended to clean his plate, so that he might be offered a huge hunk of that sweet-smelling gingerbread for dessert.

His face the absolute picture of innocence, Bart gazed over at Maggie and muttered, "Oh, did I happen to mention to you, just in passing, of course, that I might be required to make a trip to London, England…fairly…soon?"

"Oh, is that right?" Maggie raised smooth brows and met his gaze, her face as straight as a poker.

"Yes. It seems that I have come into...some sort...of inheritance. Some properties...I believe. I received a letter from a firm of London barristers. Did I fail to mention that to you? Well, I suppose I did. Sorry. At any rate, the thought crossed my mind...just a flicker of a thought...you understand...that perhaps you...and young Johnny here...might be of a mind to accompany me."

"Why, Mr. Logan...!" Maggie gaped at Bart as if he had lost all reason, "How could we *possibly* do that? And us not even married!?"

"Well, it did occur to me, that in order to keep the whole trip on a proper keel, you could invite along...someone to act as chaperone. Such things, in the very politest of societies, are done all the time. I would, of course, cover all expenses. We would maintain separate staterooms, and separate quarters at whatever lodgings or inns presented themselves upon our journey. But there would be the dire necessity, I suppose, for a...chaperone."

"Oh?" Maggie gazed at him with amazed eyes, "And just whom, Mr. Logan?...did you have in mind for an ever so onerous task? No." Maggie cast her gaze sorrowfully down at her plate. "On the face of it, it sounds like a marvelous trip. But totally, totally out of the question, Mr. Logan. The way things are here at the inn...I don't see how that could possibly work out. I'm sorry. But I fear I must decline your generous invitation outright. And, if you don't mind, Mr. Logan, darling, in order not to get our hopes up for no cause at all, I ask that you not speak on this subject again."

"Maggie!" Barbara Jo dropped her fork with a loud clatter that brought all eyes to her face. "How can you refuse an opportunity like this? All your life, you've talked, you've dreamed of just such a trip. Now...*you blithely dismiss it...out of hand?*!"

"But...Barbs..." Maggie gave her sister a look of gravest concern. "Whatever would you do? How would you possibly manage? Left all alone, here at the inn? Here you are, still languishing in such deep grief over your loss of *poor Fred* that you're scarcely able to drag yourself out of bed, dress, and stumble down the stairs. I wouldn't *dream*, Barbs, of sailing off over the wide Atlantic, and leaving you here...alone...in such a state of—"

"Well, no. I don't suppose you could...do that...but then...I could always…force myself to go along. I'd most assuredly hate to think that *I* was the cause of your missing such a grand journey…yes…that's it…" Barbara lifted her little chin and stuck her small, upturned nose in the air, as if making the grandest sacrifice ever known to mankind. "I shall travel along…as chaperone," she announced. "When do we leave?"

Maggie was initially thrilled at the prospect of a voyage to England. But over the next week, as the reality of actually leaving the inn beneath someone else's care for such an extended period, of traveling in close companionship and in such close quarters in company with Mr. Bartram Logan sank in, Maggie began to entertain grave doubts as to the state of her sanity, in leading Mr. Bartram Logan to the conclusion that she and Johnny would, could, make such an extensive, such an expensive journey. The more thought she devoted to the matter, the more absolutely ludicrous the entire idea became, until she burst out from beneath her covers one night and hissed into the darkness:

"I *must* have been *out of my mind!*"

"I must have been out of mind!" were the exact words that came out of Maggie's mouth, the following Sunday afternoon, after she had spent a restless night tossing over and over in her mind the countless impediments to such a trip. "I can't even begin to imagine, Mr. Logan, whatever possessed me to arrive, albeit for only a few days, at such a ridiculous conclusion—as to think that I could leave the inn, could leave that girl and her child. Could take ship to London, England! I must have been out of mind!"

"Oh?" Bart had seated himself across from Maggie before the huge fireplace in the dining room of the inn. He leaned forward now in his chair and repeated softly, "Oh?"

"Yes. I mean, no. I absolutely cannot go. It is past all reason for a…"

"And why is that, my dearest?" Bart continued to stare at her with dark eyes, as he slowly stroked his smoothly shaven chin and spoke ever so softly. "Why is that?"

"Well…as I have just said…and there is…the inn…and also the expense …and Johnny…he is so small."

"The running of the inn is taken care of. And I can well afford the expense. It is not, as the old saying goes, a drop in the bucket, sweetheart. And as to Johnny, I do believe his little heart would break, if now…after he has as good as been told outright that he is to make this trip, and then to crush his dreams…would be cruel beyond belief."

"Well…" Maggie hemmed and hawed, "And what about Barbara Jo? I'm certain that she doesn't really feel up to this trip."

"Well, why don't you call her downstairs, my sweet, and ask her?"

Maggie rose from her chair, gathered her full skirts in her hand, and moved to the base of the narrow staircase, where she proceeded to call up to her sister. Barbara Jo almost immediately appeared on the stair landing. Though she had not accompanied Maggie, Bart and Johnny to church, she was now fully dressed; her hair had been combed, and her face washed.

"Well," Bart called up to her, "it's wonderful, indeed, to see you, Mrs. Moss. Though we did miss you at the church service. And I was sorry to hear that you were…indisposed…and lacked appetite to partake of luncheon with us. I trust…that the afternoon finds you of a more salubrious state of health than did this morning?"

"I am feeling quite a bit better, thank you for your kind interest, Mr. Logan." Barbara Jo stood staring down at them with an impatient frown on her pale, freckly face. "As a matter of fact, I was just in the process of sorting through my clothing. My gowns. I was just wondering, Mr. Logan, will there be occasion aboard ship, or at this estate of yours in Surrey, any need to pack along a…dress for formal evening wear?"

"Well…I don't quite know how to reply to your inquiry, Mrs. Moss," Bart called up to her, wondering why they were required to shout at one another. "But, yes, if you were going, there would be ample occasions, I feel sure, to dress in your finest gowns. But, unfortunately, Margaret Ann, here, has just advised me that she no longer…has in mind…making the voyage with me. She says—"

"*What?*" Barbara Jo, in one short moment, bounded down the stairs, reached the lower step and now strode on into the dining room, where she stood stock still, eyes wide, mouth open, gasping and staring, as if about to fall into a dead swoon. Her face, already pale, had gone as gray as ashes, causing the freckles across her nose to stand out like marching brown sentinels.

"But...*Maggs!* You can't *mean* it? I mean...would you *deny* yourself...would you *deny* Johnny...*would you deny me this one opportunity in my entire lifetime* to...Oh, Margaret Ann McKinnon...you will *never* change! You are still as *selfish*, as *self-centered*, as hard hearted and uncaring as you were as a ten-year-old! If you deny me this one simple pleasure in my life, *I shall never, ever, forgive you!*"

Not taking the bother to cover her mouth with her hand, Barbara Jo simply burst into great wailing sobs, gathered up her skirts, whirled about, and fled upstairs, her moans and shrieks of abused outrage echoing in the dining room and up the stairs, minutes after her slender form had disappeared at the head of the landing.

"Well, my dearest," Bartram, not seeming at all taken aback by his soon-to-be sister-in-law's verbal and emotional outburst, continued to speak in a soft, reasoning tone of voice, "there I would say you have your answer...as to how your sister feels...about making this trip."

Maggie, who stood beside the massive fireplace gazing at the landing from which her sister had just disappeared—leaving her dramatic declaration echoing so loudly behind her—seemed for the moment speechless. Then she gathered her wits, gathered her voluminous skirts in her hand, and walked forward to face Mr. Bartram Logan, who had risen and stood lounging nonchalantly against the rock of the opposite side of the fireplace, a pleased smirk on his handsome face.

"*You*..." she began, eyes squinted, lovely face flushing crimson, "You knew...you knew all along just exactly how Barbara Jo would react. Didn't you Mr. Logan, *darling*!? This was your way of making your point...without uttering a word or lifting a hand. This was, shall we say, your *ace in the hole*, your great *trump card, concealed up your sleeve*—"

"Have you been gambling or playing at cards, Margaret Ann?" Bartram Logan's dark brows arced in mock surprise.

"No! I have not! But when one operates an inn deep in the mountain country of North Georgia, one is bound to hear...certain terms...bandied about the tables and the fireplace, Mr. Logan, darling! So! Seeing how the land lies...Seeing that I am to be forever hereafter noted for all to see as the world's most *villainous*, most *uncaring*, most *monstrous* ogre, I suppose, then, Mr. Logan, *darling*, that you can just simply go right ahead...and purchase the tickets!"

"Yes, my sweet. I shall put myself on that very task, bright and early, tomorrow morning! And you heard what I informed your sister, as to the occasions for wearing…"

"I, Mr. Logan, darling," Maggie retorted, her anger still burning hot at how easily he had foiled her, "am not the widow of a rich merchant. I do not possess a trunk full and a wardrobe full of gowns ordered from…"

"Well…never fear…my sweet." Bart gazed down at her and mused softly, "You shall find yourself truly in the heart of the world's most fashionable shopping districts! London! And with Paris itself…just across the Channel! We shall all, immediately the ship anchors at the London quay—and we rest ourselves a bit at St. George's Inn—take a carriage to Oxford Street, where lays a fine shopping district…Well!…come to think of it, we can take the coach easily on to Broad Street!…where the tailors are world famous, and have been for centuries, for their finely-crafted men's suits. I could use a few new—"

"Oh!" Maggie put her hands over her ears, wagged her head, sank into the nearest maple rocker, and wailed softly, "Oh! Lord, have mercy!"

———————

As Maggie lay in bed that night, tossing and turning, she attempted to envision in her mind the very real possibility of walking out the front door of The Sparrow Inn, knowing she would not reenter it for several weeks to come. She attempted to envision traveling up to Philadelphia, and on to the coast, probably Boston Harbor, where Mr. Logan had indicated that they would board a great liner, to cross the vast Atlantic. She could not. She attempted to envision standing on the deck of a great ship, Johnny at one elbow, Mr. William Bartram Logan at the other. She could not.

And when it came to envisioning herself shopping in fine stores on London's Oxford Street, or any of its teeming thoroughfares, she chuckled aloud at the laughable audacity of such an imagined situation. And there still awaited the fine estate Mr. Logan had inherited…

Finally, in the wee hours of the night, Maggie drifted off to sleep, only to be awakened by the insistent cries of Samantha.

Maggie dragged herself out of bed. Planting her feet on the colorful rag-braided rug covering the planked flooring, she forced herself to her feet, felt for and lit a taper, then plodded down the narrow hallway to the room occupied by Bethany Lee and her little daughter.

Maggie stuck her head in the door. "Bethany Lee," she hissed in a loud, angry whisper, "can't you hear your child crying? She needs to nurse! Aren't you going to rouse yourself up and at least attempt to allow the child to satisfy her hunger?"

"Oh, it's you, Mrs. Evans. I got nothin' ta offer th' poor little tyke," Bethany Lee mumbled disinterestedly. "Maybe you could fix one o' them …them bottle things…fer her?"

Without a word, Maggie turned, closed the door and made her way along the narrow stairway, and down to the kitchen. The goat's milk was in a small pitcher…out in the well, along with the sweet milk. She'd have to light the lantern, go out and draw it up, kindle a small fire in the cookstove, warm the milk a bit…

With a heavy sigh, Maggie lit the kerosene lantern, and made her way out to the well. She removed the iron rod scotching the windlass, drew up the well bucket with its precious contents, and filled a clean bottle with the goat's milk. Then she tied the milk cloth back about the top of the jug with its stout cord, placed the small brown earthen jug back in the oaken bucket, and lowered it down into the cool depths of the well, and re-scotched the windlass.

Back inside, she lifted an eye from the black iron cookstove, dropped a few pieces of kindling into the stove, and lit it up. The pine sparked and sizzled and caught, sending up a fragrant odor of fresh resin. Maggie set a pan with a bit of water directly over the small blaze, and plunked the bottle in. Who was supposed to do this…when Maggie was sailing the high seas? When she was traipsing through Europe's finest shopping districts? When she was viewing a vast English estate!? Maggie tested the milk for warmth, and replaced the stove eye with a bang

Then Maggie was trooping back upstairs, gathering the tiny squirming, whimpering infant into her arms, into her own room, when she flopped down into her rocker before the cold fireplace, and, with an old quilt tucked snugly about the both of them, held the bottle for little Samantha, who slurped and cooed appreciatively, one tiny hand on either side of her meal as she greedily swallowed, and required burping. Maggie placed the tiny baby girl against her left shoulder, and felt the little head doddering against her neck. The child felt warm, precious, a new life, a new beginning. A catch in her throat, Maggie whispered a little prayer that God would keep the child safe in the palm of His great hand. Exhausted from a long day, and as yet an almost sleepless night, Maggie wondered idly if she would ever hold another infant of her own…in her arms…like this…

Then she forced her mind back to the present. She needed to get the baby back in bed with her mother. Her mother… Maggie heaved a great sigh. What was wrong with that girl!? Couldn't she see what she had here? But it was clear that Bethany Lee was not at all interested in the child. She was pining for *that man*. That unidentified coward! That soulless fiend! The baby's father, who evidently had not the backbone of an earthworm!

Maggie flung back the quilt, rose and made her way back down the hall. She deposited the sleeping infant in bed with her mother and ordered sternly, "Bethany Lee? Can you hear me? Don't you roll over in the night and…"

Maggie just left it there. Made her way back to bed, and lay there wondering if she had had sense enough to slide the well lid back in place after lowering the bucket back down? That's all she'd need right now! To leave the lid off the well! And find some night roaming critter had fallen in—to drown and stink up the water…which would then be unusable for days, until the well had been thoroughly emptied and cleaned—

Maggie re-lit her taper, back down the stairs, out to the well, where she found the lid firmly in place.

She re-entered the inn. Banged the back door shut. Back up to bed. As she passed through the dining room, she heard the eight-day clock on the mantel strike four. And preparations for breakfast at The Sparrow Inn began promptly, most days, at five each morning.

———————

By seven o'clock, the dining room of The Sparrow was packed. Maggie felt as if she had been clubbed in the head. And Samantha still waited upstairs to be fed and changed and bathed. She wondered if today Mr. Logan would be by with the date of departure for the voyage. She wished her head didn't ache. But at least, since her sister had begun planning for the trip, Barbara Jo had revived up. She was down for breakfast at the crack of dawn each day now, her light blue eyes bright, her pale face flushed. She still had made no effort or indication or said the first word about returning to her fine yellow brick house. But, at least, to Maggie's great relief, neither had she mentioned again the possibility of selling the place off. Maggie wondered if Benjamin Noah had found time to make his way down to the pasture behind Trap's wheelwright shop to milk the goat this morning. And was Johnny up yet? Had she bathed him last night, before tucking him in bed? No. She had found him asleep beneath one of the tables, had not the energy or the heart to disturb him, and had simply carried him up the stairs and tucked him in. He'd need...and what else had she forgotten?

"I have the tickets," he whispered excitedly in her ear.

"Oh! Mr. Logan. How are you...this morning?" Maggie replied wearily.

"I'm fine. Didn't you hear what I just said?"

"What? Oh. Yes. The...tickets."

"Don't get yourself *too* excited, my sweet," Bartram Logan smiled wryly. "After all, it's only...a trip to Europe..."

"What? Oh. It's...wonderful...too wonderful...to be quite true. I...still can't quite imagine it all. And there's so much to do here. So much yet to be done. And I wonder...who on earth will do...all this..."

"Sweetheart," Bartram Logan took Maggie's arm, ushering her past several filled tables to a vacant one in the corner before the fireplace. He motioned her into a chair.

"You appear...lovely...but utterly exhausted. Are you the only person in the place capable of lifting one finger?"

"That's untrue, Mr. Logan, darling," Maggie snapped tiredly, "and unfair. Liza Mae and Benjamin Noah..."

"I know, my sweet," Bart said softly, "but you do far too much. I worry about you. Always taking the entire world onto those slender shoulders. You need this trip. You need to get away. Let that girl take care of her child—"

"But will she?" Maggie gazed at him with worried sapphire-blue eyes. "She appears not to have the slightest instinct of motherly love or compassion. She will let the poor little thing whine and root and fuss, and it all falls on deaf ears. All Bethany Lee does is dawdle in bed. And when she is up, she stands staring out the window, eyes scanning the street, as if searching...waiting..."

"For what?"

"I...don't know. Maybe she thinks...*he*...is coming for her. Maybe he has *promised* to come for her. I don't know. All I do know is that she's practically worthless, as far as caring for her child."

"Well, if he's coming, he's certainly taking his own good time about it," Bart heaved a long sigh. "But that's not your problem. When you're not here to see to the little one, she'll roust herself up and take on the role of mother. You'll see."

"I wish I could believe that as blithely as you seem able to. But, then you aren't *here*, hearing the infant's hungry cries in the night...trooping down the stairs and out to the well—heating up a bottle..."

"And neither will *you* be...very shortly. Our ship sails on the tenth."

"So...soon?" Maggie stared at him, a startled look darkening her eyes, putting a slight flush in her cream-smooth cheeks. That's..."

"We need to leave...the end of next week, so we can swing by Philadelphia, on our way to Boston."

"Boston?" Maggie asked.

"Yes, my sweet. Don't you recall that it's from Boston that the particular ship I wish us to board makes its departure? So, it's to Boston we must needs go. So leave the child to its mother, and you begin packing for you and Johnny. I believe your sister informed me days ago she was about all ready to go."

"Yes," Maggie murmured, recalling the vigor with which Barbara Jo had gathered her dresses, gowns and bonnets and spread them all about the upstairs, then walked from room to room, squinting her eyes and pursing her lips, in a harrowing attempt to make the very difficult decision as to which of her sumptuous garments to pack for the voyage—and which she must leave behind. Apparently, this was a most onerous task, as Barbara Jo would brook no advice or suffer any interference, and would scarcely deign to make conversation, whilst engaged in this arduous pursuit.

Maggie glanced down at her own dark cotton frock, donned fresh this morning, but now splashed with a bit of goat's milk, a dab or two of flour. She raised her eyes to Mr. Bartram Logan's and sighed, "I fear, Mr. Logan, I shall not be nearly as well attired as my dear sister. You shall no doubt prefer that she accompany you to...whatever functions...you plan attending, on board ship, or in the fine city of London."

"Don't talk nonsense," Bartram Logan smiled at Maggie, his dark eyes alight with frankest admiration, "I will adore you, always, even should you be encased in a tow sack, and wearing a straw hat on your lovely little head! Which I am sure, my darling, shall not be the case. Have you had breakfast? No. Keep your seat. And I shall make my way into the kitchen, and return shortly with plates for the both of us."

Which is exactly what he did. And in no time at all, Maggie found herself seated before the fire, partaking of a delicious breakfast of hot ham and eggs, drinking deliciously hot coffee, and listening to Mr. William Bartram Logan spin his magic tales of Philadelphia, Boston, London, Paris… All the while he talked, Maggie sat, elbows on the table, a small hand propping up her chin, gazing dreamily into his dark eyes—recalling the warm burden of the child against her shoulder in the night, the two of them cozily bundled beneath Mama's lovely flower garden quilt…

Chapter 22

Fog drifted off the River Thames and hung thick over Fleet Street as the heavy coach carrying Lady Marilyn Eveline Drayton threaded its way slowly, laboriously along the crowded cobbled streets of London's richest financial district. The coach swayed from side to side. The iron-shod hooves of the steeds struck the cobblestones with dull claps, echoing through the coach and off the surrounding buildings. Seated on the cracked leather upholstery, Lady Marilyn stuck her beautifully bonneted head out the coach window, her gaze taking in the startling sights of London—that never failed to amaze her. Everywhere Lady Marilyn looked, wealth was on display—in the dress and tenor of the fine, proud gentlemen who paraded the streets, as if their sole purpose in life, Marilyn thought, was that their high social status and fantastic fortunes should be openly displayed. Other grandly attired gentlemen alighted from rich carriages sporting liveried drivers and footmen. With their tall beaver-felt hats, their silver-tipped canes, and carrying large leather pouches, they breached the entrances of the towering stone edifices that reeked of prestige, influence—and vast wealth. And along London's finest street, as out of place and unwelcome as rats in the king's pantry, scampered the usual rag-tag mob of prostitutes, cut-purses and cape-thieves, gnawing and nibbling their way about the edges of London's upper-crust.

It all gave Lady Marilyn Eveline Drayton a sour taste in her mouth. As the rattling coach lurched to a stop before a particularly impressive stone building, Lady Marilyn glanced down at her hands, at the worn fingertips of her best gloves. And then down at her small feet—the faded silk stockings, the little spool-heeled leather slippers with crimped bows that had once been the best London shops had to offer, but…now… the shoes appeared scuffed about the toes and along the edges of the heels, and the bows were a bit frayed. Oh, well, mayhap her dress tail would hide all that.

The driver dropped down from his box, and waddled to the coach door to pull it open and lower the step for her. The driver took her hand, and she alighted. The man then lumbered to the rear of the coach, where waited her baggage. "Whar 'e be wantin' these, Mee'laidy?" he asked, his accent reeking of impoverishment and stupidity.

Like the ignorant cockney idiot he was, not bothering to wait for a reply, he began carelessly tossing out her trunks and packs and bales, as if they were bales of hay, Lady Marilyn thought, he was offering to the cows!

Lady Marilyn sought but found no reply. What could she tell the man?!

Instead, she grated her teeth, and stood looking up and down Fleet Street. Then she swung her gaze to the large pile of baggage—strewn but a few inches from the flowing filth that was the London gutter. *Those bags! They held all she possessed in this world!*

Oh, what was the use of it all, Marilyn sighed to herself. Then she pulled from her tiny purse the torn and crumpled letter she must have read for the hundredth time. She checked the address with the bronze figures over the front door, then stood scanning the letter again. Blood rose past the neck of her best gown, up into her lovely white throat, suffusing a face that had stood many a gentleman on his ear in some of London's most richly appointed drawing rooms and loveliest gardens and salons. But, Marilyn thought wryly, *those* days, sadly, were behind her. She turned *twenty and seven*, this past fall. Indeed, the bloom was rapidly fading from off the rose.

Marilyn clutched the letter to the bosom of her lavender silk gown, closed her eyes, and had she been a praying person, she would actually have prayed. Instead, what Marilyn did was utter a few very unladylike curses. She, who had once been the toast of the best London circles. Now... Now, this tattered letter was her sole hope of salvation, of redemption...from poverty, ignominy ... and total and utter social decline and ruin. To say nothing of the looming specter of starvation. After receiving the letter from the firm of Sullivan & Sullivan of Fleet Street, London, advising Marilyn that she was one of the heirs of Sir Feldon Bartholomew Hurston, Fourth Earl of Windsfield, she had clung to it, as a drowning person clings to a single limb floating past in a fast-swirling stream against which they are utterly helpless, and that is fast drawing them under.

Lost in thought, continuing to ignore the coachman, Marilyn stood staring at her luggage, wondering how on earth she was going to keep it safe, while she made her call at the offices of Sullivan & Sullivan. Had she possessed more than a few paltry coins in her thin, flimsy little purse, she would have tucked her things safely away in some inexpensive little inn. With a rueful smile, Lady Marilyn wondered whether or not there was such a thing in London as an *inexpensive* inn. Perhaps in the Seven Dials District—where she would not be caught dead! Well, one thing was certain—she couldn't leave the stuff just sitting beside the sewer that was the curb of Fleet Street.

"Mee'laidy?" the coachman stood waiting.

Perhaps if she popped inside, she could secure permission to have it hauled into the attorneys' suite of offices—until she could, hopefully, get her hands on at least a portion of her coming fortune. Yes. Just enough to see her through—until the final reading of the old duffer's will. Lady Marilyn was fully aware that she was not the sole heir. Somewhere in the backwards country of America, so Sullivan & Sullivan had informed her, resided a second heir—one *William Bartram Logan*, who was now, so she understood, making his way towards London to claim his share.

Lady Marilyn felt certain that since she was of fine English stock, and had visited Sir Feldon from time to time over the years, and was thus somewhat acquainted with him, that she would receive the lion's share of whatever the old fellow had left behind. As to this American, this William Bartram Logan, until she received the letter from Sullivan & Sullivan, she had never known he existed. Therefore, he must be of distant kin, indeed, a most comforting thought.

The coachman stood glaring at her ever so rudely, dark bushy brows knit in a deep frown, coal-black eyes glinting greedily, one large, grubby hand extended palm up. Lady Marilyn noted with disgust that his uniform was none too clean, either. How on earth did such a foul dolt obtain a license to work London's finest streets?!

Not wishing to cause a scene on a public street of London, especially not before the very door of Sir Feldon Bartholomew Hurston's barristers, reluctantly Lady Marilyn dug forth the bulk of her remaining precious hoard of funds, and paid the man.

A liveried footman for the building had noticed Lady Marilyn standing on the curb, her luggage piled willy-nilly about her little feet. Now he stuck his head out the door, and asked politely:

"May I help you, milady?"

"Oh, yes! How very, *very* kind of you!" Lady Marilyn gushed, plastering on her most charming smile, batting her stunning violet eyes rapidly beneath their lush dark lashes. A gloved hand flew to her throat, as if she had been completely taken aback by some recent happenstance.

"I need to get…my things…inside, my good man, for just a few minutes. I don't know what came over me. I completely forgot to send them on to my lodgings—whilst I kept my appointment with the Messrs. Sullivan. Could you by any chance be a fine fellow, and help me with them?"

It grated on Lady Marilyn's proud sensibilities, to be forced to cow-tow to paid help, but what else could she do under the circumstances? If she told the richly-liveried footman exactly how she felt right now, he would probably blanch pale as death, duck his head inside like a frightened turtle, and leave Lady Marilyn to her own frightfully inadequate devices.

The footman's sharp black eyes did not miss the stunning face, the lovely form clad in a very expensive silk gown and bonnet. "Of…course, milady. And with whom, might I ask, did you have an appointment?"

"Why…!" Insolent sod! What business was that of his!? Lady Marilyn bit back the scathing retort pushing itself against her very white teeth, and smiled. She did not actually *have* an appointment. She was here on their doorstone out of pure, raw, desperate need. "With the *Messrs. Sullivan*, of course, my good man! Now…are you going to see to my things…or not?!" Lady Marilyn failed to keep the angry impatience from her voice. "My appointment is now upon me, my dear fellow," Marilyn lied, "and I haven't a moment to spare. I will leave you, then, to your task."

And with that Lady Marilyn gathered up her violet silk skirts, attempting, all the while, to hide the sorry state of her shoes and stockings, and stood waiting for the footman to hold wide the door to accommodate the voluminous spread of her garments.

The footman, meanwhile, was struggling and grappling, attempting to gather up her luggage and swing the door open for her. Marilyn glanced up at the sign that gleamed in huge brass letters *Sullivan & Sullivan, Attorneys at the Bar*. As she stood impatiently waiting, she fought to compose herself and appear every inch the grieving, concerned, deserving heir of Sir Feldon Bartholomew Hurston, Fourth Earl of Windsfield. She drew her small frame up to its full height, plastered on a smile, and stepped inside.

The heavy door swung shut behind her. Lady Marilyn released hold on her froth of crinolines and skirts, patted them down, heaved an angry sigh, and stood fuming. Couldn't he see that she was in dire straits and in need of immediate assistance? Wasn't that what the dunce was paid for? You would think that stupid footman did not have a single brain in head.

As the footman filed in and out, piling Lady Marilyn's trunks and bales and bags in one corner of the vestibule, Marilyn stepped into an outer office, where sat a thin, pre-maturely balding young man whom Marilyn assessed in a flash as being a mere underling, a lowly-paid clerk. He rose to his feet, and ushered Lady Marilyn in.

"Yes, milady?" the balding clerk peered at Lady Marilyn through a tiny but unbelievably thick pair of spectacles set in thin wire rims.

"I am here at the summons of Messrs. Sullivan & Sullivan. I am Lady Marilyn Eveline Drayton, *heir* to the *late Earl of Windsfield.* Would you please announce me immediately? I have been traveling for some days, and am tired and weary, and in need of finding accommodations and taking my rest. Besides, there are other pressing business affairs that demand my attention," Lady Marilyn lied very smoothly with a haughty lift of her little chin.

Lady Marilyn was shown to a rich leather chair, where she sat twiddling her thumbs and bouncing her small feet impatiently, while the balding clerk rifled through a thick stack of papers on his huge, highly-polished desk. Why on earth didn't that half-blind fool just get on with business, *and show her into the barristers' offices?!* Did he think she had traveled for days in filthy, lurching coaches shared with the off-scourings of the country, and had slept in cheap inns, just to be kept dawdling in an outer office the bulk of the morning!? She was exhausted from three harsh days of a rocking coach that churned through fog and mud and rain, and had at one point gotten hopelessly stuck. She was hungry because her funds were so low that all she could afford on her journey from South Hampshire was poor fare indeed—a bit of bread and cheese, a few bowls of weak tea, along with a bit of watery gruel. She wanted to get her inheritance, and get herself a hearty meal of roast goose and blood pudding, and a fine bed in which she could stretch herself out and catch some sleep—in a fit accommodation that was not located above some cheap pub roaring with loud chatter and drunken laughter!

Finally, in a fit of exasperation, Lady Marilyn erupted to her feet. She could feel blood hot, rushing up into her cheeks. But this, Lady Marilyn was well aware, only enhanced her attractiveness. She was fully aware that she had, in her early twenties, been reputed to be the most charming, most beautiful woman in all London. She approached the balding clerk's desk, and demanded with a flutter of long, dark lashes and a pretty pout:

"Well, am I to be kept waiting the entire day long?! I *do* believe, if you will be so kind as to *consult* your calendar, good sir, you shall discover that the *time* scheduled for my appointment *has been passed by at least half an hour!*"

The balding clerk gazed up at her, stunned at the accusation. Quickly he adjusted his spectacles and with nervous little flips of paper, rechecked his schedule.

"Are you...*quite* certain...milady...that you have come on the appointed morning? I mean...I fail to find your name listed... anywhere... today...at all?"

"Well!" Lady Marilyn pulled an aggrieved little sigh, making certain that her bosom heaved and fell just enough to capture the balding clerk's eye. Then she gave her chin a haughty little lift and demanded in a highly injured voice: "*And* my good sir, is that due to any failure on *my* part, that you are so inept as to not include me on the morning's schedule? I am certain that *your employers* will be *highly interested* to learn of this *failure on your part,* in the performance of your duties. Would you please inform—"

Since they dealt only with the upper crust of English society, this was *most* uncommon, in the offices of the Messrs. Sullivan & Sullivan, that any slightest detail should be overlooked or mishandled. And certainly not the scheduling of an appointment—with an heir to the Fourth Earl of Windsfield! How could this have happened?! *This could possibly cost him his position...!*

"I...will...check...to see...if...one...if...Mr. Sullivan is...free...to see you, milady."

A moment later, the thin, balding clerk reappeared, twisting his neck to peer at her from beneath his tiny wire spectacles, as he stood holding the door wide for Lady Marilyn to enter. Without a glance in his direction, Lady

Marilyn swept past the harried clerk, and her small right hand extended towards the tall, elegantly attired gentleman moving towards her, she gushed, "Well, at last! I meet the gentleman in charge of my dear, dear late cousin's affairs!"

"Lady Marilyn Drayton, I understand?" His eyes cold, a frown pinching his long, somber face, the barrister took her gloved hand, bowed stiffly, and gave Lady Marilyn the strained semblance of a smile. "Milford P. Sullivan, at your service."

Lady Marilyn quickly withdrew her hand from his, fearing he would see or feel the thinness of her worn gloves. It appalled her, how she had lately fallen into such grating poverty. It made her absolutely ill. When she had married that old fool, Winston Drayton, she had been of the opinion—as had most of London—that Sir Winston Drayton was one of the richest men in the South of England. His family had for years controlled business and shipping interests all up and down the River Thames. Then, shortly after the marriage, Lady Marilyn learned to her total chagrin and utter horror, that all those business and shipping interests were the property of, and beneath the control of, Sir Winston Drayton's mother, Lady Olivia Stanforth Drayton. Her only hope, then, was that Sir Winston would gain control upon the old shrew's death. But, alas, Lady Olivia refused to die.

Then Winston Drayton, this past spring, not five years into the marriage, had had the audacity and gall to up and die on Lady Marilyn. Leaving her to the not-so-tender mercies of his mother. Shortly after Sir Winston's untimely death, a grieving Lady Olivia had thrown her out, and Lady Marilyn found herself for all intents and purposes homeless, and with scarcely a farthing to her name. She had been forced to cast herself, all the past several months, upon the merciful charity of what few friends she retained, telling them that since losing poor Winston, she simply could not bring herself to reside in any of the fine mansions that held such tender memories of their all-too-fleeting time together. The summer had gone passably well, staying about amongst her few friends; but by fall, most of her welcomes had worn thin. Thus, she had passed a cold, harsh fall and winter, foisting herself upon her few remaining acquaintances. But given Lady Marilyn's personality and temperament, she had quickly worn out what little tolerance had awaited her.

"I…fear…madam…." Milford P. Sullivan stammered. Then, recalling his manners, he graciously offered, "Won't you take a seat, madam. I fear that… your…visit…is quite…unexpected. Catching me a bit…off guard. The reading of the will is not scheduled for almost another three weeks. If you would be so kind as to check your correspondence, I believe you will find— that the reading of the will is to be scheduled later in the month, after the arrival of Mister—"

"Oh? Is that so?" Marilyn rudely interrupted, as if this bit of information was so startling as to have taken her completely by surprise. "Well!" she prattled with a little flourish of one hand, palm inward, to hide the worn fingertips of her glove, "How careless and thoughtless of me. But, you know, Mr. Sullivan, how we women often are. Our pretty little heads are not attuned toward business, you see. No. Not at all. So perhaps I have appeared in your office a bit…prematurely. But, now that I am actually *here*, now that I have made this arduous journey all the way from South Hampshire— that has robbed me of all comfort and worn me to the bone—cannot you go ahead and assign unto me some of the properties that I have coming?"

"Madam?"

"Can you not, sir…" What was wrong with this idiot? Was he as dense as a post? "Can you not forward me a small…*advance*…on my coming inheritance? Say, ninety or one hundred pounds? To at least *somewhat* offset my expenses in coming here?"

"No, madam, no!" Milford P. Sullivan vigorously wagged his head. "I…fear…that is *totally* out of the question. Until the formal reading of the will, *nothing* will be distributed…to any of the heirs. And, as I understand from my last contact with your cousin, Mr. William Bartram Logan, he was not even taking ship until—"

"And just what, *sir*…" Lady Marilyn hissed between clenched teeth. She shoved back tears of desperation, fought to suppress the panic coursing through her like stabs of an icy knife, strove to keep the panic from bubbling into her voice. But she found this impossible.

"You…! You…! *Almost a month!?* "

Quickly she recovered herself, lifted her lilac eyes beneath dark lashes that fluttered and shivered like the wings of a broken dove; her lower lip trembled slightly.

"And just exactly what, may I ask you, Mr. Sullivan, am I supposed to do with myself!—for three full weeks? Whilst I am waiting for this errant, thoughtless clod of a cousin?! You see, sir, the truth of the matter is, that I failed...to bring along...sufficient funds...to see me through such an extended wait for my inheritance." Despite Lady Marilyn's best efforts, her voice rang with raw desperation.

"Well, madam, what you are supposed to do...that is completely out of my hands. I can only tell you that this firm will abide by the terms of your late cousin's Last Will and Testament. Until Mr. William Bartram Logan arrives, everything is sealed. The estate, the documents. *Nothing* will be—"

Marilyn leapt from the rich leather chair, gave an exasperated stamp of one foot, spun on her heel, and flounced out the door, past the startled clerk, and to the front vestibule—where awaited her pile of luggage.

At the front entrance, beside her luggage, Marilyn halted. What on earth was she to do now!? Without opening her purse, she knew exactly what few coins lay therein. Not enough for a single night's lodging and a decent meal. Not in the city of London. Not in any section of London where she would not be instantly set upon, robbed, raped, or worse. She had assured herself a thousand times over, that if she showed up here, though she was almost a month early, Sir Feldon's legal representatives would advance her a reasonable sum to tide her over until she actually received her estate. With one delicate hand encased in a threadbare glove, she brushed away tears of rage. She was a blithering, bloody idiot! She shouldn't have let him put her off like this! She should have stood her ground! Demanded her property! Demanded her rights! She was *certain* that the bulk of the estate was coming to *her*. Therefore, it all belonged *to her*—and not to Sullivan & Sullivan!

But she knew that look. Cold. Calculating. Tight-lipped. Tight-faced. Unyielding. She had seen that look in Winston Drayton's eyes on more occasions than she cared to recall. She would not get one thin farthing from this cursed law firm, not until this Cousin William what's-his-name showed up! The devil take him! Hopefully, if she were lucky, he would fall overboard and drown himself on the voyage over!

As Marilyn stood yanking on her bonnet strings, pondering the awfulness of her situation, the footman was already busying himself tossing her bags and bales back out onto the side of the street, one of them landing in the filth-laden gutter.

Then Lady Marilyn found herself ushered out into the thin mid-day sun, across which gray puffs of cold clouds suddenly scudded. Lady Marilyn gazed up at the clouds and shuddered. Of all the rotten luck! It was sure to spout a deluge before she could find any suitable shelter! Down at the corner of the street, she hailed the first empty coach, and the coachman had almost loaded her bags, when the skies opened, and barrels and buckets of cold liquid fell in sidewise drifts, across the stone faces of the buildings along Fleet Street. The burly coachman tossed in the last bit of luggage, offered Lady Marilyn a hand up into the coach. As she settled her slight frame into the cracked leather of the worn coach seat, Marilyn muttered, "Well, at least I'm not soaked to the skin! Only my cloak is wet, and for that I suppose I should be grateful! Though to *whom* I haven't the remotest idea!"

Almost, when she had received the notice from Sullivan & Sullivan just when she was at the lowest ebb of her life, Marilyn had entertained the faintest notion that perhaps, after all, there *was* a God in heaven seeing to the affairs of human kind. And perhaps, just perhaps, *He* was seeing to her affairs.

But this was a faint notion, and very fleeting at that. And! Now—! Oh, well. She would manage somehow. On her own. Without the aid of this invisible, unseeing, uncaring, empty entity some fools chose to worship. How could she have believed even for one millisecond that anyone or anything gave a care about *Marilyn Drayton*!? Even as a child, she had been unwanted. Her own mother had been jealous of her, jealous of a beauty that so vastly outshined her own, even when Marilyn was very small. And her father…*No!… She refused to allow her mind to go there…! To that awful man…!*

Just as the bottom fell out of the sky, the coach driver poked his head in her door, "And where 'tis it to, mee-laidy?"

"Are you familiar with the Estate of Windsfield?" Lady Marilyn shouted over a loud clap of thunder following a bolt of lightening that had just split the clouds in a jagged line of white heat that arced over the stone buildings.

"Yaaas, mee-laidy! And is that whar e' be goin'"?

"It *is*!" Marilyn emitted a loud, defiant reply. "How long?"

"A good ways out, it is, mee-laidy, in the rolling hill country of Surrey. Take mos' th' addernoon ta git thar? Do 'e 'ave—?"

240

"How *dare* you, you fool?" Marilyn's lovely face went livid, screwing into an ugly, hateful scowl. "How dare you question a lady so?! You'll *get* your fare! Mount your box, and off with you, impudent oaf!" Out of that lovely mouth there issued a vile string of curses—

The coachman's face went pale beneath the rivulets of rain pouring over his dark face and down his scruffy beard. He'd heard his share and more of rude language, but who'd ever heard a grandly dressed lady speak so?!

He doffed his soaked hat, scrambled onto the driver's seat, and gave a fierce snap of the reins. The heavy rig lurched forward with such force that it caused Marilyn's head to jerk back in her bonnet as she grasped for the sides of the coach and her luscious lips emitted another loud string of curses that sliced through the coach walls, "*You...!*"

By the time they had reached the outskirts of London, the cloudburst had passed. The skies cleared, with just a few puffy wisps of white visible. The countryside rolled past the coach windows, fields and pastureland, verdant green, fresh-washed and sparkling. But the beauty of the English countryside was lost on Lady Marilyn, as her tired brain spun about chasing its own shadow. A fearsome sum the coachman would be demanding at the end of this afternoon's journey, she knew. A sum Lady Marilyn was far from possessing. What, then, was she to do? She must put her crafty, cunning little brain to work.

Cool air whipped off the rain-sparkled fields and pastures rolling past and blew into the open windows of the coach. With the pleasant air and the rocking of the coach, Marilyn, despite her worries, nodded off. She was awakened by the slowing of the coach. She opened her eyes and peered out. Her mouth fell into a small "o" and she let out an amazed gasp.

There on a slight rise at a little distance stood one of the grandest residences Marilyn's jaded eyes had ever beheld. She had been here before, but not in a great while. When she had run up debts that Winston refused to pay, she had come here, hand out to her cousin. But had departed with her hand still empty. Tight-fisted old... And she had forgotten how very splendid Windsfield was. But now that it was about to be *hers*, she saw it with new eyes. A veritable palace! A great, gray stone pile that rose and rose, and went on and on! Its turrets and chimneys split the skies. And surrounded by lovely formal gardens that, though it was still winter, boasted every hue of color in the rainbow and beyond. A shimmering lake lay off past the westward gardens, with a cottage, or boathouse. Marilyn wasn't sure which. In the other direction, rose the gigantic barns and stables. She was so bedazzled by the splendor and elegance of the place that she was speechless for several moments. Then finding her voice, she hailed the driver as he pulled the rocking coach to a full stop in the graveled circular drive before a massive front door and bounded down from his seat.

"Are you…certain…driver?…that you have brought me to the correct place? I don't recall Windsfield being …quite…so…"

"Aye, 'nd 'ave me not lived a' but London Town since I drawed me furst gasp of breath? Aye, 'tis Windsfield 'e asked fer, and 'tis Windsfield 'e got! And that, milady, will be five pounds, and sixpence." He removed his hat that had lost every vestige of color it may ever have possessed, and extended a grimy hand, palm up.

It was a small fortune! "Well, then…" Lady Marilyn made a great matter of arranging her voluminous skirts just so and picking up her tiny purse. She then sat fiddling with the ribbons of her bonnet, while the coachman waited ever so patiently. Then she stepped lightly down from the coach, turned on him, ignoring the open hand.

"Just wait about unloading my things," Marilyn ordered imperiously, "while I make my presence known. A servant will be out shortly…to pay you your fare and to take care of the luggage. Good day to you, then."

And with that, she picked up her skirts and hurried up the massive stone steps to the broad front door.

At the first clatter of the huge brass knocker, the great oak door swung wide. A solemn-faced butler appeared.

"Yes, madam?"

"Would you kindly pay the coachman, and then see to my things!" Lady Marilyn instructed the startled butler.

"But…" Joseph's mouth fell open. He gasped out, "What!? But…who be ye…madam?"

"I am the new owner of Windsfield, you stupid idiot! *Your new Mistress*! Or at least I soon shall be. Now! On with you! On with you! Don't just stand there like a dumb donkey! Do my bidding! At once! This instant! That is, my good man, if you value your job! Now—!—Remove yourself from the doorway! I am tired."

"No, madam! I cin't let you in. By order of Himself's barristers, this estate is closed to al' comers, until the last Will of Himself be read, and the estate be settled. That's my certain, sure instructions."

"Stand aside!" Marilyn ranted, violet eyes blazing. Behind her, she could hear her luggage being unceremoniously flung off the coach. "Are you deaf?! *I am the heir!*"

"No, madam!" the servant muttered, his eyes set, his face implacable. "I cannot open the door to every—"

"My good man—!" Marilyn shouted, scarlet in the face. "I shall have a *horse whip* taken to you!"

"What's going on here? Joseph? What's all this?"

"It's this...person...trying to push her way inta th' house, Mr. Ridley, if you please, sir. And I don't know her from a sheep. And she is tryin' ta push her way inta th' house. And I am just following your instructions—"

"Yes. Quite, Joseph. I shall attend to this. You go on about your other duties. Yes, madam? And just...what...business do you have at Windsfield?"

"You...blubbering...bungling...oafish..."

"Madam, I am Albert J. Ridley, steward of Windsfield. A position I have held very honorably for the past twenty-odd years. And during that long course of a score and more of years, you are not the first loud, strange woman to come banging at the door with no business in particular to speak of. If you have business here, then it is certainly my duty to aid you in that business. And if not, then perhaps you would be wise to hail your coachman—before he departs the drive. It is, indeed, a long and arduous hike back into town."

"*Loud!? Strange?!* You—! You—! I am Lady Marilyn Eveline Drayton! *Heir to Windsfield!... you idiot!*"

"Madam," Albert J. Ridley, completely unruffled by this outburst, informed her coldly, "That cannot be. We were informed by the estate's attorneys to prepare for a visit from the heir—one Sir William Bartram Logan, Fifth Earl of Windsfield. And until Sir William's arrival, not one soul was to be permitted entrance past this door, lest properties be carried off prematurely. Of you, madam, I have received *no* instruction. Not one soul is to be allowed entrance, madam, until the arrival of Sir William—"

The words fell on Lady Marilyn's ears like piercing stabs of icy knives cutting through her tired brain.

"No! No! It cannot be! That…bloated…aging…frog! How could he *do* that to me?! That…..that…."

Words failed Lady Marilyn. What with the past few almost sleepless nights, coupled with poor or no nourishment, and the cold shudders of outrage that shook her slight frame, Marilyn felt sure she was on the verge of falling in a dead swoon.

Which she promptly decided was a most excellent idea.

A gloved hand flew to the brim of her violet silk bonnet. With a slight cry, "Ohhhhhhhh…!" Lady Marilyn closed her lovely violet eyes, and collapsed in a dead but graceful heap—at Albert J. Ridley's feet.

"Madam! *Madam? Joseph!"*

Joseph, who had been lingering quite nearby, hastened to the steward's side and replied immediately, "Sir? What…shall we do with her…sir?"

"I don't suppose we can in all good conscience leave her lying on the steps, now can we, Joseph?" Albert J. Ridley observed coolly. "We shall bring her inside. Revive her with a glass of cold water. Make absolutely sure she…touches nothing. Then send her on her way."

That's what you think! Lady Marilyn fluttered one delicate eyelid to catch a glimpse of the steward's stiff, closed face. *You…cold hearted, fish-faced donkey!…just you wait until I settle with this interloper…this William Bartram Logan! Fifth Earl of Windsfield, indeed! We shall just see about that!*

"Ohhhhhh! Water! Water! I must lie down! I do believe…I'm…dying…!"

Somewhere in the east wing of the huge mansion situated atop a slight knoll on the Estate of Windsfield a massive grandfather clock chimed the hour. Eleven o'clock. The families occupying the jumble of thatched-roofed cottages running along the lanes and roads of Windsfield Village in the valley situated southwest of the mansion grounds had been up and stirring hours ago. Cocks had crowed, milkmaids had stripped the village cows' udders of their precious load. Cattle and sheep grazed. Oxen and mules had been hitched to ancient plows and furrows were even now being laid open in the

244

rich vales and over the slight hills of soil fertilized with manures from nearby byres and barns. Mothers tended their young and children played amongst garden plots and chicken coops.

Older children bent over the low desks of the Windsfield Village School, and earnestly applied themselves to the scratching of their lessons on charcoal slates and papers. Books and schooling were free and readily available for any and all of whatever age who cared to read and learn.

Cottages and roads were well maintained in Windsfield Village, and shops and stalls were plentiful, where one could buy fresh fish, bread or cheese or a shank of lamb or have one's shoes mended. Weavers of cloth and hawkers of thread occupied one end of the main street, so that no soul needed be in want of decent coverings and clothing at more than reasonable prices. It is true that jewelers and bankers and money brokers and lenders were not to be found in Windsfield Village, but this bothered the village's citizenry not one whit.

The steward of Windsfield Estate—and thus of Windsfield Village, its schools, its farms and dairies and sheepfolds and tiny cottage industries—was a wise, prudent, generous-hearted and compassionate manager. He did for the residents of Windsfield what they were incapable of doing for themselves—insured them a market for their products and produce, managed the financial affairs of the village, advanced monies as loans to those unfortunates who had unexpected expenses due to ill health or crop loss, paid for a bevy of trained teachers to run the Windsfield Village School, a physician to be in ready attendance for the populace, and for a protestant minister to stand in the small whitewashed church each Lord's Day and bless and instruct the people in the Holy Writ as set forth in the King James Version of the Holy Bible.

The citizens of Windsfield Village—that morning as Lady Marilyn awoke from the sumptuous bed to which she had, a few days prior, been bodily carried—were, all in all, happy and content with their lot in life.

But there had been, since the death of the Fourth Earl of Windsfield, a breeze of anxious unease rippling across the cottage rooftops and over the fields, pastures, and orchards of Windsfield Village. Even those in attendance at the tiny white church on The Lord's Day each week since the Earl's death lived beneath the looming shadow of the Fifth Earl of Windsfield.

Would this *Fifth Earl of Windsfield* keep the present steward on? Would he be wise, compassionate and of a generous nature? Would life at Windsfield Village continue to offer productive employment to those souls willing to work? A comfortable cottage with fuel for winter fires and shanks of lambs for the pots of those willing to rise early and raise their own bread and meat?

Would the spring festival of May continue, when the farmers and their wives and the milkmaids and plowmen and all the children grasped colored streamers of ribbons, and danced merrily about the maypole, welcoming the spring and summer with the new growths, the joys and warmth they brought? Or would the dance about the maypole be banned as heathenish and pagan by some stiff-faced, straight-laced steward or by his employer, the Fifth Earl of Windsfield?…as it had been in the days of their grandfathers? And the fall festival of harvest home? Would the farmers and shepherds of Windsfield Village still be allowed every Sunday off, to attend worship services or sit about their cottage fires and rest their feet and play with their little ones? Would the children still be allowed their books and their leisure on cold winter days to sit and read and learn and dream?

Oh, dear Lord above—!—the villagers of Windsfield prayed—*send us a kind, wise, benevolent Fifth Earl!*

And thus it was that when word flooded out of the main house—from the kitchen and stables and out over the lovely formal gardens—that a sour-faced, shrill-voiced, shrivel-hearted shrew who labeled herself *heir to Windsfield* had suddenly appeared at the door of the mansion house and announced herself the new mistress of the estate, that the hearts of the villagers all squeezed in their chests. Their breath caught painfully in their throats, and everyone walked beneath a shadow of dread and unease— what about this *man* of whom they had all been told?…this *Sir William Bartram Logan*? Was he not, then, indeed the new Earl of Windsfield? Was this selfish, sharp-tongued interloper to be allowed to take control of the estate and the village, and make life a hell on earth for each and every one of them, down to the tiniest babe at its mother's breast?! God forbid!—that this woman who called herself *Lady Marilyn Eveline Drayton* should be truly heir to the Windsfield Estates…!

All this dread had been generated in the short space of one week's time. Immediately she appeared at the door, where she collapsed in a helpless heap, Albert J. Ridley had taken horse and ridden hard for London, for the office of the barristers, Sullivan & Sullivan, where he learned to his horror that there was, indeed, such a personage as Lady Marilyn Drayton. And that such a personage was indeed one of the heirs to Sir Feldon's estate. Exactly *what* her part in the inheritance, the barristers were not at this time at liberty to divulge. Albert was, therefore, instructed by the barristers to allow the person to stay in residence at Windsfield, but he and the household staff were warned to keep a sharp watch on her, to make certain that Lady Marilyn did not 'appropriate' to herself anything of value, since the lady seemed bent upon having her inheritance prior to the settling of all the legalities of the case.

The stone and marble sculptures that adorned almost every room, nook and cranny of the massive mansion were deemed to be safe, due to their heft and bulk. But a sharp eye was kept to the cabinets where exquisite silver services gleamed, and to the closets where rich linens were stored amongst dried leaves of roses and lavender bulbs. Close watch was also maintained on the library, where many rare first editions nestled on dust-free, well-polished shelves. Then there were the many canvases done in charcoals and fine oils by the masters of Europe that adorned the mansion's grand salons, winding staircases, and broad halls.

For although the woman who termed herself *Lady Marilyn* appeared, in the presence of Albert the Steward, as benign, as harmless, as helpless as a newborn colt, complaining of some unnamed malady that kept her largely abed for the greater part of each day, when the head steward was not in attendance, the staff of Windsfield saw a different side of Lady Marilyn.

She was seen up and about—but not until almost noon of each day— appearing hale and hearty as you please. She roamed the halls and climbed the staircases, carrying in her hands a large ruled pad, and a sharply trimmed pencil with which she was constantly scribbling upon her large pad—as if upon the business of taking a complete and thorough inventory of the mansion's rich contents.

Then as soon as Albert the Steward appeared, due to her weakened condition brought on by stress at being denied her rightful heritage by the greedy firm, the brothers Sullivan & Sullivan of Fleet Street, London, Lady

Marilyn would again find herself unable to deal with even the slightest of her daily needs. All her meals must be fetched to her. Up the stairs. Her hair must be combed and arranged each day by one of the chamber maids. Her clothes must be cleaned, laid out properly and her bedding refreshed and arranged. If she deigned to leave the house for a stroll in the gardens, she must be aided up and down the grand staircase over which she usually flew as lightly as a dove.

And all this assistance was procured by a tongue as sharp as a two-edged sword, that lashed out and bit and carved and carried from almost one end of the fine mansion to the other—although there were altogether more than three-dozen rooms total in the vast place. But not one soul dared breathe a word to Head Steward, Albert, for they had all been warned, in a voice, loud, clear, and dripping with venomous rage, that *if* they foolishly forgot, and foolishly spoke out of turn—*heads would roll*.

How it was, then, that the cloud of darkness, the foul and abusive language, the fear and frustration rose from the rooms of the great mansion and drifted down the grand halls and staircases to the Village of Windsfield below, no one seemed at all certain. For not a soul, they all swore to one another, dared breathe a word of derision about the witch that had taken up abode in the mansion at Windsfield.

Chapter 23

An air of enthusiastic expectancy, of sheer joy of being seemed to emanate from Barbara Jo McKinnon Moss, rise above the steeply gabled roof of The Sparrow Inn, waft over the little town, and on up over the surrounding blue mountain ridges.

She hummed a low tune, as she bustled about, packing her largest trunk with her finest dresses and gowns, and her best, softest chemises and under things. She was about to embark upon a transatlantic voyage! Something Barbara Jo McKinnon Moss had never envisioned—not even in her wildest dreams! She scurried about the room she still insisted upon occupying in the upper story of her sister's small inn. A room that could no longer be gainfully let out for rent, but Barbara Jo gave that not a second thought. After all, *she* was Maggie McKinnon Evans' blood kin, the one surviving sister. Surely, this entitled her to some rights.

Including the right to be invited along on this voyage across the ocean, to a country called *England!* Barbara Jo was so excited she had scarcely slept a wink for the past three or four nights running. Often, she was up in the wee hours of the night, prowling about the narrow corridor leading from room to room in the upper floor of the inn. Often, in her wandering, she would lift the corner of a curtain, and peer out into the darkened dirt thoroughfare leading past the small inn. Once or twice—perhaps it was only her imagination?—she had thought she spied a figure on horseback, a figure that inevitably, once the curtains of the upper story of the inn gave the ever so slightest flutter, faded back into the sides of the plank buildings flanking the main street of Rhyersville.

A frown on her pale, narrow face shadowed by light brown hair that, until recently Barbara Jo had left to its own whims and devices, Barbara Jo

249

mentioned this oddity to her sister, Maggie, on two separate occasions.

"Oh, Barbs!" Maggie chided her gently, "How you do carry on! Why must you roam the hallway…! And then…! Forget it, Barbs. Don't go conjuring up mysterious figures in the night. Why on earth would some poor, benighted soul sit his horse, night after blessed night, just to peer up at our windows?"

"I don't know, Maggs!" Barbara Jo wagged her head in warning, "But…believe me when I assure you most strongly…he is out there! Every night! Rain or shine! And he is watching this inn—like a hawk watches the hen coops!"

"Barbs!"

"I think you should *say* something…to the sheriff!"

"The sheriff?! What in the name of heaven would I *say* to the sheriff? My darling sister, who by the way has been for the past few weeks so stricken with grief that she could hardly stand upright…has now taken it into her head…now that she is not only up out of her bed, but constantly roaming the hallway night after night…has taken to seeing dark doings in the street of Rhyersville?! On a nightly basis?!"

"Maggs! That was cruel and heartless of you! Yes, indeed! Cruel…and heartless! Make all the fun of me you want, but I know what I saw! You could at least speak to Mr. Bartram Logan."

"To Mr. Logan?"

"All right, Maggs. Let's just let the matter drop. But believe me…" a finger wagging in Maggie's startled face, "You can just believe me when I say that one of these fine days…these words will come back to haunt you!"

"How many changes of under things, Barbs, do you honestly feel we should take?"

It was the following afternoon, and Barbara Jo had just mentioned the mysterious rider, again, to which Maggie made no response; she simply stood staring at her sister oddly. Was Barbara Jo going mad? Imagining strange riders in the darkness of the night?

"What? Oh…I don't know…half a dozen or so, don't you suppose?" Barbara Jo mumbled, deliberately turning her back. Maggie could ignore her all she wanted, but she knew what she had seen. She *had* seen him, again last night. Who *was* he? *Why* was he here? Spying nightly on The Sparrow Inn? Maggie failed to believe her. And perhaps with just cause. She hadn't seemed able to pull herself together, rid herself of the melancholy that had afflicted her since Fred's passing. Now that he was gone, she often felt twinges of guilt, that she had never *truly* loved the man, not the way a woman *should* love a husband; but, in her own way, she realized after he was gone, that she had...deep feelings for Fred Moss. When she most needed someone, he was there. He had filled a great, gaping void in her life. Had given her days meaning and purpose. Together, they had made a *life*. Now, that life was gone. Now, that void, that purposelessness had returned; drifting, vast, yawning, gray clouds of fog threatened, day by day, to swallow her up. She had no talent for sewing, or tatting, or any sort of needlework. She cared nothing for cooking and housework. In short, she felt useless—without Fred, and the mercantile... She was twenty-two years old! A lifetime of emptiness yawned ahead of her.

Barbara Jo realized that Maggie was saying something, some lame excuse of an apology, and then exiting the room.

Barbara Jo heaved a sigh, turned, moved slowly to the front window, lifted the curtain, and peered out into the coming darkness.

Oh, yes! He would be there! She was sure of it. Again. Tonight. Maybe she should say something herself...to Mister William Bartram Logan. No. Not now. It might hinder their departure. This trip to London was ever so important to her...a bright ray of sunshine striking through gray clouds, and they would be leaving in only a few days. Taking the train, Mr. Logan said, first to Philadelphia, where Barbara Jo understood he had some business matters to attend to. Plus, he had voiced a desire that Maggie and Johnny visit his boyhood home, in the fine suburbs of Philadelphia. Then from there to the coast. To the city of Boston, to the port, to board a transatlantic liner.

Whoever it was, lurking like a black devil in the night, peering constantly up at their windows, surely an investigation of him could wait. Yes, he could wait. Until they returned from Europe.

Barbara Jo dropped the lace curtain back in place, turned her back on the window, and resumed her packing. Surely, whatever his evil designs, nothing bad could come of them...not in the next few weeks.

Chapter 24

"Will we be having the joy of your company this Sunday, Mr. Logan, darling?"

Over the remnants of breakfast, Bart gazed at Maggie across the kitchen table. "I am not quite sure yet, my sweet. There, is, darling, one thing…here in Rhyersville that will demand…a bit more of my attention…before we depart for Europe. Did I perchance mention to you, that I have…taken on this big…order…?" He turned his coffee cup slowly in one tanned hand.

"Order?" Maggie gazed at him quizzically.

"Yes, sweetheart. For building materials, and so forth…you know. I told you about it. About this fellow…he's…building a new house for his…wife? But…I…dread the thought of putting this huge project on hold, even for a few weeks, as he is most anxious to have it go forward with all speed. But…never mind…I'll probably just leave all my business interests in Giles' most capable hands. I'll meet with him, Saturday or Sunday, and we'll work it out."

"No, Mister Logan, you didn't breathe a word to me about any big order…that I can recall. Where is he, this man, building this new house? Here in town?"

"As a matter of fact, it will sit right outside town. Down past the schoolhouse. Where the creeks runs through that…lovely large valley. Yes, I…that's where he's raising his new…log home."

"A *log house*? Oh, how exciting! Has construction already begun? I'll have to walk on down there, one day, and take a look. Do you think this man would mind? I would love to see it!"

"I am most certain he would be delighted to have you visit the building site. In fact, I believe he…told me…the place is already well into the building process. I understand that the foundations have been laid, and parts of the log walls raised. I do believe I might just have a copy of the architect's drawing…of the place…in my saddlebags. Would you care to have a look at them? He might appreciate getting a woman's opinion…on the place."

"Architect's drawing?! He must be a man of some means. Oh! Of course! I can't wait to see them….!"

Bart hurried out, then strode back inside. Drawing a long sheaf of papers from a leather bag, he spread them carefully out on a table near the dining room fireplace.

"Well. Here they are. What do you think? *This* shows a view of the finished house…the front of the place."

"It…looks almost…like…Cottonwood, doesn't it?"

"Oh, but darling, this is nothing like Cottonwood, do you think? I mean… see? The veranda columns…these are huge, square-cut logs, not round, and Cottonwood is white clapboard. And this…this is the chinking between the logs."

"They…certainly are *huge* logs! Each one appears to be…"

"Yes, they are large, but that's because they have to support the upper story. See? And there's to be a veranda…and above it…"

"Oh, Bartram! It's just…simply grand! It has these gigantic square columns, rising up from the veranda, and …what's that?"

"That's a sort of second veranda. It will run along the upper story, so that, of a morning or evening, he and his wife can step out of the upper bed chambers, for a good view of the surrounding mountains."

"How wonderful!" Maggie felt as if her breath had been stolen away.

"You really like it?"

"Anyone who wouldn't… has something wrong with his head!" Maggie sighed. "It's a dream…"

"Yes. That's exactly what he said. It's been his dream…for some months now…to build this place. It's to be a surprise…he told me…for his wife. He might appreciate, therefore, a woman's opinion, as to the layout of the interior. The outer walls are pretty much settled, except that a window might be moved or a door, here or there, without a great deal of bother. But the interior partitions, the layout of the house, it's still pretty much up in the air…so he told me. He…asked if I had any ideas…and I just thought I'd run the entire thing by you…maybe get a woman's viewpoint on it. Impossible to ask his wife. That would spoil the surprise."

"Well…" Maggie bent her head over the drawings, as Bart flipped through them.

"Ah! Here we have a…suggested…plan for the interior partitions of the downstairs…"

"What is this?"

"Let me see…I suppose…that would be…yes, I think that's the main parlor. And over here, he mentioned something about a music room, or library and music room combination…"

"A room…for books…and music? Who *is* this man? Is he from *Rhyersville*?"

"No, darling. I don't believe he is…but moving on…what do you think about the kitchen? And a dining area large enough for entertainment? Where should those be located?"

"Well, how will the house be situated on the property? An eastward facing kitchen would be nice, to catch the morning sun."

"That's an excellent idea. I'm sure…he would be delighted with that…and darling…what do you think about—"

The two of them bent their heads, mulling over and discussing various room layouts and arrangements. Time flew, and finally Maggie lifted her head and stared off into nothing, muttering dreamily: "She is certainly a fortunate woman. The lady whose husband is building her such a marvelous place."

"You…really think so?"

"Yes, Mister Logan. He must love her—*very* much."

"Yes…that could well be the case. Would you care to…walk down there…and have a look at the building site?"

"You mean…now?"

"It's not far. The man said that he wanted to be close enough that his family could easily attend Sunday services, as his wife is very much into…the church. And the children could…easily attend school…even in inclement weather, when he was unavailable to transport them."

"Oh? How many children do they have?"

"Only…one, I believe he told me, thus far…a little boy. But…they are young, and have plans…"

"It would be a wonderful home in which to raise a family. They certainly wouldn't be tripping over each other's toes. Look at all the rooms! It's...as big as Cottonwood!"

"But...it's not...Cottonwood. This is...a new house. There's not one like it in the country, that I know of. He had it designed...especially...for his family."

"It is certainly...but there's something so familiar about it...I feel as if I've already seen the place...and walked about in it."

"Perhaps...that's because of the...square-log construction...like McKinnon Valley? With the veranda, and the upper floor. But, this, sweetheart..."

"I know. I'm being silly...it's just that..."

"You really like it, then?"

"It's perfect!"

"Why don't we go and find Johnny? Where is he? We'll walk down and check out the location?"

The three of them strode down the hill, past the little schoolhouse, the addition Thomas Byers was tacking on about half completed.

Then a quarter of a mile or so farther on, as they left the little country lane and headed across a field that had lain fallow for many years, Maggie caught the murmur of the creek. Past the field, they came to a vast meadow, drenched in sunlight, against a backdrop of purple mountains.

"Over here," Bart Logan was saying, "See, there, before you get to the creek, that's the rock foundation."

"*Foundation*?" Maggie muttered, "Why...the walls of the lower floor...are already built!"

"He mentioned this project...months ago. So I've had the crew on the lookout for just the right timbers...for the walls...support beams...and...well...he's farther along with the project than I had supposed."

"And the house, it goes on, and on! Who *needs* a house this size?"

"I don't know," Bart shrugged. "But it's *his* idea...and I understand that he has the money...to build it this size. I suppose this is what he wants.

255

Perhaps, what he believes will make his wife happy."

"She will love it here," Maggie murmured. "She can sit on the veranda of an evening, and hear the frogs croaking, and the creek murmuring by. It's just, too, too, perfect. Thank you, darling, for showing it to me."

"He will be very pleased, the owner, to have a woman's approval. And I'm sure he'll appreciate all your suggestions, about the layout of the interior."

"Yes...well..." Maggie smiled wistfully up at Bart, "I can assure you, Mr. Logan, darling!...the pleasure was all mine! And now, the sun seems to be sinking over those magnificent mountains. I think we have dawdled quite enough for one afternoon, pushing ourselves onto someone's property, and invading the privacy of their new home, half-finished or not. Perhaps we should head back for the inn, and think about getting Johnny a bit of supper? Where is Johnny?"

"I think, my sweet, John Thomas, Jr. has tired of our company, and has run off to go wading in the creek."

"Johnny!" Maggie was screeching as she flew across the meadow, dark hair streaming out from beneath her bonnet as she ran, "Those are your *best* shoes! And *look* at you! You're getting them *all wet*!"

"Whose goin' ta live in this place, Maggie? I sure do like it here!" Johnny had leapt to a sandbar far out in the middle of the creek that was very wide, and in some spots, very deep. His shoes and stockings all appeared soaked.

"I don't know, sweetie. Some people we never even heard of. I think...they're from up north, somewhere."

"You mean...a bunch of *Yankees* is comin'....?"

Maggie leapt across the flow of the creek, landing firmly on the little sandbar, reached and took Johnny's small, warm hand, pulling him along behind her, from sand bar to sand bar, out of the creek, and along the path to where Bart Logan waited, a huge grin on his face.

"Oh! *You!* You think this is *funny*?" Maggie demanded. Dragging Johnny along behind her, fuming, Maggie stomped past Bart and flounced back up the hill, past the little schoolhouse. She forgot all about the grand house that was being constructed—in the vast grandeur of the sunlit valley just outside Rhyersville.

Chapter 25

"Don't you think you should *rouse* yourself, Bethany Lee, and feed little Samantha? I have already given the baby her bath."

Maggie laid the tiny infant down beside her mother. The little girl looked up at Maggie, her blue eyes wide, her button of a mouth open like the beak of a little bird.

"Bethany Lee? Did you *hear* what I just said? Mr. Logan will be here in a few minutes. And I simply do not have the time…*Bethany Lee*!?!"

"Whut…!?" The girl turned over, brushing gold-blond hair back from a face that was, even at this hour of the morning, very, very pretty, Maggie sighed to herself. What a pity the girl had nothing inside that matched her outward appearance!

"Arouse yourself!" Maggie shouted angrily, "And see to your child! I am leaving! This morning, my dear girl! And there will be no one…no one but you, do you hear me?…to see to this infant! Now! Get up! And see to your gorgeous little daughter! I hear Mr. Logan's voice, downstairs. And I do believe that's *his* tread on the stairs, to fetch down our luggage. *Get up!*"

With a heavy heart, Maggie gave Bart the faintest of welcoming smiles as his handsome head appeared over the stair railing, Benjamin Noah a few steps behind him. Bart smiled at her, dropped a soft peck on one cheek as he topped the stairs and met her in the tiny hallway; then he and Benjamin Noah bent strong backs to the gargantuan task of shuttling Maggie's, Barbara Jo's and Johnny's luggage down the stairs and into the waiting carriage.

Her heart twisting, rising up into her throat, Maggie bent over the baby, gave her a parting kiss, turned her back and hurried down the stairs. A hug and a kiss from Liza Mae, a huge grin and a wave from Benjamin Noah…and just like that…Rhyersville fell behind them in a swirling cloud of early-morning dust.

And they were off.

The train rumbled and clattered down the tracks, at the amazing speed, Bart advised the two women and little Johnny, of at least thirty to *thirty-five miles per hour!* In no time at all, Johnny grew bored with sitting sedately on the seat beside Maggie, so he bounced back and forth—between Maggie and Mr. William Bartram Logan, who sat in the seat immediately behind them. Johnny would kneel on the seat from time to time, peering back at Bart Logan, making weird faces at him, just for the fun of it, which Bart promptly returned in kind. Then he would bounce over Maggie's booted feet, around the end of the seat, and leap up beside Bart, or onto Bart, whichever was the result in each case, until he about wore out the floor boards of the train car.

The traveling quartet had all sorts of problems, immediately they boarded the train. Bart certainly had no intentions of sharing a seat…for hours on end…with Maggie's sister, while Maggie herself sat within arms' reach…just in front of him.

But Johnny absolutely refused to sit beside Barbara Jo, and share her seat, unless Maggie also occupied the same space. So they ended up with Barbara Jo, Johnny, and Maggie, all crowded onto one seat, except for the short spaces of time when Johnny deigned to dash back to keep Bart company. Johnny did, in fact, seem torn between his desire to sit beside his sister, and Mr. Bartram Logan at one and the same time. But the length of the seats did not readily permit such an arrangement. And Barbara Jo, Maggie knew, would have been highly insulted, had the other three deserted her, and left her to herself on a seat all alone.

As Johnny scooted over and around her feet, times too numerous to count, Maggie grew weary, and found it difficult to concentrate on the loveliness of the countryside swirling past. At thirty-five miles an hour! What was the world coming to!

She tried to lay her head back, but the train seat which was at best firm and at worst hard, did not lend itself to such a physical arrangement. *I would rather,* she mumbled at one point to herself, *be sitting in my rocking chair, on the back porch and staring at McKinnon Mountain!*

"What's that, darling? Did you say something?" Bart inquired, leaning forward so as to speak above the roar and clang and rattle of the iron wheels whirring against steel rails. "Are you enjoying yourself? Are you comfortable? Want to come back here? And sit with me, for a spell?"

Maggie glanced over at her sister. Barbara Jo's light blue eyes met hers. "No!" Maggie yelled in reply, "Not…right now…maybe…later."

By now, Johnny, who had been awakened very early this morning, had begun to slow in his meanderings back and forth from seat to seat, and he sat now, very still, the blue eyes beginning to occasionally drift shut, and his little head to bob about on a tiny frame, against his most manly attempts to stay fully awake so as to miss nothing.

The next thing Maggie knew, Johnny had fallen fast asleep, and had sunk in an awkward slump, half in, half out of her lap.

Maggie's side and leg grew absolutely numb, even beneath his slight weight. Bart, immediately behind her, peered over, and saw that she was getting uncomfortable.

He rose from his seat, lifted Johnny, and stretched the little boy out on the seat with him, his head resting on Bart's leg.

Then, in a few minutes, Bart removed his coat, folded it neatly into a soft bundle, slipped this beneath Johnny's slightly sweaty head, rose and reached for Maggie's hand.

Gratefully, she gave it to him. He pulled her to her feet, led her down the train aisle, and out onto the rear platform.

Here the two of them stood, wordlessly watching the countryside speed by. Then Bart spoke.

"The country's changing so fast! I can't believe it!"

"What?" Maggie asked, looking up into his tanned face.

"The way towns and farms are springing up. Just a few years back, I could travel this route, and only seldom see a farm cottage, or a village or town. Now, the country's pushing in from the seaboard. Forests are being turned daily into farms. Some of the farmland, into towns. Folks are daily crossing the mountains to the west. The Territories of Wyoming, and of Washington, are seriously talking of seeking statehood. Soon, we'll stretch from sea to sea."

"Rhyersville hasn't changed all that much. Not at all. Not since I was a child," Maggie mused.

"Well," Bart surmised, "Rhyersville's a bit off the beaten path, so to speak. It may not change very much for years to come. But have you looked at the countryside about Cottonwood lately?"

"You mean...Logan Town?"

"Yes. Logan Town. There's more to come there. I can feel it in my bones. I can feel it...in my heart...a voice, telling me..."

"Telling you...what?"

"I don't know. Even in the remotest mountains, people need jobs. They need a way to make a living for their families. To put a roof over their heads, food in their mouths. Give them hope for tomorrow..."

"And you see all that...at Logan Town?"

"I don't know. Do I sound daft, to you?"

"No. Not at all."

"Good. I'm glad we agree on that. You all right? You want to go back inside?"

"Maybe we'd better, and go check on Johnny. He's sure to wake up hungry."

Bart smiled. A comforting warmth spread through Maggie, giving her heart an unexpected jolt. Bart's hand firm on her arm, they turned to reenter the coach car.

When the sun stood directly overhead, Maggie broke open the picnic basket Liza Mae had packed. Fried chicken, biscuits, apples, cold potato wedges.

Then Bart pulled from beneath his seat the jug of water drawn fresh from the well this morning.

They roared up the country, the lovely, rolling hills and wild-flower-sprinkled valleys of North Georgia soon falling behind, outside their windows. They rolled on, over the *East Tennessee, Virginia & Georgia Railroad*, into the cedar-dotted hills of Tennessee. Then, as darkness was settling over the surrounding hills, they roared into Knoxville. They laid over for the night, at a fine Knoxville hotel. As soon as their heads hit their pillows,

Johnny and Barbara Jo sank into deep slumber. But as Maggie lay in bed in the cool darkness, she found it difficult, despite her bone-deep fatigue, to fall asleep, as the sound and motion of the train continued on in her head.

The following morning, as boilers were stoked red hot, they re-boarded the train, and away they roared. By noontime, as it had yesterday, Maggie's face felt tight and drawn, coated with flying cinders and coal dust that wafted through the train cars and landed on every passenger. Then into Bristol, Virginia, where the train halted, to take on coal, wood, and water. Bart did not mention the fact to Maggie, that this was the only railroad line crossing the Appalachian Mountains; it was, in fact, the line used by the Union Army during the War, to strike lethal blows deep into the belly of the South. It passed up between the Holston and the Nolichucky Rivers, through wild, unsettled country. Mountains rose on either side. Maggie stared out the train window at the wilderness that was Virginia Ahhhhh... *Virginia*! She wondered, as they entered the state, whether they would travel anywhere near that awful field or forest...where Grandpa Thomas Shawn McKinnon had fallen...and where his bones still lay... .

As they rolled into Richmond, she wondered if they would *ever* reach the town of Philadelphia!

By mid-afternoon Johnny had gotten bored to total distraction, and was bouncing from seat to seat. Bart pulled out of his duffle bag a big box. Out of the box, came a book.

"What is it?" Johnny asked, blue eyes wide.

"It's a book about flora and...about trees and other plants. I thought, if you planned on becoming a physician, you might like it."

"Who wrote it?"

"Why...a man named *William Bartram!*"

"You mean..." Johnny gazed up at the tall man beside him, eyes wide in disbelief, "You mean...there's another man...named just like you?"

"No. Not *just* like me. You see, my last name is Logan. But his last name was Bartram."

"Oh. How did you go and get his name?"

"Well...Johnny...it wasn't me who went and got his name. I believe it was, in fact, my great-grandfather. He was a friend, you see, of Mr. Bartram, the naturalist. He did, in fact, if I understand correctly, travel with him, about

261

what was then still Indian Territory. And he liked the man…and obviously his name…very much. So much, you see, that he named my grandfather after him….William Bartram Hurston."

"Oh. Why did he write a book?"

"He loved plants. He studied them. And he wanted other people to love them, and to study them. That's why anyone writes a book. So that other people can read and enjoy it."

"Did you n'joy the book?"

"I certainly did. I was just about your age, you see, when it was given to me…a gift from my mother's father…whom…at the time…I had never seen. But, after I read the book, I knew that if my Grandfather liked a book written by his own father's friend, Mr. William Bartram, who loved nature so much, well…then…my grandfather…couldn't be…*too* bad of a man."

"When did you git to meet him?"

"Oh, I was almost grown. Seventeen or eighteen, I think, the first time I came for a visit. I even attended a party of some sort, thrown by one of the local farm families."

"The *Bidwell's corn huskin' party*?" Maggie turned fully about, staring at Bartram Logan over the back of her seat.

"Why…yes…I do believe…it was! How did…you…know that?"

"Oh…" Maggie's smooth brows shot up slightly, "Seems…to me…I heard…about it."

"Don't tell me…!" Bart cried in amazement, "You were *there*! *Weren't you?* Well…?"

"Yes…and she told a fib…and she nearly drowned a *whole* wagonload of girls!—just to get there!" Barbara Jo chimed in.

"All that time…" Bart breathed, "*You…were…so…close…*"

Chapter 26

After three days of the rattle, roar and smoke of the train, Maggie found the city of Philadelphia to be altogether lovely, but far, far too crowded for her liking. She absolutely could not imagine… "Actually…living in such close quarters, with so many other folk, all rubbing and jostling elbow-to-elbow, so to speak," she told Bart. Bart only grinned, "Whatever you say, sweetheart."

She found the Logan mansion, situated not far back from a broad avenue shaded with elm trees, charming. Even grandiose. Almost as large as Cottonwood. But there, she quickly noted, the similarity ended. No row of slave cabins dotted the south lawn. Just something called a *tennis court*. Here, Bart informed her, folks swatted a little ball back and forth over a net, at one another. Trying their best with each turn, he informed her, to make the other fellow miss.

"When on earth do they find the time to bat a little ball around?! And how… unseemly and downright ungracious of them! To deliberately attempt to foil their companion's every move!" Maggie had replied indignantly. And Bart had, again, shrugged, and grinned, "It's…sort of…like playing horse shoes, like you do in the South. Except with a ball. No, not really."

There was scarcely any front yard, to speak of. And no sign of any veranda graced the front of the two-storied structure. Which to Maggie was a shock. Every southern house worth its salt, even the meanest of sharecropper cabins, boasted a front porch, and a huge front yard. But the back of the house did host a vast expanse of neatly-clipped green lawn, and a formal garden, in the English style, so Maggie was informed by Bart. All the hedges sprinkled with arbors, rows and rows of them running this way and that, beneath spreading shade trees, past fountains and benches, invited one to drop down and spend the day. And the profusion of lovely flowering shrubs took Maggie's breath away. Viewing Eleanor Hurston Logan's gardens—neatly maintained by a caretaker who lived in the downstairs west wing of the fine house with his wife, the housekeeper—Maggie immediately felt a great kinship with Bart's mother, though she had never met her.

Bart spent a few days going about whatever business he had to attend, leaving Maggie, Barbara Jo and Johnny to their own devices. The three of them wandered about the huge Philadelphia mansion, oooiinnnggg and ahhhhiinnng over this and that. Then they would march outside, and stroll about the lawn or wander about the winding paths of the garden. Maggie, all the while, felt at loose ends. The housekeeper prepared their delicious meals and did all the cleaning. She even gathered their clothing from their luggage, and took it out back to the wash house, returning it fresh and smelling of sunshine.

What did women who lived in such houses do with themselves all the blessed live-long day? Maggie wondered.

Then Bart showed Maggie into the library, where, over the huge mantel, hung portraits of a man and a woman. "My parents," Bartram Logan whispered reverently.

"They…he is handsome. You…show great favor for him. And your mother, she's…lovely. You…have her eyes."

"Yes," was Bart's muted reply. He hastened her next door, to the music room. And Maggie began to discover what it was that the women who resided in such houses did all the blessed, live-long day. They read. They entertained their friends at card games, teas, and dinners. They did needlework, and took long, leisurely walks in their lovely gardens. They probably even batted the little balls back and forth at each other. Maggie, running a finger over the little pieces of embroidered and crocheted works dotting the fine furniture, could almost see Bart's mother…sitting in one of the rose-damask covered chairs, of a late afternoon, the western light glancing across her face and gown as her hands moved. She envisioned Eleanor Hurston Logan sitting at the grand piano that filled an entire corner of the huge music room. What had life been like for this daughter of the South? Transplanted so traumatically, in the midst of a Civil War, from home and hearth, deep into northern enemy territory?!

Maggie thought then of the War. Of the *devastation* it had wrought on the South. Of its still-lingering effects on so many families. What had all that death and destruction *accomplished?!* And that line…that had delineated North from South—enemy territory—now train coaches roared across it. In remote areas, stagecoach lines struck across it. Riders and farmers and millers hauled their produce and products over it. Now there was no more line, except in the memory of so many who had fought…and lost…so much.

———————————

The Port of Boston bustled with carriages, wagons, and horsemen, vying for a spot to draw near to unload their industrial and human cargoes. Longshoremen shouted, racing up and down the docks, where a great row of ships lay queued at anchor, about half still boasting towering masts, rigging and sails.

It was a bright, almost summer-like day. Maggie had thought the city of Philadelphia a boggle to the mind, with all it furious human and animal activity. But, this, the Port of Boston, made Philadelphia pale in comparison!

The hired carriage dropped them off, and Bartram Logan, Johnny clutched tightly in one arm, hustled Maggie and Barbara Jo along the boardwalk, up the broad gangplank, and onto the steamer.

Finally, after most of the morning had expired, the four stood at the rail of the great steam-driven, screw-propelled ocean liner, and gazed back at the spires, chimneys and rooftops of the city of Boston.

"I can't believe we are *actually…finally…here!*" Barbara Jo muttered, fiddling nervously with the ribbons of her dark blue silk bonnet. She still refused to wear black, traditional to mourning, but had decided that deep navy blue did not make her light complexion appear too sallow. Having secured her bonnet against the slight breeze moving over the crowded quays, Barbara Jo lifted both thin hands in vigorous, flitting little waves to the people thronging the docks.

"Gracious goodness," Maggie laughed at her sister. "To whom are you waving, Barbs?"

"Oh, no one in particular," Barbara Jo demurred, "I'm…just telling this place goodbye. I hope I can sail away, and leave it all behind."

"Oh, Barbs!" Maggie heaved a great sigh. "Have you, in all your years, learned nothing? We don't *sail away* from our problems and heartaches. I fear, dearest Barbs, that we indeed haul them along with us."

"That's *just* like you, Maggs! Anytime I attempt to experience the slightest bit of joy, you have to become all solemn and philosophical, and spoil it all for me!" Barbara Jo's lower lip began to tremble. Her light blue eyes grew moist. She sniffed. She produced a small handkerchief from the folds of a voluminous sleeve, dabbing quickly at her eyes, noisily blowing her nose.

"I'm...sorry....Barbs," Maggie muttered, chagrined. "I certainly didn't mean to..."

"Forget it, Maggs," Barbara Jo pulled a weak smile. Twisting the small lace-trimmed square, casting her gaze back across the teeming quays, vigorously she began flouncing her little handkerchief up and down in the salt-sprayed air.

Maggie reached out and laid an arm lightly about Barbara Jo's thin shoulders, drawing her close, wishing with all her heart she could...somehow...make everything all right.

No, that did *not* lay within her power. She would just have to trust in God, to somehow bolster her sister up, help her learn to accept what had happened, to deal with it—in a logical, reasonable, rational manner. Logical? Reasonable...? Rational...? *Barbara Jo!? Dear Lord,* Maggie breathed, *do have mercy...!*

Soon a huge barge drew alongside, so close, to tow and herd the huge liner out into the deep shipping channels of the Atlantic. Slowly, ever so slowly, *The Lady Ann* turned, and pointed her great steel prow out to sea.

Chapter 27

They rounded the tip of Cornwall, into the English Channel, and headed into the Dover Straits. The white, white cliffs came into view, rising off to their left. They stood, the four of them, staring up at the cliffs. All silent. All fatigued from days and days of the ocean rocking beneath their heels. Once the ship entered the Thames Estuary, the sea-reach was straight, the river's banks desolate and deserted, except for the seagulls circling lazily overhead, and a cluster of houses which they were told was Southend-on-sea. Now and then a lonely wooden jetty jutted from the river's edge, constituted of mud-flats, a black and shining marsh that went on for miles. Beyond the marsh rose wooded slopes, overgrown with vines and bushes.

As they were towed farther upriver, to their left, clusters of chimneys came into view. On the right bank rose a building which Maggie thought to be hideously ugly, of no definable shape. An ugly pile of red bricks filled with windows and topped with a tile roof. Then on the left stood the Village of Gravesend.

The houses of Gravesend crowded right up to the river's edge. As if they had been unceremoniously dumped there by some giant, careless hand, the houses appeared in imminent danger of toppling down the hill to which they so precariously clung—and off into the River Thames. In the distance, a church reared its lofty spires above the chaos of rooftops and warrens that was Gravesend. Hundreds of ships stood queued up at the quays. Some of them steamers, others proudly sported tall masts, spars, sails and rigging. Tugs moved in an out. Like the one guiding the *Lady Ann* in to berth.

"Well, darling, I think we are finally here," Bart whispered into Maggie's ear. Maggie gave him a faint smile and heaved a sigh of relief. She was tired of the confinement of the ship, though it was indeed huge, and offered its passengers various amenities, diversions and entertainments. The food had been excellent. The weather perfect. The company…

Maggie had spent more hours staring up into the eyes of Mister William Bartram Logan than she cared to recall. It made her nervous, this physical closeness to the man whose ring she wore. He was laughing, charming, keeping Johnny occupied, attempting to keep her occupied.

But Maggie's mind had constantly wandered back, over the taffrail, over the roiling wake of the sea…back to the little inn she called home…back to The Sparrow—and McKinnon Valley.

How on earth were they managing…without her? Was Bethany Lee feeding and bathing the baby? Was she keeping her bottom clean? Had a small animal somehow found its way beneath the tightly-closed lid on the sheltered well back of the inn, fallen in, drowned, decayed, and fouled the water? And poor Barbara Jo! The first few days aboard ship, Barbs had been beneath the weather. Sick to her stomach, unable to eat, unable to stand upright. Unable to come on deck and take the bracing salt air and watch the gulls drifting like white dreams in a blue sky, following the ship all the way across the broad Atlantic, waiting Bart told Maggie, for the scraps from the meticulous ship's galley to be tossed overboard into the gray-blue waters that appeared to Maggie deep as the sky was high. It was almost a week into the sailing before Barbara Jo, face pale and drawn, eyes lighter than the blue, blue sky, finally set tentative feet onto the deck of the ship, which seemed to Maggie as long and as broad as some of Papa's cotton fields.

Maggie would oftentimes stand at the tall railing, gaze down into the endless waters, then up into the sky, and feel that she was suspended between heaven and earth—in some other-worldly realm. Across the Atlantic waited the continent of Europe, and their destination, the green shores of England. Behind her lay…all that was near and dear to her heart. The Blue Ridge Mountains of North Georgia, the small mountain town, her small business, McKinnon Valley. What on earth was she *doing* here?

But now she was here. As they stepped off the liner and began mounting the cold, steel, salt-sprayed steps of the pier, Maggie peered down into the River Thames, still swift here, due to the awesome pull of the tides, the waters lapping at the pier fouled and dirty. She turned her eyes forward, and soon saw their luggage being piled into a huge coach. She was being lifted inside by the strong, sure hands of Bartram Logan, Barbara Jo beside her. Bart sat opposite, Johnny settled beside him, as much so as Johnny ever settled anywhere. Then they were lurching along Watling Street, through the Boroughs of Lewisham and Greenwich, through the Village of Blackheath, in South London.

"This road once thronged with highwaymen and cut-throats," Bart mentioned off-handedly. "Especially during the reign of Queen Elizabeth."

"Who was Liz-a-bet?" Johnny asked.

"A strong, fine queen, some years ago," Bart smiled down at the tiny boy tucked beneath his arm. "It's…safe enough, now." He had, Bartram Logan realized, gotten closer to this little boy, had come to love him more than he had ever dreamed such a thing possible. His heart swelled in his chest. In May…Johnny…and Maggie…would be his. "What's that you were saying, darling?" Bart smiled over at Maggie, seated across from him, his heart in his eyes.

Maggie almost gave a gasp, and could not help but avert her gaze. What she saw…in his eyes… She had no desire to ever again have a man gaze at her with such longing and passion. It almost frightened her. She had no desire to be *totally possessed, ever again…*

"I…said…" Maggie forced her eyes back to meet his gaze and snapped rather tartly, "how far is it, to the inn?"

"Not that far, darling," Bart continued to smile patiently. What had he just seen, for one short instant, deep in her eyes? What had he heard in the voice? Anger? Surely not…fear? No. She was just tired. He could see that she was exhausted. "Just on the outskirts of London, so I have been informed. I'm certain that we shall arrive there shortly."

But just then, even as Bart spoke, the sun disappeared behind a bank of dark clouds to the north. Beyond the coach windows, rain began to fall in thick sheets across the black heath. Wind whipped the great coach, rocking it from side to side. Barbara Jo gave a small, frightened yelp.

"It's just a spring storm, blowing in off the Channel. It'll soon pass. I understand such storms are frequently experienced…and are to be expected, in England," Bart said.

Maggie met his gaze, smiled at him. Whatever he had seen, the instant it came, it was gone. She appeared totally at ease, as she reached over to her sister. "Of course," she patted Barbara Jo's thin hand reassuringly, "This is not one tad fiercer than the storms moving over the mountains back home, eh? Barbs? Here," Maggie patted the thin hand, cooing as if Barbara Jo were a two-year-old, "Here, here! Now! Everything's going to be…fine."

Her warm hand resting atop her sister's cold, thin one, Maggie frowned slightly, turned her gaze out the window, into the sheets of rain that pounded against the glazed film that served as a coach window and wondered whether she would ever be able to banish the ghost of Len Evans. *Don't think about Len Evans!* Think about the countryside. Now and then she could see ancient buildings, like cold, faceless sentinels, marching past in the lowering gloom. *Dear God!* she thought, *How I wish I were home! Sitting before the fireplace, in the dining room of the inn…*

Bart Logan, his lank, lean frame swaying with the movement of the coach, watched the two sisters. How very different, he thought, these two are. Maggie, if set down in the middle of the Atlantic, minus boat or sail, would hitch a ride on a passing whale, or hail a passing gull or more likely, an angel, and find her way, *somehow*, safely to shore, practically unscathed.

While Barbara Jo, even in the shallowest of familiar waters, seemed daily to be on the imminent verge of sinking.

Maggie gazed out the blurred window, her thoughts winging back across the ocean, to Rhyersville. Suddenly, clearly in her mind, she saw Thomas Beyers, smiling at her, his right hand outstretched, as he stood on the stair landing of Barbara Jo's fine yellow brick house, his eyes dark and troubled, asking: *Are you or are you not…going to marry Mr. Bartram Logan…?* Maggie narrowed her eyes, put a hand to her throat. She wasn't sure why, but lately Thomas Beyers' handsome, earnest face had been intruding itself more and more into the fringes of her thoughts.

Suddenly feeling Bart's intense gaze resting upon her, Maggie turned from the window, flashing him a sweet smile…

Instantly, Bart wondered…*now what!?* What lay behind that smile? Guilt? Was that what he had glimpsed? Was she riding in this hired coach, so close to him that he could reach out at any moment and take her hand firmly in his, and all the while was she thinking…*daydreaming*…about some other man? *Who?* He was aware that every man who laid eyes on Maggie McKinnon Evans could scarcely draw his gaze away from such stunning beauty. But he could not conjure up in his mind the first man that he considered an actual *rival*, unless, of course, he frowned slightly, the widower... Thomas Beyers?... wavy blond hair, dark, intense eyes, educated, cultured...crazy in love with Margaret Ann McKinnon. But she never mentioned him. She, not to Bart's knowledge, ever saw him...except for the times he came into the dining room of the inn...to have his supper. And even then, she seemed to pay him little more heed than any of the other customers.

She never spoke to Bart about her emotions; she never confided in him. He had not the slightest notion what her feelings were...towards Thomas Beyers...or for that matter...towards himself...Would he ever reach behind that smile? That smile that sometimes rested upon him as brilliant as sunshine, making his blood run hot and his heart to thump madly against the walls of his chest. Then again, her smile would be almost cold, sad, mysterious, far away, difficult to read...no...make that *impossible*!

Little Johnny sat suddenly up from beneath Bart's arm, asking with wide, sleepy eyes, "Are we there yet?"

"No, son," Bartram smiled a bit sadly down at the little boy, "I'm afraid...we're not...quite...there...yet."

Johnny settled his slight frame back against Bart, and Bart turned his gaze out the window, scarcely aware of the passing scenes wreathed still in sheets of drifting rain.

Then, as quickly as it had swept in, the violent storm subsided, like a whimpering child, reluctantly withdrawing itself back onto the sea. The sun burst out through white, puffy clouds. And the heavy coach, drawn by four enormous steeds that were tossing their manes and flicking their tails, was slowing to a clattering halt in the foreyard of the dark, impressive bulk of the St. George's Inn.

His charges safely and comfortably ensconced in the inn, Bartram Logan felt free to go on about his business, visiting the offices of the Barristers, Sullivan & Sullivan, in a fine stone building fronting on Fleet Street, just off Trafalgar Square.

Bart stepped lithely down from the light hired carriage, strode to the door, which was immediately opened for him by a uniformed doorman, and entered.

He was greeted by the Messrs. Sullivan, who both wrung his hand warmly, and smiled at him as if he were a godsend for which they had longed for many a day.

"What's...going on?" Bart finally was able to ask.

"Well, Mr. Logan, my good sir. It appears that...your cousin..."

"My...what?"

"Why...sir...your cousin...Lady Marilyn Eveline Drayton. A very distant cousin, at that, being the daughter of a cousin of the late Earl, *thrice* removed. She simply *appeared* here one day, far, *far* in advance of the appointed time for the...for your... arrival... and when we, of course, refused to...make any advancement to her against... any possible inheritance, she made her way by hook...and shall I say it, sir?...crook... onto the grounds of Windsfield, and into the very bosom of the household. Where, we are informed by your dear departed uncle's trusted steward, she has...more...or less... attempted to...take...*unlawful* control."

"Take...control?" Bart asked, deeply confused.

"It would appear that she has shown herself, since her arrival at Windsfield, to be a lady of vile...and most despicable...temperament. And, unfortunately, to add to the confusion, she...has...developed...some sort of difficulty...with her health, we are told...which prevents us from being...able...to evict her...as law rightfully requires...from the premises."

"Well...if the poor woman is ill..." Bart frowned, his confusion deepening.

"We are not *at all* certain, Mr. Logan, that such is the case. And *that* is our point, *exactly*, not at all certain...that Mrs. Drayton is in the least bit indisposed. We are advised that at some points in time she barely seems capable of drawing herself up off her bed. Then again, she has been reported to be seen striding, hale and hearty, about the estate...as healthy as any country yeoman."

"Well..." Bart smiled confidently at them. This...cousin, Lady Drayton, sounded like a deceiver and a malingerer, a terror in skirts. But Bart had no wish to prejudge anyone, least of all some distant relative. "As soon as we finish our business here, I shall just journey on out...to the estate…Windsfield…I believe you call it, and look…the situation over. I am sure we…that is to say…my cousin and I…shall get on….most famously. Now, gentlemen, what is it that I am supposed to do? Or to know? Or …whatever?"

"Since you are, Mr. Logan, the principal heir, very little of anything going to…Lady Drayton…just some possessions of the His Lordship's long-deceased cousin that he thought she might like to possess for sentimental reasons, we shall simply read to you the will. Possession will pass immediately to you. I do not feel that she need even be present. You can simply show her your copy. That should…suffice nicely…to put any of her…claims…to rest."

"Claims?" Bart asked.

"Unfounded. *Completely* unfounded, claims, I might add," offered the older of the two Sullivan brothers. "Your dear departed uncle made his wishes very clear. Very, very clear, indeed. Unless you decline his request, you are to be executor of the estate. You are to inherit all lands, monies, etc, the title, leaving your… cousin…but—"

"Title?" Bart's handsome face creased in a slight frown.

"Why, yes, Mr. Logan. You, of course, will be Fifth Earl of Windsfield. And we shall, of course, just as a formality—your dear great-uncle did make provision for some of the staff, servants, and others—schedule a reading of the Will?"

"Oh. I…see. Yes…well…" Bart stammered, "Let us just get on with it, then, gentlemen…shall we…?"

———————

Maggie, feeling she would simply jump out of her skin if she didn't escape the walls of the St. George's Inn, made her way down the staircase and out the front door, into the street. The day was warm. She wore a bonnet, but no heavy shawl, and she carried a light parasol, one she had borrowed from Barbara Jo.

As she pushed open the massive front door and stepped outside, Maggie felt a twinge of guilt. She had more than halfway promised Mr. Bartram Logan that she, Barbara Jo and Johnny would stay put…behind the massive, dark oak doors of the inn. But, here she was, stepping lightly onto the stone walkway flanking the cobblestone street. She had left Barbara Jo stretched across the huge bed in their room, her mouth open, sound asleep on one pillow, while Johnny lay curled beside her, lost in dreamland, on the other.

Maggie strode smartly along, enjoying the feel of a cool breeze on her face, shaded beneath the bright blue, lace-trimmed silk parasol. Maggie wore her white dress, the one with the little blue sprigs of flowers with green leaves, a deep blue velvet sash spanning her slender waist.

Even on the streets of London, Maggie McKinnon, in her innocent passing, began to cause quite a stir. The parasol exactly matched the sash and the blue of her bonnet, which with white lace framed a gorgeously perfect face set off by wide blue eyes framed with dark lashes.

People turned to stare, but Maggie strode on, feeling perfectly safe. This was, after all, a huge city. Well populated, and certainly well patrolled with whatever security the city felt was proper. And she wasn't going far, and she didn't intend to stay long. She knew in her heart that Mr. Bartram Logan was a man of sense and discernment, and would not have installed them in anything that bordered on being an unsafe part of London.

But before Maggie had strolled two blocks from the St. George's Inn, she noticed that she had somehow acquired a shadow. No, make that *two* shadows. They were scuttling along behind her, now, ducking first into this doorway or behind this tree or column, and then that. No…they meant her no harm…they could not be following her? What on earth…why on earth…she glanced down at the small reticule that swung from her left hand, her right hand carrying the parasol. She attempted to hide the thing. She stuck it into the folds of her dress, but it bounced this way, then that, and refused to stay neatly tucked away.

With a sharp catch of breath, she realized that now the two dark, ragged forms had rapidly gained ground, and were almost upon her heels! *What to do? What to do?* If she were attacked, would anyone come to her rescue on this busy London street? Why hadn't she for once in her life listened?!— and stayed safely ensconced behind the door of the inn?! Mr. Bartram Logan would be furious with her…! And she saw not the first English gentleman near enough to summon to her immediate aid…!

Without giving her actions the first moment of thought, Maggie halted, whirled abruptly, and with a swift sweep of her left hand, dragged the blue parasol closed. She then thrust it out before her, in the manner of a weapon.

Caught completely off guard by these unexpected movements of their intended prey, the two thieves halted dead in their tracks. Dirty hair swinging from side to side, round orbs flicking furtively about in dark, dirty faces, they eyed one another, then the slender, awesomely lovely woman before them.

She stood with small, delicately booted feet firmly planted. The closed parasol she wielded before her, thrusting it from side to side, covering one of them, then the other, as if ready to lunge forth and plant the thing squarely in their black hearts.

Then, all at once, she swung the thing high overhead, shook it violently, while raising the other hand, her reticule dangling from it. She then began to shake both hands, reaching them far up, as if interceding with heaven. Then she opened her mouth and shrieked:

"Come! Lord Jesus! Come, Lord!—and drive the dark devils from this street..!"

!!!!!!!!! BOOOOOOMMMMMMM!!!!!

Did they imagine it…? Or did a clap of thunder roll across the sunlit sky? Did they imagine that a bolt of startlingly-white light shot out of the drifting clouds, illuminating the street for fifty feet or more about the slender figure standing with upraised hands? A light as white as any angel's wings…!

The faces of the two thieves grew slack; their bloodshot eyes widened in terror. They whirled about, and fled, ragged shreds of britches flapping about bony ankles like the wings of frightened crows.

———

"Well," Bart began, picking up his silver meat fork, attempting to initiate casual conversation over their supper in the smart dining room of St. George's inn that evening, "And just what did you ladies, and Johnny, do with yourselves during my unavoidable absence this fine afternoon?"

"Not…much…of anything…" Maggie hedged, taking a bite of the lovely roast goose, reaching with a slightly trembling hand for the crystal water goblet beside her China plate.

Barbara Jo looked up between bites, her light blue eyes narrowed at Maggie, as if to ask, *Are you going to tell him? Or shall I?*

Maggie gave Barbara Jo's left foot a none-too-delicate nudge beneath the white-draped table. Barbara Jo gave a small, startled intake of breath.

"Are you all right?" Bart Logan frowned over at her. "Can I order you some more water?"

Barbara Jo gave a slight wag of her head.

Maggie, Bart noted, was staring peculiarly at her sister. A warning? "No? No water?" He gazed from Maggie to Barbara Jo, the more likely of the two to talk.

"What…exactly…is going on here?"

All at once, a uniformed waiter appeared at Bart's right elbow. "That was sure somethin'!" His boyish face beamed with admiration at Margaret Ann.

"Oh? And just…what *was* this *something*?" Bart asked in a low, slow voice, his dark eyes glued to Maggie's lovely face. Her eyes stared straight into his. She had ceased chewing on her bite of roasted fowl, swallowed hard, and pulled a stiff, innocent little smile. The bite seemed to lodge in her throat. She needed a sip of water, but with Mr. Bartram Logan's dark eyes peeled so intently in her direction, she dared not reach again for the crystal goblet.

"Why, sir? Haven't you heard? How the lady, there, drove off two rogues intent on waylaying her and…doing God-knows-what?"

"Oh…? Is…that…right?" Bart asked, his voice so low Maggie barely caught the words.

With nervous little flicks of blue eyes, Barbara Jo swung her gaze from Maggie to Bart. Would Mr. Bartram Logan rise up in anger, upset the table, drag his betrothed out of the dining room, up the stairs, and there give her the tongue lashing she so rightfully deserved? Would Margaret Ann McKinnon Evans *never learn*? She thought she could take the world by the tail…just go sashaying off…down some foreign street…

"Yes, sir!" the young waiter replied, his enthusiastic admiration radiating from a beardless face, "Raised both her hands to heaven! And evoked the Savior! Calling down the might of angels…!"

"Angels, eh?" Bartram Logan mused, his tanned handsome face as dark as a thundercloud.

"Well…" Bart stared at Maggie, reached out a hand, grasped his water goblet by its delicate stem, and tipped the contents into his mouth. Then, as they all sat staring at him with wide eyes, he calmly glanced up at the waiter, and ordered:

"If you have quite finished your tale…of daring do…would you please refill the water glasses."

Then Bart cleared his throat, wiped his mouth on his snow-white linen napkin, replaced it in his lap, and asked, "Would you, by any chance, darling, care for a bit of dessert? Or have you not quite finished your main course?"

"Dessert…would be…very…nice…" Maggie whispered, giving a little nod of her head.

"So, Mrs. Margaret Ann McKinnon Evans, now you are vanquishing your foes by calling down upon their unsuspecting heads the powers of heaven? Thunder, so I got it from one source, someone who quite off the cuff accosted me on the stairway of the inn. And then," he waved a hand dramatically in the air, as if needing to emphasize a point, "there was also, as I have been given to understand it by another…gentleman…bolts of lightening…as it were…or was it only *one*…bolt of lightening…struck the cobblestones with such force as to give the adjoining and surrounding buildings quite a rigorous rattling of their doors and windows? Am I leaving *anything* unsaid here? Any…little…tiny bits of detail…any information you would deign to add…to fill the story in…completely…for me, my darling?"

"How you do carry on, Mr. Logan!" They were in the sitting room of the ladies' suite. Barbara Jo and Johnny had retired for the night. Maggie drew her gaze away from Bart's face, and moved to the window, where she stood, her back to him, looking out into the street below. Gaslight flickered from posts set along the street. Carriages and light wagons and carts, an occasional man on horseback, moved below her. Like figures in a dream.

She had narrowly avoided, just this afternoon, being…what *could* have happened to her? She could have been dragged into one of the alleys flanking that London street. A dirty hand capped over her mouth, she could have been viciously assaulted…raped… murdered…

She felt Bart Logan's presence as he moved up behind her. "I'm…sorry…" she whispered. "I know…it was foolish of me. I knew it…even as I pushed open the door…I knew I was inviting danger…but still…I went…I don't know why. How can I explain it to you, Mr. Logan, if I don't even understand it myself?! Oftentimes…I am…seized…by these

277

impulses. I have thus been plagued, God have mercy on my soul!…even in childhood. I could not name for you the times…I set the entire household upon its very ears. Made Papa and Mama *old* before their time…" she mused in a low, dreamlike voice. "Caused my sisters' faces to frown in fear and consternation…for my safety…and for theirs. There seems to be within me…this…unbridled spirit…"

"Yes, darling. Exactly," Bartram Logan was speaking into her ear, his mouth touching her hair, his breath warm, flowing down her neck. "I know. And that's one of the things…only one…that I love about you. You dare tread where most of us only dream of going. And I often fear…that I will never…never…be able to track you there…where you run before me…I fear I will never be able to catch, to capture that spirit…"

"*Why?* Mr. Logan? Why, do you even bother to try?" Maggie asked, feeling tears begin.

"Because…as I just said…I love you. I would rather worry and wonder and walk behind you, than to walk beside any other woman on earth."

"I make no promises…Mr. Logan…that I will ever…*can* ever…change," Maggie whispered, as she leaned her head back against him.

"Darling. Have I asked you to?"

Chapter 28

"So," Bartram surmised as the rocking coach broached the crest of the slight hill. "This is Windsfield."

"Oh! It's…breathtaking!" Maggie sighed, leaning her head slightly out the coach window to catch her first glimpse of Bartram Logan's recently inherited English estate.

"I only thought…" Barbara Jo peered past Maggie, up the slight grade, where in the distance, beyond a stretch of rolling green hills dotted with wildflowers, rose a grand, gray stone, four-story building, with tall, leaded windows, chimneys and turrets towering over a darkly-tiled roof that stretched over wing, after wing, after wing. "I only thought such things existed…in picture books! It…goes on…forever! It does quite take one's breath away!" Barbara Jo whispered.

"Well, I suppose it is…quite…impressive," Bart mused off-handedly, as if the palacial mansion were something to be met with in any locale, on any ordinary day. Removing his hat, he raked a hand through his dark hair, before setting the hat back, its broad brim cocked slightly forward over his forehead. He couldn't help but notice that Margaret Ann had made no further comments. He knew exactly how she felt about excessive wealth, though she had never expressed openly to him her feelings on money—any more than she had any other of her inmost thoughts. He well knew that she felt that the wealthy of the world were spoiled, useless, empty-headed, totally arrogant individuals. And he supposed that to a certain extent *that* included William Bartram Logan.

The coach-and-four lurched to a stop. Bartram Logan stepped lithely down from the coach—a luxurious closed carriage belonging to the Windsfield Estates, a carriage belonging, now, in fact, to *him*—that had come to call for them at the St. George's Inn as soon as a messenger had been dispatched to Windsfield, advising the resident staff of the sprawling estate that the Fifth Earl of Windsfield had arrived safely in London, concluded his business, and was now ready to visit his new holdings.

Bartram Logan reached up, placed his hands about Maggie's slender waist, and lifted her to the ground. Then Johnny. Then he took Barbara Jo's cold hand, and helped her to safely alight.

Immediately, the neatly-uniformed mansion staff, all stiff as starch in livery of black and white—as if they had all been waiting behind the massive oaken doors, peering expectantly out, ready on an instant's notice to step forth and greet the new master of Windsfield—appeared as if by magic.

Albert J. Ridley, head steward, stepped forward, greeting Bartram Logan with a slight bow, and words of deep respect for the new Fifth Earl of Windsfield:

"Greetings, to you, milord, and to those who are in company with you. And a most gracious welcome...to...Windsfield. Won't you kindly, sir, step inside, ladies, and Master Logan. We shall have your things brought immediately in, and placed in... whatever rooms you wish... to ...take for your accommodations."

Bart could see that the steward felt extremely ill at ease. He supposed it had been a very long time, if ever, that the man had greeted a new master to the mansion. The man stood before Bart, attempting to appear cool and collected, but Bart's quick mind did not miss the anxiety bordering on sheer panic lurking behind the stoic Englishman's eyes. And the way he kept fidgeting with his hands, clasping them first before him, and then, finally, seeming unsure of exactly what to do with them, tucking them behind his back.

"This be me wife, Master Logan."

The short, stout woman Bart took to be the head housekeeper, stood nervously behind the steward, the top of her head barely reaching the man's shoulder. As her husband motioned in her direction, she took a step forward, and to Bart's total amazement, gave a short, slight curtsy, as if greeting royalty. Her rotund face flushed as red as a berry, though her gray eyes when she peered up at him from beneath sparse brows appeared cold, frightened and nervous as a squirrel set for the pot.

"I am more than pleased to make the acquaintance of you all," Bart offered as a way of hopefully breaking the ice, putting the household staff at ease, as the lot of them stood on the stone steps staring at the arriving party of Americans as if they had just descended upon the estate from some distant, alien shore...which, Bart supposed, in their closed English minds...they had. Bart motioned toward Maggie, "This is Mrs. Margaret Ann Evans, my betrothed, whom I plan to marry come spring. This is her sister, Mrs. Barbara Jo Moss. This fine figure of a fellow is young John Thomas McKinnon, Jr., Mrs. Evans' brother. And now, could we step on inside. And I am certain that... whatever quarters... you have ready for occupancy," Bart continued, reaching out and pulling Maggie to him with one arm, while picking Johnny up with the other, "Mister Ridley, wasn't it?... will be...just fine with us."

"Albert, at your service, milord."

"Very well, then, Albert."

With that, Bartram Logan, Fifth Earl of Windsfield, smiled graciously down at his steward, who was a head shorter than Bart; and Maggie on one arm and Johnny in the other, he strode up the broad stone steps of Windsfield Mansion. Barbara Jo picked up the folds of her full skirts and trailed along behind. She could hear the steward issuing muffled orders to the driver and the footman, for the luggage to be brought in.

Maggie was instantly struck with the grandeur of the huge entrance hall. The entirety of The Sparrow Inn would have fit, Maggie reflected, easily into the entranceway, steeply-gabled roof and all. And though the day had turned warm, it was cool inside the vast stone mansion. Maggie noted doors—tall and broad enough to accommodate three or four persons abreast, leading off in all directions. And a grand staircase, winding up, and up, and up...

"Well..." Bartram Logan mused. He took Maggie's hand and held it tightly, as if to assure her she had not been swallowed by some mammoth stone monster. He put Johnny down, but held on to him as well. Bart stood gazing about him, thinking how this must look to Maggie and the boy. Then he was distracted as the steward's plump wife bustled forward.

Having been advised beforehand by the firm of Sullivan & Sullivan that the new Earl of Windsfield and his lady were not yet wed, she had opened, aired, scrubbed and scented for them separate quarters. Now, having met the master and his lady, having re-entered the grand mansion, she was again in her element. Her domain. She had been head housekeeper at Windsfield for many years. Here, in these vast, marble-tiled halls, she ruled supreme. There had been no mistress at Windsfield for many, many years now. Thus, her word to the household staff was law. With a jerk of her head, a lift of her brows, she dispatched the kitchen staff and the upstairs maids to their ordinarily assigned duties, whilst she busied herself with leading the new arrivals forward, toward the broad staircase.

The sound of their clicking heels echoing through the vast mansion, they reached and mounted the sweeping staircase. As they climbed, Johnny pulled his hand out of the warmth of Bartram Logan's large one, and now hung onto Maggie, lifting his small brown leather high-tops high with great effort as they mounted the stairs of the palacial mansion.

First, Mrs. Ridley showed Barbara Jo to a boudoir draped in lace and linen with walls of a light purple hue. Next Maggie was led into a room whose walls were the exact shade of early morning sunshine. The bed was gigantic, with four huge posts and a lace canopy that arched towards the grand ceiling trimmed with white carved woodwork, and sporting friezes of twining yellow roses with green leaves amongst delicate, lacy-white bunches of baby's breath. So high was the bed that beside it on the colorful Persian rug rested two steps to be mounted.

"Maggie?" Johnny muttered softly, as he gazed anxiously up at his sister, blue eyes wide, little face in a scowl. "I want to stay *with you*!" he sighed.

"Of course, sweetie. Whatever you want," Maggie squeezed his small hand reassuringly.

"But…Miss…" the rotund Mrs. Ridley turned to stare at Maggie, a cold, disapproving frown creasing her heavy brow, "We have a room all prepared…for the young master. He will have his own bath…and playthings have been *especially* brought in…"

"Fine. Good." Maggie gave the woman a firm but friendly smile. "How very kind…and thoughtful of you. I'm quite certain Johnny will make good use of that space, during the day, perhaps. Whenever he has the desire to play. But John Thomas will be sleeping in here. With me."

"Yes…Miss…whatever you say."

"Yes," Maggie replied firmly, "Exactly. Johnny's things are to brought in here, along with mine."

Mrs. Ridley, thin brows knit together, a stiff frown on her face that was round as a cabbage, exited the room. It was not a good idea, she thought to herself, to coddle the young so. If she were not *very* careful, before Master Logan's lovely lady knew it, the little boy would be wanting to accompany the couple on their honeymoon! She was very well aware that it was the custom—and had been for centuries—for the British aristocracy to push their young out of the nest, so to speak, to teach them very early on the value of independence, of meeting life's vicissitudes with a cold eye and a stiff upper lip. Most children were shuttled off when not much older that this little mite, to some fine, distant, excruciatingly strict and extremely expensive boarding school—where they would soon cease their whining for their mums, and learn to stand on their own two feet. After all, this world was not an easy place in which to make one's way. Even with money. Lots of money. And old, old money at that. The new Master's young lady had a great deal, a very great deal to learn.

Maggie stood in the center of the room, holding onto Johnny. Suddenly she felt absolutely overwhelmed with the entire thing, as if her legs would no longer support the weight of her body. Her head swam with confusion. She felt totally disoriented, as if she had become lost in a dream world, a storybook world, with castles and knights and dragons—Windsfield was the castle, and Bartram Logan was the knight, and she was just waiting for the dragon to sweep out of some vast, dark room and devour her! A world with no sure footing. Pulling Johnny along with her, she mounted the two steps and sank down onto the huge bed. Whatever had *possessed* her to accept William Bartram Logan's invitation to accompany him to this sumptuous, other-worldly English estate!? She must be totally out of her mind! How vividly she recalled the day Nellie Sue, Barbara Jo and she had ventured over the mountains to check out the grand plantation house called Cottonwood. *If Nellie Sue could only see her now…!*

Maggie swung Johnny up into her arms and snuggled him close. "Well, what do you think about all this, sweetie?" Johnny felt warm and small and very familiar, clutched close in her arms. Maggie squeezed him, as he replied, "I don't know what to think, Maggie. But it sure is *big*, ain't it?"

"Yes!" Maggie almost giggled aloud, "My thoughts exactly! If it's *anything* at all, *it sure is big*!"

Maggie gave a sudden start. "*Mrs. Ridley! You incompetent chit of a charwoman!*" A shrill scream came reverberating along the upstairs corridors, flew through the door and about the room where Maggie and Johnny sat on the big, ornate bed. "*You idiotic, moronic cow!* You mean that *he has actually arrived*? And I was *not* informed? *Not given fair warning? Nor* called forth to greet my dear, dear…cousin? I…recall…informing you, in *no uncertain terms*…that *prior* to his expected arrival, I was to be—"

By this point, Maggie had risen from the great bed, stepped down, and dragging Johnny along behind her, made her way to the huge door of the bed chamber, swung it open, and stepped into the upstairs corridor.

There stood a beautiful brunette swaddled in a sumptuously revealing white silk dressing gown. She faced Mrs. Ridley, her eyes flashing fire, her perfect face flushed scarlet. Unbelievable words laced with horrid curses issued from her luscious, full lips in a loud, heart-stopping volley.

Bartram Logan, hearing the uproar, appeared from a door farther down the broad corridor. Still fully dressed in his fine traveling suit, minus only his felt hat, he strode along the giant hall until he stood a few feet back of the beautiful brunette.

"What seems to be the problem here, Mrs. Ridley?" Bart demanded.

"Oh!" At the sound of Bart's voice, Lady Marilyn Drayton's violet eyes widened. She whirled about to gaze at him, gave a soft little gasp; a hand flew to her throat as her voice sank by several decibels. "Oh, my!" she advanced toward him, gushing sweetly, "You *must* be my *dear, dear* cousin! How very, *very* nice to at last meet you! I have been *so* looking forward to—"

"Oh?" Bart stood hands on hips, and cut in rudely, "Is that why you are crying about the upper hall?"

"Oh. Well. That. I had, *very kindly*, you understand, asked this…our *dear* housekeeper, Mrs. Ridley, here, to advise me…immediately she learned the appointed time of your arrival. So that I could…be downstairs…properly attired…to welcome you…to Windsfield," Lady Marilyn stammered on, attempting to put the best face on her fit that she could.

"I take it, then," Bart took a step forward, frowned down at her, "that you are *Lady* Marilyn Drayton? Am I correct in that assumption?"

"Oh, yes!" Lady Marilyn gushed, brushing both hands nervously over her silk dressing gown, as if to smooth out numerous clumps of offending wrinkles. Then a hand flew to her hair, which she knew was a total and complete mess, as she had been in bed and fast asleep until abruptly awakened by voices in the corridor...*she could kill that dunce of a housekeeper, who had no doubt known this entire morning that this was to be the day of her cousin's arrival...!* "I am...Lady Drayton. And you, of course, are my dear, *dear* cousin, William Bartram Logan!"

"Yes," Bart's frown lingered. "I am..." the word *happy* seemed to stick in his throat and refuse to issue forth out of his mouth. As did also the word *pleased.* He had heard the angry tirade, that volley of invectives more fit for the mouth of a sailor than an English lady, and he did not at all feel happy or pleased to meet his cousin, Lady Marilyn Eveline Drayton, who, Bart immediately decided, had a mouth like a fishwife. "I am..." Bart stumbled on, finally giving it up, and muttering, "This is my betrothed, Mrs. Margaret Ann Evans, and her brother, John Thomas. That seems to about cover the introductions to those of us here present. So. Well. Since we are all exhausted from our travels, let me say...it was...nice...meeting you...Mrs. Drayton... and shall we now all retire to our rooms. And perhaps...we shall see you downstairs for supper...should your health and strength permit. I have been given to understand that you have not been in the most robust physical condition...of late. If you find yourself unable to join us for supper, we shall most certainly...understand."

Instantly Lady Marilyn realized the awful, the terrible first impression she had made on this *usurper*, this *foreigner* who had sailed over from America to rob her of her rightful inheritance! But...he was... quite...handsome...

"Oh, no! I feel...*much* improved today! I shall, most assuredly, be joining you!" Lady Marilyn gushed, smiling profusely as she batted long, dark lashes.

"Yes," Bart pulled a grim smile, "I was..." and it slipped off the tip of his tongue before Bart, the consummate gentleman, could stop it, "... afraid of that."

Lady Marilyn's violet eyes narrowed to slits; the full lips pulled thin. *"Pardon me?"*

Maggie took a step forward, interceding with a smile. "Yes, we were...all *so afraid*...we would miss your company for supper! Weren't we, *Mister Logan, darling?*"

"Exactly," the new Earl of Windsfield turned and gave the beautiful woman garbed in some dark, nondescript muslin frock such a look of love that Lady Marilyn felt her heart squeeze painfully in her chest with sheer jealously. She would *kill!*...yes indeed...*she would kill*...to have a man like William Bartram Logan send such a look in *her* direction.

Then they all seemed to melt into their rooms, leaving Lady Marilyn Drayton standing alone in the huge corridor, lovely violet eyes narrowed beneath perfectly plucked brows, plotting in her mind just how she would erase this bad impression she had just so foolishly made, and gain the good graces of this thief and interloper, this very handsome thief, this very desirable interloper. Well, *what did they expect of her!?* With no warning of their imminent arrival, it was *their* fault that she had been fast asleep and half out of her mind with worry. But now, yes, she would have to go through her wardrobe, choose her least faded and worn gown. She still had a few at hand that should put to shame that little county bumpkin—what had he called her, *Margaret Ann?*—what a common and low name.

———————

Supper at Windsfield that night was a somber and solemn affair. Bart kept eyeing Lady Marilyn Drayton with a wary, guarded frown, not quite certain what to expect, what vile words might erupt next from the *lady*—a term which in this instance Bart found ludicrous in the extreme. A few hours ago, she had burst into that railing tirade for no apparent cause that he could identify. Then, not an hour past, as he was dressing for dinner she had appeared outside his door. When he, his shirt half buttoned, had opened the door in response to her insistent knocking, and had inquired, "Lady Drayton? Is something wrong? What can I...do for you?"

Clad in a gown which Bart felt was cut *far* too low, she had stepped very close, almost against him, lifted her face, batted her violet eyes with jerky little flutters, and whispered suggestively, "*I* might ask you, Cousin Bartram, that *very* same question!" She then pushed her way past him, floated into his room, and, in a most suggestive pose, reclined upon his bed. Bart, standing with his hand still on the door handle, had turned to stare at her in disbelief. "Should I, *Lady* Drayton, desire your...company...you shall be the first to know of it. Now, if you will kindly excuse me, I would very much appreciate it if you would take yourself *off* my bed, and *out* of my room."

Then upon entering the dining room, he had found that not only had his houseguest had the effrontery to bully Mrs. Ridley into allowing her to plan the dinner menu, but she had also made the table arrangements, seating Bart at the head of the table, and herself in the hostess' chair, immediately to his right. Not only had she offered herself to him—a man she had scarcely laid eyes on—like a pig on a platter, but now she was putting herself forth as mistress of the manor.

Barbara Jo had been placed at Bart's left. And Maggie had been seated beyond Barbara Jo.

When it became apparent that no place had been laid for Johnny, Bart rose, shoved back his chair with a frown, and ordered another setting immediately brought.

"It was my understanding…that it would just be the adults…" Lady Marilyn frowned up at him. "I had no *idea* the…*child*…would be brought into the—I mean…*it simply is not done!*"

It was all Bart could do to hold his tongue, finally, he sputtered in a voice cold and laced with anger, "This is not a formal occasion. It is merely a family dinner. In *America*, we do *not relegate* our children to—"

"It's all right," Maggie, from her seat below Barbara Jo, muttered tiredly, having no idea exactly what was occurring here. She was tired; she was unaware that Lady Marilyn had shoved her way into Bart's room. She simply wanted to have her supper. "It was just a…misunderstanding, Mr. Logan. Please, do take your seat."

But Bartram Logan did not immediately take his seat. He stood staring at Maggie, two chairs down. He wanted very badly to order Lady Marilyn to switch seats with her. But Maggie looked exhausted and confused. Johnny was hungry, and fidgeting in his chair. Bart sat down. "Mrs. Ridley, you may now serve supper," he ordered in a strained voice.

What on earth, Maggie wondered, had taken possession of Mister Logan? He looked angry and ill at ease. Oh, well. He was a strong man, but he was probably as spent as the rest of them. A lovely meal, a good night's sleep, Maggie thought, and they would all be of a more suitable temper. Maggie eyed the fine china plate before her, with its lovely pattern, a profusion of winding flowers and vines, as if, she thought with a smile, the kitchen maids had just gone out and plucked it from the garden. The elaborately patterned plate rested its expensive bottom on a delicate lace cloth that stretched the entire length of the dining table that appeared to Maggie to go on forever. The lovely cloth, probably, she thought with a little sigh, hand tatted by an industrious little woman residing in one of the tiny cottages dotting the village below the hill where rose Windsfield Mansion. As she fiddled with the strange food on the lovely plate that probably cost all by itself as much as the entire worth of The Sparrow Inn, she wondered at the odd assortment of eating utensils resting in gleaming silver beside the plate. And she wondered what the strange dishes were, that kept appearing as if by magic from the groaning sideboard sparkling with silver and gleaming crystal.

"Maggie." Johnny gazed down at the food on his plate, then up at Maggie, his beautiful little face creased in a tired frown, "What is this stuff? Can I please have a drumstick? Where's the drumstick?"

"*It's kidney pie!*" Lady Marilyn's sharp voice rang along the length of the table like an ill-toned gong.

"*Sweetie!*" Maggie whispered, aghast.

"*Tomorrow* night, Johnny, I can *personally* promise you," Bart said with a cold glance at Lady Marilyn, "You shall have all the drumsticks your little heart desires. But tonight, we are in a different place. An entirely different country and *culture*, one might say. And, here in England, so I am told, kidney pie is quite a delicacy."

"What kind of pie?" Johnny frowned.

"Never mind, sweetie," Maggie smiled down at her small brother, "You can just… eat your roll. Want a bit more butter on it? And how about some…" She stared at the dish just offered her, and grew immediately silent. What *was* that stuff?!

"It be blood pudding, milady," the serving maid at her elbow whispered. "Would you, or the little boy—"

"*No!* Thank you!" Maggie gave an involuntary shudder. What had she gotten them into? What had William Bartram Logan gotten them into!? Were English folk cannibals!? And heathens!? Didn't the Scriptures adamantly forbid the consumption of blood?

"Mrs. Ridley! Could John Thomas have a serving of scrambled eggs to go with his roll. And from this day forward, while we are in residence here at Windsfield," Bart barked to the housekeeper as she passed by the yawning length of the silver and crystal laden table, "*Mrs. Evans* will choose the menu to be served for each meal. Darling?" Bart ignored the stunned look on Lady Marilyn's flushed face—that had turned lobster red and broken out in huge beads of sweat. Since taking up residence at Windsfield, she had been issuing orders for whatever foods her heart desired.

And Mrs. Ridley looked none too pleased, either. Scrambled eggs, indeed! New master or no! This was *her* house! This was *her* kitchen staff! *She* decided—

But no. Apparently that long era was about to come to a screeching, heart-rending halt. First had appeared the sharp-tongued shrew who called herself Lady Marilyn. Ordering them all about! Like she were some grand duchess! Now here came *Himself* in the flesh, and the new master's lady was smiling at him, beaming was more the word for it, her face wreathed with a lovely smile, and her eyes...more in the nature of some lovesick school girl, Mrs. Ridley thought, shocked to the core, than the mistress of some fine English estate. Whatever was the world coming to! Heaven forbid that *these people*—

"That will be...just fine...Mister Logan, sir. Bridie be fixin' 'em, and the scrambled eggs is bein' brought *right* out." Mrs. Ridley's mouth pulled a stiff grimace, "And I shall put myself at your lady's disposal, whenever...she would care to make her choice for future meals...just let me know. And shall I have dessert served now, sir?"

"What...is it...the dessert?" Bart frowned, almost afraid to ask.

"It be a fine, smooth chocolate mousse, sir."

"A moose?" Johnny peered up worriedly at Maggie, "These people eat moose for dessert?"

"It's a custard pudding, I do believe, Johnny," Bart smiled despite himself. After all, he had Margaret Ann and Johnny to consider. Whatever was going on with Lady Marilyn Drayton, he must not permit her to spoil their first evening at Windsfield. He felt sure he could deal with her later. Bart held out a hand, "Why don't you come and sit on my lap? See, here come your eggs. You want another buttered roll? And I *might* just share my portion of pudding with you. And we can talk about tomorrow. And make lots of plans. I bet there are stables here. With plenty of horses...and whatever."

"Horses?" Johnny scrambled down from the chair beside Maggie, rushed around to where Bart, the Fifth Earl of Windsfield, sat at the head of the table, and was immediately lifted into the Earl's lap.

"Well! Now!" Bart laughed and squeezed the warm little body tight against his chest. "I'd say that's more like it! Eat your eggs, for, look! Here, I believe, comes our dessert! Could we have another spoon over here, please, Mrs. Ridley, for our pudding. Thank you! Now, Johnny, which spoon do you want? This one? Good thing, my boy, now, dig in! Ummmmmmmm!"

William Bartram Logan smacked his lips in open appreciation and gazed down at the little boy in delight. Johnny smacked his lips and burst into loud peals of boyish laughter.

As the two of them took turns, eating a bite of egg, then a bite of pudding, and loudly smacking their mouths, Lady Marilyn watched all this total lack of manners, this totally unsuitable camaraderie with the boy. He had brushed her off this evening, and now William Bartram Logan kept deferring to, and gazing into the eyes of the woman called Margaret Ann Evans! She wondered if he might have *Mrs. Evans* for dessert! *Really!* It was just *too* much! These *Americans*! Such flagrant ignorance of good table manners! Such total lack of any semblance of the finer social graces! Really! Were *these* the people that this gracious Estate of Windsfield was to fall fallow to!?

"Would you..." Lady Marilyn choked back the words pushing themselves into her mouth, and muttered between clenched teeth, "...excuse me, but I find that I am, after all, not quite up to...*this*. I must...retire to my quarters." Lady Marilyn rose, guided her chair with a practiced flourish back beneath the dining table. Lifting her small chin into the air, she turned as if to leave, then paused, heaved a great sigh, and ordered imperiously, "On second thought, Mrs. Ridley, I *will* have a dish of the chocolate mousse. Bring it to my room. Along with a hot cup of tea. And, oh, a sandwich of some sort."

"We would be *more* than happy to excuse you, Lady Marilyn." Bart rose to his feet. His smile was cold, his words clipped and measured. "But, since you are on your feet, and are yourself going up the stairs, why don't you, Mrs. Ridley, hand the lady a tray containing her pudding, along with her tea and scone, and allow her to fetch it up as she goes?"

Lady Marilyn's lovely face grew first red as blood, then pale as snow. So. William Bartram Logan was a man who did not flinch from taking control, speaking his mind. He had scorned her. Now, he was neatly clipping her wings. Putting her in her place. But, though she had to bite her tongue until it bled, she swallowed the hail of curses crowding themselves into her mouth until she thought for an instant she would choke on them. How *dared* he speak to her in such a manner! And *before the servants*! In polite society, it simply was not done! If she held no attraction for him, then she must go about this on a different tact. But their differences should be aired in private. Why must he belittle and scorn her in front of the hired help!?

Lady Marilyn stood stoically as she received her tray containing a small buttered bun, a cup of tea, and a dish of chocolate mousse. Then she spun on her heel, in such a mad swirl of tray and gown that the cup of tea rattled loudly in its porcelain saucer, and threatened to become upset.

Mrs. Ridley narrowed her eyes in dismay, and clamped her lips tight in agonized expectation of the entire affair landing on the polished oak floor of the dining hall. What was going on with *these people!?* She could but heave a grateful sigh of relief when the ramrod-stiff back of Lady Marilyn disappeared through the archway leading out into the main downstairs corridor, and up the sweeping staircase to the second floor.

"Bart!" Maggie gazed over at her intended and heaved an astonished sigh. "How…*could* you! The lady is, after all, a guest in this house—"

"*Exactly*," Bart said, "She is a *guest, and nothing more*."

In her room, munching her bun and sipping her tea, Lady Marilyn pranced and paced like a caged tiger. A fine, fine mess she was making of this entire affair! *Every* move she made proved a disaster! She had no *earthly* idea what to do next. What new tactics to try. These people! Never in her entire life had she seen the like of them! They were beyond all understanding! The more she was exposed to them, the more muddled and uncertain her position became. She had met few men who could not be captured by her charm. But not William Bartram Logan! She had planned a lovely, delicious dinner for the ungrateful, backwoods American clods! And what did the new Earl of Windsfield do?! Ordered scrambled eggs to placate a child who could not possibly be above the age of four or five!—and therefore should have been served his meal in the kitchen with the servants—then sent promptly to bed!

Ridiculous! And the woman! This…*Margaret Ann Evans* person! She had appeared at the table dressed in a gown that could have come straight out of one of London's finest shops. When first Marilyn's eyes lit on that gown, a sour taste bitter as bile had risen in her throat. That should have been *her* gown. *She* should be the woman on the arm of the Fifth Earl of Windsfield…!

At that instant Lady Marilyn made up her mind—she would *not* give up so easily. There was *far* too much at stake here. She must get her head together. It shouldn't be too difficult—given her fabulous wit, her matchless beauty, her impeccable breeding, her background and…everything about her was a *perfect* fit to be mistress of an estate such as Windsfield. What grand parties she could hold here! She could stand on the hill before Windsfield Mansion and gaze down upon the village and the villagers that were at her beck and call. She could command wealth. Replace her faded wardrobe with the latest fashions from Paris and London. Regain her standing in the upper levels of London society…she could…yes…she *would* prevail. No matter what hardships life flung at her… like a cat…she always managed to land on her feet—!

First, she had to discover some different angle. Get William Bartram Logan to gaze at *her*, the way he now gazed at that *Margaret Ann Evans person!*

Her mind in a fitful whirl, Lady Marilyn Drayton picked up her bowl of chocolate mousse—she must take food wherever she could find it—strode to the window of her room, and peered out. Beyond the meticulously groomed formal gardens surrounding Windsfield Mansion stretched the lovely, rolling English landscape, dotted with rippling grasses and sprinkled with wild flowers. But, her lovely face set and cold, Lady Marilyn saw none of the beauty. She saw only herself, if she were not *very* careful, being ushered out the door of Windsfield, with no one to care, and with no place on the entire face of the earth to go…

Lady Marilyn shivered, turned away from the gorgeous view, set down her empty bowl, flung herself face down on the lush bed, and began to violently beat the pillows with small, white, cold fists.

Chapter 29

The new master of Windsfield sat behind a huge mahogany desk that filled almost one entire wall of the master's study. Before him waited the steward, Albert J. Ridley, holding in his hands a gigantic set of ledgers, which he solemnly extended toward Bart.

Bart reached both hands and took them. Laying them carefully before him on the wide expanse of the desk, he gazed up at Albert J. Ridley. "You think I should study these, do you, Mr. Ridley? All of them?"

"It is Albert, sir. Yes, sir. I do," the steward nodded his head solemnly, his face as set as stone, his light gray eyes staring at some spot beyond Bart, on the south wall of the spacious study that smelled of old wood and leather and books.

"Very well, Albert," Bart said in a clipped, no nonsense tone. "I shall give them a go, this morning. Then I shall join my lady and her family for luncheon. Then, early in the afternoon, I thought you and I might ride out and have a look about the place."

"You think, sir, to take a look about Windsfield…in one short afternoon? It does get dark early here, if I might say so, Sir William."

"What? Oh, well, be that as it may, we can make a start at…looking the place over. And, if need be, we shall ride out again…tomorrow morning."

Albert turned as if to leave, then turned back. "One other thing, sir. I do believe that a message has arrived from the barristers. The reading of the *will* is to be here, at Windsfield, Friday, at two in the afternoon. That is, should you return them a reply that this meets with your good pleasure…sir. What word shall I send them?"

"Yes. Friday. And this is Monday. Four days hence would be fine," Bart stared at the stack of ledgers, and heaved a great sigh. He needed to study the ledgers, to see exactly what he was getting himself into, assuming full and final control of the vast Windsfield Estate. Were there any unpaid debts and obligations looming? He should have realized that this was not to be a holiday, but a large amount of work. Yes. This was going to be more of a chore than he had ever imagined. And he had intended to spend most of his time with Maggie, to make certain she wasn't miserable and lost in the vastness of all this. Breakfast, thank goodness, had gone somewhat smoother than had last night's supper. Maggie had taken her rightful place beside him at table, to his right. Barbara Jo had deigned to join them, and seated herself as it pleased her. As had Johnny, who chased about the table for a bit before Maggie could settle him into his chair, where he devoured two boiled eggs and two or three sausages—along with a piece of toast smeared liberally with jam, and a pint or so of fresh sweet milk. There were no hot biscuit and grits, but Bart and Maggie and Barbara Jo did feast on some sort of small stuffed sausages and scrambled eggs, with a delicious toast made of barley, they were told.

And though it was now well past noon, Lady Marilyn had not yet graced the household of Windsfield Mansion with her presence.

Bart shuffled through the massive stack, picked up the last ledger, turned to the very back, and saw written in neat, cramped figures, the total assets of Windsfield Estate, as they presently stood. His mouth flew open with astonishment. He slammed the ledger shut, laid it beneath the others, and sat staring about him. If *that* was the final figure, the true worth of Windsfield, it was readily apparent he would be wasting his valuable time to spend it poring over the remaining records. If the estate held that sort of worth, it was certain that Albert J. Ridley was a man of rare integrity, and to be trusted in all things. As an astute and canny businessman, Bart knew that he should, regardless of this assumption, give the records a look. But he soon found his mind wandering. He was not, at the moment, in the mood for dusty books and records. Neither was he presently of a mind to take an extensive tour of the estate with Albert Ridley. That could wait for another day. Bart pushed the ledgers aside and went in search of Maggie.

"Darling? Wherever are you?" he went calling about the east wing of the country mansion. Finally, after thirty minutes or so of fruitless searching, his ears picked up a welcome reply.

"In here, Mr. Logan. In what I suppose would be referred to as the music room."

Bart paused at the entranceway, peering into a lovely room set with ivory and pastel seating arrangements, and dotted with statues, tables tastefully decorated with bric-a-brac, and here and there, huge pots containing what appeared to be living plants. And an array of musical instruments. Sunlight streamed through tall, un-curtained windows that rose to the ceiling, almost like an atrium. "Well!" Bart smiled at Maggie as he strode in, "This is rather…nice… wouldn't you say, my sweet?"

"Nice, is it, then, Mister William Bartram Logan, Fifth Earl of Windsfield? *Nice*, is it?" Maggie put on her Scotch-Irish brogue. "Do your eyes not, then, behold that gold harp, strung with fine, strong strings, and as tall as most men? Or that array of fine fiddles, all in their original cases? Set in a fine cabinet of polished wood? Or this, Mister Logan, darling, this grand piano that—"

"Yes, I get your point, my dearest. Why don't you sit down, and play me something?"

"Here?" Maggie stared up at him, "Now? I…couldn't."

"Why on earth not?"

"I'd feel…"

"Out of place? Not at all at home? Is that what's going through that pretty little head of yours?"

"No. Of course not!" The lie slipped out of her mouth before Maggie was truly aware of it.

"You never could tell a good lie, you know that, don't you, Margaret Ann? You're no good at it. I can read you like a book."

"Oh? And just what, Mister Logan, darling, does that book say, right now?"

"That, stunning as it is, you would love to flee this room. This place. Cast a saddle across a good mare, and go galloping across the heather and the gorse. The wind tearing at your hair—"

"You, Mr. Logan, darling," Maggie smiled up at Bart wistfully, "are not far from the truth. Not far a'tall, a'tall."

"Where's our boy?"

"Our…boy? You mean…Johnny?"

"Do we have another boy, darling? Yes, I mean Johnny. We don't have another boy, yet, do we. Where is he?"

"Down for his nap," Maggie retorted shortly, feeling the blood rush to her face. She had never imagined…that she…and Bartram Logan…could have children…a boy…what would *this* boy look like? Would he be handsome? Charming? Kind and loving to a fault..?

"Now what are you thinking?"

"Why, Mister Logan! I thought you could read me like a book!"

"Well, my sweet, sometimes the words get blurred, and despite my best efforts they all run together. Maybe my vision, at times, when I stand close to you, like this, gets a bit…impaired. What do you think?"

"I think that if this place has stables with healthy horses in it, we are wasting our time indoors, arguing your visual impairment."

"I agree. Mister Ridley! Albert!"

"Sir?" As if by magic, as if he had been lurking about in the shadows, just waiting for this call, Albert J. Ridley appeared, dark hair slicked close to his head, moustache neatly trimmed. His suit and shirt and tie impeccable. Shoes shined. "Could I be of assistance, to you, then, Sir William?"

"Yes, Albert. Could the lady and I perhaps visit the stables, and see what saddle mounts might be available for a jaunt about the property?"

"You…mean…visit the stables? You mean…now, sir?"

"Yes. Now, Albert, if you please."

"Mister Logan, darling, shall we not, out of sheer good manners, invite Lady Drayton to ride along?"

"No, my darling, we must assuredly *shall not*."

"Why, Mister Logan! Your behavior, last evening, towards Lady Drayton was nothing short of…abominable…and far, far below the high standard of gentlemanly conduct you have thus far exhibited. And now, today…Might I, perchance, ask why? She has not even shown herself today. I know her language in the upstairs hall last afternoon…left much to be desired. Still…?"

"Ah, my sweet, what explanation can I offer you?…except to say that I am *not* without my sins and shortcomings, not at all the perfect knight. And, much to my sorrow, you have already begun to discover the cracks and chinks in my shining armor!"

They rode—the two of them, unescorted, unaware and unconcerned about borders—across the rolling countryside to the east. They laughed and talked, sometimes racing their mounts across the green hillsides. Other times, letting their mounts set their own pace. Heedless of the time, of the day, of the country. A man and a woman. Alone with nature. Enjoying the afternoon. Then, all too soon, Bart noticed that the sun was sinking in the west.

"I suppose...we'd better turn these horses about, my love, and head back for the stables."

"Must we?" Maggie stared over at her handsome companion. Almost, for a few wonderful hours, she had forgotten who she was. She had forgotten who he was. She had forgotten she was cavorting across the English countryside with the Fifth Earl of Windsfield. For a few hours, she had been lusciously, delightfully free, and deliriously happy.

"Yes, my sweet, I fear we must. Johnny will be up from his nap."

"Johnny..." Maggie muttered, an icy current flowing down her neck and spine. Johnny would be up *and searching for her!* It was this man, Bartram Logan, who was now reminding her of her little brother...? *What was happening to her?! She was drifting across the English countryside, as heedless, as addle-brained as Barbara Jo!*

Maggie felt the magic of the afternoon vanish away. Over those lovely, rolling green hills lay the stone mass that was Windsfield. She had meant to speak with Bart this afternoon, on this ride. She had meant to ask him what in the world he intended *doing* with the place? It was a world away from home. It was a world and more away from everything she knew and loved. Did he entertain even the slightest notion of ever actually *living* in this place? But she had asked him nothing. She had merely galloped her mount across the English countryside, as happy and carefree as a lark! A handsomely boyish Bartram Logan by her side, all the Logan enterprises seemed nonexistent. The Windsfield Estate a lovely, foggy dream.

Now, Maggie turned her mount and grew quiet, as they headed back.

They found Johnny waiting for them. He was sitting on the front steps of the manor house, with a runny nose, and a small face flushed deep pink and wet with tears.

"Oh, sweetie. I am so sorry. I...don't know—"

Riddled with guilt, Maggie was blubbering on, "Time seemed to just take wings and fly off! I honestly can't even imagine what on earth happened to the afternoon…"

"Your sister and I went for a ride, young fellow." Bart stooped down and lifted Johnny into his arms, pulling him close. "We figured you'd like some time on your own, to ramble about and make some grand discoveries. After all, you're growing up. You're a big boy now. Did you find anything to do interesting…this afternoon?"

"I did!" Johnny instantly brightened, wiping away the offending tears with the back of one small hand, his eyes beaming at Bart Logan. "Mr. Ridley let me go into the garden. I dug up two worms. And I catched a *bootifal* butterfly. And Mr. Ridley said he had a book, in the big library. And it showed how the butterfly changed from a worm into what he is now!"

"Why! Johnny! That's a marvelous adventure! I'm so sorry we missed it! You weren't too sad, when you awoke, and we were gone?"

"Nah! I wasn't scared at all. Can we go to the big library now? And see the book with the worms in it?"

"Sure. Why not?" Bart drew him close, giving him a squeeze before setting him down. "But I expect your sister might want to take herself away for a few moments, to consult with the kitchen staff. We *do* want drumsticks for supper, now don't we?"

"And mashed potatoes!" Johnny piped up, "With lots and lots of sweet butter! And could we have—"

"All right, you two! That's enough! I can see when I'm no longer needed," Maggie pulled a pretend pout, bent and gave Johnny the slightest peck of a kiss on a tear-streaked cheek. "And you…" Maggie wagged her head at Bartram Logan.

"What?" Bartram pulled an innocent face, "Don't *I* get a drumstick for supper?"

Maggie gazed up at the handsome man, then down at the small boy. Maybe it wasn't so bad, riding back to Windsfield Mansion. She had a supper to see to. Fried chicken, with mashed potatoes and creamed gravy. Surely they could scare up some vegetables to steam. And dried-apple tarts topped with sweet clotted cream might not be totally out of the question. She'd have to see exactly what she could scare up—in the buttery and pantry.

Chapter 30

Bartram Logan sat at the huge mahogany desk in the study, attempting to begin anew the task of checking the voluminous stacks of ledgers presented to him by the steward of Windsfield on the day prior. He had put himself to the task shortly after dawn, and now found that the clock in the corner was chiming the hour of two in the afternoon. He had not taken a break since taking his chair. He suddenly realized he had unwittingly missed lunch. His vision had begun to blur, from staring at all the columns and columns of neat figures parading across ruled page after ruled page—and every figure was in apple-pie order.

Bart heaved a sigh, rubbed his eyes. Pushing the stack of ledgers away, he rested both elbows on the dark, shiny surface of the desk that had probably, he suddenly thought, been used by the First Earl of Windsfield. But, apparently, from its fine appearance, like everything else connected to the vast estate it had stood the test of time very well. It had been faithfully and dutifully tended and preserved.

Bart closed his eyes, drew a hand across his face, suddenly aware of the slight stubble on his chin. He had shaved this morning, hadn't he? Oh, well…his train of thought was interrupted by the appearance of the steward, Albert, standing thin and regal in the doorway, hands clasped dutifully before him.

"Sir," Albert Ridley gave a slight bow of his balding head, "excuse the interruption, but His Lordship, Sir Wilfred Brimley, has just arrived, and wishes to speak with you, should you have a moment."

"Who?" Bart blinked his eyes, a puzzled frown crossing his tired face.

"Lord Wilfred Brimley, if you please, sir, is master of the adjoining estate, Brimley Hall."

"Oh, well, in that event, Albert, show…his Lordship in…and could you…perhaps have a word with *Mrs.* Ridley. See if she could, perhaps, prepare a…"

"A tray of tea, sir?"

"Why, yes," Bart smiled tiredly, "a bit of tea…and whatever… And, oh, Albert, would you see whether you can locate Mrs. Evans, on such short notice, and ask her if she would be kind enough to join us…for tea. And I…suppose…I should receive…Lord…Brimley…in the…"

"The downstairs withdrawing room, sir?"

"Yes, Albert. We shall receive His Lordship…in the downstairs withdrawing room."

"Yes, sir. Quite." Albert Ridley turned and hastened away.

Bart rose, stretching the tired muscles in his back and shoulders, and made his way to the downstairs withdrawing room. He strode in and walked around the room, spacious in size and grand in all its appointments. And was immediately disappointed that Margaret Ann had not appeared. Well, of course, she had not, not on such short notice. Well, he supposed he could…

"Lord Wilfred Brimley, sir…"

Bart, who had been standing gazing out a broad expanse of velvet-draped windows, turned to see Albert Ridley gesturing respectfully toward a very stout, balding, very broadly smiling fellow whose eyes were a twinkling sky-blue and whose face was fair as a child's above a snow-white cravat. His waistcoat was of tan wool, and his trousers tight-fitting and of a cream hue. He wore black riding boots.

Bart stepped immediately forward, offering his hand. Which Lord Brimley immediately grasped, and—in the American tradition—wrung soundly, his smile, if possible, growing even broader.

"Well, the Fifth Earl of Windsfield, I believe it is?"

"Bartram Logan. William Bartram Logan," Bart grinned at him. "Welcome to Windsfield. Won't you please take a seat?"

Lord Brimley did as he was bid. His broad smile never slackening one iota, he placed his hat on the nearby table, rested his ivory-tipped cane against the armrest of the couch, and lowered his huge, expensively clad bulk onto the plush damask matching the scarlet velvet drapes.

"And how, my good sir, do you find our fair England? And the estate?"

Lord Brimley leant forward from the fine couch where he had seated himself, and stared with a frank and friendly interest straight into Bart's eyes.

"England is lovely, Lord Brimley," Bart replied with a nod of his head, liking the man instantly, and staring back just as frankly at his new neighbor, from his seat opposite. "And I find the estate…in excellent hands and in fine shape. My late great uncle chose, in Mister Albert Ridley, a fine fellow, who has seen well to all affairs."

"Yes…indeed," Lord Brimley gave a slight frown. Just like an American, he supposed, all their democratic nonsense, lowering himself to the same status as his steward. "But I am sure that, now that you have arrived…" He raised light brows slightly.

"Bart Logan," Bart smiled over at him.

"Ah. Yes. Mister Logan. Now that you have arrived, I'm sure that everything will soon be…*I say…!*"

"Oh, Lord Brimley, this is Mrs. Evans. Mrs. Margaret Ann Evans, my betrothed. Darling, this is our neighbor, Lord Wilfred Brimley."

Both men had risen, and stood staring intently at Maggie, whom Albert Ridley had located in the garden, her knees pressing the dark cotton of her skirt deep into the rich English soil, as she made at some offending weeds she had found peeking out from an otherwise perfect bed of late winter blossoms.

At sight of Lord Wilfred Brimley, Maggie's brows lifted, and her lovely white skin flushed a deep rose, making her eyes, wide now at sight of Lord Brimley, appear as dark as sapphires.

"Oh!" Maggie gasped, her gaze falling in embarrassment to her skirt, boasting two wet knee-prints. Thank goodness the fabric was dark, and the soiled spots scarcely showed. But…still… And she was also suddenly and very painfully aware that several locks of hair had fallen from beneath her bonnet, and now dangled about her forehead and ears in dark, shiny, sweaty tendrils. "I did not realize…" Maggie removed her bonnet, gave a swipe at the tendrils of hair, wondering whether she had quite washed all the soil from her hands—when, at Albert Ridley's summons that Bart wished her to join him, she had re-entered the sprawling mansion. Her heart picking up a beat, Maggie murmured, "I did not realize…that we had…company…"

"It's all right, darling," Bart smiled at her, as if nothing at all was amiss, "Lord Brimley just…stopped by…"

"Yes," Lord Brimley stared at Maggie just as frankly as he had at Bart, and now he gave her a broad, appreciative grin, "I should have sent notice…but I…am given to these impulses…just popping in…you do see…where my close neighbors are concerned. You will pardon me, won't you, Lady…?"

"Margaret…Ann," Maggie murmured, giving a nervous little laugh, not knowing quite how to respond, feeling her legs might crumple beneath her slight weight. She had never met an English nobleman…if one did not count Bartram Logan. "I…"

"Do sit down, darling," Bart stepped toward her, took her arm and guided Maggie into a wing-backed chair. Bart retook his seat, as Maggie sank gratefully into the dark green tapestry near him, hoping none of the dirt from the front of her skirt-tail…

"As I was saying," Lord Brimley smiled around at Bart and Maggie, "I am most frightfully sorry to have burst in on you, like this. But, I must say, you look…charming, my dear Lady Margaret Ann. *Simply charming.* I do say, Mr. Logan, you have made a splendid choice. Simply splendid! Lady Margaret is…"

"Yes, I know," Bart said, watching as, despite the two damp, dirty blotches marring the front of her muslin frock, Lord Brimley's fair face, at sight of Maggie, had turned deep crimson to the top of his balding head. He didn't think the man was even aware of the dirt on her skirt, so taken was he by that gorgeous face. "Ah, I see that our tea has arrived. My dear," Bart smiled over at Maggie, "would you care…"

The tea was poured, and little by little the three of them relaxed, enjoying the delicious tea, the buttered sandwiches, the tiny cakes, the friendly conversation. Lord Brimley proved himself a garrulous fellow, yet every inch the gentleman, forcing himself not to stare at Maggie overmuch. To include Bart in his line of vision, and in the conversation. He made the gracious offer of his able assistance in any way that they might possibly require it.

Then Lord Brimley was rising, "I really should be on my way, and leave you two to your day's doings. But, I must say, meeting the two of you has been most *thoroughly* delightful. And, say, would you care to do me the honor of visiting Brimley Hall? I am entertaining a few friends, the evening of Saturday. Would you, by any chance, care to come? And join us? I would be most delighted, if you would—"

At that exact instant, Lady Marilyn Drayton, in a *very* revealing garment of some light, flimsy fabric, chose to appear abruptly in the doorway. Immediately, both gentlemen turned to stare.

"Oh! *Do* excuse me!" she gushed, taking one step into the parlor, her skimpy garment floating about her as she came, batting dark lashes rapidly, a delicate little hand fluttering about the soft, white expanse of an exposed bosom and throat. Bart could not help but catch that odd scent wafting up about her... what *was* that scent...not rosewater ...but...surely not...*cloves?* And her eyes seemed at one and the same time to sparkle, yet to have a peculiar glaze. Had Lady Marilyn been imbibing...? And what *was* that garment she was wearing? Bart was not altogether certain, but was that her *chemise?* Such a light, flimsy affair that he could almost see her soft, creamy skin through the fabric.

She scarcely made it through the parlor door, before making a misstep. Teetering for a moment on tiny feet clad in satin slippers, she staggered backward, clutched for the doorframe, then regained her equilibrium and continued, "But...I *thought* I heard voices. No one informed me..." she added in a highly aggrieved, childish voice, "that *tea* was being served. And I don't believe that I've been introduced ..."

Bart stood amazed that she had apparently been making freely, for some time now, at wine or some other sort of spirits that had been stored in a readily accessible place about the mansion, the scent of which she was valiantly attempting to disguise by chewing cloves. He'd have to speak to Albert Ridley—about that. Make certain that, in future, all chests and cabinets and the wine cellar, be kept tightly locked, lest Lady Marilyn, some fine morning, become besotted, come hurtling down the broad, winding staircase headfirst, and break her lovely little neck before luncheon could even be served!

He wondered whether she had been drinking when on that first evening she had shamelessly pushed herself into his room, flung herself at him like an offering on a plate without any slightest consideration of the possible consequences. But no. He had detected no odd scents when she had pushed past him. Perhaps there had been the faintest scent of rose-water, but beyond that, nothing—except the scent of a lecherous woman.

And, now, here she was, half-drunk, scantily, indecently attired, dark hair loose and flowing about slender shoulders—putting herself forward in a most unladylike fashion, to a gentleman she had never met. And intruding into a private withdrawing room, where she had definitely not been invited...

Bart searched for something to say. "We have seen so little of you, of late, Lady Marilyn, due to your constant...*indisposition*. But it seems that *today*, you have made a somewhat *miraculous* recovery, at least enough to—find your way down the stairs..." Despite the presence of Lord Brimley, Bart was on the verge of adding: *Still in your nightclothes...in mid-afternoon...more than half-drunk...on wine, or whatever, and well able to lurk eavesdropping about the halls—!*

But Maggie, detecting the yawning gaps in his knightly armor, so to speak, immediately cut him off. She was on her feet, ushering his cousin into the room. "How *thoughtless* of us! Lady Marilyn Drayton, this is a neighbor, Lord Wilfred Brimley, of Brimley Hall."

"*Yeeesssss*," Lady Marilyn's frowning scowl fled, immediately replaced by a charming smile, beamed exclusively at Lord Brimley, "I *am* Lady Marilyn Drayton," she gushed. Bart's keen hearing detected only the slightest hint of a slur in her voice, as, batting long, dark lashes she continued to purr, "Mister Logan's *cloooose* cousin. I've heard of Brimley Hall, and did I, or did I not, hear something, about an *invitation*...?"

"Lady Marilyn." Lord Brimley pulled the slightest of frowns and the shallowest of polite bows. "I had heard...some three weeks or so past...that...a...lady...was in residence...at Windsfield. And I must...apologize for not stopping by earlier. To bid you welcome. But I was given to understand...by some people of the village...that you were...unusually...wont to be indisposed."

"Village gossip," Lady Marilyn snapped, waving the words off as if shooing away pesky flies with a soft, white hand. "I can assure *you*, my dear Lord Brimley, one should *never* lend one's ears to village gossip." Lady Marilyn tilted her lovely head aside coquettishly, as if sharing some secret that was for Lord Brimley's ears alone. Lilac eyes wide and bright, she sidled closer, almost in his face, pulling a silly little smirk, peering up into his eyes, openly flirting, "We *all know* how the lower class is given over to an *inflamed* imagination. Too much idle time on their hands, would be my opinion. I can only *imagine* what those…*dear, sweet* souls…have been spreading about me, down in the village. By the way…this…dinner party…to which we are *all* being so delightfully invited…will your *wife*…be in attendance?"

"Oh? You…you…are…acquainted…then…with my…dear wife?" Lord Brimley's heart gave a flutter; he frowned, his round face coloring, and took a step backward. Did he *know* this woman?

"Oh. Well, no. Actually, I am not. I was merely…"

"Well," Bart cleared his throat loudly, ardently wishing to end this embarrassing conversation. To get Lady Marilyn out of the parlor, and safely back up to her room. He gazed over at Maggie, inquiring, "What do you…think…would be…best, darling?"

"I believe it would be most unkind of us to refuse Lord Brimley's gracious invitation."

"My thoughts exactly." Bart gave a relieved smile.

"It's all settled, then. And I shall look forward to seeing you at Brimley Hall—and, of course, your…family. Saturday. Shall we say…at seven? And should I send a carriage? And for how many?"

"We shall arrange our own transportation, thank you, Lord Brimley, and Margaret Ann does have a dear sister, Mrs. Barbara Jo Moss, who is visiting here with us. And…of course…there is…"

"Yes. Well. Of course, you must bring along Lady Barbara…" He hesitated for the slightest moment, then made a gallant gesture with one hand toward Marilyn Drayton, "and …this dear lady. And…now… ladies…" Lord Brimley, smiling broadly, bowed, took two steps backward, and, Bart now at his elbow, turned to leave the room.

Maggie could hear the two men making polite, pointless conversation, their voices fading down the huge corridors and out through the front door.

Maggie stood staring at Lady Marilyn Drayton, not at all certain what…if anything…she should say…to this…person…

But Lady Marilyn saved her the effort. Ignoring Maggie, she turned, in a whirling huff of skirts and hair, and disappeared into the bowels of the great stone mansion.

Then Bart returned. He stood in the door, smiling at Maggie, "Well, what exactly do you think…of our…new neighbor?"

"He's a nice enough fellow, I suppose," Maggie tilted her head aside prettily, her fair skin blushing bright rose, "But I wonder what Lord Brimley...*Lord Brimley...of Brimley Hall*," she raised one small hand, covered her mouth, and gave a tiny laugh, "must think of *his neighbors*— especially one who appears in mid-afternoon, the front of her gown damp with soil from the garden! Her hair and hands a total mess! Making a bumbling attempt at serving an English afternoon tea...for the very first time in her life!" Maggie concluded with a dismissive wag of her head.

Bart walked toward her. "From the look in Lord Brimley's eyes, my sweet, I don't believe the man saw *anything* past the fairest face in all England, now that you have arrived. And who cares a whit what he thinks, though on the face of it, I agree with you wholeheartedly, he appears a decent sort of chap. Deucedly good of him ...excuse me, my darling...to invite us all to Brimley Hall. Including *Lady Marilyn*. What in God's good name...is *wrong* with that woman?" Bart moved to stare out the window.

Maggie moved beside him. "I'd say, for one thing, Mister Logan, that she is frightened half out of her wits."

"*What...?* " Bart turned to gaze at her, wagged his head in confusion, "By...?"

"By being a woman...who is apparently totally on her own. And from the appearance of her gowns..." Maggie halted, not wanting to say anything *too* disparaging about Bartram's recently discovered cousin.

"Her...gowns?" Bart frowned, "But...they appear fine to me. A bit *more* than fine, if I were to hazard a guess, my sweet. And were I a gambling man, I'd lay a large wager that they are *dastardly* expensive, to say the very least."

"Yes, Mister Logan. They are. Or...should I say...were? Did you not notice...? How the braiding and laces of her fine gowns have begun to fray...just the tiniest bit, at their rich edges? And how the stunning colors of the silks and satins and brocades have lost some of their depth and luster and...no, I don't suppose, being a man...that you noticed a bit of this, did you, Mister Logan, darling? And have you seen that look in her eyes, Mister Logan?"

"Look? What look? Behind the drunken glaze, you mean? Well. No. To be utterly truthful about the entire affair, no, I did not. A look, you did say? A bit frayed, and faded a bit, and so forth...? All of which means...?" Bart waved a hand distractedly about in the air.

"All of which means, Mister Logan, darling, that the good Lady Marilyn Eveline Drayton…yes, the good Lady Marilyn is down to her last few farthings…or whatever it is they spend, here in England. In other words, Mr. Logan, Lady Marilyn is fastly joining— has she not already joined—the ranks of England's desperately poor. Yes, that's exactly the word to describe her. Lady Marilyn is, to put it bluntly…desperate."

"Desperate…?"

"Oh, can't you see, Mr. Logan? No. How could you possibly see!? You're a *man!*"

"Well, I certainly have no intentions of disputing *that* point with you, love, but I still don't see…"

"You are a man…who has power at his fingertips. A *wealthy* man who has never experienced the slightest *hint* of deprivation. Let alone that most terrible, *heart-breaking, soul-wrenching* sort of deprivation. Of being without funds to provide one's self with a roof over one's head. A decent meal…and from the look in Lady Marilyn's eyes, I would say that the Lady is frightened out of her wits, and all too well acquainted with the sour taste of poverty."

"You…really…think so? What should we do?"

"You should investigate her circumstances, Mister Logan, darling, as unobtrusively as possible, don't you think? Find out exactly where she stands in this world, financially, that is to say. Does she have hearth and home? Does she have family or friend? Or is she, as that empty look in her closed, dark eyes implies, alone, bereft, tossing on a sea with no safe shore to welcome her?"

"You…read…all that…in Lady Marilyn's…eyes?"

"All that. And more," Maggie heaved a sigh, gazed sadly at Bart. "The lady, on top of all that, I fear, is totally, totally devoid of any faith or feeling that would afford her any anchor or comfort of spirit, in her direst times of need."

"Oh. I see," Bart mumbled, totally amazed. Totally confused. Why had he seen none of this, if it was so evident in the lady's eyes, face, demeanor or whatever? He had seen only a loud, brash…was he a totally cold, uncaring, unfeeling, unseeing clod?

"Why is it, my dearest," Bart muttered in Maggie's general direction, "that I discerned…*none* of this?"

"Because, Mister Logan, darling, you were not searching for it."

"Yes. Well," Bart muttered, "I think I shall ride into London on the morrow, and speak with the Messrs. Sullivan. Early in the morning. To see if they can scare up…or have scared up…any information on…my dear cousin. You…don't suppose…my dearest…that Lady Marilyn is simply crass and mean and small at heart, do you?"

"That may be part of the problem, Mister Logan, but meanness and smallness do not put that kind of fear in a woman's eyes. Nor that kind of quaver in her voice. Nor that kind of passionate rage—"

"Yes. Quite." Bart interrupted. "You are of the opinion, then, that there is some… good in every soul…even in the soul of a sharp-tongued shrew who puts herself forth like a cheap—not my words, but those of Mister Albert Ridley—like a—"

"Yes, Mister Logan. That's exactly what I believe. The poor woman appears to be teetering on the brink—and if some compassionate soul does not throw her a rope to cling to…"

"And you expect me…to throw her some sort of…rope?"

"It would appear, Mister Logan, that you may be her sole remaining male kin of any relation. Thus, it appears to fall your lot, Mister Logan…"

"Yes. I'll…investigate…and see what…rope I might be able to toss. Money… you think?"

"Money…might help to relieve her awful anxiety. A new gown, perhaps. A new bonnet. A pair of new gloves. Any…or…all of these…?"

"Oh. Well. Then, why don't you ladies come along on the morrow, and busy yourselves at the shops, whilst I chat with the barristers? How does that plan work for you, my love? Perhaps, Lady Marilyn's…attitude could be altered…by the… mere purchase of a few…items of clothing? Is this…general… amongst…women? Even amongst those who, let us hope, are of a more genuine virtue and cold sober?"

"I would think, Mister Logan, darling, that a lifting of the spirits with a turn of fortune is general amongst the world's entire populace. But…yes…I would say it is more generally felt amongst women. Women…Mister Logan…feel this…desire to appear at their best. As much so as fortune, heritage, and so forth, allows them."

"And you, my sweet? You feel…this desire…to appear…"

"Only fleetingly. From time to time. Mostly, in the past few years especially, Mister Logan, my feelings have been more attuned to putting a roof over our heads and food into our mouths. But that is not, I don't believe, the first concerns of Lady Marilyn's heart. Not from the look on her face. No, I would say she is concerned, first of all, with her appearance to others. She, having no spiritual anchor, may hang all her worth on how she appears…to others. So, then, a few new gowns and bonnets, gloves, would seem a small trifle to pay to lift the lady's spirits." Maggie pulled the slightest frown, adding thoughtfully, "Yes. We might try that, as a beginning."

"A beginning? But…I thought…you just said…"

"I'm making absolutely no *promises* here, Mister Logan, darling," Maggie wagged her head at Bart and gave a little frown and a small, dismissive flutter of one small hand, "After *all,* I am *not* a magician or a fortune teller! Who knows…whether a few items added to her fine but fast-fading wardrobe might affect her temperament. In my opinion, what the lady really needs—"

"What the lady *really* needs," Bart ducked his handsome head slightly, said in a very sarcastic, *very* ungentlemanly aside to himself, "is to be kept away from the brandy and the wine, and given a good, swift kick in the—"

"Mister Logan! *Darling!*"

"Yes? My sweet…?"

Bartram deposited the ladies into the vestibule of what appeared to him to be the largest, the most expensively appointed shopping salon along Oxford Street, then made his way to the offices of the barristers.

"Yes," first one then the other of the Sullivan brothers, as they sat across the broad expanse of the desk from him, smiled very patiently, very knowingly at Bart, as if he were a small child with no knowledge at all of women…women with batting eyelashes, dark glances, and wily, winning ways. Whereas, they—situated as they were—were well versed in every human foible and prevarication imaginable.

"It is our earnest belief that despite what your good, sweet lady may think…well, to put it to you bluntly, we were warned by Himself, the Fourth Earl of Windsfield, not to…allow Lady Marilyn Drayton more than what he had stipulated in his final documents—to which he set his hand, and firmly placed his seal. We were advised…not to be swayed by her…in any fashion. The Lady…" here the older of the Sullivan brothers cleared his throat, very painfully, and gazed over at Bart with a deep frown furrowing his high brow, "the Lady is well known…about London. It seems…that during the lifetime of her husband…Lady Drayton was wont to visit shops and stores and salons…and rack up *huge* bills. Debts which her dear departed husband found it difficult…if not impossible…to pay. This, according to our understanding, is why she was banished from the estate of her late husband's family, this, coupled with her… unpleasant temperament…and affinity for lies, and deceits."

"Yes, Mister Logan. Should…such a…person…ever get her hands onto a fortune of any size," the younger of the Sullivan brothers continued, "Should, God forbid, the Estate of Windsfield, ever fall into such greedy, unscrupulous hands…The Almighty help…"

"Yes. Well, I knew little about the lady, until just now, speaking with you two. But, despite all this, I do feel some…duty…toward her. Now…if she has, as you seem to indicate…been truly…cast away…on the verge of being homeless and starving, what, exactly, gentlemen, can we…safely do…to come…to her aid?"

"I would suggest that upon the reading of the will you might want to—should you be of such a mind, so as to satisfy the conscience of you and your sweet lady—set a sum at Lady Drayton's disposal. A sum that would keep her for some time, should she spend it wisely."

"Yes. And then," the second Sullivan added with a stern expression on his thin face, his eyes burning, "*Wash* your hands of her."

"Well, thank you both, gentlemen. That…sounds like excellent advice. And, if it is not presumptuous of me to ask it of you, could you go ahead and prepare whatever… forms…might be required, and could we decide now exactly what sum…should be set aside…for the subsistence of…Lady Marilyn? And could you please bring these forms out with you, when you come for the reading of the will. I would *very* much like to wrap up…any loose ends, before returning to America, the end of the month."

The barristers Sullivan turned to stare deeply into one another's eyes; then they turned to face Bart, the older of them speaking: "We would suggest, if you do not consider the amount to be excessive, ten thousand pounds?"

"Well, gentlemen, not to cut the lady's living circumstances *too* close, shall we make it, say…twenty?"

"That is…indeed…generous," the older of the barristers remarked dryly. Deep-set eyes narrowed, lips pursed thin, he gave a little cough, a great swallow, as if finding the amount difficult to choke down.

"And should she, Sir William," the younger Sullivan, who oftentimes appeared to defer to his brother, spoke up with a lift of salt-and-pepper brows, "burn her candles at both ends, so to speak, and run short of funds…at some date not far into the future…?"

"Shall we take this thing, gentlemen, one step at a time?" Bart smiled into the earnest faces of the barristers, quickly qualifying his speech with, "But, I fear, should the Lady prove as foolish as that, then no amount of money would probably rescue her from her own follies and foibles. In which event, I fear Lady Marilyn Drayton shall find herself cast adrift upon a troubling sea—with neither boat nor paddle."

Chapter 31

Seated in the coach on the return trip to Windsfield, Maggie tucked securely at his side, Bart reached and took her hand, turning to glance at her, as well as he could, beneath the brim of her new, ruffled silk bonnet.

"I do say, that bonnet, it's *most* attractive, my darling," Bart mumbled in Maggie's direction, so taken with her appearance he forgot for the moment who else was riding in the coach.

"Oh?"

"And the gown, too. It's...*very* becoming. What...*color* is that?"

"It's magenta...silk taffeta, Mister Logan. You do like it?"

"Like it!? It's...stunning. It...gives...your skin—"

Maggie withdrew her small hand from the warmth of Bart Logan's larger one.

Suddenly Bart became aware that Lady Marilyn Drayton and Barbara Jo Moss occupied the seat opposite them. He clasped his hands together and smiled at the two ladies, and out of politeness asked, "And did you ladies...do as well...for yourselves?"

"Not so that you, Mister Logan, would notice, apparently," Barbara Jo pulled a wry grin. "Not that we are apt to catch the eye of any gentlemen nearby. Were that our intent and mission, it appears we might as well have stayed at home."

"Oh? No! Of course, not! You...two...are...lovely! Yessss, lovely...indeed."

Bart sputtered, pulling a broad grin. "And you, Lady Marilyn? How...did you... find...the offerings...in the salon?"

"Offerings?" Lady Marilyn stared coldly at Bart, her eyes as hard as twin stones set with dark, jeweled centers. How dared he! Was he implying

that *she, Lady Marilyn Drayton,* was some sort of *charity case*!? Her head still ached and throbbed with each lurch of the coach, from the wine she drank last evening. She closed her eyes against the probing gaze of her American cousin. His dark, disapproving gaze seemed to pierce right through her. So she *had* been a bit drunk yesterday afternoon. Foolish of her, to make a spectacle of herself before Lord Brimley in that fashion. She had, in the privacy of her room last night, wondered whether seducing her cousin was not entirely out of the question. She decided it most definitely was, given the way he gazed at her—as if she were something he had stumbled across on the street. Perhaps, then, she should turn her attentions elsewhere, at least for the next few days. She must make certain to seize the first opportunity to explain to Lord Brimley that she was not usually given to—it was just that…these people…this *awful*…situation…were driving her to the very limits of her endurance …that was why she had made at the wine, late into the night…

"What…I meant…to say…was…how did…your *shopping* jaunt go?"

"*Jaunt?* " Lady Marilyn echoed, pulling her lips thin, drawing her eyes from Bart's handsome face, and staring sullenly out the window.

"Well!" Bart leaned over and muttered softly against Maggie's bonnet ribbons, "So much for *altering* the disposition with—"

Bart suddenly felt the not-too-gentle nudge against his right ankle of a small spool-heeled satin shoe.

He closed his mouth, and kept it closed until the carriage rolled up before the huge stone steps of Windsfield Mansion.

———

"Well," Bart remarked sarcastically, when at last he was alone with Maggie in the wood-and-leather coziness of the study, "So much, I suppose for that little strategy. I would say the shopping…whatever…was a total failure…in a certain department. Not, you understand, darling, that all of you ladies don't look amazingly beautiful in your new attire. It's just that…"

"Give it time, Mister Logan, darling. Give her time. And perhaps your dear, dear cousin will come around."

"Come around? What a quaint way you have of putting things, my dearest. Yes, that's just what I'm afraid dear, dear Lady Marilyn will do. I am afraid she will *come around*... and open her mouth...half drunk...and like a dog in—"

"Bartram Logan! Stop that!" Maggie chided, frowning up at Bart as they stood gazing together out the window of the study, across the rolling beauty of the English countryside. All at once she gave Bart a playful poke in the ribs with one sharp little elbow. Bart reached down and gave her a tickle across her ribs. He felt her stiffen beneath the tips of his fingers. Instantly, as soon as his hand touched her, he knew he shouldn't have. Not so intimately. Not like that.

Maggie's face flamed scarlet; she stepped quickly away from him, to the huge window. What had just gotten into her? This was *too* much! Seeing him every day, like this! Living in the same house, though it was as big as all outdoors! She was acting as if she were already married to this man!

"I'm sorry, darling," Bart mumbled, "please forgive me. It won't happen again."

"I would like to go home," Maggie muttered through her embarrassment.

"Home?" Bart mumbled to her back, "But...darling...the *will* has not been read. We're invited to Brimley Hall, remember...?" *Home? They were thousands of miles from home! And nothing was settled! She's like a keg of powder, Bart thought to himself. One word, one touch, is all it takes...to set her off! Good Lord...!*

"Margaret Ann, I said I was sorry, and I truly am. I don't know...what else I can say to you. Except...that I love you. Sometimes...my heart races past my head. I...truly...am...sorry."

"Tell me something, Mister Logan," she turned on him, her eyes brighter than he had ever seen them. "Did your father, perchance, ever fight in any of the Union campaigns against the Confederacy... in the State of Virginia?"

Bart stared at her. They had never discussed any of the particulars of the War... she had never broached the subject of the War to him...their differing sides... why... now...?

"Well, Mister Logan?"

"I...well..." Bart could see a great chasm yawning before him, into which, if he were not very careful, he was about to plunge headlong, with no hope, perhaps of any rescue or recovery. *"No,"* he quickly denied, *"Never.* Not to my knowledge. Not ever. Never, did my father fight in any of the skirmishes or battles…against…the South…in the lovely…state of…Virginia."

He protested too much, Maggie thought. And it was the first time, she believed, that Mister Bartram Logan had deliberately lied to her.

"I think, Mister Logan, darling," she continued to gaze up at him, her eyes bright, a little smile playing about her beautiful mouth, "that I shall go into the kitchen now, to look to the preparations for supper. What do you feel you might enjoy, for your supper meal?"

"What…?" Bart mumbled, "What…whatever…"

She turned and was gone in a magnificent swish of magenta silk skirts with a flash of satin slippers dyed to match.

Bart sank into the leather chair behind the huge mahogany desk, threw back his head, and laughed.

Chapter 32

The day scheduled for the reading of the will dawned clear, unusual for Southern England this time of year. Bart dreaded the day, dreaded the thought of the last wishes of the Fourth Earl of Windsfield being echoed about the chambers of the man's grand mansion for a final time. He wished that he had known the man who walked these halls. He dreaded what he knew would most likely be the reactions of Lady Marilyn Eveline Drayton—when she heard the clear and incontrovertible directives of this voice from the grave. He greatly feared that for some unknown reason she harbored expectations that would not be met.

But mid-afternoon did arrive, much too soon for Bart, and, as the barristers, the brothers Sullivan & Sullivan, had requested, to make certain there were no future misunderstandings, all the household, along with many village officials and some local clergy, gathered in the main downstairs parlor.

They all sat about, waiting, William Bartram Logan, Maggie, Barbara Jo, even Johnny, who had been allowed to miss his nap. And of course, Lady Marilyn. The household staff, the clergy and officials of Windsfield Village clustered about along the wall behind the new Earl and his family, occasionally shuffling their feet or clearing their throats, to ease their nerves.

As the assembly waited, Bart forced himself to relax. He had seated himself on the huge couch near the fireplace, and had motioned Maggie and Johnny to join him there. Barbara Jo sat off to one side, in a deep armchair, almost in the corner, in a half-doze. Lady Marilyn had taken a seat in the wing-backed chair not far from the door. She sat stiff and straight, her lovely face pale. And to his great dismay Bart was certain that he had detected the faintest whiff of cloves as she entered the room. She must have tucked a bottle of wine or claret away in her room, before the cabinets and the wine cellar had all been locked.

When the elder of the barristers Sullivan & Sullivan at last arrived and was shown into the elegant spaciousness of the downstairs parlor, Bart rose, and moved to greet him. With curt nods, his face solemn and all business, he motioned that he was ready to proceed. Bart took his seat, as the barrister opened his leather case.

A murmur of anticipation ran through the staff and villagers clustered in the back of the room.

"If we could kindly have the attention of all present. Thank you," Mister Milford P. Sullivan began. "May I make a few remarks at the outset, that I know all present mourn the passing of the late…"

Lady Marilyn squirmed impatiently. Why didn't the thin, balding fool get on with it? She had waited for an eternity, attempting to hold herself together…until her inheritance could be received. Now, here the elder Sullivan was going on and on, with a distinctly irritating nasal twang, about the meritorious character and life of that fatuous old frog, the Fourth Earl of Windsfield. As if spouting some sort of eulogy! What did she care, if he *had* donated this and that. Had improved the lot and the lives of all those with whom he came in contact…as well as many of those he did not! And to her horror, it appeared, from hearing Mister Sullivan ramble on…that the old fool must have given away *half* his fortune—*half of her fortune!* To this and that very deserving cause!

Then she heard him droning:

I, Feldon Bartholomew Hurston, being sick and weak of body, but of perfect sense and memory, praise be to the Almighty, but knowing that it is appointed to all men once to die, do hereby make and ordain this my Last Will and Testament, revoking all other wills heretofore made, save only this. In the manner and form that followeth:

Item: I give my soul back to God who gave it, and my body to the Earth, there to be decently buried in accordance with instruction given in a separate instrument, in the sure and certain hopes of the Resurrection, and that I shall see my Savior at that last day.

Item: I do hereby make William Bartram Logan, the son of my

*grandniece, Eleanor Hurston Logan, my Executor. If he be unwilling or
unable to serve, I desire the barristers Sullivan & Sullivan to serve in
his stead.*

Item: I give and bequeath unto...

The barrister's voice droned slowly on, through a mishmash of legalese
that meant nothing to Lady Marilyn. Her mind, lulled somewhat by the wine,
began to wander. She forced her attention back to that solemn, sonorous
voice that echoed about the spacious parlor. She realized he was
enumerating the names, one by one, of what seemed to be an unending
succession *of several dozen* legatees—members of the household staff,
past members of the household staff, members of the clergy, officials of the
village, his legal representatives, and so forth. Some of these persons named
were indicated as being well past their prime. Some were ill or indisposed,
or simply too old to retain their positions, and had for some time now been
living, it appeared, on the largess of the Fourth Earl of Windsfield. And for
all these, generous stipends and annuities and allowances had been set up.
And as the barrister Sullivan read on in his rambling, solemn voice, it was the
desire of the Fourth Earl of Windsfield, that his heir would find it in his heart
to continue to honor these commitments. And that he would also find it in his
heart that those still serving the estate in whatever capacity might retain their
present employment.

Item: I do give and bequeath to Marilyn Eveline Billings Drayton—

Lady Marilyn's heart skipped a beat...at last! At long last—!
*—the paintings hanging in the lower corridor of the west wing of
Windsfield Mansion, being those created by and signed by the hand of
my cousin thrice removed, and her great-grandfather, Thornton
Glenforth Billings...*
Lady Marilyn felt all the air rush out of her lungs! *Paintings!* She had
received... *a few paltry paintings—!?*

Item: I do give and bequeath to William Bartram Logan, all the remainder, balance and residue of my estate, both real and personal, of all kinds whatsoever, to him, his heirs...

The voice droned on. But Lady Marilyn failed to hear it, so violently was her heart pounding.

Everything! That...interloper! That...! He was getting everything! While she was getting a few dusty, worthless paintings...by a no-name artist! What good would those pathetic, long-forgotten attempts at art be to her? Something she would be required to haul around and store*! Store where? She was out on the street—!*

———

Vaguely, Lady Marilyn was aware that those seated in the parlor had risen and were milling around. She heard not a word, only the loud roaring in her ears of her own heartbeat. She saw only dim shadowy figures, moving about as if in a nightmare. She doubted very much that should she attempt to stand, her legs would support her weight.

Then she realized that the room was emptying. Only the barrister Sullivan and William Bartram Logan remained. What would she do now? What *could* she do now? Where on earth would she go? One thing was certain, the worthless paintings could stay where they were! They could hang there in the west wing of Windsfield—until they mildewed, rotted, and fell in the floor for all she cared! How *dared* that old doddering fool insult her so—!

Through her fog of fear and rage, Lady Marilyn realized the barrister was bending over her, extending in one long-fingered hand some sort of document.

"Lady Drayton, the Fifth Earl of Windsfield has discussed with us...your... situation...and at his request we have drawn up this draft, providing for you a one-time payment of twenty thousand pounds. A most generous sum, that if madam will invest wisely and use judiciously—"

Lady Marilyn snatched the bank draft from the barrister's hand and leapt to her feet; face livid, she stood waving it about. "What does the new Earl of Windsfield think I am? Some sort of ignorant char maid, some *charity* case—to be fobbed off!? With *this?* Windsfield is well worth—"

The barrister's face grew pink above his snow-white collar. "Did you, madam, hear the amount the Earl is graciously settling upon you?"

"It is not *nearly* what I am due!" Marilyn screeched, her eyes wild with rage, her bosom heaving. "By rights, I should *have it all!*"

"By *what* rights, madam? Mr. Logan is a direct descendent of the late Earl's brother. You are a descendent of a distant cousin, who could not in this world ever have dreamed of holding rights to either lands *or* title. The late Earl thought you might wish to have the paintings. But, as to anything else, you have *no* rights, madam. No rights at all. It was only out of the generosity of his heart that Mr. Logan has made this magnanimous gesture. But if you have no wish to receive the draft—" The barrister extended a long-fingered hand, very adroitly plucked the wildly waving draft from Lady Marilyn's hand— and stood holding it.

Marilyn well knew it was a very tidy sum. But not *a drop in the bucket* to what she had expected. It did not in any wise assuage her deep disappointment. She had lived with the expectation of becoming vastly wealthy. Not of subsisting on just enough to keep her in bread and cheese and charcoal.

In one, swift motion, Marilyn snatched the paper from him. "I...*will* take...the draft...but I will also hire a man at the bar to look into all this!"

"Do with the money whatsoever you will, madam. But that would be a terrible waste of funds." Then, dark eyes narrowed beneath bushy white brows. The barrister added, "But let me *warn* you, madam, the Earl *did* make it very clear—*this* is a *one-time...gift.*"

With a dismissive wave of his hand, the barrister Sullivan turned on his heel, and his back to Lady Marilyn, gathered up leather satchel, hat, cane and gloves, and strode out. Marilyn could hear his voice, echoing back up the corridor, as he spoke with William Bartram Logan.

Light violet eyes dark with rage, Marilyn glanced about the elegance of the empty parlor. Without one word to her, the new Earl of Windsfield had taken himself off, along with everyone else. He was so sure of himself, was he? Now he was officially lord and master of Windsfield. And he thought himself rid of her. Well, the Fifth Earl of Windsfield had a few things to learn— about *Lady Marilyn Eveline Billings Drayton!*

Somehow Lady Marilyn made her way up the grand staircase. As she climbed, she thought glumly that she might as well go up and pack. She did, after all, hold in her hand a bank draft for quite a substantial sum. She could take a coach into London...

But tomorrow was Saturday...and there was the invitation from Sir Wilfred Brimley...to his dinner party...at Brimley Hall...

She must decide exactly what to wear...Lord Brimley, after all, might, perhaps, be more amenable to a lady's winsome charms. The most happily of married men had been known, in the swirling, crowded, filth-ridden, yet lovely city that was London, to support a beautiful mistress in the grandest of styles...

Chapter 33

Brimley Hall set atop a low hill in the softly rolling countryside of Surrey. The stone pile that was the great house was, therefore, visible for some distance about. It dwarfed the surrounding outbuildings, and reared its impressive bulk against the rosy sunset like a castle, Maggie thought. And it was not until several minutes after sighting Brimley Hall that the lurching coach hauled its occupants to the doorstone of the mansion, where they were immediately welcomed and hastened inside.

As if expecting their imminent arrival, the master of Brimley Hall was there in the vaulted entranceway to meet them. Greetings all around were followed by the ladies surrendering their cloaks to a waiting servant, and being ushered into the elegance that was the main parlor. Lady Marilyn Drayton managed to secure a position by the side of their host, Lord Brimley. She wound one small arm into his, and hung on until he led the lady into the parlor itself, unwound her arm, and deposited her into the comfortable depths of a rich settee. Lady Marilyn sat stiffly on the richly padded cushions, fuming and fretting. How dared he rid himself of her, like putting a dog to drink at his bowl of water? Despite her care at her toilet this fine evening, despite the richness of the gown for which Bartram Logan had more than willingly paid, despite the way she knew it brought out her slender figure to perfection...despite the fact that her hair was done in the very latest style...she had had one of the maids at Windsfield occupy herself with it for hours...despite all this...! First Bartram Logan...now Lord Wilfred Brimley...Was she losing her charm?! Her ability to captivate, to lure men into her cocoon of lies and looks and longings?! A chill ran down her spine.

The male guests of Brimley Hall stood about in clusters in their white cravats, fine frock coats, ruffled shirts, britches and boots, making small talk…about crops, the weather…and politics. All subjects Bartram Logan enjoyed immensely, and in which he could readily converse. But as he enjoyed the company of his male counterparts, he made certain to keep a sharp eye on Maggie and Barbara Jo…and, of course, Lady Marilyn, whom he felt, that since he had brought to this affair, and since she was family—albeit somewhat distant family—was his charge.

Maggie found herself seated beside Lady Brimley, whom she found absolutely charming. The lady was most interested in hearing all about the wild, frontier country of America.

"I fear, Lady Brimley," Maggie smiled at her hostess, "our little neck of the woods is no longer considered a frontier. The land was parceled out by lottery, you see, in the 1830's, shortly after my Great-grandfather arrived in the mountains of North Georgia. The Indians were …the Indians left…shortly after Grandfather Shawn Ian McKinnon settled in McKinnon Valley."

"McKinnon Valley? Oh, it sounds absolutely charming. *Do* tell me all about it!"

"Well, Lady Brimley, I fear that I shall bore you most frightfully. There is not a great…deal to tell…I grew up in the valley, along with my two sisters. Papa returned from the War, and farmed the valley, and we three girls did what we could to help. But I fear that oftentimes *I* was more of a hindrance than a help."

"Your father fought then, in that awful…War?"

"Yes. He did."

"And, was he injured?"

"Yes, he was. He carried a lead ball in his leg until his death."

"And you?" Lady Brimley smiled sweetly at Maggie, "You were a…precocious child?"

Maggie gave a smile in remembrance, and glanced over at Barbara Jo, who was beginning to nod off beside her on the broad settee. She was brought back to the present by Lady Brimley's urging.

"Please, do go on."

But then Lady Brimley was given a summons from a servant and excused herself, and Bart was standing over Maggie, taking her by the hand, "I do believe, my sweet, that dinner is about to be served."

Bart, Maggie on one arm, Barbara Jo on the other, gave Lady Marilyn a slight nod, indicating that she was to follow, into the vast dining room that glowed with the illumination of three gigantic candelabra.

Beautifully attired in one of her new gowns, a marvelous creation in teal blue sprinkled with seed pearls, Maggie, Bart Logan at her elbow, felt quite comfortable seated at the vast table that glittered with crystal, china and silver all polished to a high sheen until the glare hurt the eyes. The food was delicious. Soft laughter and conversation flowed. These English country folk, Maggie decided naively—at least Lord and Lady Brimley and their friends— were not all that different from the hill folk back home. Their clothes were fancy, their speech flowery, their foods a bit odd, but at heart, not that different. They only had much, much more of this world's glitter and goods. Maggie glanced over at Barbara Jo, seated to her right. Barbara Jo gave her a returning smile. Maggie's gaze swept beyond her, to Lady Marilyn, who looked as if she had just swallowed a bone, and could get it to go neither up nor down. Poor thing!

Dinner over, the entire company moved to an elaborate music room, where Maggie noticed a grand piano standing in one corner. It was a huge thing that filled the entire corner of the room. Then, to her embarrassment, Lord Brimley was speaking from half across the vast room, addressing her solicitously, "Lady Margaret, I have it on very good authority that you sing, and play, and both quite well. Would you then, Lady Margaret, favor us with some tune?"

"Oh! No! I…couldn't!" Maggie felt color rising into her cheeks, as she wagged her head in flat refusal. Then Bart Logan was bending over her, smiling, and whispering in her ear, "My sweet, they will be *enthralled* with your singing and playing. Can you in all good conscience deny them this great pleasure, after such a charming and delicious dinner?"

"But…" Maggie stammered and continued to shake her head, "It's…been…so long. And I've never even seen such a grand instrument, let alone placed my hands upon the keyboard…"

"Let's all have a hand for Lady Margaret!" Lord Brimley was beaming at her, while Bart Logan pulled her bodily to her feet, and guided her with firm steps towards the looming instrument.

Maggie was firmly plopped down onto the shiny stool. Bart Logan moved away, only a few paces, as if to give her room to catch her breath, yet still support her with his presence. Maggie stared for a moment down at the strange keyboard. Then, as if of their own accord, her hands lifted and placed themselves on the keys.

The chords rose and swelled in a sweet cadence, as a Scottish folk song Papa had played on his fiddle flew through her mind. Then Maggie found the words pushing themselves out of her thoughts and into the vast music room at Brimley Hall. Bart was stunned for a moment, when the first notes were struck; he immediately recognized the tune as being a Scottish ode to Bonnie Prince Charlie, that Scottish upstart who raised an unsuccessful challenge for the English throne. Then, as he glanced about at the rapt faces of those gathered in Brimley Hall, Bart quickly realized that that had been more than a century past, and apparently all had been forgiven, as the voice of his beloved soared beautifully:

My Bonnie lies over the ocean,
My Bonnie lies over the sea,
My Bonnie lies over the ocean,
Oh bring back my Bonnie to me.

The heather is blooming around me,
The blossoms of Spring now appear,
The meadows with green'ry surround me,
Oh Bonnie, I wish you were here.

Bring back, bring back,
Bring back my Bonnie to me, to me,
Bring back, bring back,
Oh bring back my Bonnie to me....

When the song ended, and her hands grew still on the keyboard, loud bursts of clapping rose and whirled about the room. Bart Logan stepped close, bent, gallantly took Maggie's hand, pulled her to her feet, whirling her about and presenting her to her adoring audience. Maggie smiled as her gaze swept the smiling faces. Then the smile faded, as her eyes met those of Lady

Marilyn Drayton. Never had Maggie felt such raw, cold, unadulterated hatred directed personally at her.

"Thank you. Thank you," was all Maggie could manage. She heaved a sigh, glad that in the not too distant future, they would be packing their things, readying for the voyage back to America. Thank goodness, they would be going home, leaving Lady Marilyn Eveline Drayton and her problems on the far side of the vast, bottomless Atlantic Ocean.

Sunday morning, a gray, blustery day, Lady Marilyn appeared at the door of the breakfast room in a skimpy chemise, and in a curt, clipped voice, requested the use of a coach, to fetch her into London. Bart told her that he would be more than happy to advise Albert Ridley to order her wish accommodated. A coach and steeds from Windsfield stables would be at her disposal, at the ready, if she would but kindly afford the steward an hour's notice.

Sunday afternoon, the clouds had somewhat lifted, just a few hung here and there in the form of light fog, like feathery dreams, drifting about over the village below. As Lady Marilyn took coach for London—to the biddings of farewell and best wishes for a safe and speedy journey—from Bart Logan, Maggie, Barbara Jo, and even Johnny—just before the coach door was closed, Lady Marilyn returned to them all a curt nod of contempt. Her lovely face pale as death and set as stone, beneath a veil of thick dark lashes her lovely violet eyes narrowed darkly, and seemed to warn them one and all: *You are not quite finished with me yet*! The lady's actual words were:

"Perchance…we shall all have… the great pleasure…to meet *again*."

To which Bart Logan made the sarcastically ungallant remark in a soft muted aside for Maggie's ears only, *"Dear Lord Above!—Let us most sincerely hope not!"*

Chapter 34

Maggie arose early and stepped out onto the front porch of the inn for a breath of fresh air. This was the fourth morning she had awakened in her own bed, since returning from Windsfield. It was a marvelous feeling, to be cradled in the comforting shadows of the mountains, the familiar scents of The Sparrow—of dried flowers, pine resin, burning firewood, and good country cooking—wafting about her.

Dawn was just breaking. Fog still hung low over the mountains to the west and along the basin of the creek beyond the small town, down where the tiny schoolhouse sat among its sheltering cove of hardwoods. And on past that, in the giant meadow, she suddenly recalled, set the huge log house being constructed by some man of whom Maggie had absolutely no knowledge. She must, Maggie thought dreamily, stroll down to the meadow and have a look at what progress had been made on the vast log house. Maggie paused, listening, and above the quiet of the mountains, she thought surely she must be mistaken, but was that the thudding of a hammer she heard, quite nearby? Surely Thomas was not up *this* early, hammering away at his planned addition to the school.

Maggie heaved a small sigh. Yes, it was hammering, just as she had thought. She wondered that Thomas couldn't bring himself to lie abed on a fine Saturday, and let his soul take some rest! Let work on the extra school room wait until later in the day. Not only was there still fog hanging over the mountains and the creek, but there was a distinct chill in the air. Maggie gave a shiver, and hurried back inside. That Thomas Beyers! Down there already, slaving away at his new school room, and probably hadn't had a bite of breakfast! Well, she certainly didn't have time to fetch him a ham-biscuit! But she was sure he could at least do with a hot cup of coffee. She wondered idly to herself what on earth a man like Thomas Beyers ate for breakfast, anyway. She wondered if he ever prepared for himself a really decent meal of any sort! Well, Thomas was not her problem. And breakfast at *The Sparrow Inn* was. Ham and sausage to fry; eggs to scramble; grits to boil. Liza Mae, Maggie was sure, probably already had popped a huge pan of buttermilk biscuits into the oven. And Benjamin Noah was probably out back, drawing up fresh buckets of water for brimming pots of Liza's strong coffee.

Maggie hurried into the inn, and to her amazement found that Barbara Jo was actually up and descending the stairs, albeit at a snail's pace, her head down, her light brown hair in total disarray. A deep scowl on her face.

"Well! Barbs!" Maggie chirped to her sister cheerily, "Have you settled back into your own bed? So good to see you up and about—on this fine mornin'!"

"What's fine about it?" Barbara Jo growled, shoving back the locks of hair that shrouded her vision until she could scarcely see the stairs beneath her feet. Maggie could quickly see that only a few days back from their trip, and Barbara Jo was settling, not into the comfort of a familiar bed, but into a familiar pit of despair.

"Come on in the kitchen," Maggie urged, "and get yourself a fine breakfast. Then the entire world will look much brighter."

"I don't know that the world will ever look brighter, Maggie. Sometimes you do weary me, with your eternal optimism. By the way, what time is it?"

"Why?" Maggie turned to gaze at her sister, "You have an appointment or somethin'?"

"Do I look to you like I have an appointment, Maggs? I mean, now really?!"

"You look as if you could stand to wash that stringy hair, and run a comb through it every now and then," Maggie said most unkindly. "And you could try putting on something other than that tattered morning robe you've worn for—what is it now?—the past three or four days? Since the day we got home. How about if—"

"Just leave me alone, Maggs. Let me be. Who gives a rotten fig what I look like? Or what I have on—"

"*I* give a rotten fig, Barbs!" Maggie fairly shouted. "You could march back upstairs, at least wash your face and comb your hair, put on a decent garment….and go take some breakfast to Thomas Beyers!"

"Thomas Beyers?" Barbara Jo stared at Maggie as if her younger sister had just taken complete leave of her senses. "Since when have you become so concerned about Thomas Beyers's breakfast?"

"Since he's been slaving away on that extra room down at the schoolhouse. He's much too proud to ask for help. He seems bent on finishing the entire project all by himself. Now, you just do what I said, you hear me? Go on back up, and make yourself at least halfway presentable. I'll go on in the kitchen, and get some food together. The man at least deserves a hot breakfast, if he's down at that schoolhouse on a Saturday morning, all alone—"

"All right! All right!" Wearily Barbara Jo turned, and began trudging back up the stairs, as if each step required every ounce of her energy, complaining bitterly as she went, "Why can't you just leave folks alone, Maggs? Always bossing people about! If Thomas Beyers wants breakfast, let him come into the inn and get it, like all the other self-respecting folk! Why should I be expected to tote and fetch for Thomas Beyers?!"

"Barbara Jo!" Maggie interrupted her string of grumbling, calling to her sister's drooping back, "Tell me something. Do you have some more urgent use of your time, this fine Saturday morning?!"

Barbara Jo paused on the stairs, one pale hand on the balustrade, turned and peered angrily down at Maggie, standing staring up at her, hands on hips, and that look on her face that brooked no disobedience.

Wordlessly Barbara Jo tossed her stringy hair from her face with one pale hand, and disappeared at the top of the stairs landing.

Maggie was stunned at how soon Barbara Jo reappeared, entering the kitchen, her face washed free of sleep, her brown hair pulled into a tangled pile atop her head—at least it was out of her face.

"Have you tried shampooing your hair in—"

"No, Maggie!" Barbara Jo retorted tartly. "Whatever concoction you are about to suggest, no I have not! Now, leave me alone. Give me whatever it is you want to send to Thomas." Barbara Jo frowned, extending a hand that to Maggie looked as thin and pale as death.

"You look fine, Barbs." Maggie gave her sister a glowing smile, attempting to force a show of approval, of some sort of reassurance. "Just fine. I'm sure Thomas will be delighted…to see you coming."

"Maggs," Barbara Jo heaved a dramatic sigh, "Thomas Beyers has never *once* in his life been *delighted* to see *me*. You know that. As you will well recall, Thomas Beyers thought me the *worst* of the worst of his students. All those years, when we were in school, I never *once* received from Mister Thomas Beyers the slightest notion of a hint that he found my presence—or my school work—in any shape or form…in the least…delightful. Thomas Beyers was…kind to me. He tolerated me, he was everlastingly patient with me, he endured me, but never once can I recall his being *delighted* with me. Not as with some other people I could name."

"Why, Barbs!" Maggie stared at her older sister, "I don't at all recall Thomas merely tolerating you!"

"You know very well how Thomas is, Maggs. He tolerated all the children. Even the most dirty, ignorant, ill-kempt lot from the coves. Thomas Beyers is God's angel sent to earth, apparently to sweep up the leavings of humanity, and dump them into the pot of learning, and hope he stews up something of worth. Thomas is too good for his own good. Too good for this world."

"Then, Barbs, if Thomas is such a paragon of kindness and virtue, you should feel more than honored…to fetch him a hot breakfast."

"Oh! Give me that!" Barbara Jo snatched the metal pan covered with a snow white cloth from Maggie's hand, clutched at the hot jug of coffee, then turned and swept out of the inn with a highly injured air, mumbling and grumbling as she went.

Down the steps she trudged, an aggrieved frown on her pale face, as if being led to her execution, across the narrow yard, into the rutted red-dirt road. She fairly hopped along, so angry and put out with Maggie as she was. Oh, yes, she recalled the many patient looks Thomas Beyers had given her as a young girl, trying to find her way through the world, living always in the shadow of the blond beauty that was her oldest sister, Nellie Sue, and then, Maggie, that strikingly gorgeous brunette that followed her into the world, the year Papa came home from the War. How could she, with her pale complexion with a sprinkling of freckles eternally across her nose and her nondescript brown hair that was neither true brown nor true blond, compete? Life was so unfair! She had a good enough mind, she supposed, but sandwiched in between Nellie Sue and Maggie, she made no attempt whatsoever to make much use of it. She felt lost in a shadowy valley not of her making, and felt little motivation to climb out of it. What was the use? Who ever paid her any attention!? Certainly not Papa!

But, no, she would not go there. Papa had been dead these many years, then Mama had followed. And now Fred lay in the little graveyard behind the Shiloh Baptist Church. She really should go there, she supposed, and visit his grave, at least now and then. Maggie was forever visiting the graveyard, toting up bunches of wildflowers in the spring and summer, and in winter, laying wreaths of green holly with bright red berries. But...then...didn't Maggie always do *everything* just right...?! Oh. Well. Maybe...just maybe, she might go up on the mountain back of the inn, and gather some holly, take it up to the graveyard and lay it on Fred's...

No! She didn't want to step one foot into that awful place! She didn't want to think about all those dead folks! She didn't want to think about...truth be told, she didn't want to think about the past...and certainly not about the future...!

Then the schoolhouse stood before her, surrounded by the silent sentinels of hardwoods barren now of all leaves. The creek sang along in a thick stand of trees, not far from where the little wooden building stood. Its song seemed to Barbara Jo to carry the voices of her childhood back to her. They had played in the sandy yard. At recess and lunch time, they had even waded in the creek. Their happy voices and laughter still seemed to hang among the barren branches. Well, she supposed, not all of her school days had been bad.

"Barbara Jo! Is that you!?" Thomas had spied her coming down the hill, and climbed down from his hammering on the rafters. He stood before her, his battered work hat in his hands, his handsome face drenched with sweat and wreathed in a pleased smile.

I wonder why...I had never before noticed... just quite what a handsome man Thomas Beyers is, especially when he smiles like that, Barbara Jo thought to herself. Then, instantly, she felt a guilty flush turning her face from pasty pale to crimson red. How could she?! Fred was but this past fall plopped cold in his grave! And here she was! Thinking to herself that *Thomas Beyers, of all people,* was a handsome man! *What was wrong with her?* One thing was clear, she had been far too long absent from church!

"Thomas," Barbara Jo gazed up at him, her face still a rosy pink, her light blue eyes dark now with guilt, extending the pan of sausage, biscuit, grits and eggs with one hand, and the hot jug of coffee with the other.

"You…haven't brought me breakfast?" Thomas smiled, his gray eyes lighting up.

"You are an angel! And hot coffee! God bless your dear, sweet soul!"

"Well, Thomas, I must confess…" Barbara Jo began, awash now in more guilt, that swept over her as she recalled how she had balked and fretted about bringing this man a bit of food and some hot coffee, "Really, Thomas," Barbara Jo lifted a hand as if to ward off his thanks, gazed at him solemnly, face flushed so that her freckles stood out starkly. Blue eyes wide, biting her lower lip, attempting to pull a faint smile to assuage her conscience, she wagged her head, "Please. You do not have me to thank for your food and drink. It was all—Maggie's—"

"Nonsense!" Thomas smiled his sweetest, "*You, Mrs. Barbara Jo Moss,* are the person I saw coming down the hill in the cold. Have you eaten? I see there's enough here for two or three hungry people. I could go inside, and scare up another fork, perhaps? And perhaps a spare cloak for you. That thing you have on doesn't look all that warm. And you could join me? I do have a couple of coffee mugs inside…" Thomas stared at her with such pleasure, such sweet welcome on his face, that Barbara Jo found herself, totally against her will, agreeing to eat one of the biscuits, and drink a cup of coffee. They sat on the steps. She even allowed Thomas to drape his heavy wool cloak about her shoulders, though, in truth, Thomas's kindness proved warmth enough.

"And how was your trip?" Thomas asked.

"Fine," Barbara Jo mumbled, "but, unfortunately, it's over. And life does go on."

"Yes," Thomas smiled, "Thank God, it does."

The sun was rising over the eastern mountains, burning away the fog. A few winter wrens and a couple of cardinals flitted about in the barren trees, spots of beauty and color against the blue of the morning sky. The sun felt warm. The biscuits and sausage were delicious, and the hot coffee warmed Barbara Jo inside. And who could not feel themselves coming alive when in the comforting presence of such a sweet and fine person as Mister Thomas

Beyers? He insisted upon hearing all about the trip. And he actually *listened* to her. Then, her tales of England ended, Barbara Jo found herself laughing aloud with Thomas, as Thomas explained to her how he had not placed his ladder quite properly yesterday afternoon, and had taken a painful topple into the schoolyard, his hammer still clutched in his hand.

"Oh, my! I do *declare*, Thomas! Did you see Dr. Ellis? Are you all right?"

"The part of me that was injured the most, I fear, Dr. Ellis could in no wise have helped!"

Thomas gave a loud chuckle, his eyes sparkling with amusement, and Barbara Jo found herself impulsively laying a hand on his arm to steady herself, as she fell into a fit of laughter. How long had it been, she wondered, quickly drawing back her hand, and putting it over her mouth to hold back the gushes of merriment she found erupting from her. When had she *ever* acted so outrageously?! So brazenly!? Even with Fred, her departed husband, she had never, ever, let herself go so. Fred had always been a man of cool temperament and demeanor. A very quiet, very dispassionate man, Fred Moss had not been a man for much touching, nor had he wished to be touched. Yes, that was the word for Fred. Dispassionate. She couldn't ever recall, during all their years of married life, Fred gazing into her eyes and laughing with total abandon...as Thomas Beyers was doing now...

Overwhelmed with guilt, Barbara Jo leapt suddenly to her feet, her face ablaze, her eyes wide and a deep, bright blue with chagrin and embarrassment.

"I have to go!" Barbara Jo blurted out, drawing off Thomas Beyers' warm cloak, pulling her shawl about her thin shoulders, as if to contain the waves of emotion flooding over her. What on earth was wrong with her!? She was not a giddy schoolgirl! She was a recently widowed woman, full grown! How dared she let herself go like this?! Mama would moan and turn over in her grave! How dared she smile at a man and laugh with him and enjoy his company...even being so forward as to lay her hand *upon his naked arm!*

Barbara Jo fled up the hill, leaving Thomas Beyers standing, a bewildered look on his tanned face, waving the empty pan and jug in his hands. "Don't you want to return these, Barbara Jo, to the kitchen of the inn?"

Barbara Jo appeared not to hear. She fairly flew up the hill, her dark skirts swirling about thin ankles, as if the devil himself was chasing her.

Barbara Jo fairly burst into the door of the inn. Maggie, hearing the loud bang of the heavy front door, came out of the kitchen to see who was creating such a ruckus.

"Oh," Maggie said, "it's you. Did you have a nice little walk?"

Barbara Jo stood in a huddle, shrinking into her shawl, her face averted, hidden beneath the huge dark brim of her bonnet.

"Is anything wrong?" Maggie persisted. "Did you find Thomas all right? Did he enjoy his breakfast? Did you enjoy—"

Barbara Jo flung off her bonnet. Blue eyes still dark with anger, she blazed out at Maggie, "Why, Maggs, must you *always* ask so many questions? Why cannot you simply *leave* people alone? Why *must* you..." Barbara Jo broke off, seemingly on the verge of tears.

"What has happened? To upset you so?" Maggie asked in a soft, sympathetic voice that set Barbara Jo's teeth on edge.

"See!?" Barbara Jo shouted at her, "There you go again! With all your probing questions! Well, if you must know, *Mistress Nosey Busy-body*, Mister Thomas Beyers did enjoy his breakfast! And I *did* enjoy my brief visit with him! In point of fact, I enjoyed it *far* too much! Now! You have heard the whole sad story! And are you satisfied!?"

"Well...I..." Maggie stared at her sister, completely taken aback. What on earth had Thomas Beyers done...or said...to put Barbara Jo in such a state? But knowing Thomas, knowing what a godly gentleman he was, had always been, Maggie could not for a moment imagine that Thomas Beyers had said or done the slightest thing amiss. What then had set Barbara Jo off on such a tangent?

What was it she had said...she enjoyed her visit with Mister Thomas Beyers far too much...

Wagging her head, Maggie stepped back into the kitchen.

————————

Shortly after the lunch crowd had departed the inn, the dining room and kitchen had been cleaned and straightened, dishes washed and stored neatly away in cupboards, Barbara Jo approached Maggie, sitting at the kitchen table nursing a cold cup of coffee.

"Sorry, Maggs, about the way I yelled at you this morning. But, you know something? You haven't changed a bit since you were eight or ten years old. You could ask more questions than a peddler could pull things from his pack. I'll never forget how all your questions drove the entire family to utter distraction!"

"That's not really what's bothering you, Barbs," Maggie smiled at her sister. "You like Thomas Beyers, don't you? You enjoyed talking with him for a few moments this morning, and that made you feel—"

"Let's not get into all that, Maggs,' Barbara Jo sat down across from Maggie with a great sigh. "I acted like a *Jezebel!* You should have *seen* me! You should have *heard* me!" Barbara Jo laid her head forward between thin hands. "Mama would have been absolutely appalled. I mean, here Fred hasn't been gone but a few months, and I'm sitting in the spring sun with another man, laughing like a love-sick hyena at some joke that is barely funny at the most! I even...oh, I can't even say it! Not even to you!"

"Oh, my!" Maggie grinned mischievously, "Whatever did you *do*, Mrs. Barbara Jo Moss, that was so awful!?"

"I...I actually touched Thomas Beyers!" Barbara Jo muttered through her spread fingers. "I...laid my hand on his naked arm! I can't begin to imagine what came over me! What possessed me to do anything so unchristian, to take such liberties! And me a married woman!"

"Barbara Jo, look at me," Maggie urged softly. "You are no longer a married woman. You are a widowed woman. If you choose to sit in the sun with a man, it's perfectly all right, believe me. And if you choose to laugh at his lame jokes, then, that's all right, too. And what's so brazen about simply putting a hand on a friend's arm, in a companionable gesture?"

"Because...Maggie...you don't understand." Barbara Jo raised a tear-streaked face to stare at Maggie, "When I sat with Thomas in the sun, when I laughed with him, I looked at him. I mean, I really *looked* at him. And it was as if I was seeing the man, Thomas Beyers, for the first time. He was no longer my schoolmaster. He was no longer the widower of my dead sister. He was a *man! I had these...feelings...Maggs, feelings I never had for Fred in all the years we shared the same house. Do you see what I'm saying, Maggie!? My husband has just died! And I had these...feelings....for our former teacher, our brother-in-law, Thomas Beyers!"* Barbara Jo flung up both hands and gave a dismal, unbelieving wag of her head. *"Can you believe that?!"*

"You're a woman, Barbara Jo. Thomas Beyers is a man. It began in the Garden of Eden. God made us that way. You're free. Thomas Beyers is free. There's nothing wrong if the two of you have…feelings…for one another."

"Oh, yes, there is, Maggs!" Barbara Jo wagged her head violently, "There most certainly, assuredly is! My husband has not been dead all that long! I should be grieving for him! In my own way, I suppose, I am still grieving for him. But…Fred…and I…we never…"

"Fred was a lot older than you, Barbs. You were just a girl, when you married Fred Moss. Fred was old enough…well, never mind that. What I mean to say is…Fred was…older. Thomas is a young man. Not that much older than you. You probably never had with Fred…that is to say…you and Fred…you might not have felt…"

"I know what you're trying to say, Maggs. And, yes, you're right. I didn't marry Fred for love. We all know that. But he was kind to me. I owe him some sort of…. loyalty. Don't I?"

"Barbs, I don't know what to say to you. I just know that there's nothing wrong with your experiencing…feelings…that are perfectly natural. You, after all, did not die with Fred. Your life will go on. Did…Thomas…enjoy your visit?"

"If you mean did he behave any differently than when he rose to write our sums on the blackboard or hand out the markers and the charcoal slates, no, Thomas did not. He was just the same sweet, gentlemanly soul Thomas has always been. He did not give me the first indication he felt anything…except deep gratitude for his hot breakfast. So, there. I have said it. I have made a *fool of myself.*"

"There are other single men in the world, besides Thomas Beyers," Maggie commiserated, "You are young, and not at all bad looking. That is, if you'd—"

"Ohhhhhh, Maggggggs!" Barbara Jo burst into wailing moans. "It does make my poor head ache! The very thought of attempting to—"

"I'm not asking you to become a man-slayer, Barbs, for heavens sakes!" Maggie stood up from the kitchen bench, hands on hips, staring at Barbara Jo. "All I'm…suggesting is that you…take yourself in hand! Take a sweetly scented bath, do… something…with your hair…put a little smile on your face…every now and again…"

"What…should I use on my hair…do you think? Should I…?"

Maggie walked around the table and stood staring at Barbara Jo. Then her blue- blue eyes lit up, and she leaned close to Barbara Jo and whispered, "Why don't we—"

Thomas Beyers crawled up his handmade ladder propped against the schoolroom's rafters, then turned and gazed up the hill. Wouldn't it be nice…if…someone…brought him breakfast…? He had rather enjoyed Barbara Jo's visit of yesterday morning. He could not recall seeing the poor woman smile since the recent passing of her poor husband. Thomas' heart, as always, went out to anyone who was in the least bit unhappy or in need. And though Thomas was not a man to give much notice to the apparel or appearance of the fairer sex, he could not help but notice how of late poor Barbara Jo had allowed herself to go absolutely to seed. But despite the hair that was badly in need of washing, the dress that was too big and baggy now that she had dropped so much weight, yesterday morning as he had sat in the sun with her, when she had turned to stare up at him, he had looked into her eyes, and…saw something—he was not sure what—that had *not* been there before. She seemed, right before his eyes, to come suddenly…alive. It was as if he had never really *seen* her before, though she had sat in his classroom countless days, and he had been in the McKinnon home numberless times. There was Nellie Sue…and, of course, the beautiful, mesmerizing Maggie. But Barbara Jo had always hovered in the background…like a slender shadow in his mind…but yesterday…he had looked into her eyes…and had seen…

"Mr. Beyers?"

Thomas gave a tremendous start, making him almost topple off the roof again, as he whirled about to see Barbara Jo descending the little hill leading into the sandy schoolyard.

"Barbara Jo!" Thomas lifted a hand in greeting, feeling his face suddenly grow hot. He had just been thinking about her…and here she was…it was as if…

"I'm sorry," Barbara Jo hesitated for just a moment, staring up at him from the white sands below, "I didn't mean to frighten you." She frowned beneath

337

the brim of a deep blue sunbonnet that ringed her face with white lace.

Her dress was as blue as the mountains stretching away in the distance. Her hair hung about her face in dancing ringlets of gleaming gold-brown…

"Barbara Jo…?" Thomas murmured.

Chapter 35

"The Sparrow is often so crowded, and of late, I have been forced to turn folks away—or house them on the floor!" Maggie grumbled that late March afternoon. "If I had them—now that spring is almost here and the weather is opening up—some nights, I could let several more rooms, if they were available."

"Well, then, my dearest, why don't you...simply...build on?" Bart asked, smooth brows raised, brown eyes flecked with gold smiling at Maggie.

"Simply...build on...is it, then, Mister Logan, *darlin'*? And from where...and from whither...am I to procure these funds...to simply, as you so glibly choose to put it...build on?"

"Well, I mean, darling, if you really want more rooms, then why don't we..." Bart lifted a hand helplessly into the air. "I mean, we *are* getting married...in May...and if you wish to expand the business...I've been meaning, my dearest, to speak with you about just this thing. You *do*...then...intend to...keep *The Sparrow*...in operation... after... we're... married?"

"Keep The Sparrow?" Maggie stared at Bart as if he had just dropped from the sky and knew nothing at all, "Of course! I intend to keep The Sparrow! After all...I mean...*really*...Mr. Logan, darling. What else would I *do*? Married or not! I mean... Mr. Logan...this is my business...my only means of livelihood...for me...and Johnny..."

"But...darling...after we're married...I mean...that's just the point I'm attempting to make here. You won't be forced to depend upon The Sparrow...any more...for a living...you see...so I was just wondering..."

"The Sparrow is *mine*! Mr. Logan! *I* built this business! With *these* two hands! It is not *much*, I know, in the eyes of a rich Northern-born Yankee from Philadelphia! But it is *mine, Mister Logan, mine!"*

"Of course, darling. I understand that. I have watched you…build…The Sparrow. I think you have done an absolutely fabulous job of it. And…if you wish The Sparrow to continue to prosper, and you wish to build on…well…I mean, Margaret Ann…there is all that lumber…stacks and stacks of pine and oak and so forth, flooring and framing and roofing shingles up at the camp. And with all the loggers pitching in…which I can assure you they would be most happy, even delighted…to do, you could raise a new wing…let the upstairs hall flow into the new addition. Even raise the roof…if you so chose, and add dormers…all the way across. The Sparrow could be a striking country inn."

"And a veranda, Mr. Logan? A veranda spanning the entire length of the front? With columns…?"

"Yes, darling, columns…right…and rockers…where one could sit on a summer's eve and watch the sun sink down behind the mountains…maybe a real back porch, eh, extending across the new addition…and…?"

"Fireplaces?" Maggie's eyes were deep blue and glowing, as the vision of the newly enlarged Sparrow rose in her mind in all its glory. "Fireplaces, Mr. Logan, in every room?"

"Certainly, if you wish it. That should not be hard at all to manage. Fieldstone and river rock are plentiful, and red clay surely abounds, in every hill in North Georgia. There, is, darling, only one thing. I did…take on that big…project…for building materials, and so forth…you know. I told you about it. About this fellow…who's…constructing that new log house for his wife. But…I believe I can…juggle the two projects. I'll speak with Giles. We'll work it out."

"Well, Mister Logan, how could I forget…about that big order…that huge log house that Yankee is building down in the meadows. I wouldn't want you to put yourself beneath any additional load of stress, not at all…on my account. We can certainly make do."

"It is not now, nor shall it ever be, my desire that you, my dearest darling, should ever again be called upon to simply…make do."

"Well, Mr. Logan, I scarcely know what to say."

"Then, please, don't say a thing about it. Oh, by the way, why haven't you mentioned…Liza Mae's condition to me?"

"Liza Mae's condition? Why, does she appear...ill to you?"

"Ill, my dear? Is that what you call it these days?" Bart appeared a bit confused.

"Well," Maggie turned to stare at Liza Mae, just entering the dining room, a tray of coffee mugs balanced in her very capable hands. Maggie's eyes fell to Liza Mae's middle, swaddled in a dark dress covered by a snow-white apron of her own making.

"Oh! Oh. Well, I had not actually thought to tell you, or anyone else for that matter, about Liza Mae's...condition. But, of course, we are all...so thrilled..."

What in the name of heaven was the matter with her? Where was her brain? How could she not have noticed? Because she was so selfishly wrapped up in her own life! Liza Mae was very clearly in the family way! And must have been so for *months* now!

"Why? How could you not have told me, Liza Mae? I thought we were friends? Had I known, I most certainly would not have left you with the burden of the inn, whilst I went traipsing about England!"

"That wuz 'zackly why, Mizz Maggie, I din't tell youse. I knoooowed dat youse woud't go. Anyhow, I's is fine as a fiddle, as anybody wif eyes in der heads cin see."

"Oh, Liza Mae! You are such a friend, such a treasure to me! And I know you and Benjamin Noah are just so thrilled! A new little one!"

"Ye'm, Mizz Maggie, we shore is! And this'n, Mizz Maggie, he don' gonna be borned *free!*"

Within two weeks, the new fireplaces rose, two of them, at the end of the new addition. And the frame reared its sturdy rafters over both the old and the new Sparrow. Then the outer clapboard was nailed on, and the new oak shingles found themselves, as if by some miracle, spanning the entire length of the new Sparrow. Atop the attic insulating the entire inn, and providing new storage, dormer windows glowed. Soon, Maggie could walk along the upstairs hallway, straight into the new part of the inn—that opened into the new upstairs rooms.

And new rooms waited also, downstairs, from a hallway leading out the western end of the dining room.

All sealed with sweet-smelling pine. All boasting fine rock fireplaces. All soon furnished with fetchingly carved maple and oak bedsteads, washstands, dressers, and wardrobes fashioned by Tad Horton and the other loggers, in the barn behind the mansion at Cottonwood. With some assistance, Maggie was given to understand, from Bartram Logan—as well as from some of the residents of the new settlement of freedmen clustered about Cottonwood.

As Bart, accompanied by Maggie, was touring the new wing of the inn, Bart, admiring the furniture, remarked off-handedly, "I might, since we appear to have so *many* fellows handy at the production of furniture, establish a sort…of furniture factory…you might say…at Cottonwood. Give the men something to do…during the winter months and when the weather is inclement and they are forced to remain idle indoors. Something productive. A way to pass the time….and make themselves useful…you might say. Some have never in their lives had tools and materials easily at hand…"

"I think it's an excellent idea, Mister Logan, darling. *The Logan Furniture Works…*"

A strange coach rolled along the red-dirt street of Rhyersville, deep with ruts from the winter rains. The strange coach rocked to a halt before *The Sparrow,* and a slight, well-dressed woman going on in years from the look of her, stepped down, aided by the hand of her hired driver. The woman stood very still for a moment, her tired gaze sweeping the very pleasing lines of the fine mountain inn rising before her.

"*Whar*, exactly Ma'am," her driver inquired, rolling a huge wad of tobacco about in his mouth, spitting a long stream of tobacco juice into the dirt street before removing his battered hat to rake a rough hand through his unkempt hair, "*Whar* should I take th' coach, and see ta th' hosses?"

"Just allow me to proceed inside, if you will, Jacob." The lady, quite small and slight of stature, smiled up at her hired driver, "And then I shall be soon out again, and we shall know more...about the situation...and the town. You just wait for me here, Jacob, if you would be so kind."

With that the lady mounted the broad steps of The Sparrow, and with a few light movements crossed the veranda set with a row of welcoming oak rockers, and entered the front door.

Liza Mae, just entering the dining room, drew in a loud, gasping breath, at sight of the slight, well-dressed figure.

Maggie, her back to the door, serving dinner to a group of men before the fireplace, turned, to see what had taken Liza Mae's breath away so.

Maggie felt her face drain of every ounce of blood. Her entire body went rigid, as cold as ice. All sense seemed to flee from her head. Was it...NO! *It could not be...!*

But, yes, it was...there was no mistaking that kind, thin face with the faded gray-green eyes.

"Mrs.—Evans?" Maggie took an involuntary step forward, her body responding, as it normally did, to the entrance of a new customer into her establishment. She felt her feet propelling her forward, as her right hand, of its own volition, rose to grasp that of her mother-in-law. By some miracle, she found her voice, "Mrs. Evans?" she repeated, "What on earth...are you...*doing* here? Is anyone...with you?"

"I have, of course, dearest Maggie, come to view my son's grave. And...no. No one is with me. I am entirely alone, but for the man I hired to drive the coach, all the way up here. I failed to realize it was quite so far. Do you work here, my dear, in this fine inn?" Mrs. Ida Evans was staring at Maggie with frank worry, and deepest sympathy.

"No...Mrs. Evans, I...own...The Sparrow. What can...I mean...have you just arrived? Of course...you have...you must be tired. And hungry..."

"I could do, my dear, with a place to sit down and a bite to eat. And should you, if this is your inn, should you have a room available, I would very much like to have my few things brought in. Then, tomorrow, I thought..."

"Oh, yes!" Maggie muttered, glancing over to see that Liza Mae had fled the room.

Maggie realized she was still holding the thin, cold hand of Mrs. Ida Evans. She dropped it, swept a hand up to her hair, tucking a few unruly strands behind her ears. She must look a fright! And here Len's mother stood before her…looking…she did, in fact, Maggie suddenly realized, look much better than Maggie had ever seen her. Her bonnet and dress were new, and ever so fashionable. Her face, though thin, had a bit of pink in the fine-boned cheeks. This, Maggie suddenly realized, was once a beautiful lady…perhaps …until she had married Big Carl Evans…

"And…*Mister*…Evans…?" Maggie whispered, holding her breath, as if fearful that Big Carl Evans would at any moment come barging through her front door.

"Mr. Evans, my dear Maggie, God rest his soul, passed away…a few weeks back. After…Len…well, the loss of his last son, the son he had planned to make his sole heir…it seemed to take all the…life out of…Mr. Evans. He appeared to lose all cause for living. Nothing…anyone could say, or do…"

"Ahhhhh," Maggie heaved a great sigh of…relief? What a black-hearted sinner she was! How could she possibly be relieved—at the death of a man?! "What about…your children?" Maggie was bold enough to ask.

Ida Evans shrugged thin shoulders. "When Mr. Evans began to sicken and decline, I made all sorts of efforts to find any of the children. Thus far, I have utterly failed. So, I do fear, my dear, I am totally alone in the world. Except," Ida Evans pulled a sweet, sweet smile, "of course, for you."

"*Me? Oh!*" Maggie gasped. This poor, benighted soul, so lonely, so alone, was grasping at straws, attempting to rekindle some sort of kinship with *her*? After what her son, Len, had done?

"Well," Maggie found the energy to whisper, "I…of course…we do have a room. Just…up those stairs. Should I send someone out for your bags…Benjamin Noah…or would you prefer that your hired man…bring them in?"

"Oh, that's all right, dear. We are, after all family. Don't put yourself out at all…on my account. I will call Jacob to bring them in. Shall I pay you now or…?"

"What…? Oh, no…never mind that," Maggie felt her head go into a swirl, blood roaring through her brain, as this slight woman stood before her, her mere presence ushering in a bevy of ghosts from the past. Ghosts of heartache and loneliness. Of sheer, utter desperation. *Loss* beyond all human reason and comprehension. How Maggie wanted to hustle her out the door, and order her driver to speed off, taking this person away, *away*...back to where he had found her...!

"I'll...show...you...the room..." Maggie marched stiffly up the stairs that had been widened to accommodate the flow of traffic into the new wing of The Sparrow that still smelled of sweet pine, maple and oak, the soft, light tread of Mrs. Carl Evans right behind her.

"Whut *dat woman* be adoin' here?" Liza Mae demanded when Maggie had seated Mrs. Ida Evans at a table in the corner of the dining room and returned to the kitchen.

"Mrs. Evans, Liza Mae, tells me that Mr. Evans has passed, and she is here to visit...Len's...grave. She will stay a few days, then...she'll be gone...and life will go on. Now, will you kindly..."

"T'ank da good Lawd dat sorry fool be dead! But, no'm. I's sorrie. I's *is*. But, no'm. I'sll not be sarvin' *dat* woman. Youse cin run me off, if youse wants to, but..."

"Why, Liza Mae! Oh, for one moment, I forgot. Mrs. Evans was your mistress."

"Yes'm, Mizzz Maggie. Dat woman wuz my mistress. And she *knowed* good an' well what her man wuz a doin', sneaking out ta da slave shacks eber night, most o' da nights. And she didn' do *nuthin'*, you unnerstan', Mizzz Maggie, ta stop dat devil!"

"Surely, Liza Mae, you know the kind of man her husband was. You know...Big Carl Evans..."

"Oh, yes m'am! I *knowed* that man in more ways thin' I's kere ta' eber 'member! *I knowed* that man! And I don' bore 'im a chil'! A chil' that he throwed inta da hog pen wif da rest o' da pigs!"

"Liza Mae!" Maggie hissed, "We *cannot* always forget, but we *must* forgive! This woman has lost her husband, a husband that left her as scarred...as the rest of us. No doubt, even more so. Believe me, Liza Mae, when I say...that *that* woman seated in there in the corner of the dining room, was as powerless against Big Carl Evans as you. She resided in the same house with that..."

"Ye'm, I knows dat." Liza Mae gave a stubborn wag of her head. "Still…an' all…I don't know dat I can see ma way clear ta have *nuthin'* ta do…wif' *dat* woman!"

"Well, Liza Mae, she's going to be here…at least for a few days. Then she will be on her way, and neither you nor I shall *ever* probably see her again in this world. You do work here. So, let's just get *on* with it, shall we?"

"Yes'm, if ye says so." A sullen scowl on her face, her dark eyes shooting fire, Liza Mae picked up a tray, shoved open the kitchen door with much more force than necessary, and shuffled from sight.

Maggie sank to a chair at the end of the kitchen table. What on earth…? What could *possibly* happen next? Just seeing Ida Evans again suddenly ushered in a flood of horrid memories, hitting Maggie squarely in the face like a blast of icy-cold water. She gave a shiver, and felt herself go faint with fear. Would she *ever* be rid of the ghost of Len Evans?!

Chapter 36

The figure sat his scrawny horse and shivered in the cold. It was pitch dark, and a slight drizzle had begun to fall. As he waited and watched the inn from the safety of the alley, though April was just around the corner, as frequently happened in the Blue Ridge Mountains suddenly the temperature plunged. The drizzle turned to bits of sleet and snow, striking his bony face, freezing in his drooping beard and on the long hair streaming from beneath his battered hat and down his thin back. He might just not ride back to the shack in the cove tonight. It being so dark and all, he reasoned, and with this bone-chilling cold, maybe he'd just go a piece up the mountain and pull off a few pine boughs to build himself a lean-to, maybe even build himself a little fire. Yeah, that ought to work. Then, in the morning, he'd creep down and spy on the woman at the inn. He might even catch a glimpse of his girl. She was staying here now, he knew. And, some weeks back, she had given birth, he'd heard down at the mercantile. A little girl. Seems as though he was cursed with females in his family.

He gave a shudder, as the unrelenting unfairness of life swept over his cold frame. He was hungry, too. Cold and hungry. Maybe he'd find a bit of food to scavenge, come the morrow, when the McKinnon woman threw out the peelings and the leavings of her fine meals. They were fine meals she put on her tables, so he had been told. Not that he had ever eaten any of the young woman's cooking. He never had such a thing as money, not one thin penny. Besides, if she ever found him hanging about her inn, she'd probably take a broom to him. Pulling his thin coat closer about him, he shivered, and longed for death. He was so lonely now, so alone, what with his woman long gone. And the girl. Nobody, nothing left, except for him, and his horse, and it half-dead. What did he have to live for anyhow? Maybe he'd just freeze to death in the night. Then some of the town folk would stumble onto his dead carcass, and then they'd all be *real* sorry! Sorry they didn't do anything for him! Didn't offer a disabled veteran of the War some meager bit of assistance. Not a pittance had one soul offered him all these lean years. Not even a word when they met him on the dirt street, the few times he showed himself.

A dark, thin shadow in the lowering gloom thick with drifting sheets of sleet and snow, he rode out of the alley, and made his way up the mountainside back of the inn. Once safely hidden in the trees, he slid off his horse, holding on to the stirrup after dismounting, until he was able to balance himself on his one leg. Then he hopped over to a nearby evergreen, a cedar, fragrant in the midst of winter. He drew his whittling knife out of his front pocket, opened the blade that was long and well worn from hours and hours of whittling, and lopped off a few low-hanging branches. Then he piled the branches against the trunk of a huge yellow pine standing nearby. He wondered if he could find a few dead limbs to build himself a decent fire. Then he could warm up a bit. Maybe even whittle for a while, to help pass the miserable night.

He dug about beneath the thick blanket of leaves and pine straw and pulled out some dead branches. He broke them apart, took a flint from his pocket and struck up a spark. The sight of the little fire made him feel better. A bit of light. A bit of warmth. He sank his bony rump down into the soft pine straw and leaves. His back against the huge pine, drawing the cedar boughs heavy with needles close about his shivering frame, he heaved a sigh that began at the tips of his freezing toes and erupted upwards through a deflated chest.

Then he settled his bony back more comfortably against the giant pine, fumbled about, and in his left front pocket found the little piece of yellow pine he had been whittling on the past several days. He took it out, and stared at it in the dim light of his small fire. It was slowly taking shape. It was the figure of a little lamb, like one he'd had as a small boy. Yeah, he recalled in minute detail that little lamb. But it had up and died and left him alone and grieving, just like every other living thing in his life. But the things he carved with his hands—they stayed with him. He had an entire shelf full of these things, back at his shack of a cabin. Not that anybody except him knew or cared one whit about his carvings—that took days, weeks, sometimes months to complete.

He had every animal that had ever roamed the forests and mountains. And a few people. Soldiers, mostly, from the War. Some with horribly debilitating wounds. Some with half their arms. Or with missing legs…like him. They stood silently along the cabin shelf where he placed them. Their faces set like stone. Their eyes unseeing. Their mouths mashed in tight, grim lines. And there they stayed. They were all the company he had nowadays.

Icy barbs of sleet sprinkled with snowflakes whirling about his head, by the light of his small fire, he whittled on the little lamb for a while. Then he drew his bearded face down into the collar of his worn coat, and, the sleet pelting him a bit harder despite his thick shelter of cedar boughs, he closed his eyes. Maybe tomorrow he'd scout around the tiny mountain town. See if he couldn't scare up some pieces of tin, or big wide boards. Anything to afford him more shelter from the elements. He might even rig up some sort of frame to tack it all onto. And the horse…he'd need to scrounge up a few armfuls of hay for the poor starving creature. Plenty of water in the creek just over the ridge. But no grass. Nothing for the poor animal. Yeah, he'd have a mighty busy day tomorrow. Better try to catch a wink of sleep.

The sleet continued to fall, soon coating the barren tree limbs and the needles of evergreens around him. The small fire sputtered and burned itself out. Finally he fell into a troubled sleep. Battles raged in his mind. The wintry stillness of the mountainside was shattered with the hot roar and flash of rifles and cannon, from old battles. Old, yet they filled his brain with mangled bodies and pitiful moans…as if they had occurred only yesterday, or were still being fought…tonight… He writhed and thrashed in his sleep, groans and startled cries escaping the mashed mouth.

Deep in the night, Samantha's hungry, insistent cry woke Maggie. Reluctantly Maggie left her warm bed, made her way downstairs, and stepped through the dining room and kitchen, across the back porch, out into the cold dawn. It had snowed a bit during the night! At least an inch of snow and sleet was piled about the back yard. Pulling her thin shawl closer about shivering shoulders, she stepped carefully down the back steps, each step crunching softly in the mixture of sleet and snow. Slowly she made her way across the narrow yard. She needed to pull up the goat's milk from the cool depths of the well. "Brrrrrr!" she shuddered, her teeth clattering with the chill air swirling about her. "Had I suspected it was this cold, I'd have slipped on my woolen coat!" She reached the well shelter, rubbing her hands together and blowing on them to generate a bit of warmth, before taking hold of the iron rod scotching the windlass—which she knew would be like a chunk of ice to her cold fingers.

Just as she reached for the icy iron handle, she thought she caught, out of the corner of her eye, a figure darting in and out of the trees on the mountainside just behind the inn. Surely not, she chided herself. She must be imagining things. What idiot, what dolt would be out in the woods on a chilly morning like this? But, then, it could be a hunter. No. No man in his right mind would go hunting right behind the main street of the tiny mountain town.

Maggie stood still for an instant, not even breathing, attempting to discern any movement among the tree trunks sparsely dotted with small clumps of evergreens eternal to the mountains—small cedars, hollies heavy with glistening red berries, rhododendron, and sweet shrub. Nothing moved. Well, she muttered to herself, she must have imagined it.

No. There it was again! Maggie removed her hand from the scotching rod, and crouched down behind the well curb. Peeking out, she wondered… What on earth? A thin, dark, bedraggled figure clad entirely in rags hopped out from behind the trunk of a huge pine, and to the spot where Maggie made a habit of dumping out vegetable and fruit peelings, husks and hulls, and kitchen leftovers. Why would someone be out there, slinking about in the woods, searching for other folks' leavings of apple and potato peelings, and bits of biscuit and ham!? Like a mirage, a shadow in human form, the thin figure hopped back behind the sheltering pine. And Maggie wondered if she had actually seen it at all.

She waited for a few moments, the cold making her fingers ache, her legs began to numb. Finally, Maggie rose from her hiding place. Slowly she reached for the cold iron rod, removed it quickly, and grasped the icy handle of the windlass. Then with one hand guiding the rope so the bucket would not scrape against the well walls and pick up clay from its banks, she wound the windlass slowly, drawing the bucket up so that she could swing shut the well lid beneath it, and retrieve the cold goat's milk.

The jug of goat's milk with a milk cloth tied securely about its neck safely in hand, giving one last glimpse at the mountainside back of the inn, Maggie turned and hurried inside.

"Oh no!" Maggie moaned to herself, "No lard left in the bucket! And with biscuits to be baked come mornin'! How could I have been so careless, as to let the lard run out this way." Liza Mae and Benjamin Noah had left for the day. Barbara Jo was upstairs, as was Johnny, already tucked into bed.

Maggie walked to the front door and stood peering out. It was not quite full dark out there. If she hurried, maybe she'd still be able to see her way clear, to make it to the mercantile and back, before full darkness fell. But it was very cold, so she'd need her heavy wool cloak. Nothin' for it, but to get my cloak, go down to the store, and hope I can get someone to the door at this unholy hour! She could light the kerosene lantern—no, she would need both hands free, to carry the heavy tin of lard.

"Mister McAlister?" Maggie banged on the door of the mercantile.

"Oh, is that you, Mrs. Evans? Whut ye be adoin', out at this hour? Out of somethin' important, then, are ye?"

"Yes, I fear so," Maggie sighed, hastening into the welcome warmth of the huge store. "It's freezing cold out there. And for some insane reason, I've let the lard completely run out, at the inn. If I don't want the building torn down in the mornin', I'd best be prepared with hot biscuits!"

"Aye! Mrs. Evans, and so ye must! How big a tin would ye be awantin', then, sees ye be carryin' it yeself? Or should I run it down for ye?"

"No, I certainly won't put you to that bother. I'll take it. Give me twenty pounds, and you go on to your warm bed. Sorry if I've kept you up."

"Nah. Think nuthin' of it. Was just about to lock up, but what's anuther ten minutes or so. Well, if that's all?"

"Yes, just put it on my bill. And, goodnight, then."

Maggie hefted the heavy tin of lard, pulled her cloak close, and stepped out the front door, hearing the heavy bar drop across the closed door, even before she had stepped off the narrow porch and into the still-muddy street from the melting sleet and snow.

The street, Maggie thought suddenly, lay before her as dark and unfamiliar as Egypt. What was that strange noise? Maggie halted for a second, and glanced along the street behind her. It was so dark…did something move, a shadow, disappearing between the buildings? A chill of fear crept up Maggie's spine. She turned, gave a shiver, and hastened forward. A cold wind gusted suddenly down off the mountains, blowing tendrils of hair about her face beneath her night bonnet and sending the tail of Maggie's cloak swirling about her ankles. Oh, God! Why was she so afraid? She had lived in Rhyersville almost all her life! What was there to fear here? On this street as familiar as her own face? She knew each soul that inhabited each and every business along this street, each soul that resided in each and every house for miles and miles about the tiny mountain town! What had she, then, to fear? The unknown?

Some wild animal? They seldom came down into the town. Maybe now and again a hungry bear, seeking a bit of cast-off garbage in the dead of winter…

There it was again! Steps? No, what creature walked with such an odd gait? It was a clump, thump, clump, thump…

Thank God! The door of the inn lay just ahead!

Hauling her heavy burden, Maggie heaved a sigh. She could see the lamplight, spilling its yellow warmth out the front windows of The Sparrow, falling across the broad front veranda…just a few more steps. Shift the tin of lard down to the crook of her left arm, reach with the right, and lift the heavy doorlatch….ahh…rush inside…drop the oak bar firmly into place…

Bumps of flesh rising along her arms, Maggie hastened through the dining room into the kitchen, hefted the tin of lard to the top of the meal chest. Her knees weak as water, she felt that she might fall in a dead swoon…

What on earth was wrong with her! She was being as big a ninny as Barbara Jo! That was it! She had listened to her sister go on and on about that dark figure, nightly haunting the inn. Suddenly she recalled the scrawny shadow she had seen creeping out of the forest…back of the inn…

For the love of heaven…! Get *ahold* of yourself, Maggie McKinnon! Check the doors! Bank the fires! Put out the lamps! And go to your bed!

For several days, Maggie kept close watch on the mountainside back of the inn, and to her horror one morning she again spied the scrawny, filthy figure, hopping along the forest floor. It darted behind a tree, then out, and with hands more in the nature of claws, it scooped bony tentacles into the scrap pile she had thrown out for the rabbits, the winter wrens, the cardinals and the squirrels. Then it hopped quickly back into the quiet seclusion of the thick woods.

A fleeting vision of the odd figure danced about in Maggie's brain all that day. And as dusk began to gather, Maggie stood on the back porch of the inn, and gazed up at the looming mountainside. With the rising of the sun, the sleet and snow had melted away. No precipitation on the mountain or in the valley below. So what *was* that? Was that tendrils of fog, drifting up from that patch of trees not a hundred yards from the inn yard? Or was it smoke from a campfire?

His hut in the woods was slowly taking shape. He found several large pieces of cedar planking stacked behind the cavernous building that belonged to the man called Trap. With these he had fashioned walls to keep the cedar boughs off him and out of his face and beard. He rigged himself what might suffice as a roof with scraps of tin. He had also appropriated several armfuls of sweet hay for his horse, from the wheelwright's stables. Riding up to his shack in the cove, he gathered all his precious carvings into a tow sack, and hauled them to his new hiding place on the mountainside. He'd have to be sure the tow sack with his treasures stayed well up beneath the tin roof of his new hut. He scrounged around and found several large, flat stones, to build himself a new resting place for them. With all that work he'd invested, he didn't want 'em gettin' wet and settin' in to rot. After all, they were the only friends he had in this cold, cruel old world.

As darkness began to fall, he built a small fire. Then he crouched before it, sat back on a rock he had lugged up for a seat, stretched his one leg out toward the welcome warmth of his fire, and surveyed his new domain. At least now, he wouldn't be so alone. He had the woman throwing out lots of peelings and stuff from her restaurant, though he hated the idea of subsisting on anything cast off by the clan of that John McKinnon. Still he had to eat to live. And she had even begun to put out tins of food. Maybe she had a pet raccoon, wolf, or fox she was accustomed to feeding. Whatever. At any rate, now he at least had a bit of food in his flat belly. And with Trap's stables so near, now, with any luck at all at not being caught, his poor horse would not starve 'til the grasses thickened up.

And he had seen her, just last night. He had even smelled her. She smelled good. But he had not gotten up the nerve to take her. Not yet. But one of these fine days…his opportunity would come.

Overwhelmed with pity, Maggie began to place more and more food onto the scrap pile. Then, finally, after a week or so of this, she began putting complete meals, plus mugs of beverage, onto an old stump standing a few paces back in the woods. And each time, when evening fell and she returned for the tin vessels, they were completely emptied. And licked clean as a whistle. Maggie began to leave entire loaves of bread, and small bags of turnips and potatoes.

She mentioned this odd creature, living in the forest at the foot of the mountain, at the breakfast table on a Saturday morning. Liza Mae and Benjamin Noah both shook their heads. They had seen no such creature. But Bethany Lee suddenly gave a muffled gasp. She began hacking and coughing. Almost choking on her food, finally she caught her breath. She looked over at Maggie, her face blanched pale as death.

"Bethany Lee?" Maggie asked, her voice quiet, "You have some notion *who* this person might be? This person scrawny as a bird, lurking about in the woods back of the inn, scrounging scraps for his living?"

"Well…ma'am…ummmmm…it could be that this thing…be *Pap*."

"You mean…*your father*?" Maggie frowned in amazement. "Why on earth would he be living in the woods up on the mountain?"

"I'm not sayin' fer shore that 'tis Pap. But who knows why Pap does the things he does. He's been strange—ever since comin' back from th' War, my Mam said."

"Your mother? And just what happened to her? Where is she?"

"I don't rightly know, ma'am. She done disappeared, when I was just a little thing. All I recall about Mam is that she got to where she was gone a lot. Then one day, in she marches, and Pap turns on her like a mad dog. He ranted and raved, and he run her clean off. And I 'spect she was more than glad ta go. She couldn't take it no more."

"Take what?" Maggie insisted.

"Always being cold. Always being hungry. Ever since Pap come back from the War, she said."

"Was your father...injured in the War, Bethany Lee?"

"Yes'm, I 'spect you might say that. He's got but one leg, anymore. And he can't rightly stand up none too good...on that one leg. So he says he's not a man no more. He can't grow things, and such. Some people as says that Pap's got tetched in th' head. By th' war, and all."

"He's not able to farm?"

"No'm, he ain't able to stand up right. And he says he's no good at raisin' critters, like hogs and sheep, and such. He tried his hand at just about everthin', and nuthin' worked for Pap."

"How awful!" Maggie gasped, "What...then...What does your father do, Bethany Lee, for a living?"

"Nuthin' that nobody knows of. Nuthin' nobody cin see. I guess that's why folks all say he's tetched in th' head. He goes out in th' mornin'. Totin' his tow sack. And sometimes he comes back with somethin' to eat in that sack. And sometimes he comes back with nuthin' a'tall. That's what we called the starvin' times, up in the cove."

"But, I don't understand, Bethany Lee. If your father lives...up in some cove...what is he doing, roaming the mountains back of the inn?"

"I don't know, Miss Maggie. I purely don't know. But, whatever it is he's adoin' back there, you can mark my words ta one thing—he's up to no good. He hates me now, you know. And he hates a lots of other folks. He blames 'em for his gittin' hurt in th' War, I guess. If truth be told, Pap hates most folks."

"But...Bethany Lee, why? That makes no sense at all," Maggie leaned over the table and insisted.

"Because they's got things Pap's *not* got. And, most of all, he hates 'em 'cause they's all got *two* legs."

"Bethany Lee, how can you just sit here... calmly eating your food... and saying such terrible things about your own father!" Maggie demanded in an angry, strident voice. "If he's hungry, and alone, roaming the mountains in the cold and ice, don't you think you should go to him? Don't you feel that it's your duty as his child, to go out there, and *talk* to him?! *Help* him!?"

355

The girl gave a slight, sorrowful wag of her head, sending her blond hair shimmering, "I cin't talk ta Pap. Not no more. And never could much, fer that matter."

"But, Bethany Lee, if he's alone out there. Cold. And hungry—"

"You 'spect *me* ta go out there and try ta talk ta that mean ol' devil-of-a man?" Bethany Lee's eyes narrowed to slits. "Don't you understan' one thing about us cove folks? He don't want *none* of my help! He done *hit* me! He done *run me off*! And me big with child and with no place on this earth ta go! *He hates me!* He told me he wished me *dead*! And my babe dead along with me! Why should I care what 'comes o' him? Serves him right, if he's cold now, and hungry!"

"Bethany Lee! Those are *terrible* things to say about your own father! No matter what he's done—"

"Well, it's *true*!" Bethany Lee leapt up from the table, threw her fork onto her empty plate with a clatter. Tears filling her eyes, she slammed the ladder-back chair against the scarred oak table and stormed out at Maggie, "I tell ya, he's *crazy mean*! Tetched in th' head by th' War, is whut he be! You want somebody ta talk to that mean old scarecrow-of-a-man? *You* go up on the mountain, and see how fer yore talkin' gits ye—with *Silas P. Crocker!*"

Bethany Lee spun about. Gathering in both hands the heavy skirts of one of Maggie's best cotton frocks, heaving loud, gasping sobs, she fairly flew to the foot of the stairs and bounded upward, her footsteps echoing on each yellow-pine tread.

Heavy. Angry. Filled with hurt and despair.

The girl's words rang in Maggie's head. "*You want somebody ta talk to that mean old man? You go up on the mountain, and see how fer your talkin' gits you with Silas P. Crocker…*"

So the creature had a name…*Silas P. Crocker*…Maggie sat staring at the remnants of her meal. Well, *something* surely needed to be done. *Someone* needed to check on the man…but, at the moment, nothing, and no one, came to Maggie's mind… to go up on the mountainside and try to reason with a man who was, a score of years after the last shot had been fired, still so traumatized by the War Between the States…If Silas P. Crocker was truly as confused, as filled with hatred as his own child intimated, he posed a danger not only to himself…but perhaps to the community of people living in the valley below the mountainside where he now seemed to have set up crude living arrangements. Maybe he was even now, this very moment, peering down at the inn... Maggie gave a shiver, rose, with one hand lifted the crockery plate containing her half-eaten breakfast, with the other hand her mug half filled with cooling coffee, and began clearing away the breakfast dishes. Liza Mae and Benjamin Noah glanced uneasily at one another, leapt to their feet, and dumped their breakfast remains onto a tin plate which Maggie immediately took outside, as Liza and Benjamin Noah wordlessly began their usual morning chores.

The day passed, as busy as any day they had ever had at the inn. It was late when Maggie banked the fire in the dining room fireplace and headed up the stairs and to her bed. But she couldn't help but pause, her hand on the new oak balustrade, and think of that poor man. He was out there alone in the dark and the cold, on the side of that mountain! How could she in all good Christian conscience go upstairs and climb into a soft bed and pull warm quilts up beneath her chin, knowing Silas P. Crocker was out there!?

The kerosene lamp casting its warm yellow glow before her, Maggie turned and made her way back through the dining room, through the kitchen, where she swung wide the kitchen door. Then, only in her nightgown and a thin shawl about her shoulders, she stepped out onto the narrow back porch and stood peering into the cold dark of night. Then she raised her free hand, cupping it about her mouth, and called into the wintry blackness:

"Mister Crocker! Can you hear me? If you're out there, come on in! Come inside by the fire! Mister Silas P. Crockerrrrrrrrrrrrrrrrrr!!!!"

Maggie's calls were greeted with a fierce gust of wind that whipped the name about the mountainsides, through the barren limbs of winter trees, like some sort of winged saker, and threatened to blow out the faint flame of her lamp—and that sent the ends of her shawl fluttering about her head.

Heaving a great sigh, reluctantly Maggie turned and stepped back into the warmth of the inn. Holding her flickering kerosene lamp aloft, she pushed the kitchen door closed with a frustrated bang, dropped the heavy bar in place with a flourishing thump, turned and headed for the stairs.

Upstairs in bed, Maggie stared into the darkness, and imagined a one-

357

legged man, thin and starved to the point of emaciation, eyes red-rimmed with rage, dark and burning with love toward none and malice toward all—roaming the mountains right behind The Sparrow Restaurant & Inn.

"*God*," Maggie whispered into the darkness, "*reach down your hand of love tonight. Hear, Lord! Help, Lord! Heal, Lord…*"

Her prayer seemed to be answered with a rising of the wind, sending the upstairs shutters clattering loudly against the oak clapboard walls. The fierce gusts whistled and howled down the mud-and-rock chimney, sending little puffs of ashes rising and drifting about the rock hearth.

Maggie pulled Mama's warm quilts tightly up beneath her chin, settled her head deep onto Mama's down-stuffed pillow, squinted her eyes tightly shut, and imagined herself in her own room…in the square-log house…in McKinnon Valley…Papa…and Mama…sleeping soundly in their own cozy room at the end of the narrow hallway… Nellie Sue warm and safe beside her…and Barbara Jo, on her own bed…just the other side of the small room…

The following Sunday afternoon, the two of them were sitting in the downstairs parlor. With the addition to the inn, Maggie had felt that with all the new rooms available, and with so many folk now, so it seemed, residing in the inn—she and Johnny, Barbara Jo, Bethany Lee and Samantha—and now, Mrs. Ida Evans appeared to have added herself to the growing household of the inn, as she gave no indications of making any effort to head back down country to her home in Forsyth County—a downstairs parlor was sorely needed for use during daylight hours. It boasted comfortably cushioned seating built by the Logan Furniture Works, a table or two held kerosene lamps handy for reading, and a fine, big fireplace kept the place cozy on cold days. Wide, southward facing windows looked out onto the front veranda, letting in sunshine, even on the coldest days.

"Margaret Ann, I really don't know…" Bart wagged his head sadly. "How does one go about helping someone who refuses help? This…Silas P…..whoever…he will come down off the mountain and behave himself like a human…rather than an animal…*when and if* he makes up his own mind to do so. And not before. If the poor tortured, demented soul has lived in this wretched condition for more than twenty years, how do you, my darling angel, expect to rescue him from his pit of hatred and despair? Really, Margaret Ann, I do believe you have met your match." Bart frowned at her.

"Mr. Logan, darling," Maggie began, speaking very slowly, very patiently, as if explaining something to a small, ignorant child, "Have you never read the Scriptures about the man named *Legion*?"

"Legion..." Bart knit his handsome brow in deep concentration, raised a strong brown hand to stroke his smoothly-shaven chin, and grinned over at her, "No, my sweet, I can't say that I do recall...that particular passage. But...then...you are *all too well* aware...that I am somewhat...ill versed..."

"Yes," Maggie frowned prettily at him, "I am all too aware. But this *Legion* received his name because the poor besotted creature was inhabited by not one, not two, not even three or four, or half a dozen—"

"Where is all this leading, my dear?" Bart raised dark brows to peer at her across the short space between the rockers they had drawn up before the inviting warmth of the parlor fireplace. "Pray, do go on."

"Yes, I shall gladly do so, if you will be so kind as not to interrupt me so very rudely."

"Pray, do excuse me. But oftentimes, you get hung up on the details, and never seem able to arrive at the meat of the story." Bart smiled at her charmingly.

"Are you saying, by any chance, Mr. Logan, that I am given to rattling on to no purpose at all? Is that what you're trying to tell me, Mr. Logan, *darlin'*? That I'm indeed an empty, idle-mouthed chatter-box of a—"

"What happened to Legion?" Bart interrupted with a faint smile.

"Well, what happened to Legion was very simple—"

A faint lift of his brows, Bart muttered beneath his breath, as he smiled over at her, "Oh, really? Dare we hope so?"

"Do you want to hear the story—or not!?" Maggie demanded angrily.

"Of course, my darling. I always adore the very sound of your voice."

"Then do please keep quiet," Maggie wiped the palms of her hands over her skirt, as if to smooth out numerous wrinkles, and set her mouth to continue.

"This poor creature lived amongst the tombs. Numerous tombs, you do understand? An entire huge *graveyard,* is what it actually was."

"Ummmmmmm hummmm," Bart nodded his head sagely.

"And he was of such an ill temperament, so ill-suited to keeping company with normal human society, that he was totally and absolutely shunned by the entire populace of all the surrounding villages and towns and communities."

"Nobody at all liked the poor fellow," Bart murmured.

"He was *intolerable,*" Maggie explained. "Always raging and charging out of the graveyard. Rising up from amongst the tombs like an unearthly apparition, scaring all the local folk absolutely within an inch of their lives!"

"Oh, my," Bart frowned.

"And this continued on, for…I believe…it is such a coincidence…more than a score of years."

"You…don't…say!" Bart wagged his head in disbelief.

"Yes, it did," Maggie nodded her head in return. "He continued on in this sorry state, until the Lord Jesus Himself in the flesh passed by."

"Oh, I see. And the Lord Jesus Himself…in the flesh…when He passed by, put an end to the sorry state of this poor fellow's condition…"

"Well. Yes. That's exactly what happened. The Lord Jesus just simply talked with him, and…"

"But…in this particular instance…I can see where you're going with this, my sweet," Bart wagged his handsome head. "Yes, I can see. But what I also understand is…that…in the case of this…Legion…fellow…our Lord Jesus was there…*In the flesh?* Right?"

"Well, yes. Of course," Maggie snapped impatiently. "But what does that have to do with anything?" She had ceased rocking in the huge oak chair, and sat staring at Bart as if ready to charge him. She had that certain look on her face with which Bart was all too familiar. That look that said, *I'm right about this! And don't you dare try to convince me otherwise. For, I can assure you, my fine fellow, you will be absolutely and totally wasting your time.*

"Uhhhhh," Bart stammered, "Yes, of course. But my point, my sweet, is simply this. Our Lord Jesus, while here on earth, in the flesh, was able to accomplish great feats and wondrous miracles…past all imagining. While *we*….if you get my meaning…"

"While we, Mr. Logan, darling, are totally forsaken by the Spirit, absolutely without any power from on High, forlorn and at the mercy of all evil now rampant in the world? Is that what you're attempting to say?"

"Well…no…not exactly. But you must admit, my sweet dearest," Bart began softly, knowing as he gazed into those blue-blue eyes, so wide now, and so filled with anger, that he was far in over his head…with nowhere at all to go with this conversation. Why, in the name of all that was holy didn't he ever learn to simply listen to her stories, keep his mouth shut, and nod his mute assent? But no, spiritual novice that he was, he felt inclined, always, when she began one of her gospel stories, to add his ignorant two cents' worth.

"I mean…really…darling…" Bart fumbled about, searching his mind for anything halfway intelligent to inject into this conversation that had gotten totally out of his realm. Was he still so unfamiliar with the spiritual? "I mean…really…darling…do you think anyone can simply walk up to this poor fellow…this Silas P.…whatever…and talk him into forsaking the dark clouds of hatred and insanity, coming out of the fog of the past…and embracing a sane and real future? Is that what you actually believe?"

"Well," Maggie snapped, her eyes now dark sapphire and flashing fire, "*And…why…not!?*"

"Well…because…because…because…"

"*Because* I am totally void of the Spirit of the Almighty? Because *my* prayers reach no farther than the smoked ceiling of this small, insignificant, nondescript mountain inn tucked on the backside of nowhere? *Is that why, Mr. Logan, darling?*"

"Margaret Ann! Sweetheart…!"

"Well, I will have you to know, Mr. Logan, that I have been *praying* for Mr. Silas P. Crocker. I have been praying *very* hard. *Every night.* I have *faith.* And one of these days…one of these *fine* days…he's going to come down off that mountain, and walk the streets of Rhyersville…like any other sane and sensible fellow. You just mark my word on that, *Mister Logan, darling!*"

"I…I totally and absolutely…believe you, my sweet!" Bart lied, nodding his head in supposed agreement. "And…I am joyously…looking forward to just such a time."

"Now," Maggie set her mouth in a pretty little pout, "you're making fun of me."

"No," Bart quickly denied. Reaching over, he took one of her small hands in his large, warm ones. "I believe that when you, my love, set your mind to it, you and your prayers can indeed move heaven and earth. And if heaven and earth, then what kind of chance does this poor Silas P. fellow stand, when you began your nightly assault upon the Almighty and storm the very portals of glory?"

Maggie narrowed her blue eyes and stared at him suspiciously. His eyes were dark and filled with warmth. A small smiled played about the handsome mouth. He seemed, in fact, to be telling the truth. She felt herself begin to relax. She flashed Bart a dazzling smile

Bart felt all the tension drain from his back and shoulders. He squeezed the small hand he held, reached over and drew her forward with his other arm, until their noses met. "I love you, Margaret Ann, and whatever you want…whomever you wish to pray for…you just let me know. I'll be right there beside you, praying with you, fighting beside you, when those gates of glory collapse—and you and I will go marching in, totally victorious, together always."

Maggie felt tears flooding her eyes. She gave his hands a quick, answering squeeze. Then she blessed Bart with such a smile that he began to doubt that a truly fair and loving God, or any creature in existence, could possibly deny this gorgeous angel any request.

Chapter 37

Lady Marilyn Eveline Drayton stood before the one small window in her mean London flat, gazing down into the filth-ridden street below, crowded at all hours of the day with a gaggle of odd, ugly, rough characters, making their way here and there about the great city. Like rats in a sewer, she thought sourly, most of them bent upon errands of destruction, vice, and theft. How she despised it!—that she had been forced by reduced circumstances to settle for this mean, dirty little hole-in-the-wall, where she scarcely dared show herself, lest she be set upon! A person of her station in life! A person...oh, what was the use! That William Bartram Logan had gotten the best of her, all right. He had gotten the bulk of the inheritance of that old stupid frog who had called himself *Feldon Bartholomew Hurston, Fourth Earl of Windsfield*—!

—Leaving her nothing except a few worthless canvases that no soul in his right mind would pay one pence to purchase!

The upstart American, uncouth and ill-mannered despite his achingly handsome good looks, had done her in, all right, despite his magnanimous gesture not mentioned in the will of the Fourth Earl. True, he had signed over to her a quite generous sum, just to salve his conscience. But it was not a drop in the bucket when compared to the worth of the sprawling Windsfield Estate!

And that...well, that draft he had signed...she had... She now could look back and see how very foolish she had been with that quite generous lump sum of money. First, she had rented a fine house in one of London's upscale districts. Then, she had blown an exorbitant amount on an entirely new wardrobe. After all, if she planned to re-kindle her life, re-establish herself in London society, she must certainly dress the part.

Then, she had had the terrible misfortune of meeting *Sir Roger Woolsforth.*

Woolsforth, it was, who had been so aptly named! He had certainly pulled the wool forth, and over her eyes! And she, with all her wit and harsh life experience, had not once suspected a thing. She had not seen past his lies and the smoke screen of wealth and charm he had cast about himself. He had wined and dined her, escorted her, lavished attention on her…and dared she admit it?…romanced her…out of all her remaining funds!

He knew of this great investment opportunity, he had told her. Off handedly, at first, insisting, when she plied him with questions demanding more details, that no, he would not dare risk the capital of one so near and dear to him, though just lately met. No, even though the gains were certain and sure as the sun would rise on the morrow, no, he could not, would not, be her go-between. But, in the end, he had allowed himself…to be persuaded.

He had taken everything.

And he had simply vanished from off the face of the earth.

And now…! What in the name of heaven was she to do…?

Throw herself on the mercy of some…friend? No. She had exhausted all those avenues. Months ago.

Lady Marilyn turned from the window, tears welling in her dark, angry eyes. What *was* she to do!?

What did she have *left*? She flounced over the worn fabric covering the floor that passed for a rug, to a huge chest resting at the side of the small, mean room. Slowly, with one pale, thin hand, she lifted the lid. She had *this*. She reached in one hand, and drew forth a large red-velvet bag. Opening its gold-braided drawstring, piece by piece, she drew out a lovely, lavish, extremely valuable tea service—in stunning silver.

She had *this*. She had taken it…that last night she was allowed to reside at Windsfield Mansion. Having been denied her rightful inheritance, she had, in the privacy of her room, taken out her large tablet, and scanned the inventory she had made of the contents of the Windsfield Mansion. She had searched it diligently for any items of worth she felt she could…appropriate…and make off with…without being discovered. She had suffered no qualms of guilt, no remorse, and no compunction at all, against taking something of great value, which she felt was rightfully hers.

Now, the questions loomed large before her…*what* would this silver tea service fetch? And how far, and *to where*, would its worth take her?

She could not survive for long, she knew, on the sum, though it might be quite large. No. Rents and food were too expensive. And then there were hired carriages, etc. if one was to get around in the city of London. New frocks, and shoes, if one was to maintain any sort of social dignity. Have friends…or acquaintances…to tea…and so forth. No. She could not subsist long on whatever this splendid tea service would fetch.

Her only option, then, to *invest* the sum, and hope to get some sort of future return…

Invest…?! What a laugh! Wasn't that what she had just attempted?! And look at the disastrous results!

Well, one thing was certain and clear, she had to think of something. Come up with *someone…some place* where she could go…where they would be *forced* to take her in…?

But where…!?

The only blood kin that she knew anything of, was that handsome, uncouth, tight-fisted, distant cousin—William Bartram Logan—

—But Cousin Bartram resided—she supposed, very richly so—all the way across the vast Atlantic! Would the silver tea service…carry her…all the way across the vast…Atlantic? And if so…to…*what*?!

Chapter 38

"Thar's be a…purson…Mizzz Maggie, at da front doh'. She says…" Liza Mae began, breaking off for a lack of words to describe to her the person she had just encountered at the front entrance of *The Sparrow*.

"Well, show her in, Liza Mae. And then why don't you take a break, and get off your feet, for a bit?" Maggie raised smooth brows. She was busy, and why did Liza Mae feel that Maggie had to personally greet this person…?

By now, Maggie had followed Liza Mae to the front door—that stood wide open, the afternoon light falling across a figure that Maggie had hoped to never see again in this world. And behind her, strewn across the wide veranda of the inn, a mountain of luggage.

"Lady…*Marilyn?*"

"Whom does it appear to you to be?" Lady Marilyn snapped, fighting to hold her tongue from spewing out the words…words so vile she dared not utter them. For if she expected *any* sort of cooperation from this…this…*ignorant milkmaid* that stood staring at her with a wide, idiotic gaze, her mouth hanging open…

"I am, as you might well *expect*, come in search of my…*dear cousin*…Mister William Bartram Logan. And I have spent days…no weeks…being subjected to the most *ill* means of transport. And then to be brought to this…these *dismal* surroundings… Where *is*…my dear cousin? I am dead on my feet. If I don't sit down soon, I shall swoon dead away!"

"Well! Yes! Please, do step in. And would you like something to eat, perhaps? Or do you wish…to be shown into the parlor…to rest…until word can be sent to… Mr. Logan?"

"Sent? Word? And just where…*is* this…*dear* cousin of mine? Not in this dinky, dingy little village, I trust?"

"Well," Maggie stammered, searching for something intelligent to say. How dared she...show up here...like this...and then act as if she had just been deposited in a barnyard, before some...chicken coop!?

"Well," Maggie repeated, her voice a bit sharp, "Mister Logan is a man concerned with many business interests. He does not simply lounge about The Sparrow, waiting for long-lost kin to pop onto the doorsteps! In the event that he has not ridden out to Logan Town, on some important business or another, he is, no doubt, at this time of day, up at the logging camp. If you would come into the parlor, perhaps you might make yourself comfortable there—until Mister Logan can be located...and informed of your... *unexpected*...arrival."

Maggie motioned Lady Marilyn into the dining room, past the stairs, and into the hallway leading into the front parlor, where a cheery fire always glowed on cool days. Though spring was upon the Blue Ridge Mountains, a chill oftentimes lingered in the air drifting over the mountains.

"*This?* You call *this*...a parlor?" Lady Marilyn stepped into the cozy parlor, peered down her lovely nose at the room, and almost burst into tears. Or laughter...she wasn't sure which would have been more appropriate! She had come all this way! Had paid her last pence, had sailed across the broad Atlantic Ocean with such high expectations of being received in some richly appointed mansion, in some fine city—! And *this* was the sort of accommodations she had found?! This tiny, dirty, crude town? This rustic inn? This miniscule...crudely appointed hole-in-the-wall that this woman laughingly called...*a parlor?!*

"Well, yes, Lady Marilyn, I do. If you can find nicer accommodations, in Rhyersville, then, by all means..." Maggie stood, feet firmly planted before the open parlor door, and motioned toward it, "...please... feel free to take yourself and your luggage...off—"

But Lady Marilyn, apparently dead on her little feet, had sunk down into the soft comfort of the nearest chair, and closed her eyes.

"Ohhhhhh!" Maggie muttered, flouncing out the door, and out to the kitchen to find Benjamin Noah. "Would you kindly bring in that mountain of luggage from off the front veranda. Then go up to the lumber camp," Maggie ordered her hired man, in a clipped, angry voice, "And tell Mister William Bartram Logan, that, contrary to all sane obstacles against *any* such an occurrence ever possibly happening, his dear, *dear* cousin...*Lady Marilyn Drayton*...has just...dropped down out of the clouds!"

"Say...whut?" Benjamin Noah stared at his employer, his dark eyes wide.

"Tell...Mister Logan...that Lady Marilyn Drayton...has just arrived in Rhyersville!"

Lady Marilyn, totally exhausted, had fallen into a deep sleep, immediately that her little head touched the back of the soft, inviting down cushions of the huge rocker pulled up near the fireplace. Peering in at this newly arrived...guest...Maggie saw that she was still fast asleep an hour later. And Maggie went on about her business of serving the noon meal to a dining room filled with farmers and local ladies and business owners.

As the dining room and kitchen were being cleared and swept and dishes washed out in the kitchen, Lady Marilyn Drayton appeared. She stood at the foot of the stairs, staring about her with a vacant gaze. Then her dark violet eyes seemed to snap wide, and she apparently came to herself, and realized where she was.

"I have been here...for hours...and no one has had the common courtesy to offer me a sip to drink, or a bite to eat, or any sort of refreshment!" she accused in a loud, imperious voice, as her senses came back to her, apparently in full and total force.

Maggie smiled at her newest, most unwelcome guest, "It is difficult to quench one's thirst or appease one's hunger, when deep in slumber and softly snoring, is it not?"

"*I...do...not...snore!*" Lady Marilyn exploded.

"Oh? Well," Maggie smiled very sweetly, wiping her hands on her aprontail, "then...it must have been the rain pelting against the window panes, that I heard...each time I passed by the parlor door."

"*It's not raining!*" Lady Marilyn roared.

"My point, exactly," Maggie smiled sweetly. "We do happen to have a bit of food...left in the kitchen...if you would care to just follow me?"

"I am not accustomed...my dear Mrs.—whatever your name is, I don't recall—I am not accustomed to being served in the *kitchen*. Like some...some...*char maid!*"

"Well. In that case, I suppose you shall just have to put off eating anything, Lady Marilyn, until the dining room is again open for service. You see, we have it all cleaned and swept...ready for the supper crowd—" Maggie absolutely refused to cow-tow to this...

"Oh! All right! I don't know...I cannot imagine...why I am being forced... subjected to...why I must put up with...with such...crass...abominable..."

"Yes, well," Maggie had swung wide the kitchen door, and stood waiting for Lady Marilyn to enter. "If you would, then, just seat yourself at the kitchen table?" Maggie gave a dismissive wave of her hand. "And I will fix you a plate...of whatever I can find."

"*Leftovers?* You expect me to sit here, in this shack of an inn, and to consume *leftovers?* Food over which...some other...crude...persons have..."

"Do you...or do you *not*...Lady Marilyn...wish me to serve you a plate of fine, clean, country cooking?" Maggie smiled down at her newest guest.

"Oh! Get on with it! Give me...whatever it is that I smell...*what is that?*"

"Steak with creamed gravy. Fresh collard greens. Baked yams. All the mornin's biscuit is gone, so it will be a buttered slice of cornpone."

"Ohhhhhhhhh!" Lady Marilyn laid her head forward into two small, very white, very soft hands, and moaned softly—until intense hunger drove her to lower her hands, raise her head, and reach for a fork. She devoured the stuff, scarcely tasting it, except for the deliciously tender steak, smothered in thick, creamy gravy—and the baked yams. The collards and the cornpone, despite her intense hunger, she found she could barely tolerate. Then she dragged herself up from the kitchen table, and asked to be shown to the necessary. Maggie walked to the back door and held it wide. Then slowly she raised her right hand, and pointed in the direction of the outhouse. Her head held high, Lady Marilyn sailed past Maggie, a highly aggrieved look on her lovely face, her dark eyes blazing, tromped out to the outhouse and banged the door shut. Then back into and through the kitchen, through the dining room, she floated, back into the downstairs parlor—to wait for William Bartram Logan. Surely, surely, she moaned in a low, angry snarl, William Bartram Logan, Fifth Earl of Windsfield, would soon appear, and rescue her from this awful, *awful* dump!

The afternoon sun stood not far from the western rim of the Blue Ridges, as Stephen Giles drew the heavily-laden freight wagon to a halt before the steps of The Sparrow, leapt lithely down, and strode up the front steps of the inn. On the lower step, he paused, knocking the clumps of red clay off his logger's boots. He removed his hat, bumping the red dust from its broad brim against the heavy cotton of his trousers. He then mounted the remaining steps, crossed the wide veranda, and pushing wide the heavy oak door, strode into the dining room of the inn.

Holding his sweat-stained broad-brimmed hat against the faded front of his blue chambray shirt, he stood just inside the front door, allowing a few moments for his light grey-green eyes to adjust to the decreased lighting. "Miss Maggie?" the head foreman of the Logan Lumber Company called softly.

"Oh, is that you Stephen, Mr. Giles?" Maggie came hurrying in, a perplexed look on her lovely face. "I…was expecting Mr. Logan. He did, I trust, get my message… about…?"

"He got your message, all right, Miss Maggie, and he sent me to check things out. I was headed out to Logan Town anyway…takin' a wagon-load of goods for th' store. He mentioned somethin' about me stoppin' by th' inn, to see if he understood rightly. Somethin' about a cousin of his, needing a lift on out to Cottonwood?" Stephen, out of courtesy to his Boss, did not elaborate on the puzzling instructions he had received—regarding this…cousin.

"Needing a…*lift*, Mr. Giles…out *to Cottonwood*? He's sending his cousin, all alone and unattended, out to Cottonwood? I find *that*, Mr. Giles, difficult to believe. Has *Mister William Bartram Logan* completely lost all reason? And just, how, may I ask, does he suppose his cousin is to manage— at Cottonwood—all alone?"

"Well, I'm sure I…couldn't even begin…to hazard a guess on that account, Miss Maggie. Is this fellow, this cousin…in need of special attention of some sort?"

"This…cousin…Mister Giles…I fear…is in need of more than special attention. And Mister Logan very well *knows* that. What on earth was the man thinking? I don't…believe…that…man!" Maggie stood shaking her head in deep denial. "Does Mr. Logan, perchance, plan on going to Cottonwood, to join his cousin?"

"No'm, I don't believe he does. But, well, beggin' your pardon, Miss Maggie, but Mr. Logan *is* my boss, and that's my certain sure orders, to pick up this cousin, and ferry the fellow on out to Cottonwood."

"Very well, Mr. Giles," Maggie smiled very sweetly up into the ruddy, almost boyish face of the head foreman. Stephen Giles' open, handsome face never seemed to acquire any tan, despite the countless hours spent in the sun. "Would you care to come and meet your...passenger?"

Giving Maggie a firm nod, Stephen Giles followed, as she led him past the staircase, down the narrow hall, where the two of them arrived at the door leading into the parlor. "This, Mister Giles," Maggie motioned with one sweep of her hand, "Is Mr. Logan's cousin—Lady Marilyn Eveline Drayton, lately of London, England."

Stephen Giles was aware that he was staring, his gaze sweeping the form of the trim, expensively clad figure standing between the window and the fireplace. Never had he seen a more beautiful woman. She was the only woman he had ever seen who could in any wise match the good looks of Maggie McKinnon Evans. She absolutely took his breath away.

"Lady...Marilyn..." Stephen Giles was not a boy; he had seen many beautiful women. He quickly regained his senses, knocked a lock of red-blond hair off his forehead with his right hand, and—stained hat clasped to a broad chest—gave a respectful nod. "Stephen Giles, here. Pleased to meet you, ma'am. It's my understandin'...that is...the Boss asked me to stop by...and give you a...ride...out to Cottonwood, ma'am." She was indeed lovely, but she was not a girl. Stephen naturally assumed she was a married woman. No female *that* lovely could remain very long unattached.

"Who...is this...*person?*" Lady Marilyn pulled an annoyed frown and stood staring at Bart's foreman. "And *where* is Cousin Bartram?"

"Mr. Giles, Lady Marilyn," Maggie patiently explained, "is Mr. Logan's... associate. He is in charge of the day to day operations of the lumber mill. And...more or less...sees to the affairs at Cottonwood, Mr. Logan's plantation...a few miles to the east. It appears, that Mr. Logan has been unavoidably detained...and has therefore asked Mr. Giles, here, to escort you...out to Cottonwood."

"Oh," Lady Marilyn muttered tiredly. "This is the steward of his estate? Well, then, in that event," she heaved a disgusted sigh, "I suppose you can just load my baggage there into the carriage."

"Ma'am," Stephen Giles' eyes followed the sweep of that one small white hand, as it pointed to the corner of the parlor, where firelight flickered off at least six or eight huge trunks, bales, packs, and valises.

"All *that*?" Stephen's reddish blond eyebrows shot up in amazement. "I don't know... ma'am, that I can fit *all that* onto the wagon, given th' big load she's already a'totin'. May have to leave a bit of it here, bring it on out later...when I have more space in the wagon."

"You expect me...*you*...*you*..." words appeared to fail Lady Marilyn. "You expect me to be transported several miles...to Mr. Logan's estate...in a *wagon?!* And to leave the greater part of my luggage behind? How am I to live? How am I to dress myself? If there are parties and affairs...what shall I wear for dinner...tonight? I *cannot* appear at table...in this traveling dress that I have worn...! *No!* This will *not* do at all! I *demand* to be taken out in a suitable conveyance! And I am instructing you...that *all* my things are to be taken along with me!"

"Well, ma'am," Stephen Giles scratched his red-blond head with one large, work-calloused hand, gazed down at the top of his logger's boots, then gazed straight at Lady Marilyn and said, "I don't 'spose 'twill greatly matter, ma'am, *what* you wear tonight... while takin' your supper. Won't be a *soul* at Cottonwood...but you. You can eat your supper in your shimmy, if you choose to."

"My *what?* Not a soul? But...where *is* my cousin? Does he not reside...at this place?"

"No'm. Not much...that is. Boss's too busy—to spend much time at Cottonwood. He does make a visit out there, every week or so, to check on the place."

"But...but...! Who *lives*...there?"

"Not a soul, ma'am. Not in th' big house leastwise. The freedmen, now, they live all about the place. You need anything at all, they'd be more than glad, I expect, to lend you a hand."

"But...but...who looks after the place? The staff...?"

"No'm. No...staff or nothin'. Some of th' freed women go up to the big house now and then, knock down th' spider webs and sweep out the dust wads. Other than that, th' place's pretty much inhabited by ghosts." Stephen Giles pulled a huge grin. This lady sure didn't appear to know much about

Bart Logan, or his holdings, or his living arrangements. What on earth was this London lady doin' in Rhyersville?

"Who...looks after the estate?"

"The estate? Oh, you mean Cottonwood? That'd be me, I guess. I keep an eye on things. Make sure all th' doors and windows stay intact. Make sure no...swallows build too many of their nests in the chimneys, that sort of thing."

"Then...you live there?"

"No'm. I live mostly up at the logging camp."

"But...but...how could he? I mean...it sounds like an absolutely...awful...place! How could...Cousin Bartram consign me to such quarters? I...refuse to go."

"That's fine with me, then, ma'am," Stephen Giles drawled, wondering how he was supposed to carry out the boss's orders. "You can just pay Miss Maggie here, for your room and board. In advance. For your accommodations and meals. And then you can stay on here at The Sparrow Inn, long as it pleases you."

"*Pay?* But I..."

"Well, if you'll not be ridin' with me, then, ladies, I 'spose I'll just be goin' on out to Cottonwood—"

"Mister...Giles...wasn't it? On second thought...if there *is* room for me...at this...Cottonwood...I'm sure...I shall be more comfortable there, on Mr. Logan's estate. Than here..."

"Yes, ma'am," Stephen Giles pulled a faint, thin smile, his light eyes crinkling at the corners. He thought he had handled that pretty well. He just wondered what would become of this creature...all by herself...out at Cottonwood. What *was* the Boss thinking?

Maggie stood silently at Stephen Giles' elbow, listening to this odd exchange; then she watched as he crossed the room and asked very politely, "And, ma'am, now exactly which one of these would you be needin', out at Cottonwood, for tonight?"

Lady Marilyn gave a heaving, frustrated sigh, "Ohhhhhhhhhh!" walked over and gave the toe of her little lilac satin slipper a knock against one particular piece of her worn luggage.

Stephen Giles gave a little nod, slapped his broad-brimmed hat atop his red hair, grabbed the huge valise by its frayed leather handle, and strode out the door.

Maggie heaved her own sigh of relief, as Lady Marilyn's pastel satin, spool-heeled slippers vanished out of the parlor, through the dining room, out the front door, and onto the wide veranda…

…Then, there she stood, staring in disbelief into the dusty, red dirt street, her lovely little mouth hanging open. "*Surely*, sir!" she screeched, "You do *not* expect me to ride…in *that*? It appears to be…a…a…"

Standing at the rear of the heavy freight wagon, the worn valise still gripped in a calloused right hand, "This is what I'll be drivin', ma'am, out to Cottonwood," Stephen Giles informed her. "The sun is pretty far sunk down towards the western mountains. So I suppose, ma'am, that if we intend on makin' th' place before full dark finds us, we best be on th' road. There won't be no fine coaches leaving this afternoon…or any other afternoon…for Cottonwood."

"Ohhhhhhhhh!" Lady Marilyn flounced down the steps of The Sparrow, stomped around to the far side of the wagon, and stood waiting for Stephen Giles to assist her to mount the high wagon seat.

Stephen Giles flung the huge, scarred leather valise that had once been a very nice piece of luggage—before its owner had been forced to make the rounds of the houses of her friends in London and its environs—upon the pile of store goods, strode around the wagon, leapt up on the high seat, and picked up the reins. He gazed around, to see Lady Marilyn still standing in the deeply-rutted red dirt street, staring daggers at him. "Oh," he muttered. Bending down, extending a huge logger's hand for her to grasp, he called, "Just put your foot up on the spoke," and he gave her a mighty tug upward.

"Ohhhhhhh!" she fumed, clutching at the huge rough hand that hauled her up like a sack of flour, and plopped her down on the hard seat of the wagon. Then the uncouth rogue who claimed to be steward of her cousin's estate, took the reins and gave an odd cry at the horses. The team leapt forward with such force that Lady Marilyn lurched backward on the seat, and was forced to hang on for dear life, as the horses roared down the street, raising a stifling cloud of red dust in their thundering wake.

"Have to make up for lost time!" the man shouted over at her, his voice scarcely audible over the pounding of hooves on the rock-hard road.

"Ohhhhhhhh!" she moaned.

———————————

Wordlessly, Lady Marilyn clung to the wagon seat, wondering if she would indeed reach her cousin's fine estate in one piece. The dust-filled air roared past. The horses' hooves beat a constant rhythm on the packed country road. Lady Marilyn, physically and emotionally exhausted, felt herself at one point drifting off into sleep. Then the wagon's crude driver gave a loud *hurrrroffffff*, and she almost leapt out of her skin. Her eyes flew wide. They were tearing along at a heart-thumping pace. Apparently he was attempting to beat the fast-falling darkness, as she had noted that the crude freight wagon was not fitted with any sort of lights or lanterns.

Lady Marilyn, awakened so abruptly, so traumatically, suddenly felt totally disoriented, lost, completely at sea. At one point, as the tall, muscular driver took a sharp curve, she was certain she was going to fall off the wagon seat, and be hurled into the gathering blackness. *Where was she? What was she doing here? Roaring through this strange, primitive wilderness?* Did they still have those horrid creatures she had read about in the London papers, the red creatures the Americans called *Indians*—lurking about behind the trees? Ready to fell passers-by with their crude wood and stone weapons? She was almost certain that she had heard that in some parts of this wild country called *America*, these Indian peoples still wreaked their bloody havoc.

Beneath the fine silk of her gown, her heart set up a tremulous pounding. She began to shiver. She felt cold as ice. She should have looked through her luggage and secured for herself a cloak against the night chills.

Here she was, alone with this uncouth rogue, ripping along this rough road that had rattled her bones like stones in a tin pot ever since roaring off from that horrible inn!

Then after hours of jostling and bumping against the unforgiving hardness of the wooden wagon seat, Lady Marilyn was vaguely aware that in the blackness and fog of the mountain night, the driver had somehow apparently located their destination—her cousin's fine country estate, called Cottonwood.

The man was, at long last, drawing the team to a bouncing halt. As the heavy freight wagon ceased it headlong plunge, Lady Marilyn heaved a sigh of relief, straightened her bonnet on her head, and strained her eyes, to see what on earth the place called *Cottonwood* looked like.

At that instant, the cold clouds that had obscured the moon on their drive out scudded away, as if shifted by some giant hand. And the great house rose before her out of the fog, in all its southern splendor.

But Lady Marilyn had seen Windsfield, and though Cottonwood was grand, it did not match the size and scope of Windsfield.

"It's quite…quaint," she muttered beneath her breath.

"Quaint, did you say, ma'am?" Stephen Giles stared over at his passenger. He had heard the big house at Cottonwood called many things, but *quaint* was never one of them.

"Mister…whatever your name is, I am tired. I feel as if my mouth were stuffed with dirty, well-worn wool, if you get my meaning. My…body has been beaten and battered with many sticks and stones. Would you please be kind enough to summon the staff? I will, immediately, be requiring my supper. A warm bath. My bed changed and turned down—"

"Ma'am?" Stephen stared at Lady Marilyn in the thin white moonlight. She appeared lovely, lovely, but tired. And none of the things she had just mentioned were going to be afforded this silly, spoiled creature.

"If you will recall…I just this afternoon warned you…there is no staff…at Cottonwood. I'll carry in your valise for you, then, I fear, ma'am, you will be strictly on your own."

"And just where…Mister Giles…will you be? Whilst I am left to my own devices in this…this…great white ghost of a house that is bereft of all life?!"

Stephen Giles, who as head foreman of Logan Lumber Company, and principal caretaker of affairs at Cottonwood, usually slept in the big house, answered softly, "I'll be beddin' down in th' carriage house, ma'am. Good night to you, then."

And with that, the 'steward' of Cottonwood lifted the brim of his sweat-stained hat the slightest bit, leapt down off the wagon seat, hoisted off Lady Marilyn's heavy, scuffed valise, and with long, sure strides hefted it onto the spacious veranda. From the pocket of his heavy cotton trousers, he produced a huge black iron key which he stuck in the door lock. Immediately the door swung open, he stood aside, waiting for Lady Marilyn to enter. The instant she did, he tipped his hat brim, spun, leapt off the veranda, re-mounted the wagon seat, and drove off.

Lady Marilyn hauled her valise inside, banged the heavy door shut, and stood in the darkness of the foyer of the empty mansion. She could see absolutely nothing. Which way lay a light? An oil lamp, a candle, anything that might illuminate the place a bit so that she could see her way about?

Nothing met her eyes except dense, velvety darkness. Suddenly overcome with all her rotten luck, Lady Marilyn collapsed into a tired heap atop the bulk of her worn leather valise. She gave herself over, for several minutes, to angry, wailing sobs. Then, at last, she arose, felt her way to a wall, and then along it, until she felt beneath her fingertips the certain form of a huge fireplace mantel. Then, a few inches farther on, and she felt a candle sconce. "Oh!" she muttered, "That rogue! That horrid, huge creature that dares to call himself a man! That crude, uncouth, ill-mannered—I could most gladly, very happily strangle him—"

Words failed her. Glancing about her in the yellow, flickering light of the candle, she spied a giant staircase. Reaching up with one tired, trembling hand, she snatched the sputtering candle from its ornate sconce, scooped up her worn valise with the other, tromped over to the staircase, and barely able to put one tiny foot before the other, Lady Marilyn dragged her thin body up the staircase of Cottonwood.

She reached the upstairs landing, made her way along it, pushing open the first ornately carved door that offered itself. Peering gingerly in, she spied a huge bed carved of some dark wood and spread with a snow-white counterpane. Its softness called to her from the door. Lady Marilyn immediately answered the call.

Without eating a bite or drinking a drop, without washing the first grain of dirt from the road off her tired, drawn face, leaving the candle to flicker and die and burn itself out, Lady Marilyn fell face foremost into the soft depth of the bed with a disgusted moan, and was soon snoring loudly.

———————

She awoke to sunlight streaming in the window. How long had she been asleep? She was starved! She was absolutely ravenous! Was there anything, *anything* at all, in the house to eat?! Sheer panic closed its clammy paws about her throat, choking off her breath. What had she gotten herself into? These *people*...these *crude Americans*...they knew *nothing* at all!

Nothing at all about how to receive company! She had sailed halfway around the world, to be greeted with such a—

She would think about all that later. Now, she needed something to eat. She had had nothing...since eating the steak and gravy at that awful inn. But the more she thought on it...perhaps...she should have simply stayed put...there at that crude inn. At least, there was food there. At least that milkmaid that called herself William Bartram Logan's betrothed had offered her food. And had not charged her one pence for it. She could probably have wrangled and manipulated her way into staying there...without having to pay...but then it *was* a business. And businesses did not operate without receiving payment. And that awful person, the man, Giles, had made that perfectly clear. After all, Mr. Logan's betrothed was *not* family to Lady Marilyn. No. She had no one. She had only Mr. William Bartram Logan himself to depend upon.

But, here, at this place, if there was no staff... No one to clean and fetch—and cook—what was she to do, especially concerning food?

She rose from the bed, smoothed down her wrinkled gown, and stumbled toward the door. Then through the upstairs corridor she glided, down the broad staircase, as grand as any she had seen in England, and down to the lower floor. Now...to locate the kitchen.

And search as she might, she could locate no room that appeared to resemble anything near a kitchen. No pantry. No buttery. No...

Then, as she opened the back door and peered out, she spied a large structure, the exterior exactly matching that of the mansion, with a covered walkway leading toward it.

Mincing her way along the rock-lined walkway, Lady Marilyn cautiously approached the door of the large structure, reached for the doorknob, and attempted to turn it. Despite several moments of twisting, turning and tugging, swinging her slight weight against it, it refused to budge. The door was obviously locked tight. Glancing to the side of the structure, Lady Marilyn spied a stack of what was unmistakably firewood. Wood chopped for a cooking stove. This was, then, indeed the kitchen. But how was she to access it, if it was locked? Was there food in there, and if so, how much, and how to reach it? And who was to prepare it for her? She had done very little cooking in her life. When living on her own, she subsisted, for the most part, on stale bread and cheese, with a bit of watered ale to wash it all down.

"So! I see you're up! And how did you rest? Did you fare all right? Have a good night?"

Lady Marilyn whirled about, her violet eyes wide with fear. But it was only that…Giles…fellow. The so-called *steward* of Cottonwood.

"I, at last, after stumbling about in darkness thick as soup, found a room, you…you…no thanks to you!" Lady Marilyn took two steps towards Stephen Giles, wagged a cold, white little finger in his face, and scowled darkly. "I shall, *immediately* I have opportunity to speak with my cousin, inform him of your *abominable* behavior towards me! I shall *in no uncertain terms,* inform him…that you are to be *dismissed! Do you hear me*? Never…in all my life…have I been treated… mistreated…in such a vile, repugnant manner!"

"The Boss might just be out, later this afternoon. You can tell him…anythin' you want to…then. In the meantime, would you like some breakfast?"

"You…you have…*food?*"

"They got plenty down at the freedmen's cabins. When you get hungry, you can just mosey on down that way, and sit a spell with the ladies of Logan Town, and fix yourself a plate of sausage and grits?"

"Ladies? I thought you said no one resided here?"

"I believe I told you that nobody lived in the big house. But I do seem to recall telling you that the freedmen lived here."

"Who are these…freedmen?"

"African folk. Freed after the War. Or should I say…freed *by* th' War."

"You…mean…servants…?"

"They used to be. Not any more, though. They been makin' it on their own now, for some weeks, here at Logan Town. And makin' a right smart job of it. And some of them ladies make a mighty mean pot of grits. Maybe some fried hog jowl?"

"It sounds…*horrible*! And prepared by…*those…people*…"

"Suit yourself. Just thought I'd offer. You change your mind, just let any of 'em know. I told 'em you'd most likely be here for a spell. And that whatever you needed, you'd be sure to ask 'em. Well, guess I'll be leavin' you then, to your visit at Cottonwood. Have a good day, now!"

"You…*Mister Giles*! I cannot *possibly* stay here! I find my…position here…completely…untenable. No staff! No food! No water!"

"I just told you about th' food. And there's a fine, deep well right there behind th' back veranda, just off the dog trot? See th' shelter, over there? And you can draw up cold mountain water, bucket after bucket—for your cookin', drinkin', washin' up and such—out of that well. Or if you prefer it, there's always the spring, out there in the pasture a spell. A hundred yards or more, no more than that, up back of that barn. Good, clean water. Clear as crystal and cool as a fine January day!"

"Did you not *hear* what I just said, *you blind and deaf* idiot!? *I cannot stay here!*"

"But…ma'am, this is th' only house th' Boss has got in this neck of th' woods. So, if you're here to visit the Boss, where else you plannin' on stayin'?"

"Mayhap…back…at…that…inn…place."

"Sure. Alrighty. You can just grab your purse, whatever you got handy to pay your bill, and bring out your big leather bag, then. And we'll be off, before you can say 'howdy'."

Stupid, stubborn ox! He was still of the obdurate opinion that she should pay…at that inn…place. "On, second thought, Mister Giles, perhaps I shall stay here…for a few days. You did say, didn't you, that Mr. Logan would be coming here…soon?"

"Maybe could be." Stephen Giles shrugged broad shoulders, the muscles rippling across his chest and back as he raked a big hand through his shock of red hair that glinted wet in the sunlight, like fire, as he moved toward her. He smiled amiably as he leaned his muscular frame against the side post of the dog run. Lady Marilyn was shocked that he had not donned his shirt this morning. Then she noticed a wash basin of some sort, resting atop the well curb. Evidently, she had found him at his morning toilet. Was he not aware that there was a *Lady* of breeding and gentility in residence now at Cottonwood?! Yet here the man stood, like a half-naked yeoman in the morning sunlight, grinning at her like a cheese-eating cat.

"Maybe could be?!" she screeched at him. "What sort of *stupid* answer is that?"

"Well, I just work for Mr. Logan, ma'am," Stephen Giles grinned. "He does as he pleases. And sometimes it don't please him all that well to keep me informed of his comings and goings."

"But…if you are his steward…"

"I never said that, ma'am. You did. I'm head foreman, is what I actually am, up at the lumber camp, up th' mountain, th' other side of Rhyersville, just a few miles, actually."

"Then *why* am I wasting my valuable time talking to you?! Just…get out of my sight…go on with you! And leave me to…*whatever*…"

"Yes, ma'am!" With a cool smile, he shifted his big frame off the post, walked over, emptied the washbasin, slung his damp towel over one shoulder, spun with some alacrity for a man of such size, and strode off, whistling some senseless little ditty.

As he walked away, Stephen Giles almost burst out laughing. This one was sure a fish out of water! What in the name of all that was holy was *Lady Marilyn Drayton* doing in Rhyersville, Georgia, a sleepy little, go-nowhere mountain village tucked away in a remote valley of the Blue Ridge Mountains of North Georgia?!

He frowned slightly as he walked away. Boss sure had this one pegged right! What had been his exact words to his head foreman, when he issued the terse order to "go check out the situation…regarding the possible arrival of my cousin?

"And, Giles, if…indeed…it is *unfortunately* true…that my…selfish, untrustworthy, thieving, lying, back-stabbing cousin is here…in Rhyersville…then *let* me give you fair warning, Giles. Do *not* let yourself be fooled by appearances. In other words, watch your back. Or you'll find yourself carved up into mincemeat and served up for breakfast to the frogs and the fishes. I picked up my mail the other day, at the post office in Rhyersville. It included a letter from the barristers Sullivan of London, informing me that, after having enjoyed the fine hospitality of Windsfield House for more than a month, my dear cousin made off with a most valuable silver service, secreted in some trunk or chest, upon departing Windsfield. Had the service been so much desired or so greatly needed, all my cousin needed do was simply *ask* for it, like any honest, law-abiding—not to sneak off with it buried in some piece of baggage. In other words, no welcome mat is to be unfurled. The visitor is to be hauled out to Cottonwood…and *deposited there*. My heartfelt desire is that this…visit…be…as *short* and as un-notable as possible. Do I make myself clear, Giles?"

Stephen Giles had opened his mouth to make inquiries of the Boss about this thieving fellow, this black-hearted, unsavory character that enjoyed gracious hospitality, then took things without permission. But one of the loggers had come up at that point, and their strange conversation had been concluded. Shrugging off the comment, Stephen had crawled up into the freight wagon and driven off.

Then when he had caught his first shocking glimpse, and discovered that this thieving, back-stabbing, dark and dangerous cousin was a gorgeous brunette, Stephen was completely confounded—until Lady Marilyn Drayton opened her pretty little mouth. So Stephen had done as instructed. He had safely removed her from the inn, and deposited her at Cottonwood. How to get rid of her…? Well, the rest was up to the Boss. Somebody needed to wash her mouth out…with lye soap. Stephen Giles felt that he had done his part. He had shown her as unwelcome a welcome as he possibly could, and still lay down and sleep at night. She did look rather small, and pathetic, standing there…was she truly…? *Don't even go there, Giles*, Stephen warned himself. *The Boss is an excellent judge of character. If he says the lady is a liar, a thief, and a blackguard, then, without a doubt, she surely is.*

Chapter 39

Lady Marilyn Drayton rattled about the huge mansion called Cottonwood for *five days*. When, at noon of the second day, hunger drove her to sheer desperation, she forced herself to quell her pride and walk down to the freedmen's cabins.

On her first visit, she was greeted with polite nods and low, deferential murmurs. She was offered a chair, and heaping plates of food. Which she consumed voraciously, having not the slightest notion what, exactly, she was ingesting. But it was food. And she had been consuming it now at every mealtime. And she had not yet succumbed to any dread disease, or death, as a result of eating the Africans' cooking.

Each morning, after her meal, she would stumble back to the big house, wrestle a bit of water out of the ground well, haul it into the big house, take a cold bath, as she had been unable to enter the closed kitchen to kindle a flame of any sort to heat her bathwater. She thought of attempting to walk to a neighboring estate, but could not recall having seen a single estate in passing along the dreadful road running out to this place.

And for these five awful days, all those dreadful, horrid, empty hours, her cousin, William Bartram Logan, had failed to put in an appearance. Lady Marilyn was on the verge of bursting an artery out of sheer anger and spite. It would serve him right! Should he at last deign to ride out to her rescue, only to find that she had passed away, in dire want and sheer agony, in all her misery and pain. It was as clear as the nose on her face, she pouted to herself, *Cousin William Bartram Logan thinks I will grow weary of waiting, and simply up and fade away, back over the sea to England's fair shores! And he shall be easily shed of me. Well, he does not rid himself of me quite so handily! Quite so easily! Mister Stephen Giles thought to put me off, and to put me out, by his cold, crass manners, but neither shall that rogue succeed with his crude, offensive, insensitive…!*

As she wallowed deeper and deeper into the pit of her despair and self-pity, Lady Marilyn became so desolate, in such an agonized state of loneliness, desperation, and abandonment that she was at one point almost tempted to pray.

I am not yet that far sunk into the mire of idiocy! She scolded herself, her lovely face set and cold with rage. *I will yet think of something! They cannot treat me in such a fashion—not and get away with it! Fob me off like a soiled rag!*

————————

Then, on the seventh morning, when Lady Marilyn arose and made her way down to the Africans' camp, there was Stephen Giles, hale and hearty and as big as life, seated at an outside table among the hoards of Africans. Busy at shoveling food into his mouth, he glanced up, noticed her, and hesitated, his huge hand in mid air, holding a fork filled with some sort of meat or other. He at least had the decency to rise at sight of her. He then proceeded to pull out a nearby chair, and motion her into it.

Lady Marilyn, so starved for food, so starved for human companionship of another soul that she considered in any, shape, form or fashion of her kind—though she longed more than anything to slap that smirk off his ruddy face—gave him a weak smile. If she played her cards right, *if she humbled herself, and groveled, and crawled* before this man who seemed now to be her only contact with a civilized society, perhaps, *just* perhaps, she might finagle a ride with him back to the inn. Once back at the inn, Lady Marilyn was very certain she would soon see her cousin, Mister William Bartram Logan. For it was abundantly clear that Cousin Bart would not remain long absent from that woman…that… Yes, that was it. She must talk this Giles person into returning her to the inn. She could make the excuse that…

"I…need…to return to the village, Mister Giles, if you would kindly allow me to accompany you, on your return trip? I would be…most grateful." Lady Marilyn batted her long dark lashes, and heaved her small bosom beneath the scarlet silk of her low cut gown. "What do you think, then, Mister Giles?"

"Well, ma'am. There's but one problem…with that particular

arrangement…you see. And that is…that when I leave here, I'll be leavin' with a full load of produce from the fields you see stretchin' about you. And th' wagon will be loaded to th' gills. I mean, every inch of her covered with fresh bunches of lettuces and radishes, and so forth. Otherwise, I would be most happy to oblige. Perhaps, then, ma'am, another time."

And with that, Stephen Giles hefted his lean bulk from out of the ladder-backed chair, and strode off. With an agile leap, he mounted the high seat of his freight wagon, and went rattling across the yard and into the nearby fields. Africans of every size, age and gender, streamed along beside the wagon, loading it down with bunches and bunches and more bunches of some sort of vegetables.

But Lady Marilyn was not so easily fooled. Stephen Giles, she was certain, would not be piling cabbage heads, bunches of lettuce and radishes and what not beside himself on the wagon seat. As she had stared into Giles' open and honest eyes, she discerned that he was not exactly lying. But neither was he telling her the truth. Looking the man in the face, it had become clear to Lady Marilyn: *He had strict orders—not to return her to the inn.*

As Stephen Giles drove the heavy freight wagon away, he felt those stunning violet eyes boring twin holes deep into his back. Sweat popped on his upper lip. His heart twisted in his chest. He *despised lying,* even to a person like Lady Marilyn Drayton. And to make matters worse, it was written all over her. She was clearly lost…entirely out of her element…wretched and lonely… So she was a pest. A thorn in the Boss's craw. A silly, spoiled…*thief! The woman was a liar and a thief! Why,* then, did he feel this great, growing pity for her? This huge lump rising in his throat? Almost choking him! He was getting soft in the head! The Boss was not being hard-hearted and heartless…

But, then…*she was family.* And from what Stephen Giles understood, she had no one. No one in the whole wide world… And she was not all that bad to look at.

Chapter 40

Lady Marilyn dragged herself out of bed. Then she sat absently on the side of the huge feather mattress, and she wondered dismally, *why?*

Why did she bother…to drag herself through day after dreary day? Shut away in this huge, empty, desolate mansion that had probably once rang with the happy voices of a family…

A family…? What did she know of a family? Hah!

She felt anger, followed by cold rage sweeping over her in paralyzing, sickening waves. It was *his* fault. It was *all his fault* that nobody wanted her. He called himself her father, yet when her mother died, he had *used* her! He had *sold* her! It was a *miracle* that Winston Drayton had married her! But her father had died, and she was still very young, very beautiful. And she had dragged herself up by her own boot strings—and Winston Drayton had been a fool in love…now Winston Drayton was gone. *And look at her!*

Nobody on the face of the earth wanted Marilyn Eveline Billings Drayton!

Attempting to bury the past, shove her angry, morose thoughts into the back of her mind, somehow she dragged herself through each day. Down to the African community, to eat a few bites. Back to the empty house. To wander. And wonder. And watch the road that led to…nowhere. *Where was there that she could possibly go?* Where could she find… a friendly face? Comfort…? Warmth…? Welcome…?

———————

Late in the afternoon, as dusk settled over the empty rooms of Cottonwood, Marilyn sat on the wide veranda and watched the fireflies flit about amongst the neatly trimmed hedges. And she watched the dark-skinned African children, flitting in and out amongst the cabins nestled snugly beneath the sheltering limbs of giant oak trees that lifted their limbs to the sky. At dusk, as they were each evening as she watched, lamps would be lit. And the warm yellow light would flood out the windows of the little cabins, in patches of light that danced about the sandy yards. Usually of an evening she would catch snatches of hymns, sent drifting up on the light evening air. Voices of men, women, and children, talking and laughing as they sat down to their suppers after a hard day's work in the fields would come floating out those windows, too. They were tired but happy voices, filled with warmth, and contentment, and something Marilyn had never had, and had always wondered about…that thing called *love.*

It was fully dark now. No moon lit up the night sky. Pitch blackness was closing in about her. Wearily Marilyn hefted her slight frame out of the huge rocker, and dragged herself into the house. She felt along the mantel for the candle, lit it, and mounted the stairs.

"But…what is she…*doing*…out there, Mr. Logan, darling?" Maggie asked Bart that rainy Sunday afternoon, more than a hint of anger in her voice.

"Frankly, my dear, I have not the slightest notion, and not the slightest wish to know. Just as long as she is safely *out of our hair.* Just as long as she doesn't go into a petty fit of rage and burn the place to the ground."

"Have you even as much as been out there…to see about her? Just to see how she is faring…out there…all alone? I mean, *really*, Mr. Logan!"

"Are we speaking here of that shrew who—"

"Maybe I should go out there," Maggie worried, a small frown creasing her smooth brow, "I mean, after all, Mr. Logan…"

"Margaret Ann! The woman had enough to last her a lifetime! She could easily have lived in comfort on the interest alone! She shows up here, a few weeks after receiving that more than generous settlement. Penniless! Wanting…*what?* What does she *expect* from me? I tell you, darling, I wash my hands of her. Let her stew in her own juices. And when she has had enough…of Cottonwood…I'll book her passage on some sturdy ship, and send her back—"

"Back to whom? To what?" Maggie inquired, her voice low and somber, her frown deepening.

"Margaret Ann…darling…I have come here, to the inn today, especially to spend some *pleasant* hours with you. To, hopefully, I might add, get some agreement from you on a…date."

"A…"

"A date…for the wedding?"

"Oh….I don't know…Mr. Logan, I cannot seem to put my mind on anything—"

Maggie heaved a great sigh, "except poor Lady Marilyn!"

"All right. I'll send Giles out there…tomorrow…to see how she fares."

"And…he could…perhaps…invite her to church…next Sunday?"

"*Church*, darling? I don't know that Giles himself attends church. I've never seen him…in the Shiloh congregation? Have you?"

"Perhaps, then, he worships…in his own way. Just because you haven't seen him in the Shiloh congregation, Mr. Logan, darling, does not mean he would refuse to attend, if issued a warm invitation to do so."

"Don't you mean, my dearest, *if ordered by his boss to do so?* And to bring along a most unsavory…lady? Of ill repute and poor standing?"

"Not in *this* community, Mr. Logan, darling. No one in this community has even *heard* of Lady Marilyn Drayton, or so much as laid an eye on her. Who knows? Given half a chance, she might—"

"Now, let me get this straight, my sweet. You wish me to order Giles to ride out, on his day off, all the way to Cottonwood, and fetch this…lady…and haul her to church, then return her all the way back out to Cottonwood….still all on his only day of the week off… You think, then, my sweet…to convert…to reform…Lady Marilyn Drayton…?"

"When you put it like that, you make it sound…absolutely impossible. But it's…not. No one is beyond the reach of God's tender mercies, Mr. Logan. Not even Lady Marilyn Drayton, whom you appear to consider as being as cold, as calculating, as dangerous as some…snake in the grass."

"My sentiments exactly, sweetheart." Bart pulled a grim smile.

"Stephen, Mister Giles, how very nice to see you. And would you care to haul yourself out into the kitchen for a nice hot cup of coffee, before you start your trek back up to the logging camp with breakfast for the men?"

"That sounds good, Miss Maggie! And how are you faring these fine days? How's business, now that the inn has taken on such a grand size and appearance?"

"Business…is good. I was wondering, Stephen, Mister Giles, just how… things…are progressing…at Logan Town?"

"Good, good," Stephen nodded his head, his blond-red hair gleaming, a broad smile on his ruddy face, as he lowered his muscular frame to the backless kitchen bench.

"And Cottonwood?" Maggie gazed at him expectantly across the narrow expanse of the scarred oak table.

"Oh. I think I take your meaning. Lady Marilyn? She…I don't know quite how to say this, but she appears…miserable as all get-out. I think…she's a bit lonely…out there. She doesn't…take…to the Africans all that much. She goes down and gets just enough food to keep a bit of meat on her bones, then hurries back, as if they might just grab her and gobble her up. It's…really…pathetic."

"Pathetic…Stephen…Mister Giles? What a shame…" Maggie mused. "What a shame…someone doesn't…oh…I don't know…maybe offer to drive out and bring her in…to a church service…now and again…"

"A church service?"

"Why, yes, Stephen, we hold services at the Shiloh Baptist Church *every* Sunday of the world. And the new pastor, the good Reverend David Whitcomb, is a fine man of God. You *really* should stop by yourself…and hear him some fine Sunday. He can raise the hair right off your head with his fiery preachin'. And th' singing's pretty good. And sometimes, I play the organ…now and again."

"Sounds wonderful. I might just do that very thing."

"Sunday services always start, Stephen, Mister Giles, promptly at ten o'clock. Shall we expect you then, this Sunday?"

"Sure. Why not. Be something to do to pass the day. Gits awful quiet, up at th' camp."

"Wonderful! And you will, of course, take Sunday dinner with us. Here at the inn, afterwards."

"Well, Miss Maggie, I wouldn't want to intrude…on your Sunday…or your family…or anythin'." Stephen Giles' ruddy face flushed a distinct scarlet. He well knew that Sunday was the day the Boss always came calling.

"Don't be silly, Stephen, may I call you Stephen? Thank you. And should you have a… friend…who might also wish to get out and about on a lonely Sunday…a lady friend…please feel free to bring her along, won't you?"

"A…lady…friend? I don't have no lady friend, Miss Maggie. The only *Lady* I can think of right now who is about to die of loneliness, is…"

"Oh? And who would this lonely lady be, Stephen?"

"Well, I sometimes look at the Boss's cousin, the one out at Cottonwood. She sure is like a lost little lamb."

"Why, Stephen, what a…sweet…thing to say. Why, then, don't you, Stephen, invite this lost little lamb to come closer to the fold?"

"You *what?*" Bart stared at Maggie. "And…they're…*what?!*"

"I merely invited your foreman to step into the warmth of the kitchen, while he waited for the order for the loggers, and to partake of a hot cup of coffee. And, somehow, the conversation turned to church attendance and the…loneliness of Sundays…when one is off and with nothing at all to occupy one's time—"

"The subject just *happened* to come up. And I suppose, Stephen Giles just *happened* to be seized with the sudden, irresistible impulse to attend church, Sunday next. And on top of that, he suddenly envisioned himself making the long drive out to Cottonwood, to pick up a lonely lady companion—"

"Why! Mr. Logan, darlin'!—That's *exactly* how the conversation took place."

It was Saturday evening. Lady Marilyn Drayton sat on the huge veranda of Cottonwood, staring out into the gathering gloom. She felt empty as a shell, cast off as a broken egg. Useless as a soiled rag pitched into the ditch. She could have wept of sheer loneliness, had she the energy or the will to muster up a tear. Lethargically she pushed herself up from off the huge rocker, and turned to enter the house.

"Lady Marilyn! And how are you…this fine evening?"

"Mister…Giles? What…on earth…what are you *doing* here?"

"I…well, I was here late on business…and I got caught by the darkness. So…I just thought I'd overnight in the carriage house. Have you had your supper? I was just about to sit down to mine." He produced out of the darkness a large basket of some sort. "I wondered if perhaps you'd care to join me for a late bite? Or were you just on your way inside, to call it a day?"

"Oh, no! No! I would love…I would just *looovvve*…to join you. Let me just step inside the door…and fetch a wrap."

Lady Marilyn's heart had skipped a beat. No. Not one, but two…beats…when she actually heard a *human voice* hailing her out of the falling dusk. Even if it was the voice of that awful man…that grinning jackass that called himself Stephen Giles.

But he was here. He was a person. He was alive. And he was asking her to sit with him for a few moments as he consumed a late supper. And she was going to do it. Yes, she was dying on the inside. Weak in the knees for the sound of another human voice…any voice…any voice…

A wool shawl about thin shoulders, unaware and unconcerned about her appearance, Lady Marilyn emerged back out onto the veranda, pulling the door to the big house firmly shut behind her. "What were you just saying, Mister Giles? Mayhap…I misheard you?"

"I was just remarking, Lady Marilyn," Stephen Giles repeated, shifting his muscular bulk from against the giant column where he had been leaning, holding his basket, "that I had decided to leave quite early in the morning, to go into Rhyersville, to attend church services…I believe the little church is called *Shiloh Baptist*. I will probably be up and away by the crack of dawn. And I was just wondering…since you had expressed to me on one or two separate occasions your desire to visit Rhyersville, if you would care…to accompany me? We have been invited to Sunday dinner…by Mrs. Evans…at the inn…immediately following services. I am uncertain who, but most probably there will be other folk present at Maggie's table—"

"Mister Giles! I would be…*simply delighted*!"

"Well, awrighty, then! Want to sit out here on the veranda…and eat?" Stephen Giles suggested with a grin. He could certainly not enter the big house, just the two of them. Nor could he invite her into the carriage house.

As he waved her to a chair, Lady Marilyn wondered for a moment why they were balancing food in rockers on the veranda, and not sitting at a table in the fine mansion behind them. Then a wry grin tipped up the edges of Lady Marilyn's lovely lips, as it suddenly dawned on her—Stephen Giles, the backwoods American logger, had no desire to put her in a compromising position, to perhaps sully her reputation. *If only he knew—!* But, let sleeping dogs lie, Marilyn calculated. *No way on earth was she about to tell him!*

The rim of a silvered moon and a few distant stars began to peek faintly over the ridge of darkening mountains to the east, as they ate cured ham and baked yams, and some other foods Lady Marilyn was unable to identify. One of which Stephen Giles informed her was something called *ground nuts*. Stephen Giles produced from his basket some sort of crude bottle containing water, from which the two took turns sipping, Stephen Giles gallantly offering Lady Marilyn the initial sip.

Then, all too soon, he was picking up his sweat-stained hat and his willow-withe basket. Bidding her a good night, boot heels clicking distinctly down the broad steps, he disappeared into the darkness.

What to wear! What to wear! What did these country bumpkins wear to their dreary, boring, mind-numbing church services…in that dinky little village?

Something…dark…perhaps. She would like to appear respectable, in hopes of securing future invitations, if at all possible, to the church services, followed by lunch at the inn. Being out here…all alone…it was beginning to fray her nerves. She was actually beginning to fear for her sanity. She could see no way out of her present predicament. Yes, she would tolerate the church services; she would tolerate luncheon at the rustic little inn. Anything… *anything…was better than this!*

Something not too low cut. The emerald satin taffeta, a dark material. It was the most conservative thing in her closet. It was horribly old. Horribly out of style, but it would simply have to serve. And did she have any shoes, any gloves, or a bonnet to match?

Fog floated, swirled, drifted and settled into the folds of the Blue Ridge Mountains overlooking the valley where the little white church set, its bell tower reared against a backdrop of green-green trees marching up ridges that grew blue as they drew off into the distance.

At exactly nine forty-five on Sunday morning, as it did every Sunday morning, the great iron bell swinging in the tall belfry began to peal out its call:

Come to the church in the valley...

And in carriages, and in wagons, and on horseback, and on foot...they came. "Mornin'. Nice to see you. Fine weather. Yes, it is," Bart nodded and spoke, Maggie on one arm, Johnny on the other. He had grown accustomed to attending the Sunday meeting. He had come to enjoy the gathering together with the men and women of the small community nestled high in the North Georgia Mountains. Sometimes it seemed to Bart that here, in this remote place, he had at last found Paradise on earth. Here everyone knew everyone else. Here, men greeted you on the dirt street, with a broad smile of welcome recognition and a warm, hearty handshake, looking you straight in the eye. Here, most men spoke truth, and spoke it straight from the heart. They were men who wrestled their living from the mountain valleys six days a week, and came to church to thank God on Sunday.

And the women...their collars stood high up to their necks, their bonnet strings were tightly tied, and their skirts dragged their shoe-tops. Honest, hard working mothers, grandmothers. Sisters. Sweethearts. Most serving the needs of their families from dawn until dusk, keeping the house, milking the cows and caring for the gardens and fields along with their men. But, come Sunday morning, they were up, their families fed, bathed and dressed, and they came to meeting.

But who was that...there on that back row? NO! It couldn't be? *Could it?*
Giles! And Lady Marilyn?!
Margaret Ann had made her ridiculous suggestion, but he hadn't said one word to Stephen Giles about ferrying his cousin to church, nor did he intend to! How on earth...then? *Why*...on earth...then...were the two of them sitting back there like that?!

Bart's mind began a mad whirl of investigative thinking. Then the congregation was rising to its feet, singing the opening hymn. Automatically, with all the others, Bart rose. His eyes glued to the hymn book Maggie held between them, in a fine baritone, he began to solemnly intone the words. But his mind was not on the song.

Maggie! But…*how*…what could she possibly have said…to bring *this* about? And hadn't he specifically and explicitly issued orders to Giles!? *Not to bring that woman off Cottonwood?* Wait until he got his hands on Giles…! Bart felt his anger rising. He could feel heat creeping past the starched whiteness of his collar, flushing his face. It was one of his chief failings, he knew, sometimes letting his anger get the better of him. But…this time…he felt certain the anger was more than justified…!

How to deal with this?!

He was in church. They were all in church. And apparently Maggie had not even glanced around. Perhaps she just assumed that…with whatever manipulating of the situation she had managed…the two of them would just miraculously appear!

She stood beside him now. As she felt his gaze, so intense on her, she looked up, her face so perfectly at ease, so beautiful, so innocent.

But, for Bart, all peace, all innocence had been shattered on this bright Sunday morning. *He would not have that woman…here in this valley…here in this church…disrupting his life…disrupting their lives…not with the wedding, hopefully…just around the corner…*

When peeee-ace like a riiiiiv-er…
atten-eennnndeth my soul-lll…
When clo-uuuuds like the seeeee-ea…
billows roooo-ooooo-ooollllll….

Yes, he would certainly give Stephen Giles a good piece of his mind…!

What…evvvver my lot…
Thou hast tau-uught me to saaa-aay…
It is welllll! It is well-llll…
withhhh… my soouullll…!

"Would you care for another serving of the pork roast? Lady Marilyn?"

"What? Oh, no. Thank you. *Everything* is so...*delicious*."

Was *this* the same woman who had stood in the entrance of the inn, her beautiful face a thundercloud, ready to take on the entire world, and conquer it with sheer will...?

Maggie stared at Lady Marilyn, unable to take her gaze from the woman's face.

A face that had grown, in the space of two weeks, pale and drawn. She seemed to have aged, shrunken into herself. Her right hand, Maggie noticed, actually trembled, when Lady Marilyn reached for her tea. She appeared...frightened...afraid to meet anyone's gaze, or to speak, or to scarcely lift her eyes from her food.

"Lady Marilyn?" Maggie importuned softly, "Would you care...to give me a hand...in the kitchen?"

"What? Oh...of course," anything, *anything*...so as *not* to be sent back to Cottonwood... to live all alone in that huge, empty house, day after day...

Like a whipped dog, Lady Marilyn rose from her chair, and obediently followed her hostess into the kitchen of the inn.

Having arrived in the kitchen, Maggie motioned her guest to a chair near the table. "Why...don't we sit down, for just a moment, Lady Marilyn, and have a woman-to-woman chat, so to speak. How are things...at Cottonwood?"

"Things? I don't know what you mean?"

"Well, I mean, how do you find it... out there? How do you spend your days? Why haven't you been into town, just for a short visit? I was delighted...to see you at church this morning. Are you...ill...Lady Marilyn? Is there something...anything...I can do for you? You appear..."

"I'm...all right," Lady Marilyn hastened to say. She didn't want to draw any undue attention to herself. She didn't want to give her cousin, William Bartram Logan, any cause, real or imagined, to send her back to that huge empty house... "I haven't... been in for a visit, because...it's so far. And there's no transportation..."

"Stephen Giles, so I understand, is out that way, hauling produce into town, at least once a week. Why can't you hitch a ride with him?"

"Hitch…a ride?"

"Why don't you ask Stephen to bring you along with him, when he brings the produce into town, Lady Marilyn? I harbor not the slightest intention to pry or to get personal here. But, I'm worried about you. Out there all alone. With no one to talk to."

Maggie's commiserations, coupled with Lady Marilyn's self-pity, burst open the floodgates. "Ohhhhhhh!" Lady Marilyn wailed, her eyes flooding with tears, "It's *terrr-rible!* Out there! *All alone!* And Bartram Logan has ordered Stephen Giles not to take me off the place! I just *know* it! But…don't let him know I said that! He might…not let me come back…to church…!"

"What?" Maggie stared at Lady Marilyn. The image of Len Evans flickered through her mind. She felt herself going rigid as a fence post. *Bart?!…could Bartram Logan do that? Would he do that?!*

"Well," Maggie forced a smile and laid a hand over Lady Marilyn's. Lady Marilyn quickly snatched away the hand that beneath Maggie's warm touch had felt as cold as ice. Then Maggie smiled at her guest, and asked in a soft voice, "Shall we carry in the pies?"

Bart looked up as Maggie re-entered the dining room, where two tables shoved together were crowded with her lunch guests. She refused to meet his gaze. What had…that *woman*…that *shrew*…been telling her…out there in the kitchen…? Whatever it was, from the look on Maggie's beautiful face, Bart knew it did not bode well. Not… well… at…all…

Pie was about to be served, when suddenly Margaret Ann looked over at Stephen Giles and inquired, "Mr. Giles, I was just wondering why it was that you hadn't brought our guest into town…on one of your many return trips from out at Cottonwood?"

Stephen Giles felt his face grow hot. He sputtered and gasped and almost choked on his food, before finally looking up, and managing to mumble, "Well, Miss Maggie, I…uuuuhhhhh… th' wagon is always so…loaded…"

"I see," Maggie said very sweetly. "Why, then, *now* that the wagon is apparently empty, why don't you just ride on out there, and bring Lady Marilyn's things back *now*—so that she can have a lovely visit, with us, here at the inn?"

Stephen Giles sputtered, turned red in the face, and gazed over at his boss.

Bartram Logan dropped his fork with a loud clatter, shoved back his chair and strode out onto the front veranda.

Maggie immediately pushed back her chair, laid her napkin carefully beside her plate, and followed him.

"All right, Margaret Ann. Exactly what is going on here?" Bart demanded as he heard her walk up behind him. He stood booted feet spread, arms crossed against his chest. "How in the name of heaven did you manage to pull off this morning's little coup?—and why in the name of all that's holy would you issue that woman *an invitation* into the bosom of your household?!"

"Is it true, Mister Logan?" Maggie began, her voice cold, hard, dripping with hurt and disbelief, a voice Bart had never heard.

"Is what true?"

"Is it true that you have been holding Lady Marilyn prisoner at Cottonwood?"

"What?" Bart whirled to stare at her.

"She *told* me. Just now. In the kitchen."

"She told you just now in the kitchen *that I was holding her prisoner at Cottonwood?*" Bart took a step toward her, and leaned close, to stare down at Maggie as if she had lost all her senses.

"She said you had instructed Stephen Giles *not* to give her a ride into town."

"Well. Yes. I certainly did. I admit to that. I don't want her here at the inn. She's *trouble*, Margaret Ann. I don't want you to be burdened with her. You have enough without taking on my relative's problems. I mean, Good Lord…!"

"You don't have to *swear* at me, Mister Logan. I find it *unacceptable*. What you have done. Do you realize what it's like to be a woman—held hostage—at the whim of an overbearing man?"

"Overbearing man? I'm simply attempting, my darling, as I just told you, to *protect* you!"

"And I have told you, Mister Logan, that I do not need protecting! Especially from another woman! Did you take a good look at Lady Marilyn, Mister Logan? The woman is lonely. Being isolated at Cottonwood…"

"*Isolated?* There are sixty or seventy souls living within a stone's throw of the house. Everything she needs is there…at her fingertips…and she is safely…out of our hair…until I can decide…exactly what to do about that dratted woman! And you are inviting her *here*? Already you have the girl and her child, your mother-in-law, *and* your sister—I mean, Good Lord, Margaret Ann where is it all going to end? I mean, when are we ever going to have any time to ourselves?!"

"You are *shouting*, Mister Logan. They will hear you inside. They will think we are having a terrible row."

"Well?! *Aren't* we? Isn't that just exactly what this is? You have called me an overbearing man! You have insinuated that I am a…cold…uncaring…heartless clod…while I…I was merely trying to protect you from yourself! You have an inn full of people you have taken beneath your wings. When, my dearest darling, am I to be invited to join them? When am *I* to be brought beneath The Sparrow's wing?" Bart stood staring down at her, his handsome face flushed, a few strands of his usually perfectly-combed dark hair falling across his forehead. "No, darling, that's not what I meant. What I meant to say is…you…I…we…."

"Yes, Mister Logan?" Maggie stared up at Bart. "You know very well that Lady Marilyn is a stranger in a strange country. Without transport from Cottonwood, she is virtually a prisoner there. Do you dispute that, Mister Logan?"

"Are we going to let *Lady Marilyn Drayton* come between us? Margaret Ann? *Are we?*"

"Perhaps," Maggie sighed, "we should go back inside."

"You…go on back inside," Bart said, giving a tired wag of his head, averting his gaze, refusing to allow her to see the pain in his eyes. "I…think I'll just go on down to Traps."

"To Traps?" Maggie asked.

"Yes." He raked a hand through his dark shock of hair. "I'll…just go…have a look about the place…make sure the horses…and goats…are all right."

Without another word, without a backward glance, Bart stepped off the low porch and, broad back stiff, strode down the rutted dirt road. Maggie wanted very much to call after him, and ask if he didn't want dessert. And when…when would he be back?

Maggie returned inside. They finished the meal in silence. Stephen Giles finally pushed back his chair and stood to his feet, insisting that he must leave—to fetch Lady Marilyn back to Cottonwood. Maggie stood silently by, and let them go. What could she do? Stephen Giles, after all, had his orders.

———————

Bartram Logan came by the following morning. Standing on the front steps, he informed Maggie in a clipped, cold voice, "I'm sending Giles out— to bring Lady Marilyn and her belongings to the inn—for a visit. And, while Lady Marilyn is in town, you might just want to take your guest out to the kitchen...and have another little *chat* with her. Ask her *exactly* how much it is...that she wants...*this* time."

As Bart walked away, his back stiff, his heart breaking, he wondered why it was, that just when you thought you had all the chess pieces in place, and it was a sure bet that you were going to win the game, something came along to upset the board...and send all your pieces flying.

———————

Bart was back at The Sparrow, for his usual Sunday visit. He could not stay away. He had sat stoically through the morning church service, all too aware of the presence of Stephen Giles, with Lady Marilyn Drayton close beside him, on the last bench beside the door of the little church. He needed to take his head foreman aside, and give him a few pieces of sage advice, where Lady Marilyn was concerned. He feared that all Giles saw was the lovely, well groomed, expensively clad exterior, and not the cold blackness of the heart...

Then at the inn, they all sat down to Sunday lunch; then Stephen Giles had left. And Giles did not take Lady Marilyn back to Cottonwood, as Bart had hoped he would. No. It appeared that Lady Marilyn's invitation to The Sparrow was one of length and standing. She had been here the entire week, and when Giles had indicated he was leaving, she merely stood, walked him to the door, said a brief goodbye, and gave no indications of vacating the place. But Ida Evans did rise to her feet, and announce that she had at long last heard from one of her children. She had received a letter from one of her daughters. She was coming for a visit; therefore, Ida must needs go home. Now she must go and pack. She planned on leaving the following morning. At this news, Maggie was not certain whether to be happy—or sad. She had grown very fond of Ida Evans during her extended visit. But, yet, that sweet face often stirred such terrible memories.

Bart finished his dessert, pushed back his chair, and carried his plate and coffee mug into the kitchen. Maggie stood at the dry sink, her back to him. She had put her hair up, and now, free of her bonnet, he could see the warm whiteness of her neck, several strands of dark hair falling across that vision.

"Well, at least one of your…guests is departing." No reply. "Could…someone else do that, darling? And could you join me in the parlor?"

"In a few minutes, Mister Logan." She did not turn to look up at him, but continued her…whatever it was she was doing. Was that a long, sad sigh?

Bart walked through the dining room, into the parlor, and over to the fireplace, where he bent and threw on a well-dried oak log. The fire sputtered, caught, and sprang up with a welcoming warmth. Bart straightened his tall form, and stood, hands on his hips, staring out the window. Had something changed? No. They had not spoken much, since their terrible argument, but he refused to believe anything had changed. It was late April. And today, this very afternoon, he intended to hem her in, to pin her down, to get some sort of date…for the wedding.

Hearing a soft snore, Bart whirled, and found to his dismay that Lady Marilyn had settled her slight bulk into a comfortable chair in the corner of the parlor, and had evidently fallen fast sleep. How had he missed seeing her there, when he came in? Was he that preoccupied? His brain that addled?

He would awaken her…and…and what? Surely, there was some *other* spot in this building that now consisted of ten or so rooms, for her to take her afternoon nap! Bart felt the heat of angry frustration creeping up past the whiteness of his collar, into his neck and face. *That woman!* Was there simply no getting rid of her?! Barbara Jo, Mrs. Evans, even that ignorant child, Bethany Lee, knew that the parlor was more or less off limits, of a Sunday afternoon. He was always here!

"Lady Drayton?" Bart walked over, bent, and attempted to rouse her with a tap on the shoulder with his right hand.

"Ummmm…what?" Lady Marilyn muttered in her sleep.

"Lady Drayton?" Bart then shouted close to her left ear. She gave a start, her eyes flying wide.

"What…is it?" She stared up at Bart blankly. "Oh, Cousin…Bartram…it's you. What do you want?"

"I want *the parlor*, Lady Drayton. Could I then, perhaps assist you to…your quarters? I could perhaps build a fire for you…"

"No, I am very comfortable right here. Now, would you kindly just go away, and leave me alone." The dark eyes closed, and her lovely head drooped to the side.

Bart gave a grunt of disgust. Maggie walked through the door. "Oh, I see that…your cousin…"

"Yes. Well. I suppose there is no room in the inn…so to speak…where you and I, darling, can have a few moments to ourselves. If it were not so cold today, we could perhaps sit on the veranda."

"Johnny is down for his nap. We could sit in the dining room, before the fire?" Maggie suggested.

Bart took Maggie's arm, guiding her firmly out of the cozy parlor, and as he passed Lady Marilyn, he wondered grimly just what he was going to have to do, to get her out of The Sparrow, and back at Cottonwood, until he could decide just what future arrangements…could be made.

They settled themselves before the dying fire. Bart rose, tended the fire, so that it sprang back to life, casting a warm glow over the two occupants of the huge oak rockers.

"You had something, in particular, Mister Logan, to discuss with me this fine Sunday afternoon? Are you not then, still angry, with me?"

"No, my sweet, I am not angry with you. I am…merely…frustrated…but let's not go into all that right now. This, you do realize, sweetheart, is the last Sunday in this month."

"Yes. So…it is," Maggie murmured.

"Then? The month following April, my darling, is…May."

"Yes, Mister Logan. I am well aware of that, and have been since, I believe, the second or third grade. Yes." Maggie flashed him a brilliant smile that set Bart's heart to pounding. Maybe he was actually getting somewhere, here…

"Yes. Well. So…which day…in May…have we…do you…?"

"How about…" Maggie smiled over at him, a sweet, open smile of utter, absolute beauty, her blue-blue eyes wide and sparkling as sapphire. "The…last Sunday in the month?"

"The…*last* Sunday, darling?" Bart raised dark brows, a slight frown forming above them in the tanned forehead, over which Maggie noticed that a lock of dark hair had fallen. "That…will…be…fine." It was a date. It was not the date he had hoped for. He had, in fact, had his heart set on the first Sunday, but it was a date! And, perhaps she needed to order a dress. Perhaps, he should offer, to assist her …with ordering a dress…or some other things? Yes…whatever she needed. Perhaps he could take her shopping…next week…somewhere out of Rhyersville. Down to Atlanta…perhaps?

"Will…you be…needing anything…then, darling?"

"Needing…anything?" she gazed over at him with such innocent eyes.

"Yes…you know…a new dress…or whatever. I have no idea…what you had planned…to wear."

"Oh, no. I don't believe so, Mr. Logan. I have all those lovely things…from those fine shops in London. Enough has already been spent on me, Mister Logan. I'm sure that I can find something to wear, out of all those…things."

Something to wear…she made it sound as though it were just another day… another Sunday…go to church in the morning…back to the inn for lunch…and oh, by the way, throw on some old something…for I do understand there is to be a wedding of sorts…some time this afternoon?

"That sounds…fine…just fine…darling…whatever…you wish. Would you care…"

And somehow Bart made it through the remainder of the afternoon, reminding himself constantly that he should be content. Satisfied. That she had at long last actually set a *date*! What did it matter, what she wore? But he had somehow thought… that the event of their coming wedding would carry some special significance for her. He had thought that women always required a new wardrobe for…these things… He had felt sure that she would want to…

Well, never mind that. She did have new things, just purchased in London.

He wasn't exactly sure what all she had bought in the shops there. The bills had been quite large…but…then…they also covered purchases made by Lady Marilyn…not that the money meant anything to Bart. At least she had set a date. *The last Sunday of May.* His heart almost skipped a beat.

He would go immediately to his office at the logging camp…and mark that date…in bright red…on his calendar…

———

Maggie stood holding her copy of the *Grier's Almanac*, an annual publication that had been in circulation in the South for more than fifty years, a publication that, along with the Bible, was about the only printed material found in most every plantation and farm house. This particular issue, Bartram Logan had brought her from the mercantile. Maggie recalled how that as a child she always saw the annual copy dangling from a peg beside the fireplace of the square-log house in McKinnon Valley, so as to be handy when Mama needed to consult it for Papa, who could not read, as to the weather, cycles of the moon portending propitious planting dates, and of course there were the advertisements. The front cover, as it had with the earliest issues, which began in 1807, announced in bold letters that the almanac was for the South: *For the States of North Carolina, South Carolina, Georgia, Florida, Alabama, Mississippi, Tennessee, Louisiana, Texas, and Arkansas.*

Flipping the small publication open, Maggie's gaze was immediately greeted by a wide assortment of advertisements for patent medicines, proffering a host of remedies to cure whatever ailed you: *Lydia E. Pinkham's Herbal Medicine*, for 'women's complaints', the advertisement bearing an oval likeness of Ms. Pinkham herself; *Black Draught* for constipation of man or beast; *A Life Saver—Cheney's Expectorant*, to cure chills, fevers, and croup. Tincture of senna, spirits of hartshorn… And *Raleigh's Brown Salve*, in huge tins half as big as a hat, to cure scrapes and cuts and bring painful carbuncles and boils to a quick head. What was good for man, in the instance of the salve as with the Black Draught, was also good for beasts—Raleigh's salve for their wounds and sores.

Maggie flipped on, through pages listing weather forecasts, showing the phases of the moon and how they related to planting crops. If only these pages filled with healing and planting advice could give her guidance…for the following weeks. Finally she located the page containing the calendar for the Year of our Lord 1886. With a flourish of quick, decisive strokes, she marked that Sunday in May, with a stub of lead pencil.

She had actually set a date! *She had actually...*

Maggie slammed the little farm magazine firmly shut. It was, after all, only a date marked on a calendar. Things could always change. A lot of things could happen...it was almost an entire month away. Yes, a lot of things could happen...in one entire month...

Maggie never dreamed, as she tucked her *Grier's Almanac* safely away on the parlor mantel, just how prophetic those words would prove...

Lady Marilyn Drayton rose from her bed, and stood peering out a window on the second floor of the inn, where she had been stuck away...but the window of this room did afford her a splendid view of the mountains rising behind the inn. She felt the urge suddenly to use the outhouse, or should she simply pull out the chamber pot with which her hostess had afforded her? No. It was not all that dark outside. She could see the shapes of the trees, but not the buds they were putting forth on every limb and twig for the coming of spring.

Yes, she could well do with a breath of fresh air. She would wrap herself in a thin shawl, then creep down the stairs, and out into the back yard.

Lady Marilyn made her way down the hallway, the staircase, still quite narrow to her way of thinking, through the dining room and kitchen, across the back porch and steps, down into the yard. With small, sure steps, she hastened towards the outhouse. Amazing, she thought, how cold it got here, in these wild, remote mountains, once the sun had set. Now, she had almost reached the door. She lifted one small hand—

A set of scrawny fingers closed like a vice about her wrist, yanking her backwards so violently, that had the figure not come up behind her, his stinking, bony frame giving her support, Lady Marilyn Drayton would have found her lovely form flopped flat on her backside.

Another hand immediately clamped over her mouth. She could smell the stink on him, of...vile things. Like death. He...it...whatever it was...was cutting off her breath. Lady Marilyn gave a violent yank, in a vain attempt to free herself from her unknown assailant. Though she did feel him rock and sway like a tree bent by the wind, she could not throw him over. He was too strong. Then Lady Marilyn felt a hard thud on the back of her head...and everything went black.

He had her now, all right...but how to get her back into the woods? She fought him. She was like a cat, this one. Knock her out. Drag her. That's right. Up the slope.

He had her now, secured tightly with a scrap of rope he had found in his ramblings about the town. He had her tied up good. She'd not escape now. He built up a fire, so he could see her...keep a sharp eye on her...decide exactly what it was...he was going to do with this feisty offspring of that John McKinnon...

Ah, she was opening her eyes. For one minute there, he thought he might have killed her. But, no, she was opening her eyes.

Attempting to bring her gaze into focus, Lady Marilyn stared at him with disgust and loathing.

"Who *are* you?" she spat. "You...you... vile creature!?"

"Wouldn't ye lack ta know?" Silas P. Crocker drawled in his best backwoods lingo. "Thought ye'd git away with it, didn't ye? Thought ye could just take m' girl, and m' gran'baby away from me, and git clean away wif it!"

"What? What on earth, you...you *raving, insane, besotted lunatic*...are you raging about? There's been some mistake here..."

"No mistake here...missy. I don'bi awatchin' ye too long—not to know who ye air. I've been awatchin' ye...for all these months, now."

"*Months?*" Lady Marilyn squawked, anger choking her; fear making her eyes almost cross in her head. That's when he hit her. Hard. And square across the mouth, rocking her head back against the hardness of the tree, almost rendering her senseless again.

"Ye cin't lie ta me, missy! Don't ye think I got sense 'nuf ta know how long ye been here?"

The creature stared at her, his red-rimmed eyes hot with rage. He truly was insane! She had been...*kidnapped*...by a *madman*...why?...and who would know it? Who would come searching for her? No one. They had all retired to their rooms for the night. They wouldn't miss her, or come searching…not until morning. And, probably not even then, since she often lay abed until almost noon, and had let it be known by one and all that unless the building was on fire, she was not to be disturbed.

"Look! You're making a—" It was a whine, a low whimper, but it brought his hand up, hard, across her mouth, again. Her vision blurred. Her ears rang like a gong from the blow. She tasted blood. She had bitten her tongue.

"I don't like ta have ta hit no woman. But yo're forcin' me ta do this." With a wag of his head, he reached down and picked up a piece of filthy, tattered rag, which he wound about her mouth, tying it so tightly it almost gagged her.

The rag beneath her nose reeked of all sorts of filth, almost taking her breath away with its foul stink. What had he been *using* the thing for?—before cramming it into her mouth?! Marilyn felt true terror rising up in her throat, threatening to suffocate her. She must not panic. She must use her head. She must *think*. She had been in bad situations before…but never…*never* anything like this.

Why had he done this? What had he said? Whom did he mistake her for? He said something about a girl, and a grandchild.

Yes, there was a girl at the inn. And a child. But they did not appear to be his targets. He mentioned that someone had taken them from him? Who? It had to be a woman. A woman about her size, with—

He had mistaken her for *Margaret Ann Evans! She must tell him!*

She struggled against the ropes. She felt sick. She might throw up. Swinging her head violently from side to side, she made desperate, groaning, gurgling sounds that began deep in her innards and erupted up through the gag.

He lifted a filthy, bony fist, and swung it ominously near her nose.

Recalling the two vicious blows that had all but decapitated her, Lady Marilyn sagged back against the hardness of the tree and grew quiet.

———————

Marilyn awoke with a start, and realized she had dozed off. Her back hurt. Her head felt as if she had been hit by a dray. Then it all came flooding back. She *had* been hit…not once…but twice. Thrice, counting the time down at the outhouse. Yes, she had been hit, all right. Mouth filled with blood, violet eyes glazed with terror, she glanced dazedly about. Where was that fiend? What had become of him?

She couldn't see him. Then suddenly he appeared, like a bony, rag-tag specter rising out of the darkness. One arm loaded with dead wood for his meager fire, the other grappling from tree to tree, he hopped and dragged himself along. Illuminated by the low flicker of the campfire, Lady Marilyn got a full view of her captor. *He was half a man!* She had been abducted by some crazed creature with only one leg! He dumped his load of wood, hobbled a pathetic step closer, leered down at her through tags of filthy hair, the face scarcely more than a skull with sunken eyes, wild and red-rimmed.

Balancing his bony carcass all askance on a single appendage and a makeshift crutch, he glared down at her with such hatred in his eyes that she wondered…what had William Bartram Logan's betrothed ever done to this creature…to make him loathe her so?! *What did he intend doing with her?*

Lady Marilyn felt a surge of blinding, brain-numbing terror. She couldn't breathe! She began to tremble from head to heel. Her insides melted. Had her life depended on it, she could not, at that moment, have stood to her feet. She was *nothing*. She saw it in his eyes. *She was as good as dead.*

Then something spoke to Marilyn, some voice warning her she must get control of herself. She blinked and attempted to focus her eyes, to cease the trembling.

He stared at her a moment longer, then dropped his crude crutch. The thing hit the dried leaves. They popped and snapped. Then the one-legged blackguard literally fell to the ground, the dead leaves crushing like claps of thunder beneath the sudden weight of his bony frame.

From his awkward position, half sitting, half reclining on the ground, he reached out and poked at his fire. Sparks scattered and danced off, falling into the dead leaves. Suddenly Marilyn experienced another spurt of terror. That *fool!* That *idiot!* Didn't he realize how dangerous it was? What he was doing? It had not rained for weeks, in the mountains. Everyone in the small town was talking about it. How it had been such an abnormally dry spring. But they were used, they had said, to unpredictable weather, here in the mountains. Still, the past several weeks had been so dry…No moisture had fallen, since that freak snowstorm. Lady Marilyn was again tempted to pray…that the thick blanket of leaves spread across these mountains ridges did not catch fire. Tied to this tree, *she would be roasted alive! Oh, God…!* She was tempted to pray…

But despite her awful predicament, despite the paralyzing fear robbing her of all hope, she could not find within herself the strength to surrender her own will to that of another…. If there was indeed a God, *why didn't he simply come down and rescue her!*

She wanted to rant, to rage and scream at her captor, but the gag remained as tight as it had been…how many hours ago? She had no idea how long she had been here. She sagged helplessly back against the tree, and felt tears gathering in her eyes. It was clear that she would not make it off this mountain alive. *She did not want to die!*

Alone on this mountainside!

With a hate-filled madman!

She had made friends here…!

She might make a life for herself…here…!

Where were these thoughts coming from?

Who in this tiny burg cared a *tinker's drat* about her? She had long ago admitted to herself that she had no one. This cousin—albeit as distant as their relationship was—was her sole remaining blood kin of any ilk on this earth. And he clearly found her nothing but a despicable intrusion into his life. He had made every effort to drive her from this remote mountain village. Except telling her flatly to go. He did in fact, find her abhorrent. She could see it in his eyes. The way he looked at her…She wondered what he knew…? Probably *far, far* too much. But the Evans woman had taken her in…

And then, there was Stephen Giles. He had been…kind…yes…that was the word. Stephen Giles had been kind to her. Perhaps much kinder than she deserved, given her…*where were these thoughts coming from?* What was *happening* to her? Since when was she in the habits of chastising herself for *any* of her actions? Wasn't she due her share of whatever this world offered, on any terms and by any means she could obtain it!? She had been attending that stupid church too much. Listening each Sunday morning to a man expounding upon the corrupt and sinful nature of mankind…the only hope of redemption…a risen Savior…

Well, now, and wouldn't *that* be nice! Wouldn't it be nice…to be all clean and forgiven! Saved and bound for an eternal heaven! To live in hope…surrounded by love…and warm and faithful friends… who waited for you at the inn at the foot of the mountain. And wouldn't it just be nice…to be there now…in the warmth of that inn…rather than stuck on the side of this mountain with a madman who seemed bent…

The scene—the odd man, the fire—swam before her like a surreal nightmare. She blinked to clear her vision, fought to staunch the tears. Her nose had begun to run, dribbling down into the gag. She gave a few snuffling sobs. Her thoughts trailed dismally off. Her captor dragged himself forward as best he could, sinking his bony rump deeper into the dead leaves, to thrust the upper part of his filthy, rag-draped frame forward enough to reach his small stash of firewood. With one claw-like paw, he managed to snare a dead limb, but he was still too far away to quite reach the small fire to lay his fuel on, so he flung the dead wood towards the small pile of dwindling coals.

Fool!

The moment the limb struck the fire, thrown from such an odd angle, the fire literally exploded in every direction. Hurtling here and there, red-hot coals leapt amongst dead leaves, waiting heaps of dried tinder. Falling coals began to ignite flames that licked hungrily at the dead leaves.

Beneath the canopy of budding hardwoods, tiny wisps of smoke began to curl upward, here and there, about the makeshift camp. Her captor sat staring glassily into nothing, unaware that a dozen or more fires had sprung up about him.

Lady Marilyn wanted to scream at him, to point a hand…to stomp, to rave, to do something…*anything*…to get his attention. But her mouth was gagged; her hands were bound behind her; she was lashed tightly to the tree. Only her legs were free. Frantically she began to writhe and twist and kick.

The one-legged creature stared at her; then he glanced wildly about, to see if all her kicking meant that someone had located his hiding place. At sight of the spreading fires, his eyes flew wide. Even his sick mind instantly registered the danger. He groped for his crude crutch. Dragging his bony frame as upright as possible, he began hopping pitifully about on his one leg. Grasping his makeshift crutch with one hand, ranting and raging, bluing the air with curses, he beat and flailed at the spreading fires with some sort of filthy sack.

Lady Marilyn watched with mounting horror. He was never going to be able to put all those fires out! It was the middle of the night! And the town below was locked in deep sleep! Suddenly the prospect of hell became all too real...*where the worm dies not and the fire is not quenched—!*

Oh, Dear God...! She was going to be burned alive on this mountainside...!

Benjamin Noah tossed and turned in the little two-roomed cabin just down the street from the inn. He sniffed the air. His nostrils flared. What was that he smelled? Was it...*smoke?*

Benjamin Noah rose, careful not to wake Liza Mae snoring softly beside him.

His feet firmly on the floor, he shook himself awake, then crept to the door of the cabin, and flung it wide...

The mountain behind the town was ablaze!

"Fire! Fire...on th' mountain!" Benjamin Noah went racing down the narrow dirt street, screaming to the top of his lungs.

Maggie sat straight up in bed, the hair rising up on her neck and along her arms. *Fire!?*

She raced to the front window. No fire showed itself along the street. She raced into the hall, to peer out an upstairs window towards the mountain—

Oh! Dear! Lord—

"*Fire! Fire! Everybody...* " Maggie was banging on doors, screeching to the top of her lungs.

"Maggie! For heaven sakes! What is it?" Barbara Jo came stumbling down the hall, a lit taper in her hand.

"The mountain's on fire, Barbs! The mountain's on fire! We have to get everybody out of the inn!"

With all the banging and screaming of Maggie and Barbara Jo, soon every soul in The Sparrow had evacuated the place, racing down the halls, down the stairs, and out into the street, to stand and gape open-mouthed up at the mountain behind the inn—

Then there was Benjamin Noah, racing back into the inn, and out again, Maggie screaming at him as he leapt off the veranda, and ran toward her, dragging a heavy object behind him.

"Benjamin Noah! What on earth—!"

"It be yore *trunk*, Mizz Maggie. Th' one done been brot' over from—"

"Oh, Benjamin! How sweet of you! But...don't you dare go back inside! Don't you dare risk your life for anything in that inn!"

"No'm. But don't ye 'spect we should draw up some buckets o' water, or somethin', just in case da far' don' 'scapes down off da mountain, dere, and down inta da town?"

"Look at it, Benjamin! I don't think we could get the water to the roof, if it *were* on fire, or even to wet it down enough to prevent it from catching. I just don't know...but look...the wind seems to be carrying it northwestward, back of the town. Maybe it will just stay up on the mountain...and burn itself out."

"No, ma'am, Miss Maggie, I don't believe that's gwin' ta happen. See, there, it's beginning to creep along, closer now, to da buildin's further down da street."

"Yes! It's not that far now! From Barbara Jo's house! Oh...can't we do something?"

"Whut, Miss Maggie. Pray, 'tis all's I knows ta do!"

But farther down the street, men were streaming out of buildings, dragging ladders and carrying buckets.

"How close is it, do you think?" one man shouted to his companions.

"Too close! We need to wet down the grass and weeds along that stretch, there, maybe...to keep it contained. Maybe if we had a few shovels over here. We could dig some trenches. Keep th' thing from spreadin' down into town!"

Suddenly Thomas Beyers appeared out of nowhere. His face worried, his eyes searching. Then he was beside them. And Maggie could not help but notice...that it was to Barbara Jo...that Thomas Beyers spoke...

"Are you...all right? Is...everyone...else...all right?"

Maggie saw Barbara Jo reach out and take Thomas Beyers' arm, and tuck it into her own.

"Yes, Thomas!" Barbara Jo leaned into Thomas Beyers' strong shoulder, and felt suddenly...and immeasurably...comforted.

Then she heard someone shouting to her—"It's the Moss place, Miss Barbara!"

Her house was on fire!

411

And it was true. Not one building about the fine yellow brick house was burning. But drifting embers had fallen onto the oak shingles of the veranda, and had caught.

Ladders were immediately hauled out of nowhere, and men were ascending them and descending. Buckets of water were being hauled out of wells, and handed, hand-over-hand.

But despite all the best efforts of a score or more of men, the roof covering the wide veranda collapsed with a roar and fell onto the front porch, setting it ablaze.

More men appeared out of the awful night, their eyes wide with terror.

The battle continued, to save the fine yellow brick house.

Then slowly, ever so slowly, they began to win the battle.

Thomas Beyers approached Barbara Jo, standing in line in the bucket brigade. She was pale and distraught, but she was not wailing and moaning. She was hefting heavy bucket after heavy bucket along the line, with all the others.

"I think they have it stopped, now. I think it's pretty well under control. The front veranda's gone. Some damage to the front parlor, but the back of the house, the upstairs, appear to be in sound shape. And, thank the Good Lord, nothing else has caught. Why don't you…"

Maggie watched as the two of them walked away, arm in arm.

Lady Marilyn Drayton awoke groggily, as if from a nightmare. She was no longer bound to the tree. She was splayed face foremost on the ground. She pushed herself up, dazedly recalling that as the fire had burned out of control, he had loosed her from the tree, and dragged her farther up the mountain. She had absolutely no idea where he was. Where she was. She rose groggily, and found that she could actually stand. But…where *was* he?

It didn't matter! *Get away!* That was her only thought! Get off this mountain! Back to the safety of the inn! "Please God…please, God! Let the inn still be there! Let everyone be all right! *Please God!*"

As she stumbled and cried and moaned, working her way down off the mountain, Lady Marilyn realized that she was actually *praying!* Where was it coming from? She realized, as she shuffled blindly along, that it was *not* coming from her, but from some *other place*. By all logical reasoning, she should have been dead. She recalled as she ran, how that at one point, she looked around, to see that she and her captor were entirely surrounded by roiling flames that raced through the dry leaves and limbs, licking hungrily up the trees, exploding into an inferno. The flames had encircled them, like a hungry beast, chased after them. *There was no way of escape!* For the first time in her life, she had prayed. Then… Something! *Someone*…beyond her. *Someone!* had seen her, had shown mercy, and had lifted her safely from that hellish nightmare of flames!

Praise God! She had been saved!

As she sought to escape the fire, Lady Marilyn was in such a state of shock that she was totally unaware of her injuries, of the pain shooting up from her left hand, and across her neck.

She did not recall, at this point in time, having fallen, then frantically attempting to stumble to her feet, her hand landing in a pile of burning brush, a burning limb tumbling, end over end, from the looming canopy of flames, and landing across her neck. There was too much terror, too much trauma to mind such things, when her very life was at stake. And she had somehow risen to her feet, and stumbled on…

Now, she could see the shadow of the town, spread out before her in the little valley. Behind her smoke rose in black and gray billows, and flames raced on over the mountains to west and north. But never, never in her life had any place on earth looked more beautiful, more welcoming, than did the little town of Rhyersville, that April morning.

She was in her room at the inn. The doctor had been promptly summoned to tend her burns. She had been carried up to her room by the hired man, Benjamin Noah, wasn't that his name? As he hauled her up the stairs, she could hear with each step his deep, melodic voice echoing in her head, muttering her name in prayer. *"Dear Lawd! Do bless this Laidy Mar'lin! Do tetch 'er wif yore big han's o' mercy…!"* And his wife, Liza Mae, her black eyes swimming with tears, had hastened up behind her husband, to check out her burns, then to fetch her something cool to drink, bustling and murmuring constant prayers, as the doctor salved and dressed her burns.

413

"Bad enough, I spose," the country physician surmised shortly, as he peered at her through tiny, wire-rimmed spectacles and made at his work. "Could have been worse. These burns on the hands...may leave a few scars. Especially the left one, here. Pretty deep. And those on the neck. Need to keep that well salved. Covered with clean, boiled cloths, until new skin forms. Hope you're not all that hung up on appearances. May scar, too. But you'll live. I would surmise that you, young lady," he peered steadily at her with squinted eyes, "are a very, *very* lucky person...to have survived...this night's doings! And just what do you think could have happened to this...one-legged man? Who did you say you thought he might be, Maggie, my dear? Silas P. Crocker...?"

"Thomas Beyers...and some of the men...are out searching the mountain...for either Mr. Crocker...or his corpse..." Maggie murmured. "Poor, poor benighted soul...whatever got into him?"

"Th' devil, more than likely," Dr. Ellis muttered philosophically. "Does strange things to men's heads—when they let him have his way with them."

"Yes," Lady Marilyn smiled up at Dr. Ellis, despite the bite of her pain, "And, I fear, oftentimes, the havoc he wreaks with men, he also wreaks— with women."

"What's that, my dear? Women, did you say? Oh, yes, I suppose. In some cases..."

The good doctor rambled on, but Lady Marilyn failed to hear. He had given her more than a few drops of laudanum sprinkled in a little water, and she drifted off into a deep, peaceful sleep. She was home.

"What did you say...happened to Lady Marilyn?" Bart frowned over at Maggie.

"I...don't exactly know. I can't really explain it. And she hasn't said much about that night, except how *awful* Silas P. Crocker was. How frightened she was. The way they were trapped, with no way out, and the fire raging about them...oh...and she did add that she had been...saved."

"Saved? You...don't...you can't...believe...that she...means? No." Bart wagged his handsome head in sharp, final denial. "*Not* Lady Marilyn. Did I ever tell you about the *file* the barristers' office in London raised on her, after she made off with the silver tea service from Windsfield?"

"No, Mr. Logan, darling, you did not. And I don't know that I wish to hear of it. Time will tell, if there is indeed a change…in Lady Marilyn. The *proof of the pudding*, as Mama always said, *is in the eating*. And, by the way, Stephen Giles has been in to see her."

"Oh? Perhaps…I need to have a *good* talk with Giles. Perhaps…I need to show *him* Lady Marilyn's file…"

"Mister Logan! *You…will…do…no…such…thing…*! Else I shall *never* in this life speak to you again! Give the poor woman a chance!"

"Yes. Well," Bart rubbed a tanned hand thoughtfully across his chin, "We shall wait, then, and see. But should she revert to her…old ways…I don't want Giles to be hurt…"

"Mister Logan, Stephen Giles is a man full grown. And who it is, exactly, who is meddling, now?"

After two days of searching, Thomas Beyers and some of the other men discovered Silas P. Crocker's filthy, rag-shrouded form. Shivering and shaking with fever, near starvation, he lay huddled in a wash, near the creek. But miraculously he was alive, and only had a few minor burns on his body. There was talk of locking him up in the jail. But when Maggie heard of it, she raised such a row that an emergency town meeting was called, and the criminal, Silas P. Crocker, was reluctantly released—into the custody of Mrs. Margaret Ann Evans.

"What else was I to do…?"

The sheriff looked Bartram Logan in the eye and demanded, "It was not at all what I would have *preferred* to do, you understand, but…I mean…after all…there are *laws*…Mister Logan. When it came to the kidnapping charges, well this Lady Marilyn Draper, or whatever…well…she went back and changed her story. And she refused to press charges. And then, there were the matters of being a public nuisance, setting the woods on fire. But no one was killed or badly injured…and your lady, she demanded to know the amount of bail the judge had set, which was very low, given that I had scarcely anything left to charge the fellow with…and when I told her…well, your lady marched straight down to the bank, and here she came back with it clutched in one of her little hands! I don't *make* the laws, Mister Logan!"

––––––––––––––––

Maggie had rented a small house, down near Benjamin Noah's and Liza Mae's little cabin. Now with the baby coming soon, she had moved Benjamin Noah and Liza Mae into the small house, and had put Silas P. Crocker into the little two-roomed cabin.

"Benjamin Noah keeps a keen eye on him," Maggie explained to Bart Logan, "And he takes down his meals. I mean…the poor man is *sick*…Mr. Logan, darling! *Dead* on his feet. In his present condition, I would consider poor Mr. Crocker to be a threat to no one…least of all…me."

Bart drew in a long, deep, weary breath, and simply stared at her. There were a *million words* crowding themselves into his mouth, demanding to be spit out, but…what was the use?!

He drew another deep, weary sigh. "He may…somewhat…recover…his health…with all this good food and shelter, and so forth, darling. But then…who knows…about his *mind*…" Bart lifted his right hand helplessly, let it wave dramatically about his head for just one moment, then dropped it at his side.

"Did you, by any chance, Mister Logan, darling, get a glimpse of all the beautiful carvings they found, in a scorched tow sack, alongside Mr. Silas P. Crocker?"

"Carvings?" Bart stared at her.

"Yes, Mister Logan. Some of them are *exquisite*. If they were taken down to the mercantile…and displayed on a shelf…or something…I do believe people…when people *see* these exquisite carvings…I mean…Johnny has been playing with a set of the soldiers…ever since we found them."

"Soldiers?" Bart asked.

"Yes, darling! And there are little animals! So beautiful! So true to life! The man is…he is an artistic *genius*! There is even a carving of the *Christ Child*…in His little cradle!"

"We are…still…my dearest one…speaking here…of this…*lunatic*…this *kidnapper*, this *insane man* who hauled a woman off in the dead of night, clad only in her shimmy and night slippers, almost succeeded in bringing about her demise, set the mountain ablaze, and came within a gnat's hill of burning the entire town down to the ground? Is…*that*…whom we are still…speaking of, here?" Bart shook his head, his dark eyes wide with disbelief.

"Would you…then…object…to my choosing out…some of his best pieces… taking them down to the mercantile for display…and possible sale, darling?"

"Now I'm to be a *marketing agent* for this…*kidnapping lunatic*? Is that what you're asking of me, my sweet?"

Maggie gazed up at Bartram Logan, her eyes soft and misty, as if seeing some vision, far beyond his mere mortal understanding, "Remember, Mister Logan, darling?" she cooed into his ear, as she moved very close, lilac water overcoming his senses. She was standing now almost against the fawn wool of his jacket, "Remember…in the Gospels? *The story of Legion…?*"

Bartram Logan reached out, and pulled her close against him. "Of course, darling. And how could I forget? Why don't you show me these wondrous works of art? Together, perhaps, we might choose out…a few pieces…or…we might…just take…the entire sack full, down to the store…"

———

Silas P. Crocker sat in a small, ladder-backed chair with an oak-slat bottom he himself had fashioned. Sunlight flooded through the small window of his rented two-room cabin. The silence of the sunlight was broken only by the soft scrape, scrape of his carving knife. He had to be very diligent now. He had to be up early each morning, to have his breakfast, shave and wash up a bit in the washbowl. He had a business to attend to. He had orders to fill. People wanted two of this, and three of that. Children…they said…loved his toys. There was sure to be a big market by Christmas. He had only a few months to build up his stock. Women loved his carving of the Christ Child in his own little cradle.

John McKinnon's daughter, the lady who ran the inn, had been by to check on him, several times. She had, on a couple of occasions, fetched along her Bible, and read to him from the Gospel of Saint John. She had invited him to her inn for Sunday dinner several times. And to sit in on some lessons being taught in her kitchen. He was learning to read and write. She bragged and boasted mightily about the quality of his work. She had even been kind enough to furnish him with some pots of dyes and stains that brought out, very nicely, the wood grain of some of his pieces. She even commiserated with him, about the fact that Union veterans had, for the score of years since the War ended, been receiving Federal pensions for their service during the conflict between the states. Southern veterans, having been the enemy, were, of course, shut out, and had received nothing. The Georgia Legislature had mentioned doing something for their veterans, but they still had their hands full, just trying to get the State back on its very wobbly feet. So, thus far, nothing had come of their talk. Maybe…someday…if he lived long enough, he'd see a pension for his service, for losing his leg. But Silas had already turned forty. How many more years would it take the State of Georgia to get things all sorted out? Get enough money to do something with? He doubted he'd live that long.

Still, as he worked, Silas P. Crocker began to hum an old hymn. He had a roof over his head, money in his pocket. But still he couldn't help but wonder where his daughter was… He had heard, a few days back, that she had up and disappeared in the night, leaving her child behind.

A few days later, John McKinnon's daughter, the one that ran the inn, dropped by again. She had a woman with her, carrying a small child. It was…yes…it was little Bethany Lee, carrying her child. *His grandchild.* John McKinnon's daughter explained how that Bethany Lee and the baby's Pap had up and run off together, a few days back. But God got to niggling at them, and God, she said, had brought them safely back home to their child. And now the boy—Samuel McAlister, that was the baby's pap's name— and Bethany Lee had gotten hitched. And Samuel had made up with his Pappy, and was again working with his family back in the mercantile. The young couple and their child, so Silas understood, were living in some rooms back of the store.

418

Chapter 41

With the strong aid of Benjamin Noah, Lady Marilyn had made her way down the stairs from her room, along the narrow hallway, and had sunk into a chair in the cozy front parlor. As she sat ruminating, Maggie announced that she had a visitor. Lady Marilyn lifted her dark violet eyes, and became painfully aware of Stephen Giles, as his tall, broad logger's fame suddenly filled the doorway, painfully aware of his kind smile, the warmth of the calloused hand he extended toward her...containing a handful of wildflowers he had plucked on his way down from the logging camp. In the other hand, he held a large box.

"A little something I picked up for you, to help pass th' time." Stephen Giles said, bending to place the box on the lap of her gray muslin morning dress. Lady Marilyn laid the wildflowers carefully on the side table, lifted the lid of the box resting on her lap, and gave a little gasp of delight. Sheets of paper. Some charcoal pencils. A pen, a tiny brush, and a few pastel blocks of water colors.

"Oh! But...how did you know?"

"I just figured it out. Truth be told, I saw some of your...doodlings...drawings, I mean. I was checkin' things out...at Cottonwood. I just happened onto 'em, layin' right out in th' open, there on a table. With nobody else there, knowed they had to be yours. Thought you being laid up, and all, you might like to have this here box...of things. Like I just said...to help pass th' time. 'Til you're up and about ag'in."

How handsome he looked, standing tall and lean before her, his clothes soft and faded, the sun coming through the windows and lighting his open, earnest face, his eyes...

Dropping her gaze from his, Lady Marilyn was suddenly painfully aware of how she must appear to him. Her left hand, her throat, were still swaddled in thick bandages. She had not been able to actually wash her hair for days now. The salve used on her burns had a distinctly unpleasant odor. It was difficult for her to dress. Her choice of clothes, and arranging her hair were things to which she had not given the first thought—since that night on the mountain. She was just thankful she was alive, here in this charming mountain inn…warm and safe…with people about her who actually appeared to care whether she lived or died.

"I must look a fright!" Lady Marilyn sighed, her gaze floating about the room, wondering if she should apologize for the medicinal odor.

"Ah!" Stephen Giles pulled a smile as he bent his tall frame, reached and clasped her uninjured hand, and held it for just a moment between his own large, calloused palms. She could feel the warmth, the roughness, of his palms. She knew that these hands had turned many a log, sending it splashing and plummeting down the spillways into the river. She knew they had fashioned fine furniture, and built fires, and saddled mounts and harnessed logging horses. He was a fine, hard-working man. And he was standing above her, tall and strong, smiling down at her, his eyes warm, his face open and friendly.

Unable to meet his eyes, Lady Marilyn slipped her hand from his, let her own gaze drop, and raised the hand to her throat, to fiddle self-consciously with the thick white bandage. "You don't have to flatter me, Mr. Giles. I know how I must look." *Thank God for the protective covering of the bandages! If this man could see what her neck actually looked like…he would flee this room in revulsion. Always, since she was a small child, she had prided herself on her appearance. She had been very beautiful, and she had been well aware of it most of her life. But this morning…when she had drawn back the bandage across her neck…and taken a good look into the mirror of the dresser in her room upstairs…she had almost fainted.*

Marilyn wanted nothing more than to run and hide, slamming the door shut behind her. But she pasted on a smile. This man, it appeared, had, out of the decency of a good heart, ridden quite a way just to visit her. The least she could do was to be civil to him. She batted the tears from her eyes, lifted her head, and forced her gaze to meet his. "Well, Mister Giles! It is so…very nice…of you to visit. And to come bearing flowers and a gift! Do sit down, and tell me…how are things…out at Cottonwood?"

"*Mister Giles?*" Stephen Giles sank into a chair near her, elbows on knees, and attempted to joke, "And what happened to *Stephen*?"

"Well. Then. Stephen…how are things…?"

Stephen Giles leaned forward out of his chair, locking her eyes in a penetrating gaze.

"The question is, *Marilyn*," he said softly, as if actually interested, as if peering deep into her soul, "*how* are things with you?" When had he ceased to address her as Lady Marilyn, and begun to call her…in the American fashion…simply *Marilyn*? She wasn't quite sure, but she suddenly found that she liked the sound of it.

"I'm…healing…so the good doctor tells me…very nicely." The lovely violet eyes flicked away, then back.

"Good," Stephen Giles pulled a little smile that turned up the corners of his mouth, and then reached all the way up to his eyes. "It's good, then, to hear that. When…do you suppose…then…that you'll be able to attend church services? I've…missed you."

"Stephen," Lady Marilyn said, ducking her head, fiddling with the contents of the box still in her lap. "To be quite honest with you…" Wasn't this a switch! When was the last time she had been *honest* with a man—!? "I don't know that I would be…welcome…at church services. Once these bandages come off…I may not look…to suit. That is…I saw myself in the mirror this morning! And I look—*horrible!*"

"Not look to suit? Who gives a hang how you look?" Stephen Giles stared at her. "I'm lookin' at you. And you look just fine ta me. I thought…th' very first time I ever saw you…well, I thought…there is one of th' finest lookin' women I ever did lay eyes on."

"Well, Stephen, I am flattered, but…once these bandages are removed, you may no longer think me…so…fine…looking."

"Says who?"

"Says me, Stephen." Lady Marilyn gazed straight at him, raised her right hand, and though it required all the slight courage she possessed, deliberately lifted off the heavy bandage protecting the deep burn wounds on her throat.

Eyes wide, Stephen Giles leaned in close. "Seems to look good enough to me," he speculated. "Don't see that there's goin' to be much of a problem there. Still a bit red and puffy…about th' edges…but…like Doc Ellis says, it all appears to be healin' real good."

"This…this doesn't fill you with…revulsion?"

"No'm. Why should it?"

"Because…I'm…*marred* for life!" Lady Marilyn wailed, "I'll *never…ever…* be…beautiful…again. People will *stop and stare and gawk* at me! Just look at my hand!" She ripped off the bandage and stuck out her left hand. "I'll be this grotesque, awful…sideshow *freak*! Like something one sees at the Piccadilly—" Tears filling her eyes, she turned away.

Stephen Giles took the burned little hand that somewhat resembled a dark claw, and laid it gently in his big, calloused palm, careful not to touch the fragile skin. "Awwwww! *Marilyn!*… With that face…and them eyes…?!" Stephen Giles wagged his head, "Nobody…*nobody*… Marilyn… will *ever* think those awful things about you. Not nobody, leastwise, that I can think of. People in these mountains… well…..they pretty much judge folks by their *actions,* and not that much by how they look on the outside. Not that you don't look just fine. Like I just said, with that face, who's goin' to even notice a few little dents and dings in your neck? Or on your hand. I…mean…*none* of us is perfect."

Dark violet eyes flooded with tears, Marilyn turned to look at him. And for the first time that she could recall, her face lit up with a genuine smile. Why couldn't she have met this man…before…?

"Thank you for that, Mister Giles…Stephen."

"Why don't we, then, just re-wrap these burns, and d'you feel like standin' up? Maybe takin' a little walk down th' street? Sure is pretty out there. Even where the fire burned the mountain, stuff is starting to sprout up. Wildflowers and such in bloom. Fresh air might do you good."

In another week, the bandages were off. When she appeared in church with Stephen Giles that Sunday, her scarred throat swaddled beneath the protective covering of a frothy silk scarf, her withered left hand thrust into the voluminous folds of her dress, Lady Marilyn was most warmly welcomed.

After church, Bart and Maggie took a stroll through the graveyard back of Shiloh Baptist. Then Maggie led Bart through the forest of hardwoods budding green behind the graveyard, on to the little spring that rose at the bottom of the mountain.

The water sprang icy cold out of the mountainside, and gurgled and splashed beyond the tree roots into a deep, lovely, rock-lined pool that reflected the colors of each rock—a kaleidoscope of ambers and oranges, reds and yellows, dancing through the crystal water, a dazzling feast for the eyes. A few leaves left from winter drifted lazily about the mirrored surface of the pool.

"Beautiful, isn't it, Mr. Logan, darling?" Maggie whispered, in a hushed, reverential tone.

"Yes. It's lovely. Why…or who…built this lovely rock-lined pool for the spring to feed into? And why are we whispering?" Bart muttered, his dark eyes fixed on the glittering depths.

"Well, it…this pool," Maggie explained, "this is the *baptizing* pool, for Shiloh Baptist. Many a poor sinner saved by grace has been drawn forth from these icy waters. Rising from the dead…to new life."

"Baptizing…pool?" Bart turned and gazed fixedly at Maggie.

"Yes, Mr. Logan. Shiloh *Baptist*…? The *members* of th' church get to *be* members by pledging to join the church. And their membership is solemnized by being baptized… It's a thing we Baptist…do."

"I…see," Bart murmured. "Then, unless one is…and this, I seem to recall reading…it serves…some greater purpose…than mere church membership…"

"Yes, Mr. Logan. It indeed does. As a matter of fact, I do believe I recall hearing that Stephen Giles and your Cousin Marilyn have both requested that the rites be administered them, weather permitting, Sunday next."

"Well!" Bart reached and took Maggie's small hand, squeezing it firmly. He gazed directly at her, pulled a broad smile, "We certainly would not wish to miss that. Now, would we, my sweet?"

The following Sunday, the weather proved perfect. Warm for mid-May.

The bell of the church tolled its invitation across the valley, and up the mountainsides. Rather than filing into the church at the usual time, the congregation marched through the little graveyard, up into the tree line, to the spring gushing from amongst gnarled tree roots in a small green glade on the mountainside. The women in their best dresses and bonnets, held their red-backed hymnals. The men all stood about, holding their hats in their hands, looking on. Children romped and chased one another amongst the freshly-leafed trees that cast flickering shadows across the cold depths of the rock-lined baptizing pool.

A hush suddenly descended, as Reverend Whitcomb raised his right hand, and began solemnly intoning the old hymn:

Shall we gather at the ri-ivver,
Where bright angels' feet have tro-oooddd
With its crystal tide forevvvvv-ever
Flowing from thhhhe throne of-ffff Goddddd....

Maggie stood with Barbara Jo and Thomas Beyers, and wondered angrily whatever had happened to Mister William Bartram Logan!? He had faithfully promised her that he would be in attendance. How could he miss such an important occasion?! Maggie attempted to hold onto Johnny's small, damp hand. But the task proved difficult, and then impossible, as Johnny's small, damp hand slipped from hers, and he went charging across the clearing, yelling to the top of his lungs:

"Bart! Bart...!"

Suddenly there came striding up through the trees William Bartram Logan, the rich Philadelphia businessman. Bareheaded, his expensive wool jacket and tie thrown across one arm, he wore a snow-white cotton shirt open at the neck and dark trousers ...and was in his stocking feet, his shiny black boots carried in one hand...what on earth?...Maggie wondered, her eyes growing very wide. For behind Bartram Logan marched Stephen Giles and Marilyn Drayton.

Maggie stood stunned, ignoring Johnny who ran and yelped and bounced up and down at the very lip of the rock-lined pool, until Barbara Jo showed the good sense to step forward and draw him discreetly back.

Then Reverend Whitcomb was removing his good Sunday shoes, and in his long cotton stockings, stepping down into the frigid waters that eddied about dark cotton trouser-legs. Maggie watched as if in a dream, as the tall, lank form of William Bartram Logan stepped down the rock steps behind him. Then Stephen Giles was holding out a hand to guide Marilyn in, to stand between him and Bart, in the bone-chilling, chest-deep waters...

Maggie felt frozen. She heard the familiar words the pastor was intoning. She had heard them dozens of times, but now, as she heard the slight splash and watched Bart Logan disappear below the rippling surface of the icy waters to emerge smiling, wiping the waters from his face and hair with tanned hands, she felt sure she would swoon away in a dead faint.

Maggie stared at the man sitting across from her at the kitchen table. Bart, Stephen, and Marilyn Drayton had risen dripping out of the baptizing pool, been handed towels and had disappeared to change into dry clothing, before assembling with the congregation in the little Shiloh Baptist Church, where the three of them were seated on the front bench...and solemnly charged by Pastor Whitcomb: *"Now that you have followed your Savior into the grave...been buried with him in baptism, risen with him from the dead...to walk in the newness of life, see that you conduct your lives accordingly..."* Now, Sunday dinner had been served, the food and dishes cleared away, and the others had disappeared into the afternoon. Still, Maggie felt that the day was a dream.

"Why did you do it?" she suddenly asked, her blue-blue eyes fixed on that handsome face that was becoming very familiar to her. "Tell me that, Mister Logan? Why?"

"What do you mean, darling? I don't understand...? Are you questioning...my...motives?"

"You heard me, Mister Logan, darling. *Why* did you get yourself baptized?"

"Well...I...wished to join the church."

"You did it...just to become a member of Shiloh Baptist?"

"No, darling. I read my Bible. I gave the matter a great deal of thought...and more than a bit of prayer. Then I went beneath the waters...to signify to the world that I am a true believer. Reborn. An eternal creature. A member of the family of God. Because I would not miss for the entire world…being with you…not just upon this earth…but throughout…all eternity. Do you think, my sweet, that my…motivations…will suffice?"

"Yes, Mr. Logan." Maggie whispered through her tears. "Those will suffice…quite nicely."

Chapter 42

They sat on the back porch of the inn. Maggie could *feel* the date marked on her Grier's Almanac calendar creeping up on her, almost as if the date was a living, breathing creature, slowly stalking her. And nothing had been settled…about Barbara Jo. Maggie snapped a string bean with a smart flip of her wrist, and dropped the pieces into the huge dishpan that stood waiting. "Have you decided, then, Barbs," Maggie prompted her sister in a curt voice, "what, exactly, you're going to do with…your property? Your house? Fix it up? Move back in?"

"I don't know, Maggs." Barbara Jo lifted one thin hand and flicked a lock of light hair from off her forehead. Maggie had noted that since Barbara Jo had been diligently shampooing her hair in *Octagon* soap, and applying the cider vinegar rinses, her long tresses had lost their drab brown color, and had lightened to a becoming deep-gold blond.

"Well, Barbs, have you…" Maggie paused, a snap bean held firmly in her hand, staring at Barbara Jo. "What I mean to say is…"

"I know exactly what you mean to say, Maggs. And to be quite honest with you, I have not the slightest notion what I should do. Thomas thinks…"

"Thomas? You've been…discussing…your problems…with…Thomas?"

"Well…yes…you said…I mean…Thomas *has* offered to look into getting the place repaired. So that I could…do something with it. I…mean…it's certainly no good to anyone in its present condition. And Thomas says that it would be a shame to let a fine property like that just rot and fall in. Thomas says…"

"Yes, Barbs, go on….what is…it…exactly…that Thomas Beyers has to say…about your property?"

"Thomas says I should fix it up. And either…move back into it…or put it up for sale…and make…other living arrangements."

"Other…living…arrangements? Barbs, are you attempting to tell me…that *Thomas Beyers*…is interested in…assisting you…in making…other living arrangements? I know that the two of you have been sitting at the kitchen table, your heads together over this or that book…after Thomas completes his teaching sessions with Liza Mae and Benjamin Noah. But I…had…no idea…how long has *this* been going on?"

"Nothing…is…*going on*, Maggs! You do have a most *awful* way of putting things! You sound as if…Thomas Beyers…and I…were…"

"Well, Barbs. How…*are* you…and Thomas Beyers? Are you friends? More than friends? Has he…said…something…anything…?"

"Maggs! No! Of course not! You know Thomas! He…well…sometimes…he…"

"Talks to you? Smiles at you? Touches your hand? Any of that?"

"He…I think…he…likes me…Maggs. He hasn't said this, in so many words, you understand. But…he has been asking me to walk with him, sometimes. And he has sat with me in church…several times…I don't know…I think…he might like me…just a little." Barbara Jo's thin face flushed a rosy pink beneath the sprinkling of gold freckles across her cheeks and nose. "At least, I think he does," she concluded lamely. "I don't know that much about…such things."

"Well, I'm sure there's quite a lot I may not know…about…such things…but I do know this, Barbs. When a man sits with a woman in church, when he requests the pleasure of her company, to walk with her, it means just *that,* Barbs. Thomas Beyers takes pleasure in your company."

"You…really…think so?"

"I know it, my sweet sister. And you should listen to Thomas Beyers. He is a well-educated man. He has a fine head on those broad shoulders of his. He could be…"

"He could be what, Maggs?" Barbara Jo fixed Maggie with a narrowed gaze.

Maggie stared back at her sister just as intently, "He could be the thread of gold that God is attempting to weave into what you consider to be the drab fabric of your life, Barbara Jo McKinnon Moss!"

"What, *exactly*, is going on?...between your sister...and the schoolmaster, Beyers?" Bart gazed over at Maggie, as they sat on the front veranda of the inn, watching the sun sinking behind the western rim of the Blue Ridge Mountains.

"Whatever do you mean?" Maggie ceased the motion of her rocking chair, and stared at Bart Logan with wide, innocent blue eyes.

Bart leaned forward in his rocker, elbows on his knees, and stared back, "You know exactly what I mean, my sweet. I mean, what is going on...between your widowed brother-in-law, and your sister, Mrs. Barbara Jo McKinnon Moss?"

"Have you...heard...something?"

"I don't have to *hear* anything, to know that something is afoot between those two. I do have eyes in my head. Your sister has abandoned her bed of suffering, and has blossomed forth like a rose in summer. They have been seen taking the evening air together, more times than a few. As they are even now...*this* very evening, in the process of doing. And, I don't know whether or not you may have noticed, but *Mister* Thomas Beyers has chosen, at church, in the past few weeks, to abandon his customary seat on the *right* side of the aisle. He has, in fact, crossed the single aisle of the church, and has moved himself, very discreetly, to the left, so that he sits, more often than not, either just behind or beside your sister. Mister Beyers even approached me one day last week, asking about the current prices of lumber, roofing shingles, and so forth, along with labor estimates, to do the requisite repairs to Mrs. Moss's damaged residence, to make the place inhabitable once again. Now, tell me one thing, my sweet, since I see your sister on a *very* regular basis, at least once every week and oftentimes more frequently than that, why didn't *she* approach me on this matter of such personal importance and financial import?"

"I am quite sure, Mister Logan, darling, that I would not have the faintest notion. My sister discusses none of her business with me. Barbara Jo did happen to mention, quite in passing, that she...that they...that Thomas..."

"Yes, my sweet? Are we then, to have a double wedding?"

"I don't believe things have progressed...quite to that point!" Maggie stared at Bart Logan as if he had lost all reason. "After all...Fred Moss has only been gone..."

"Oh…yes… How heedless of me. How could I forget…the grieving widow does have to observe…the proper mourning period. How long was that? I forget. Wasn't it…?"

"You know exactly how long it is, Mister Logan. So wipe that silly smirk off your face, and tell me—word for word—what you told Thomas Beyers!"

"About what?"

"Ohhhh! *The repairs to Barbs' house!*"

"Oh. That. I had Tad Horton bring down a load of—"

"She's really doing it! She's really *doing* something with the house?!"

"Yes, my sweet, she is. Or should I say, *they* are. Thomas Beyers is the one who showed up to receive the lumber…and I might add…Mister Beyers counted every board, and then rendered payment for it. All of which leads me to believe that the schoolmaster holds more than a passing interest…in the repairs. Now, what the two of them plan to do with the place… *that* you shall have to ask your dear sister."

Chapter 43

Maggie awoke with a start. Her head began to pound. Her vision blurred so that she could scarcely see the familiar rock fireplace, as she hauled herself into a sitting position on the softness of the feather mattress and then swung her legs over the side of the bed to let her toes dangle against the familiar warmth of the braided rag rug.

It can't be!...she moaned to herself...but then her logical brain added...*but it is!*

It's the last Sunday in the month of May!

Her heart racing, Maggie pushed herself to her feet. She wasn't quite sure how, but she had slept as if she'd been hit over the head with a heavy timber. How could she?! When today was her wedding day?!

Maggie sat very still for a few moments, willing her heart to cease its harsh thudding, willing her vision to clear so that the rocks of the fireplace came into clear focus. She could hear a flurry of activity. People were scurrying like mice along the hall just outside her door. Was that an iron skillet banging against the cast-iron of the big black stove in the kitchen? Did someone drop a huge pan, and send waves of sound reverberating throughout the entire inn? What on earth was going on?!

Maggie drew on a faded robe, stuck her feet into light leather slippers, and went padding over to the door, down the hall, and then the stairs. By the time she had crossed the dining room and opened the kitchen door, all activity seemed to have ceased.

Liza Mae stood at the black iron stove, as round as she was tall. Benjamin Noah turned from the dry sink, where he had just deposited a wooden bucket filled with fresh well water. Johnny and Barbara Jo sat staring down at their plates of sausage, grits and eggs. It was just a morning. Just a normal morning. Like every other morning since she opened The Sparrow—

But…no…it was not. On the meal chest in the corner stood a huge cake. Beside it rested jugs and jugs of punch. Stacks of plates set at the ready beside the cake. Rows of glasses sparkled beside the punch jugs. A pile of forks…

Maggie mumbled, "Good mornin'." She sank down onto the bench beside Johnny, who stared up at her with eyes as wide as ever she'd seen them, and as blue and deep as the ocean.

"What's wrong, sweetie?" Maggie muttered, "All that looks mighty good to me. Why aren't you eating it? Why is everyone suddenly not eating…and staring at me!?"

"No…reason," Barbara Jo muttered, ducking her head and making at her scrambled eggs like a starving person. Maggie saw Johnny give a start, and knew her sister had given her small brother a non-to-gentle nudge beneath the battered top of the kitchen table.

"What is wrong with you people?!" Maggie demanded. "This is… just…another day…now, Liza Mae, would you kindly pour me some hot coffee, and then come and sit yourself down? And Benjamin Noah, have you spread the new table cloths on *all* the tables in the dining room? And…have the extra tables been set up on the back porch, in the event we have an overflow…we are….after all…expecting…" Maggie stopped talking, took two or three bites of her breakfast, then she leapt up and fled up the stairs.

"Whut does you think?" Liza Mae asked of no one in particular. *"You think* Mizzz Maggie fer shore gwin' ta' go throu' wif' it?"

"Of course," Barbara Jo snapped tartly. "Maggie doesn't know it yet, but she's *madly* in love with William Bartram Logan."

Somehow the morning passed. Maggie had bathed, dressed, and walked to church with Mister William Bartram Logan. She had sat, very sedately, if she did say so herself, on the bench beside the man, as the hymns and the sermon rose and floated about her as if in some dream world. Then they were up, walking out of the little church, every board and log and plank of which were as familiar to her as her own hands. In only a few hours, she would make a trip back into the church…

She wouldn't think about that now. That was *hours* off! She would hang on to Bartram Logan on one side, and to Johnny on the other, and she would walk the short distance back to the inn. Then they would all sit down to a lunch that Liza Mae and Barbara Jo had prepared...

Lunch?! How could she possibly think of eating *lunch?! She had scarcely touched her breakfast! And her stomach was lurching and roiling...!* She felt Bart Logan's hand, large and warm, enfolding hers, and her stomach seemed to settle a bit.

Lunch passed. She made her way up the stairs to her room, where she stood beholding her image in the mirror. Some person she did not even recognize stared back at her. She was twenty-one years old. Her eyes were wide and blue, her skin creamy and fair; hair hung in thick, dark tendrils past thin shoulders. How could she look so young, when she felt that she had lived a thousand years!? Vivid images of another wedding day, when she was a girl-child of sixteen, intruded themselves into her mind. What was she doing?! Should she do this?! *Could she do this?!*

Then Barbara Jo was beside her, getting her out of her plain church dress, and into the simple but elegant gown of dark blue silk she and Barbs had chosen as her wedding dress...in that fancy shop on Oxford Street, in London...then Barbs was fiddling with her hair. Instructing her to slip on the satin slippers dyed to match the dress.

Suddenly Maggie put up both her hands. Pushing Barbara Jo away, Maggie sank down on the bed. She was on the verge of tears. Torn between elation...and despair....

"I...I can't...Barbs! *I...can't...*"

"*Oh...yes...you can!*" Barbara Jo ordered in a strident voice. "You can! And you will! I will not...I simply...*will not*...let you ruin the rest of your life...do you hear me, Maggie? That man waiting for you down at the church loves you past all understandin'! And you love that man more than your own life! And why don't you go ahead and just admit it!? Remember what you told me, about God creating the first pair, there in the Garden of Eden? Well, Maggie, my dear, sweet, frightened sister...what if God created *this* moment...and *this* man...just...for you...? Can you fling God's wondrous gift back in his face?! Well?! Can you?!"

Bart stood waiting, his heart in his mouth. He had never, in his deepest heart of hearts, believed that this moment would actually arrive. But here it was. No. Here she was. She was moving towards him, a vision in blue silk that made her eyes look deep as sapphire. Her hair was piled atop her head in a dark, shining halo wound with some sort of flowers and ribbons to match the dress. Lovely slippers, peeking from beneath the floating volume of the skirt, perfectly matched the dress. Then he realized...she had bought this dress, the slippers, the ribbons, in London. Especially for this moment. And they were perfect. She was perfect.

Then she was standing before him, and the good Reverend Whitcomb was speaking the words that would join them for all eternity.

On Bart Logan's arm, Maggie floated down the aisle of the church, and out into the brightness of a May afternoon. The grand carriage waited, the matched bays chomping and tossing their magnificent heads, as if anxious to be off.

Where are we going? Maggie wanted to ask. But no. She was afraid to ask. She had not asked before. And she had not asked this time.

Bart Logan was lifting her into the carriage. They would, of course, be going to The Sparrow. Everyone had been invited—to attend a reception. Of course, how silly of her. This was not like the other time. This was different. She was not in some strange town. She was at home, in Rhyersville.

Bart pulled the carriage up before the inn, tied the team to the oak hitching post, and lifted Maggie down. They were up the steps, across the front veranda, and into the dining room. Friends and acquaintances, their faces warm and familiar and filled with good cheer, crowded in, clapping them on the back, grasping their hands. Dr. Ellis gave Maggie a wet kiss on the cheek, his bushy gray beard and mustache tickling her chin. Maggie thought he looked as regal as General Robert E. Lee. Then Silas Crocker came limping by on his new artificial leg, though he still was forced to rely heavily on his crutch. Next came the preacher, the good Reverend Whitcomb, face fresh and young for a pastor, grasping their hands with a sure, firm clasp. Then Thomas Beyers, holding Maggie close, but not too close. It was, Bart thought to himself, a rather brotherly kiss Thomas Beyers bestowed on Bart's new wife, for Thomas Beyers had Barbara Jo on his arm. Johnny came bouncing up, to be lifted into Bart's waiting arms.

The dining room of The Sparrow filled to overflowing. Punch flowed and cake was sliced. Little sandwiches of some sort appeared along with the cake and punch, and Maggie, who was ravenous, talked and laughed, and stuffed herself with sandwiches and cake. Then Silas Crocker propped his lean frame against a table and surprised them all by producing a homemade flute from his back pocket, and piping a lovely tune. Soon a banjo or two joined in, along with a fiddle and a juice harp.

When the sun began to sink to the west, the music ceased. Folks began to saunter by, offering their best wishes, and their farewells. Kisses for Maggie; handshakes for Bart. And they drifted away. Maggie went upstairs to her room, to change into a comfortable frock. She looked for something into which she could change, but all of her things seemed to have...disappeared! Vanished! Everything was gone! It had all been here this morning!

She clomped back downstairs.

Bart Logan stood staring at her, as she descended the stairs, still in her wedding gown. "Ready to go, darling?" he grinned up at her.

"Go? Where? I assumed we would be staying *here*. No one said *anything*...you said *nothing* to me...about...going...*anywhere*!"

"It's not that far," Bart Logan grinned at her.

Suddenly Maggie went cold, rigid as an ice icicle. Where had she heard *that* before!?

Bart Logan led her out of the inn, to the carriage, where the magnificent team waited impatiently.

Bart was lifting her in, stepping lithely up beside her. Maggie had the almost overwhelming urge to bolt down from the grand carriage, and flee up the rutted dirt street...still in her wedding dress...

Bart was turning the team, heading down the slope towards the schoolhouse... what on earth...where was the man going? Had he lost all reason? Then he was passing the schoolhouse, turning down the narrow lane into the big meadow...

...Where sat the huge log house.

Maggie turned to stare at Bart. He had leapt off the carriage seat, strode around, and stood waiting to lift her down. Her mouth hung open. Her eyes were wide and staring.

In one swift motion he lifted her down into his arms, turned, carried her up the low steps, across the broad veranda, pushed open the door, and stepped inside. As he stood holding her, her arms tight about his neck, Maggie gazed about her, past the spacious entryway, on into the main parlor.

A gigantic rock fireplace spanned the center of the east wall. On one side of the fireplace rested the bulk of Katherine Ann's big brown leather trunk. On the other side stood the great pipe organ Papa had won for her in the log-splitting contest at the Hiawassee Mountain Fair…

"Welcome home, darling," Bart whispered.

––––––––––––

Maggie awoke to sun streaming in the window. Her eyes fluttered open, and scanned the interior of the room. *Where on earth was she!?* Then the memories came streaming back.

She was married! To William Bartram Logan!

Suddenly her new husband appeared framed in the doorway, white shirt open at the neck, bearing in his tanned hands a heavily laden tray that emitted delicious scents.

"Well," Bart smiled at her, "I see, my dear sweet Mrs. Logan, that you are at last awake! Hungry, darling?"

Maggie recovered her senses, and asked tartly, "And since when, Mr. Logan, did you learn to cook?"

"Well, my sweet, I believe my adventure into cookery was forced upon me by the sudden and precipitous departure of my camp cook…some months past. For no apparent reason that I could find, she simply fled the logging camp in a tiff, leaving behind her a gaggle of starving men, myself, unfortunately included amongst them. And in fear of my health, and indeed my very life, I took to creeping into the camp shack in the dead of night, striking up a fire, brewing myself up a decent cup of coffee, stirring myself up a hoecake and a few eggs. That alone has helped me to survive, lo, these many months. Would you care to join me, my sweet?"

Bart had settled himself, cross-legged on the foot of the bed, and sat staring intently at Maggie, the tray resting precariously on his knees between them.

"If I refuse, I fear I shall soon find myself covered in—"

"Now, now. None of that. Be nice to me. After all, I did fix you your first breakfast here at *The Meadows*."

"Oh, so," Maggie muttered biting into the delicious buttered bread, "it's *The Meadows*, now, then, is it?"

"Oh, yes. You've been calling the place that, from the first. Remember?"

"I have? Well, and all this time I was totally unaware. In point of fact, I was totally unaware—"

"That, my dearest one," Bart muttered, taking a sip of hot coffee, "is the entire idea behind a surprise?...is it not?"

"*The Meadows...*" Maggie murmured between bites of the hot buttered hoecake and the delicious scrambled eggs. "I had thought that perhaps we might... you might... have wished to take up residence...at Cottonwood?"

"Would you rather have awakened at Cottonwood this morning, my sweet, than here at The Meadows?" Bart asked, staring straight into her eyes, his coffee cup balanced on one knee.

"No," Maggie replied.

"And why not?"

"Well...Cottonwood is...a bit far out of town...from..."

"And Cottonwood is a bit of the past, right?"

"What do you intend doing...with...Cottonwood?"

"You know that Lady Marilyn is living there full time...now that Giles has been assigned there more and more, you understand. And Giles informs me that Lady Marilyn has taken more and more to bringing the people of Logan Town into the big house, for medical care, and I believe I've been informed that she's also been doing a bit of teaching and training...the children, you know. And, actually, anyone of any age who wishes to attend these...sessions...of drawing and letters...is more than welcome."

"Marilyn is establishing a school...of learning...and art...at Cottonwood?"

"It does sound like it, doesn't it? The place was, after all, *built* by slaves. And I think it most fitting that now...after all that has happened...freed slaves and their descendents reap some sort of...benefit...from all that labor."

"Well, what about...McKinnon Valley?" Maggie asked.

"That's for *you* to say, my sweet. McKinnon Valley is yours. Would you rather have awakened this morning in McKinnon Valley?" Bart asked.

"Waking there would be…nice…for a few mornings…but McKinnon Valley, is…so much has happened there…"

"And McKinnon Valley is also a part of the past. Yet, I know you wish to keep it…"

"Oh, yes, I most assuredly do, Mister Logan, darling. It's Johnny's heritage."

"Exactly. And The Meadows will be the heritage of *our* children." Bart whispered, his voice gruff with emotion.

"Yes," Maggie whispered back, "And it's…perfect."

"I'm so glad, and would you care for another cup—"

"No you don't, Mister Logan, darling!" Before Bart could catch her, she leapt from the bed, coffee cup in hand, raced out the door and down the broad oak staircase, towards the kitchen, Bart right behind her, crying as he ran, "Why is it, my sweet, that you never allow anyone to—"

Reaching the last step, Maggie halted, whirled and stood gazing up at him, "Because, Mister Logan, darling, I am *perfectly* capable of waiting upon myself! Now, when I get to the point where I am no longer capable of doing so, then you, or someone else, can fetch and carry for me!"

"I hope that will be…soon. I'd love to see you incapacitated," Bart stood four steps above her, grinning down.

"You'd…*what?* That's…a *horrid* thing to say!"

"Well, I do understand that childbearing puts a woman off her feet…at least for the space of—"

"Oh, well. Yes. That," Maggie mumbled, glancing down at her satin-slippered toes, feeling her face grow hot. "When…and if…"

"Not if…just when," Bart stepped down, caught her, picked her up in his arms, and carried her into the sunlit kitchen. "Well!" he gasped, turning to peer out the rear kitchen windows after plunking Maggie unceremoniously down onto a finely carved oak chair. "Will you just look at that…!"

"What is it?" Maggie leapt up to join her husband at the long row of eastward facing windows. "Why…it's a log house…a small replica…of this one! Who on earth…? What on earth…?"

"Well," Bart Logan ran a tanned hand over the dark stubble on his chin, "When you do become…indisposed…when children come…you *will* be needing help…close by…"

"And just who…Mister Logan, darling…is to supply this…help?" Maggie demanded. "I simply will not have…some *stranger*…"

"How about…Bethany Lee? She's certainly no stranger."

"*Bethany Lee?* But…she's as lazy as the day is long! And she married the McAlister boy. Sam. And they're living…back of the mercantile…"

"Well, my love, I have been given to understand that since becoming a married woman, living in the safety of her own home, Bethany Lee has undergone an amazing transformation. As industrious as a bee, I am told. And she…they…won't actually be moving into the little log house…not for at least a week. I told them to give us at least a week. To settle into the place. Is that all right with you, my sweet?" Bart drew Maggie close, nuzzling her neck as she stood peering at the charming little log house.

"What can I say, Mister Logan? That you are an amazingly brilliant person? The most generous, most…the absolutely most perfect of husbands? I mean…what do you expect me to say, Mister Logan, darling?"

"Any *one* of those, my sweet, would be fine. You don't have to pile it on *too* thick. Wouldn't want to give me a puffed up head, or anything like that, now would you?"

"No! Of course, not!" Maggie pulled out of his embrace, plunked herself back down at the kitchen table, banged her cup on the polished oak, and ordered sternly, "More coffee, if you please, Mister Logan. And how about poking up that fire, while you're at it. Get at it, now! Don't want the coffee going cold on us, now do we? "

They wandered the meadow in their bare feet. They waded far down the creek; then climbed out onto the grassy bank to sit and allow their feet to dry in the sun. Then they raced back to the huge log house, to drink cold buttermilk and eat fried chicken, snap beans, and potato salad that had miraculously appeared on the kitchen table during their prolonged absence.

"The place is haunted, you realize that, don't you, Mister Logan?" Maggie muttered to Bart as they sat munching on the food.

"Yes, that may well be true, but at least the ghosts, or whatever they are, have the good sense to make themselves scarce, except, it would appear, at mealtime. As I did make it clear…"

"Yes, Mister Logan?"

"I did make it clear, my sweet, that we were *not* to be disturbed for the space of at least one week."

"One week, is it? I'm not to see my brother or my sister for one week? Is that what I'm to understand, then, Mister Logan, darling?"

"Well, Mrs. Logan, those were the *explicit* instructions I left. But if you feel the overwhelming desire to escape…me…and to go racing up the hill to town, I shall not in any shape, form, or fashion make any attempt, or put forth the least bit of effort, to stop you. Do you think you will be escaping into town any time soon?"

"Perhaps not. Not for…at least…a week. I did tell you, didn't I…"

"Yes, you did. But it's perfectly all right, if you want to tell me again…and then, again. I can always go and wrap my head up in a turban, or put on a tight-fitting hat to hold down the—"

Had he not ducked, and very quickly, Bart would have been hit by that fast flying biscuit that leapt out of Maggie's hand and went sailing across the kitchen table. Then, a startled look on her beautiful face, Maggie let out a squeal, and was up out of her chair in a flash, and dashing out the kitchen door, and across the meadows…

Chapter 44

"What do you think, my sweet?" Bart Logan whispered into Maggie's ear. Her hair, he noticed, hung in damp tendrils about that most beautiful of faces, and her usually rosy cheeks were pale as snow. "What shall we name him?"

"I was thinking of Ian Bartram Logan. What do you think of that, Mister Logan, darlin'?"

"Ian?"

"Yes, you know, Ian is the Scottish form of John...?"

"Oh, yes, of course. Frankly, my sweet...I think Ian Bartram Logan is just perfect."

"Well! Thank the Good Lord! Finally! We can agree on something!"

"At this particular moment, Maggie McKinnon Logan," Bart whispered, with one fingertip tenderly pushing the tendrils of damp hair off her forehead, "I would have agreed to almost anything. You could have named him....Jonas Trap—"

"*Jonas Trap*—?!" Maggie squealed.

"It's...a joke—"

"I *must* say, Mister Logan, darling, oftentimes you do have the most *peculiar* sense of humor."

"I know, dearest, but it's one of the things you love about me, now come on, and admit that it is?"

"Oh, all right. I find you an absolute *riot*! A *clown* in the nth degree! You keep me in *stitches*...ninety percent of the time! Now, are you satisfied, Mister Logan?"

"Hmmm....maybe I'd better... just go and put on my turban. What do you think? And can I carry Ian Bartram along with me? And show him off to all those poor souls waiting downstairs, drooling piteously and with their tongues hanging out in anticipation?"

"Well…" Maggie gazed down at the baby boy swaddled in the crook of her arm. She lifted one finger and drew it across the warm softness of his tiny cheek. And at this moment, she felt that that was about all she could do. But never…never…in her entire life had she been happier. He was perfect. And he was hers. Hers…and Bart Logan's. He looked, bless his little heart, exactly like his father. "I wonder, she mused," flashing Bart a brilliant smile, "I wonder whether little Ian will possess his father's *fine* sense of humor…"

"You never quit, do you?" Bart bent and kissed her full on the mouth, "Give me my son, and you…my fine wife…lay back now and rest. I'll send someone up—"

"No," Maggie murmured, reaching out and laying a hand on his tanned arm, "don't you *dare* send anyone up. You just come back up…yourself, Mister Logan, and bring our son back with you."

"And Johnny?"

"Yes, of course, Johnny."

Chapter 45

"What on earth is this? Does anyone know where this came from?"

Maggie picked up the small package, wrapped snugly in brown paper, and tied with a soiled piece of cotton twine. "Liza Mae? Do you know what this is? Who left it here? Is it perhaps yours?"

"Whut be dat, Mizz Maggie? I's don't ever seed that lil' thin' before. Why don't youse jes' open it up! And see whut it be?" Liza Mae, her little son, Willie Noah Daniels, held across her right hip, stood frowning at the little bundle.

"All right, then, since no one seems to lay claim to it, let us just see here. Give me a knife, Liza Mae. This twine is wrapped tight as…"

When Maggie snipped the cotton twine, the brown paper fell open…revealing a stack of bills.

"Why! Lok'it dat, Mizz Maggie! It be a whole bunch o' monies! How much you 'speck dat be?"

"I…have no idea, Liza Mae, until I count it…let me see, it's exactly—one hundred…and fifty…one…two…three…*one hundred and fifty-three dollars! Dear Lord!* And what is that odd scent? *Pipe tobacco?!*"

"Whut da matter, Mizz Maggie? You don' turned white as cotton 'bout da mouf!"

"One hundred and fifty-three dollars, Liza Mae! It's…the exact amount…Papa got for the cotton crop!" Maggie's hands began to tremble. She flung the badly soiled, odd-smelling bills onto the scarred oak tabletop and stood staring at it, as if it would jump off the table at any moment, and bite her—

—The exact amount! Where did it come from? How did it get here?

Her head in a whirl, her knees quaking, Maggie stared at the money for a moment, raised a hand to push the hair back from her face, then she backed away from the table, spun, pushed open the door, and fled into the dining room. She yanked a chair up before the fireplace and sank into it, hands clasped in her lap, rocking slightly back and forth, attempting to warm herself, still the hammering of her heart, collect her senses, stop the awful quaking of her insides. *Papa's cotton money?! After all these years, how could it be? How could it simply appear on the kitchen table of The Sparrow?! Where did it come from?*

Maggie sat for several minutes, her heart and mind racing. Then she collected herself. She would go back into the kitchen, pick up the brown paper wrapping, and check to see…if there was anything to indicate where it came from, where the money came from. Yes, that's exactly what she would do.

Back in the kitchen, she stood staring down at the table, the money. She reached out a trembling hand, and picked up the brown paper. With both hands, she spread it out on the table. There, scribbled in a barely legible black charcoal scrawl…two words:

Am sorrie

Sorrie? Sorry? I'm sorry!

Sorry, is he! Sorry! Maggie shot out a hand, snatched up the offending bills, and flung them with such fury they scattered like the wind, into every corner of the kitchen. Then she whirled about. Giving a loud screech, she fled the kitchen, flew upstairs to the first room and fell across the bed. She wanted to cry and scream and bang her fists on something, on somebody…on the person who had taken Papa's cotton money…and left him sick and drunk and in the rain…left him to sicken and fade and die, a beaten man with a broken heart. Now, all these years later, he—whoever *he* is— wishes to salve his guilty conscience. To return the money. To apologize. To say he's sorry! *Sorry!!!!??*

Such anger, such cold rage rose up in Maggie that it frightened her. She thought of all the terrible things she could *do* to this person…if only she could reach him…could get her hands on him…! *Papa!!*

"Mizz Maggie? Is you aw'rite?" It was Liza Mae, worried about her, at the door.

"*Go away, Liza Mae!* I'll…talk to you…later!"

"Yes'm." Liza Mae's footsteps faded.

"Margaret Ann?" Bart was pushing open the door, crossing the room, reaching and drawing her into his arms. "What is it, sweetheart?"

It rushed out of her. The whole sad story. All of the pent up rage. The hurt. The hatred.

"I'm...*awful*...aren't I?" she sobbed into Bart's jacket front. "I shouldn't *feel* this way about another human being. No matter who. No matter what...he's done. I shouldn't *feel* this way!"

"It's all right, darling. It's perfectly natural. You're human, just like all the rest of us. Rage at him. Rant at him. Get it out of your system."

"I don't *want* the filthy money!" she wailed. "What is *one hundred and fifty three dollars to me now? Papa is gone!*" she sobbed. "I wish he hadn't returned it! Not after all these years! I wish he'd thrown it into the fire! I want him to be *sick*, and to *suffer*, and to *pay* the way *Papa paid!*"

"You don't mean that. But the money belongs to you, and Barbara Jo, and Johnny. He did the right thing. Whoever he is...he *has* paid. Then finally, he mustered up the courage, and he did the right thing, no matter how long it has taken him to do it. No matter how many days and nights he stared into the fire, like a worm writhing in his own pit of hot ashes."

"You...think so?" she stared up at him through her tears. "But...I *don't* want the money," she insisted. "I don't ever want to *see* it again!"

"Then give it to Barbara Jo and Johnny. It was their Papa's. Now it belongs to them. Your Papa worked hard for that money. He would want it that way."

"I don't ever want to *see* that money again. I don't want to *touch* it! To *smell* his filthy hands on it!"

"I'll go down and gather it up. Put it away until you can speak with your sister."

But when Barbara Jo, sitting at the kitchen table of the inn having a morning cup of coffee with Bart and Maggie, heard the startling news of the sudden appearance of the cotton money, she wagged her head, and refused to have any part of it. "I didn't earn one cent of that money," she insisted. "Give it to Johnny."

"I'll take it down to the bank, and open an account in Johnny's name, if you'd like, if the both of you agree. It will simply sit and draw interest. Then when Johnny is of age, he can decide for himself, what to do with it. It will be something from his father. I think your father would like that." Bart looked from Maggie to Barbara Jo.

"Yes, do that," Maggie nodded her head, "Barbs?"

"I think that's…the best solution."

"Good," Bart nodded and pulled a solemn little grin, "Yes, I believe John Thomas McKinnon, Sr., would greatly admire the idea of helping to set his son up in his first medical practice. And then, Margaret Ann, we will put the matter to rest. No staying awake nights, wondering. No watching folks on the street, puzzling as to whether it was this man or that. Not another word about it. Agreed?"

"Of course, Mr. Logan, darling, but I just wonder…" Maggie tilted her head aside and mused softly, "*if* it *might* be… No! It couldn't *possibly* be *him*. But what about…ummmmm…I won't think that. If *he* did it, I don't want to know…or I fear…I could never… *never*…forgive him…but…could it be…?"

"Well," Bart sighed, "so much for putting the matter to rest, eh, my sweet?"

"What did you say, Mr. Logan? I have *completely* forgotten what it was we were even speaking about!"

Chapter 46

Slowly, one by one, the bright green sweet peas hit the kitchen floor.

"Young sir!" Maggie announced sternly, hands on hips, "These sweet peas are for putting in that cute little mouth! Not bouncing off the kitchen floor! Whatever am I to do with you?"

"Maybe…if you…" Barbara Jo, seeing the look in Maggie's eyes, halted in mid-sentence. "I was only…trying to help," she finished lamely, covering her mouth with one hand to muffle the giggles.

"Well, I *know*, Barbs," Maggie began tartly, "that you are a *bottomless reservoir* of useful information on the care and training of children! I'm sorry, Barbs. I didn't mean—"

Barbara Jo removed her hand from her mouth and said solemnly, "Never mind. I'm not offended. Not offended at all, Maggs. Mayhap…I might have been…a few months back. But now—"

Maggie stared at her sister open-mouthed. "And just what, if I may make so bold as to ask, Mrs. Thomas Beyers, is so different *now*…?"

"Well, if you *must* know, Miss Busybody…" Barbara Jo tucked a strand of gold-blond hair behind her ear and cast her eyes down to the cold cup of coffee resting before her on the scarred oak table. Then she looked up, "*Now* your dear, dear sister is set to give you competition…in the form of a small cousin for little Ian Bartram."

"Oh…! Barbs! I'm…speechless!" Maggie dropped into the nearest chair, reaching for Barbara Jo's hand. "This is…well, it's just…splendid! When?"

"Hopefully not until the house is finished."

"What house? Finished? Where, for goodness sakes! Tell me! *I'm dying here!*"

"Well, Maggs, it seems that Thomas purchased the land along the creek just below the schoolhouse, some years ago. In the hopes of one day building himself a house there."

"You'll be…my neighbor…! What are you doing with the yellow brick house? Thomas has it all fixed up. I thought for certain…?"

"No. Maggs, I don't think I could…I wouldn't want to rear my family in that house. It holds…too many…memories. Thomas and I, we want a place that's ours. We want to make our own memories."

"That's exactly what Mister Logan gave as the reason for building The Meadows," Maggie muttered.

"And Bart's right, Maggs."

"What are you doing, then, with the yellow brick house?"

"It's up for sale. Not much of a market, though, in Rhyersville. Most of the folks who live here have been here for all their entire lives, and they're settled in their own places. Who knows when, or if, the house will sell?"

"That's not at all true, and you know it, Barbs! Look how the town has grown. Of course, it will sell!" Maggie encouraged her sister, "Look at how Logan Town is growing. And folks are coming through Rhyersville on their way to the furniture works there. So someone will see it, and want to buy it. It's a lovely house. A grand house."

"Maybe *too* grand for anybody in Rhyersville, I'm afraid," Barbara Jo sighed.

"She's back…at th' front doh', Mizzzz Maggie. Says she wonts ta' talk wif' you." Liza Mae, having just deposited Willie Noah Daniels down for his nap, stood frowning grumpily in the kitchen door.

"Just a moment, Liza Mae." Maggie lifted the tiny boy with the mop of dark hair down from the highchair, and set his small feet on the wood planking of the kitchen floor. Ian Bartram Logan grinned up at his mother, his hazel eyes flecked with gold wide beneath long dark lashes. "Don't give me that mischievous look of your father's young man," Maggie warned, giving the little boy a firm kiss on the forehead. Then she called:

"Johnny! Come here for a moment, please!"

"What's wrong, Maggie?" Johnny stuck his head in the back door.

"What have you been doing, Johnny?" Maggie demanded, "And are your hands clean?"

"I…was…just…"

"With that look on your face, don't tell me. I'm not sure I want to know. Just go and wash your hands, will you? Then keep an eye on your nephew here. Can you do that for me, please?"

"Sure, Maggie! I'd love to watch little Eeeeeeannn!"

"Good," Maggie muttered over her shoulder as she left the kitchen, "And don't let him pull the water bucket down on his head, or fall into the wood box, or anything? All right?"

"Maggie!"

"Mrs…Evans?! What a…pleasant…surprise. What…ever are you doing…back…in Rhyersville? Oh, won't you come into the parlor… and…take a seat. We have a fire going in there. You must be tired. Is it still cold outside? It was freezing out there this morning…Can I take your cloak…?"

"I received a letter," Maggie's former mother-in-law whispered in a soft, shy voice as she sank down to the cushioned settee near the fireplace.

"A…letter?" Maggie sat down in a nearby rocker and leaned close, "May…I inquire…from whom…you got this letter?… that brought you… back to Rhyersville?"

"Why, from *Jeremiah*, of course," Ida Evans said in her soft, gentle way.

"Jeremiah…?" Maggie wagged her head in complete confusion. "Do I…know…Jeremiah…?"

"Well, of course you do, Maggie. Doctor Jeremiah Ellis!"

"Dr.….Ellis? I had no idea…I mean…that….*Jeremiah*…was his Christian name. I have known Dr. Ellis all my life. I don't recall ever having heard his given name, or if I did…which I most certainly … probably… did… it slipped my mind completely. And you say…that Dr…*Jeremiah*…Ellis has been…writing to you?"

"Oh, yes! I do believe that Jeremiah is very lonely. Has in fact, been lonely for many years now. I sensed that in the man, immediately I met him."

"You…met…Dr. Ellis…?" Maggie stammered.

"Well, of course I did, dear. Right here, in this very inn. He was here for dinner…several times while I was visiting you, remember? And then, there was that day I was not feeling particularly well…and you carried me to Jeremiah's office…" Ida Evans smiled, and Maggie realized how blind she had been. This was not an aged woman. No, Ida Evans was probably in her late forties. And now that she was no longer crushed beneath the cruel fist of Big Carl Evans, the woman had made an amazing transformation. Her thin form had somewhat filled out; her face had taken on a healthy pink; and her eyes, once such a faded green that they appeared to disappear in her pale face, had taken on a lovely color, the sprightly color of spring leaves.

"Yes," Maggie muttered, "Now that you mention it…well…what a surprise…this is. Will you…be…staying…long?" Maggie gazed at Ida Evans expectantly.

"Well, yes, dear, I suppose…I shall. You see, Jeremiah has asked…for my hand in marriage. And I have said…yes."

"Oh!" Maggie gasped, eyes wide, her chest feeling suddenly deflated, as if she could not catch a breath of air. "*Married?* You…and…Dr. Ellis? Why…that's…absolutely…astonishing! I am so…happy for you, dear Ida! God does indeed, does he not…?…work in mysterious ways!"

"Oh, yes, my dear!" Ida Evans' green eyes sparkled, a sweet smile spread over her lovely face. "He most certainly does! Who would ever have dreamed, when I came into this lovely little mountain town to view my son's grave, that I'd be coming back…to marry again. And make a new life here."

"What about your family…your daughter…"

"Oh, Geraldine. She stayed for a visit. Then she returned home to Arkansas. Or was it Mississippi? Anyhow, she's gone. And there's nothing to keep me in that empty old house. There are so many…sad…"

"Yes," Maggie reached out and took Ida's hand, "I understand. You don't need to say another word. I do understand. And…what can I say…but welcome to Rhyersville, and congratulations! Doctor *Jeremiah* Ellis…! He's such a fine, such a good…such a very fortunate man…to have found as lovely a bride as you, dearest Ida!"

"Thank you, Maggie. You are…you have always been…special to me…from that first moment I saw you."

"Yes," Maggie was able to smile, "And you, to me. Now, it appears we have a wedding to plan! But, Dr. Ellis's house, it is so small. I mean, you know…and his practice and his patients…take up the front of the little place…"

"Oh, didn't I tell you? Jeremiah is buying a larger place. You recall that fine yellow brick house, just down the street... behind that huge mercantile? I do believe he has his eye on that place. He plans to use the upstairs for living quarters, and to take the downstairs for his practice. He would have plenty of room, in that huge, fine house, he says, to put in a few beds, for patients who require overnight care... and those able to be up and about part of the time, they could lounge on the grand front veranda, or walk about the back gardens..."

"He plans on opening a... sort... of hospital...?"

"Maggie!" Johnny popped his head in the door, his little face grim, Ian firmly clutched by one small hand tottering in behind him. "Eeeeeaannnn will not do *nuthin'* I tell him to!"

"Well! So, young sir, your little nephew has a mind of his own, does he? And I wonder exactly *where* he got such a thing? Where do you suppose?"

"I don't know!" Johnny piped up in utter exasperation, "Maybe God gave it to him!"

"You think so? Is that where you got yours? Come on over here, you two, and say hello to Mrs. Ida Evans."

"Oh! Maggie!" Ida Evans' eyes grew very wide, her mouth hung open, "He's... beautiful! God has been *very good* to you!"

"Oh, yes, Mother Evans! He indeed has!"

Bart and Maggie occupied their usual pew, Bart holding Ian, while Maggie kept a sharp eye on Johnny, who, though he was all of seven years of age now, squirmed and wiggled incessantly beside her. Thomas and Barbara Jo sat behind them, Thomas holding little Robert Thomas Beyers. At the end of the same bench, Benjamin Noah sat sedately with Willie Noah perched between him and Liza Mae. A few rows back, sat Stephen and Marilyn Giles, Marilyn being large with child. Silas Crocker sat across the narrow aisle, with his daughter and her two children, Samantha and Silas Patrick. The Shiloh Baptist Church was filled to its capacity, with some folk milling about outside, as Dr. Jeremiah Ellis and Ida Evans spoke their vows. Then everyone was laughing and talking, spilling out into the sunshine warming the little mountain town. Then they all trooped in a cluster of warm bodies down to The Sparrow Inn.

"Well," Bart Logan announced to one and all, "Despite the fact that this is an occasion and a gathering of merriment and celebration, I have a very solemn announcement to make to you…one and all."

"Oh?" Maggie gazed at her handsome husband sitting at her elbow and asked, "If it is such an occasion of merriment and celebration, why would you go and spoil it, with some somber, solemn declaration?"

"Well, if…you'd…all prefer…to wait…to hear about it…?"

"Well, no. We would *not* wish to wait, Mister Logan," Maggie smiled at her husband sweetly. Bart had risen and was standing, an uncertain look on his handsome face, at the head of the table. "*Now*, Mr. Logan," Maggie continued speaking very sweetly, "now that you have opened your can of worms, so to speak, we would not prefer to wait. We are all dying…now that you have begun your solemn declaration…to hear the conclusion of the matter."

"Well! In that event, my sweet, I would hereby like to declare to you one and all that come this fall, I shall be standing for election to the State Legislature!"

"You….*what?!*" Maggie sputtered, rising with a great scraping of chair legs and a clattering of her fork. "And just *when*, Mr. Logan, did you come to this startling decision? Why am *I*, Mr. Logan, *darling,* always the last to know? Do you realize, Mr. Logan, how many nights that will take you away from…hearth and home?"

"Yes, I have given that quite a bit of thought, my dearest, but don't…you feel…that we should…discuss this…very private…matter…at…some later time…and in a…more appropriate…?"

"If you mean, Mr. Logan, do I want to wait until you can get me home, and then work your magic charms on me…before we discuss this…then no, Mr. Logan, I most certainly do not! We are amongst friends here!"

"Well, darling, then out with it. What is it you wish to say to me?"

"What I wish to say to you…Mr. William Bartram Logan, is just *this*…when the polls open, the day of the election, *if* ladies were allowed the right to vote—which as you well know, we are not—you should find me first in line to cast a ballot for you! And, should you be elected, I say…then God go with you…bless your efforts—which I am certain shall be for the good of us all—and grant you a safe and swift journey home! Now…what do you have to say to that!?"

Bart Logan stood speechless, tears in his dark eyes, but those gathered in the dining room of The Sparrow Inn were not so emotionally encumbered:

"Hear! Hear!" the citizens of Rhyersville roared in one long huzzah. And when the cheering ended, Bart made an apology to the newlyweds.

"You must excuse me, Doctor and Mrs. Ellis, for stealing the attention away from you. But I have no idea when so many of the citizens of this part of the state will be thus assembled. Again, my most humble apologies." Bart nodded his head to Dr. Ellis and Ida; then he took his seat.

Thomas Beyers gazed over at Bart and surmised softly, "I am sure that the hearts of the populace of Rhyersville and its environs are large enough, and intelligent enough, to hold the good news of your forthcoming candidacy, along with that of our joy for Dr. Ellis and dear Ida. Now, let us all raise our glasses…"

And forty or fifty glasses of punch and tea were hoisted into the air for a rousing toast—in honor of both occasions.

"Well, now that you have become a deacon of the Shiloh Baptist Church, a member of the local school board…and are standing for the legislature, what should I expect from you next, Mister Logan, darling? And shall I again…as always…be the very last to know?" Maggie asked as she snuggled in Bart's arms that night.

"Well, darling, I certainly have no wish to get you…over excited, or anything like that, not in your…very delicate condition…" Bart whispered.

"Just because we are expecting another child, Mister Logan, does not mean that I am to be shut out of all intelligent adult conversation. And, by the way, do you intend…?"

"Let's not discuss my political intentions or ambitions, right at this particular moment, my sweet. What are we going to name him?"

"Him? How on earth…why on earth would you suppose it's a *him*?"

"Because of the way he kicks. Just feel that! Did you feel that?!"

"Oh! Mister Logan! Already twice a father! Yet you *do* have a lot to learn! Now, will you kindly blow out the lamp!?"

"See? Didn't I tell you it would be a boy? So, have we settled on a name for him?"

"I do believe so. How about Caleb William?"

"Caleb…? But…there's no one in either of our families…named…Caleb!"

"Well, then, in that case," Maggie, her face damp with perspiration, cuddling the tiny boy in the crook of her arm, smiled up at her husband, "he shall be his own man. What do you think, Mister Logan, darling? Caleb William?"

"Hmmmmm…he does *look* like a Caleb, doesn't he? Wasn't he the fellow…that…?"

"Yes, indeed, he was. He was one of the two warriors who entered the Promised Land, wholly free of fear, and with a total dependence upon God."

"Hmmmmm…for such a little fellow…those are mighty big shoes to fill, don't you think?"

"Well, we shall see, Mr. Logan. We shall see. Not that the shoes of his own father aren't enough to fill…"

"I shall not ask anything of my sons, my sweet, and you know that, except that they be men of strength and integrity, and follow their own hearts—to whatever it is they wish to be."

"You harbor no dreams for them, Mister Logan? Deep in your heart? No grandiose expectations? You don't expect…say…one day…for Ian Bartram to sail for England, to take up the Estate of Windsfield, and the Title of Earl? You never harbor such thoughts, Mister Logan? That maybe small Caleb, here, might one day take over the Logan Enterprises strewn all along the Eastern Seaboard? Be honest with me, now."

"I'm…certainly…not denying…such thoughts might…occasionally cross my mind. I'm just saying…that I want them to follow whatever destiny God has in store for them. Far be it from me, my sweet, to attempt to play god myself, to cram or shove them into some life for which they do not themselves yearn. Is that honest enough for you?"

"Yes. But, you'd very much like, some day, to take the boys to England, wouldn't you? I see it in your eyes. I hear it in your voice."

"Ah, my sweet! What can I hide from you!? You read me so well! There is that magnificent college of Oxford, in—"

Maggie gave an exasperated grunt. She reached over and grasped a pillow, and hurled it with all her might at Bart's head. "He's not *an hour old*! And already you're enrolling Caleb William in *Oxford?!*"

Bart put up both hands in defense, halting the mad flight of the feather pillow.

Grabbing the pillow, he held it against his chest as a shield, "Actually, my sweet, I was thinking more of *Oxford* for Ian Bartram, and the *University of Pennsylvania* for young Caleb William here."

"Oh?! And just what did you have in mind for Johnny?"

"Oh, I thought you and he had that all settled. The Medical College of Augusta is the nearest place I know of…but if there's some other good institute that teaches the medical profession…some other place you'd rather send him…? Why are you looking at me like that?"

"And what about the *girls*?" Maggie asked tartly.

"Excuse me, dearest…but…*what girls?*"

"What about the girls?" Maggie gazed at Bart over the breakfast table.

The twins, Eleanor Ann and Kathleen Sue, age two, sat in duplicate high chairs at the end of the kitchen table. Eleanor Ann, Maggie imagined, was the spitting image of what her eldest sister, Nellie Sue, must have looked like at that age. A blond angel. And Kathleen Sue…well…Kathleen was a different story. She stared now at her mother, her blue-blue eyes narrowed, her beautiful little mouth puckered in a determined pout.

"What about them?" Bart asked, his face the perfect picture of male innocence.

"*What about them*…? Mister Logan, darling…? I did just hear you correctly, did I not? That you intend taking the entire family…on an extended holiday…to England? Did I hear you correctly, Mister Logan?"

"Well…yes…my sweet, I suppose…you did," Bart muttered.

"And…let me get this straight…Mister Logan, you expect me to travel across the vast Atlantic…with three young, rambunctious boys…and two beautiful, spoiled little girls who are not yet out of diapers…to England? Did I hear you correctly? You plan on taking the two girls? To England?"

"I don't see why not. The liners nowadays…they're equipped as well as any modern city. They have amenities on board, my sweet, that you do not have here at The Meadows. There are…"

"Never mind that, Mister Logan. Never mind all these…whatever…these… amenities… are…the girls are still too little to go…*out onto the ocean…!"*

"But…sweetheart…there will be a vast ocean liner beneath their little feet! To buoy them up! I am not expecting all of you to *swim* to Europe!"

"Ohhhhhhhhh!" Maggie moaned into her hands.

"There, there…" Bart had risen from his chair, and came to bend over Maggie. He patted her solicitously on the shoulder, then raised her face and gave her a resounding kiss. "I knew you would agree with me…my sweet…that it is a *fantastic* idea, to take the children to see the land of their—"

"*Fantastic, did you say?"* Maggie quipped.

"Just a figure of speech, my darling. We shall all have a marvelous time, believe me. And you should start packing straightaway. The ship sails, so I understand, the end of the month."

"*Kassie wants…"*

"Yes," Maggie muttered, lifting Kathleen Sue—Kassie being the name Johnny, Ian, and tiny Caleb all had tagged her—from her chair, "*Kassie always* wants something she *should not* have!"

"I wonder," Bart muttered from the doorway, a pleased little grin on his handsome face, "just *who*, Mrs. Logan, does that remind you of?"

"*You! You*…get out of here! Before I hurl this bowl of oats…what little of it that has not already hit the kitchen floor…*at your smirking face!"*

Chapter 47

They all stood solemnly about, Bart, tall, strong, a sprinkling of gray at the dark temples beneath his fine felt hat. Maggie, slender in a blue silk bonnet and dress, beautiful beyond belief. Motherhood, Bart constantly assured her, suited her so well.

Ian Bartram Logan—going on twelve years of age, tall, dark, the image of his father—just as intelligent and strong-willed and yet a gentleman to the core—stood smiling in the sun, poking his younger brother, Caleb William—going on ten, fair skinned, hair a light brown bordering on blond—playfully in the ribs. All his life Caleb William had trailed about in Ian's shadow. And he loved it. But, Caleb William had of late, Maggie noticed, begun to lay down a path of his own. While Ian walked in his father's shadow, taking a fervent interest in the family's business ventures, Caleb had begun to show an interest in growing and living things. Like Ian, when not in school, several hours each day were spent outdoors, working at chores—caring for the horses stabled in the big log barn back of The Meadows, fetching and carrying, up at the logging camp. Or in inclement weather, stocking shelves at the mercantile, or out at the furniture works at Logan Town, sweeping up or carting away scraps and shavings.

Though they were but boys, Bart insisted that his sons, as well as Johnny, not idle their hours away. By the time they were men, he wanted them to be well versed in the ins and outs of doing a day's work, and of running a business. But Caleb William had recently been given a microscope for his birthday, and now he sat up long of a night, peering into its thick lens by lamplight.

The twins—Eleanor Ann and Kathleen Sue, soon turning eight. Ellie, just as Maggie had imagined, was growing into a girl too beautiful, too sweet tempered for this world. She did lovely needlework. She loved books and music, was learning to play both the organ and the piano equally well. But drawing and painting were her first loves. Along with their lessons and their diversions, the twins both had simple chores at The Meadows, as well as at the inn. Gold-blond hair shimmering in the early morning sunlight, Eleanor Ann stood chewing her lower lip, gazing at her Uncle Johnny, sky-blue eyes brimming with tears. They were so close, more like sister and brother, Ellie and Johnny, streaking their horses across The Meadows, or across McKinnon Valley. Swimming in the river. And when sometimes Maggie looked at her daughter…her heart twisted in her chest. This world, she well knew, could be *very* tough on angels.

Kassie—creamy skin, long dark hair, deep blue eyes—the spitting image of her mother, and Maggie knew it, and this also gave her heart pause. Kassie could master almost any musical instrument she chose, and sang like an angel. But Kassie did not light for any long period of time on any one particular occupation or diversion…except reading. She had taught herself letters almost by the time she could toddle about, and loved books. She had a vivid imagination, and dabbled at writing verse and what she called her *journal*— page after page, all written in a large, childish scrawl. Kassie, Maggie knew, would be capable of carving her own path. But Maggie knew from personal experience that the world could be a very tough, very dangerous place, even for a determined, high spirited girl. Maggie had gone through rough patches in her life, and had weathered the storms. She was in the arduous process, with the very able assistance of William Bartram Logan, of rearing five children; she had operated her own business for years now, yet she still could not go to the polls and vote for her husband in an election. Still she counted herself fortunate…most women did not have a husband of the caliber of William Bartram Logan.

But, of the two girls, Maggie was certain that Kathleen Sue would be the more able to confront whatever difficulties life hurled in her path. Kassie was elusive and unpredictable as a spring breeze, sapphire eyes alight with mischief, always playing tricks on Johnny, putting tadpoles in his drink, frogs in his bed, dumping a cat then a cup of cold water on him as he lay fast asleep, teasing him unmercifully about having to take up shaving…to catch the violet eyes of the little beauty…Stephanie Evelyn Giles…

Then the train was pulling into the depot, and Maggie's thoughts were drawn back to the present. Back to this day, *Johnny's last day at home.* Oh, he would be back from the medical college on holidays, and for the summers. But it would not be the same. It would never be the same. He would board this train…a boy. He would return to her on holiday…a man…well on his way to becoming a doctor. Johnny, meantime, was shaking hands with his nephews and thumping them on the back, more like brothers to him, and bending down, kissing his nieces, who seemed like sisters. Kassie, when she gave him a hug, dropped a wiggling earthworm down the back of his collar. "Why you…little…!" Johnny was flinching and hopping about. Kassie, eyes dancing with delight, chased after him. He picked her up, pulled her close. She grinned, reached up a deft little hand, and plucked the slimy worm out.

Johnny put her down, and came to Maggie, rubbing the worm residue from his neck, folding her into his arms. So like Papa! John Thomas McKinnon, Jr.! So like his Papa! How could this be *Johnny,* holding her now against his warm, muscular chest. How could Johnny be six feet tall and going on eighteen, and going away to *medical college?!* It could not be true! How well she recalled the day he was born…! With Papa not cold in his grave…

"You can let go o' me…now…Maggie," Johnny was whispering into her ear, stroking her hair with a big, warm hand. "I'll write. And I'll…be back…"

"Yes, darling," Bart was whispering into Maggie's other ear. "You must turn him loose. Give him into the care of the Medical College of Augusta…"

"How…do I know that I can…trust them…at that medical college…?" Maggie muttered. Then Johnny hugged Maggie tighter, and she began blubbering into the wool of his new fawn colored jacket.

"We have to let him go, sweetheart," Bart was saying softly. "Let him go, and trust God…to keep him safe…and bring him back to Rhyersville."

"Sure, Sis, once I make a doc, I'm goin' ta live out at McKinnon Valley! And keep my office in Rhyersville! So I'll be seein' ya a lot."

Maggie released Johnny and gazed up at her tall, handsome brother, demanding in a choked voice:

"And just exactly *how on earth*, John Thomas McKinnon, Jr., do you propose to manage that!? Living out in McKinnon Valley…and with your medical practice in Rhyersville?"

"Maybe I'll buy myself one o' them new fangled wheeled things...called *bicycles*. Or take up horse breeding. Maybe a few Thoroughbreds? I hear tell they can run like th' dickens, and never grow tired. What d'ya think?" Johnny grinned down at her.

"Oh! *You!*" Maggie pushed him gently away, "Go on with you, John Thomas McKinnon! Go on now...before you miss your train...and I have to put up with the likes of you for *another* seventeen years! Oh, Johnny, just a moment, sweetie. I have something...for you."

Maggie reached into her reticule, drew out Papa's bent tobacco tin, and handed it to Johnny.

"What...is it?" Johnny asked, turning the battered thing over in his hands. His eyes misted up, as his heart told him what it was.

"It's...Papa's tobacco tin, Johnny. Never a day passed that Papa didn't carry it in his pocket. Remember, when you get lonely...should you get lonely, just open the lid...and smell Papa. He'll be right there with you, and so will I, sweetie."

"Wow, thanks," Johnny mumbled. "Ya sure ya want me ta have this? What if somethin' happens ta it?" Johnny drawled, each word drawn out long and slow, smooth and slow as sweet molasses. *He even talks like Papa, despite all his years of schooling. He speaks the language of the Scotch-Irish,* Maggie thought. She had given up years ago on trying to change it. It was in his blood, in his heart, just like Papa's—just like Great-grandpa *Shawn Ian McKinnon's.*

"Nothing had better happen to it! And nothing had better happen to you, young man! Now, go on with you, before you miss your train."

Maggie placed a small hand against Johnny's chest and gave him a gentle push, just the way Grandma Mary Margaret had pushed her son, John Thomas, age sixteen, Johnny's papa, off the porch of the square-log house in McKinnon Valley that hot, dry July day of 1861, to march off and fight four long years in that War Between the States, and catch that ball of lead in his leg that he carried the remainder of his life. The train's whistle sounded over the small depot, the engine gave a belching roar, raining a hail of soot and ashes on those waiting on the platform, and over the buggies, carriages and horses hitched to the depot's rail. Johnny stuck the tobacco tin in his coat pocket, snatched the handles of his trunk and hefted it onto one shoulder.

Hurrying along as best he could, balancing his new leather trunk with one hand, and clutching in the other the brown paper bag filled with the fine lunch Maggie had packed for him, he scrambled aboard, raced through the coach cars to the rear platform, where he stood waving his cap and yelling to the top of his lungs as the train roared around the curve.

"See ya soon, Maggie…!"